PRAISE FOR SHARON POTTS

"This is thriller writing the way it is supposed to be."
—Michael Connelly, *New York Times* bestselling author, on
In Their Blood

"Rich with high-concept, captivating characters, and a relentless plot that simply won't go away."
—Jeffery Deaver, *New York Times* bestselling author, on
The Devil's Madonna

"A complex plot that builds believable suspense on every page."
—*Sacramento Bee* on *In Their Blood*

"With lean, spare writing that maintains suspense throughout, the author deftly weaves the various characters' stories into a plot that explodes in revelations."
—*San Francisco Book Review* on *Someone's Watching*

SOMEONE
MUST
DIE

OTHER TITLES BY SHARON POTTS

In Their Blood

Someone's Watching

The Devil's Madonna

SHARON POTTS

SOMEONE MUST DIE

THOMAS & MERCER

Published by Thomas & Mercer, Seattle

www.apub.com

Amazon, the Amazon logo, and Thomas & Mercer are trademarks of Amazon.com, Inc., or its affiliates.

ISBN-13: 9781503936676
ISBN-10: 1503936678

Cover design by Jason Blackburn

Printed in the United States of America

To my family—Joe, Ben, and Sarah.
Nothing matters to me more than you guys.

CHAPTER 1

The centrifugal force hit her harder than a couple of Cuba Libres on an empty stomach. Diana Lynd gripped the rim of the giant teacup as it spun around so fast she became queasy and disoriented. On the other side of the cup, her six-year-old grandson, Ethan, howled with delight, his golden curls flying out like a halo.

The booths, rides, crowds, palm trees, and blue sky rushed around her in a blur, the carny music earsplitting. She focused on the white steeple of the local church as it went past, like a ballerina spotting her mark, but it didn't help her dizziness.

"Please stop," she muttered, not sure how much more she could take. She was a sixty-three-year-old grandmother, a retired physician, for God's sake—no longer a daring, adventurous girl.

The music became funereal and sour as the teacup finally slowed, then came to a jerky halt. Ethan tugged on her fingers. His hand was sticky with the ice cream she had tried unsuccessfully to wipe off. "Come on, Grandma. Let's go to the fun house."

Diana stood, her legs wobbly. The air smelled like cotton candy and corn dogs, but then she caught a whiff of vomit. Apparently some other grandmother had succumbed to all this fun.

"Are you okay?" Ethan's dark-brown eyes were wide and serious. His New York Mets baseball cap had left a faint indentation in his forehead. He'd finally surrendered it to her on this last ride, worried it might fly off. She had tucked away the worn, dirty cap in her hobo bag.

"I'll be fine, honey," she said. "But let's take a little break."

He frowned like a grown-up, old beyond his years, just like his dad used to when he was a little boy. Kevin. She was sorry she had given her son so much to frown about.

"We can go home now if you want, Grandma," Ethan said, his crystalline voice trembling. "I had a wonderful time."

She laughed. *Irresistible child.* How happy and grateful she was that Kevin and his wife, Kim, had accepted her back in their lives after that awful misunderstanding about her illness and their wedding. But how she wished she had seen her only grandchild take his first steps, had heard him speak his first words, and had been there for his first day of kindergarten.

"I'm glad you're having fun," she said. "We don't have to leave yet."

He grinned, a child once again. He had lost one of his upper baby teeth, and there was a ridge from the adult tooth pushing through.

She reached into her bag for her phone. "Let me take your picture."

"Again?"

"Just one more." She had taken a dozen since his maternal grandparents had dropped him off in Miami yesterday. The Simmers had helped Ethan settle into his dad's old bedroom, with barely a glance in Diana's direction, while the chauffeur waited in their limo to drive them to their winter home in Palm Beach. Diana knew Kevin's in-laws carried a grudge against her over missing the kids' wedding and didn't approve of Kevin and Kim's decision to let Ethan stay with her. She had been careful not to say or do anything that might give them an excuse to flee with Ethan in tow, and had let out a big sigh of relief when they had finally left.

"How's this, Grandma?" Ethan posed, wrinkling his nose—a natural ham. He was wearing the sky-blue T-shirt she'd gotten him. It had a picture of a jumping dolphin. She hoped it would remind him of her when he was back home in New York.

She took the photo, then Ethan came around and snuggled into the crook of her arm. She marveled at his complete acceptance of her, a grandmother he hardly knew.

"You can take a selfie of us," he said.

"A *selfie?*"

"I do it all the time. I'll show you." He examined her iPhone with adult concentration, then pressed something on the screen. "Hold your arm like this," he instructed, demonstrating, "then touch the circle."

She stretched out her arm, and the two of them came into view on the small screen.

"Well, aren't you smart?" she said. "Smile."

She took the selfie and studied it. Ethan resting against her white blouse, the roller coaster, merry-go-round, and carnival booths with crowds of people in the background. Her shoulder-length dark hair, caught by a gust of wind, obscured part of her smile. One of the ticket takers had mistaken her for Ethan's mother, but maybe he'd just been flattering her.

Then again, perhaps her bliss was apparent to others.

After years of bitterness toward Larry for discarding her like a broken car, she finally had everything she wanted in life. A man she loved who also loved her, time for herself since retiring from her medical practice, reconciliation with her son, and the joy of being with her grandson. If only her daughter weren't going through her own difficulties, everything would be perfect.

"I'm going to text this to your Aunt Aubrey, then we can go to the fun house."

"Do you need help?"

Diana laughed again. "Thanks, but that much I know."

She tapped out a quick message to her daughter. **At a church carnival. Having a lot of fun. I love this child.**

She started to smile at him, but he was no longer standing in front of the teacup ride.

Her heart stuttered, and she spun around.

"Ethan?"

A group of boisterous children darted in front of her, balloons bobbing behind them.

"Ethan!"

"Here, Grandma."

She turned toward his voice, her legs shaking, as she released a sigh of relief.

Her grandson stood beside a booth a few feet from her where a bearded man with tattoos covering his arms was throwing darts at balloons. Dozens of gray stuffed animals hung from the rafters.

She hurried over to him. "You can't run off like that."

"I didn't run, Grandma. Look. They're dolphins." He pointed up at the hanging stuffed animals. "Can we go swimming with the dolphins?"

She had overreacted. Ethan had been nearby the whole time. She took his hand, fear evaporating. "Of course I'll take you to swim with the dolphins."

Her phone pinged. Probably Aubrey texting back. She glanced at the screen. Her daughter had written, **U r both beautiful. Makes me very happy.**

Diana wished Aubrey could be here with them, but she had to stay up at Brown to prepare for the classes she would be teaching. The winter semester began this week.

It saddened her that Aubrey was dealing with her rat boyfriend alone. Diana well understood betrayal and could have offered advice, or at least empathy, but Aubrey had always been stoic and didn't like burdening others with her problems.

Ethan tugged on Diana's hand and pulled her along through the crowd. They passed booths of local sponsors handing out pamphlets, balloons, T-shirts, and hats—Bob's Flooring, Tia's Latina Café, Dr. Gary's Bright Smiles. But Ethan was focused on getting to the fun house, a one-story building painted neon-pink, green, and blue, with the mouth of a giant laughing face as its door.

When they reached the entrance, he dashed over to a placard of a measuring stick with the admission requirements:

UNDER 36 INCHES—WAIT UNTIL YOU'RE TALLER.

36–48 INCHES—COME INSIDE.

Ethan stood beside the measuring stick, making himself as tall as possible. He put his hand on his head, then stepped away to look back at his hand. It almost reached the forty-eight-inch mark. "See, Grandma? I can go inside."

Several young children ran up the ramp leading to the laughing face. A group of adults watched them, but Diana wasn't about to let her grandson go by himself.

"I'll come with you," she said.

"It's okay. I'm a big boy now."

Diana had occasionally been accused of being overprotective with her own two kids, but she'd worked long hours then and had needed strict rules for when she wasn't around. She didn't want to be unreasonable with Ethan.

Still . . .

"Pleeese." He held the *e* like his dad used to do, then pointed to twin boys around his age who were climbing the ramp to the fun house. One wore Harry Potter glasses. "I can go with them. I promise I'll stay with them."

"That's fine, but I'd like to go, too." She would give him a little space but make sure he stayed within her sight.

"Okay, Grandma," he said, catching up to the twins.

She handed the man at the doorway their tickets, then stepped through the gaping mouth a little behind Ethan and the two boys.

Cacophonous organ music punctuated by fake screams played too loudly from speakers. She blinked to acclimate to the darkness, then followed Ethan's blue dolphin shirt into the first room.

The floor shifted beneath her feet—a fun-house gimmick, not her own instability. She struggled across the moving floor as quickly as she could, but Ethan and the twins were already exiting the other side of the room.

A group of children came toward her, going the wrong way. She tried to push past them—she didn't want Ethan to get too far ahead of her. But when she finally got out of the room, he was gone. No sign of him or the twins in the giant barrel that spun slowly on its side.

Diana ducked into the barrel, the only way to the next room, grabbing at the inside walls to keep from falling. Dizziness and disorientation similar to what she'd experienced on the teacup ride returned. This time it felt like her old inner-ear injury acting up, the debilitating vertigo that attacked when she was stressed or some fresh trauma disturbed the balance in her life.

I need to get out of here.

She made it through the barrel, but everything around her was still spinning. At the end of a narrow hallway, she pushed through a curtain of leather strips into a pitch-black space. She stumbled forward, reaching for the walls, but her hands touched nothing.

"Ethan," she called over the screams and too-loud music, hoping he would hear and wait for her.

Ahead, she could see red-and-yellow lights flickering. She entered a small room where flames licked the walls and the sound of explosions shook her to the core. A wave of nausea rushed over her.

She squeezed her eyes shut, trying to block the memory of the worst day of her life.

Jets of hot air spat up through the floor, shocking her into action. She ran out of the fiery room and through winding hallways of distorting mirrors. Images of herself bounced back at her—bloated, emaciated, stretched out, shrunken. With each mirror she passed, her terror grew.

"Ethan!" She ran forward into blackness. Her hands touched something hard, then a door flew open. Bright light blinded her. She blinked until her vision cleared.

She was out. *Safe.* She drew the fresh air into her lungs and almost laughed with relief.

She looked around for her grandson. Children everywhere—running, eating cotton candy and ice cream.

"Ethan?"

There was no sign of him, but the twin boys stood by a woman, probably their mother. Diana hurried over. "Excuse me. The little boy who went in with you. . . do you know where he is?"

The twins shrugged. "Don't know," the one with the glasses said.

"He didn't like the mirrors," the other boy added.

"He's my grandson," she told the mother, not sure why she felt the need to explain. "He ran ahead of me in the fun house. Did you see him come out? Curly blond hair, blue T-shirt with a jumping dolphin. This tall." She gestured to the top of her chest.

"I saw a little boy come out by himself."

"Where did he go?" Diana could hear the panic in her voice.

"I don't know. A few kids came out. Most of them went over there." The woman pointed to a group of adults near the exit door, then put her hands on the twins' shoulders and led them away.

Something crawled through Diana's gut. She returned to the exit, watching as other children streamed out. Could Ethan have somehow gotten lost in the fun house? She caught the door as a couple of kids came out and stuck her head in.

"Ethan?" she called into the darkness. "Ethan!" she repeated, her voice rising.

But he couldn't be inside. She would have passed him on her way out.

She walked around the side of the fun house to the rear of the building where a number of electrical cables snaked across dirt and brown grass toward the temporary carnival booths. A few cars and trucks were parked in the alley. A sickly stench rose from a nearby dumpster.

He wouldn't have come back here, but she called his name anyway, listening for his voice. Nothing except the distant shrieks of children and off-key organ music.

It had been almost fifteen minutes since she'd lost sight of him.

The booths, cars, cables, and dumpster whirled around her as though she were trapped inside a tornado.

Fifteen minutes.

So much could have happened in that time.

CHAPTER 2

Something was missing.

The emptiness in the front foyer of their loft apartment caught Aubrey by surprise. No man's clunky boots waited on the doormat to trip her. Jackson's fleece-lined suede coat wasn't draped over the brass coatrack. And Wolverine's worn leather leash was gone from the hook beside the door. She listened for the skittering sound Wolvie's toenails made against the wood floor when he ran to greet her.

Then she remembered.

Not their apartment. Hers.

Jackson didn't live here anymore. *He* was what was missing. He must have come by to pick up the rest of his things this afternoon while she'd been at the university library.

She ran her finger along the bookshelf by the brick wall, erasing the lines of dust that marked where the thin volumes of Jackson's tormented poetry had been. But erasing six years of living with Jackson wouldn't be so easy. She could still smell amaretto pipe tobacco and Wolverine's dank doggy scent.

She missed Wolvie. She did not miss Jackson.

She shrugged off her parka, damp from melted snow, and hung it on the rack. Flurries had been coming down thick when she left the campus. She'd hidden in the library all afternoon, unaware the weather had taken a turn for the worse. Thoughts about Jackson's treachery had preoccupied her when she should have been preparing for the Perception versus Reality class she'd be teaching this coming semester.

Perception versus reality. How ironic. Here she was, almost finished with her PhD in social psychology, with a specialization in interpersonal relationships, and she had completely missed the signs that the man in her life was a lying scumbag.

She went into the kitchen and poured herself a glass of merlot. The hanging copper pots and vintage blue-and-white porcelain canisters she'd found at flea markets were still in their places. She wasn't surprised that Jackson hadn't taken them. He'd always scoffed when she came home with a new "find," calling her treasures kitschy dust collectors. Well, she no longer had to justify or make excuses for what she wanted. This was *her* home now.

A knock on the front door broke through the silence. She started, nearly dropping her wineglass.

Jackson?

She'd changed the locks yesterday and had told the doorman to let Jackson in when he came by for his things. Had he forgotten something? The thought of seeing him made her stomach churn.

Another knock, more urgent.

Aubrey took a fortifying gulp of wine, then went to check the peephole. Instead of a wiry man with a salt-and-pepper beard, her good friend and neighbor, Trish, stood in the doorway, swaddled in her heavy down coat, her round cheeks afire from the cold.

Aubrey opened the door.

"What the hell is going on?" Trish barreled past her into the apartment. She glanced around the foyer, then studied Aubrey's face. Trish was a few years older than Aubrey and an associate professor in the psych department at Brown. She noticed things.

"Everything's fine," Aubrey said, hoping Trish didn't observe that her eyes were still red from yesterday's crying bout.

"Bullshit." Trish picked at her spiked black hair, as though she were angry at it. "I saw Jackson going in and out of the building all afternoon, loading cartons into a U-Haul. What happened?"

"I kicked him out." Aubrey tried to sound matter-of-fact.

"Shit," Trish said softly, then glanced at the glass Aubrey held. "Got any more of that?"

They went into the kitchen. Trish unzipped her coat and climbed onto a counter stool.

Jackson had sat there a few days before, drinking his morning coffee, the newspaper spread out on the counter, acting as though everything were perfectly normal. His royal-blue bathrobe had hung open, revealing dark chest hair sprinkled with silver.

Where were you last night, Jackson?

Out with the guys. I crashed on the sofa.

Why didn't you answer your phone?

Sorry. Must have left it on silent by mistake.

But there was no such thing as a mistake. Everything was a choice, even the one she had made to ignore what was happening around her.

Trish took a sip of wine from the glass Aubrey handed her. "So what did The Great Poet do?"

The Great Poet. It had been a nickname Jackson seemed to enjoy, but *The Great Pretender* would have been more apt. "He was cheating on me."

Trish raised an eyebrow.

"You seem surprised," Aubrey said. "So was I."

"Nope. Not surprised at all. I always thought he was a little too smooth."

Her friend had suspected but never said anything. A spark of anger flared, then went out. Trish would have known Aubrey wouldn't have listened, that she hid in her little world of denial, rejecting any information that conflicted with what she wanted to believe.

"How did you finally figure it out?"

"He clearly wanted me to know," Aubrey said. "Left his laptop open on the counter. I went to look something up, and there was his Excel spreadsheet waiting for me." She tried to keep her voice light to hide the hurt. "A list of all his conquests over the past twenty-two years, starting with when he went to college. Forty-eight of them. Very orderly. Like he was collecting data for a research paper. First name, age, brief physical description." She paused and swallowed a lump. "And a rating on a scale from 'one' to 'ten.'"

"How do you know he slept with them?"

"I was on the list." Aubrey tossed back the rest of her wine. "Number thirty-six."

Which meant Jackson had been intimate with twelve women in the eight years since they'd known each other. And when she'd confronted him about the spreadsheet, his answer had been, *I'm dealing with insecurity issues. I thought you, of all people, understood that.*

She had screamed at him and called him names, but that hadn't changed things. She'd allowed herself to be duped.

She ran her fingers over the ruts in the butcher-block countertop. Jackson didn't use cutting boards. She remembered him slicing limes with a giant knife, each cut slamming against the wood top, chipping away a bit at a time. Just like he'd been doing with her all these years with his nasty barbs about her going into psychology because she was so screwed up.

Maybe he'd been right. If so, dumping him had been a great first step to fixing herself.

Trish rubbed her back. "What a dick. I'm sorry."

"And he didn't even give me a good rating." Aubrey attempted a laugh as she shifted away from Trish. "A 'seven.' Of course, I was only twenty at the time, and practically a virgin." She refilled her wineglass.

"You realize he took advantage of you," Trish said. "The older, sexy, charismatic professor preying on his student."

"No, Trish. This isn't about the halo effect, and I wasn't a victim. It was right after my dad left my mom. I was angry with him, worried about her health, upset my family had just fallen apart. Jackson helped me through it."

She thought back eight years to the first day of the elective poetry class she'd signed up for because she had needed emotional relief from science and statistics. To when Jackson had stood in front of the class and recited, in his deep, sonorous voice, one of his poems about ice-covered love.

It had been as though he'd written it just for her.

"If you say so," Trish said. "But I see a master predator at work."

"He certainly had plenty of help from me," Aubrey said. "I was looking so hard at what I wanted to see that I ignored everything else. Like in the *Invisible Gorilla* video we show students. Most can't believe they don't notice the person in the gorilla suit walking across the court because they're so intent on watching the players pass the basketball."

"What did you want to see?" Trish asked.

Aubrey took a sip of wine. "I suppose I wanted to believe Jackson and I had an honest relationship. Something truer than what my parents had." She shrugged. "But you and I both know the tendency to repeat behaviors we're trying hard to avoid."

"Good news is you're no longer repeating them," Trish said. "You saw the problem with Jackson, and you're moving on."

"Hear, hear." Aubrey clinked her glass against Trish's.

But was she really past the problem? Even before college, she had ignored situations she feared would blow up if examined too closely.

Her parents' marriage had clearly been fragile, but she'd been so desperate to keep her family intact that she had spent her childhood afraid to do anything that could cause their relationship to implode.

But growing up a "pleaser" had come with consequences. She had gone off to college with no sense of who she was or what she wanted. It was why she had decided to go into social psychology, hoping once she learned to perceive herself in relation to her family, she'd be better able to sort herself out.

Apparently, she was still a work in progress.

She held up the wine bottle. "More for you?"

"No, thanks," Trish said. "I'm heading over to the Deep Sleep to meet Sarah and Julia. Come with me. There's nothing better than a cheeseburger and sweet-potato fries for a heartover."

"Thanks, but I'm fine. Really. The toughest part is losing Wolvie."

Trish hugged her. "You were far too good for that louse."

Aubrey blinked rapidly before any tears leaked out. She hated when anyone felt sorry for her. "You're a good friend."

"Call if you need anything," Trish said, heading toward the foyer.

"I will."

"And lock the door after me."

"Don't worry. I'm not letting Jackson in anymore. I'm done with being hurt by him."

Trish gave her an approving nod, then left.

Aubrey locked the door, retrieved her wineglass from the kitchen counter, and then stretched out on the weathered leather sofa. It had scratch marks from where Wolverine liked to dig. She glanced at the beige shag rug, expecting to see their scrawny, gray, long-haired mutt panting at her, begging with his black button eyes to be allowed on her lap.

That empty pang again. Wolvie was Jackson's dog. Part of the package.

The best part.

The snow was still coming down, blurring her view of the old red-brick buildings in downtown Providence. It was as if she were inside one of the snow globes she had collected as a child. Silent glass bubbles, each preserving a safe world—what she had always wanted for herself. What she'd believed Jackson would provide.

But was that all Jackson had been? A safe haven? Had she even loved him, or had she loved the idea that she had someone to come home to, who would take care of her?

She tried to understand her feelings. Was she hurt, angry about being deceived, or heartbroken? Then it hit her. She hadn't loved Jackson. The distress came from something else. With Jackson gone, she no longer felt safe and protected. *That* was what was missing. The lovely bubble world she'd created for herself had cracked, and just like when her father had left, the snow swirled around her in a blizzard.

She took another sip of wine. Snow had accumulated on the lower half of the windows, but she could see fuzzy lights in the neighboring buildings and street. It was only a little after five, though it felt much later.

Maybe she'd light a fire in the fireplace. Jackson usually did it with great showmanship, as though it were a tricky, subtle task, but she could get a flame going just as well and with a lot less fuss. She'd order a pizza and finish the wine while she binge-watched *The Gilmore Girls*, the mother-daughter TV series she had loved as a girl and had occasionally watched with her mother when Mama wasn't working late. It wasn't a cop-out, or reality avoidance. There was nothing wrong with spending a few hours in the safe, fictitious world of Stars Hollow.

She was alone, with no one to take care of her. But that was okay—she could take care of herself. Nothing was missing as long as she had herself.

Her cell phone rang. *Our love is stronger than the pain.* The words to the song Mama had requested as her ringtone on Aubrey's phone years ago. But the old, sad ballad from the sixties no longer seemed fitting for her mother, who was happily engaged to Jonathan and had surely gotten over her husband's betrayal by now.

Maybe it was time for a new ringtone.

For both of them.

"Hi, Mama." She brightened her voice so she wouldn't worry her mother. "Are you enjoying Ethan?"

Her mother was panting, as if she couldn't catch her breath.

Aubrey sat up straight. "Mom. Are you okay?"

"He's *gone*."

Aubrey's heart skipped. "Who's gone?"

"Ethan," she said, her voice breaking. "Ethan's missing."

Chapter 3

Aubrey hurried to the taxi stand at Miami International Airport, dazed by the midday heat and humidity. She hadn't slept since getting the phone call from her mother the previous evening. She had quickly packed a bag and called Trish, who'd promised to arrange for someone to cover Aubrey's classes while she was gone.

It had taken almost two hours to get to Boston's Logan Airport on the snow-clogged roads. All flights had been canceled due to the storm, so she'd camped out in the terminal hoping to get on the next flight out. Throughout the night, she had texted her mother for updates, until Mama had finally written, **I'll let you know the minute I hear anything.**

This morning, flights had resumed out of Boston. Aubrey had sent her mother one more text as she'd boarded the flight to Miami. **Getting on a plane. Any news?**

Her mother hadn't answered, and Aubrey had spent the next three and a half hours trying not to think about what might have happened to Ethan, praying this was nothing more than an innocent scare. That her nephew had wandered away from the carnival but would have been found, frightened but safe, by the time she landed in Miami.

She checked her phone again as she waited in the taxi line in the stifling heat. Nothing from her mother, but her heart skipped when she saw a text from Kevin. She skimmed it. He and Kim had made it out of New York before the storm in Kim's parents' private jet. They were in Coconut Grove at Mama's house. The rest of her brother's message hit her like a punch to the gut. **Ethan still missing. How could I have trusted her with him? I should have known better.**

Oh, Kev. It wasn't Mama's fault.

She wished she could convince him that their mother wasn't the villain he believed she was. But Aubrey had been coming to her defense ever since Mama had missed Kevin's wedding, and that had only further strained her once-close relationship with her big brother.

It had taken Kevin eight years to finally forgive Mama.

Now Ethan had disappeared on her watch.

Aubrey started to text her brother back to tell him Mama wasn't to blame, then changed her mind. This was a conversation they needed to have in person.

She reached the front of the taxi line, climbed into the waiting cab, and threw her small suitcase and winter coat on the seat beside her. After giving the driver her mother's address, she leaned back, the wool from her sweater stinging her like a hair shirt. She had spent the last few hours focused on getting to Miami, afraid if she thought about Ethan she might break down, but now she was almost home. She pulled up the photo on her phone of Ethan and her mother, taken a few minutes before he disappeared.

Ethan resting happily in the crook of his grandmother's arm, a crowd of carnival-goers behind them.

The first and only photo of the two together.

She was struck by the resemblance between grandmother and grandson. The same large, fudge-brown eyes, the same dimples as they smiled, the same heart-shaped faces.

Before this weekend, Mama hadn't known this beautiful, delightful child, but Aubrey had. She'd enjoyed Ethan several times a year ever since he was a baby, taking him to Central Park, boating on the lake, visiting the animals at the zoo, and even teaching him how to ice-skate a few weeks ago.

Where was her nephew now?

A dark memory surfaced.

When Aubrey was eight years old, a boy named Jimmy Ryce had gone missing a few miles from her house in Coconut Grove. Jimmy had been nine, and she could still recall the photo of him on the newscasts and in the newspapers—a grinning child in a baseball cap, gripping a bat. Mama had tried to keep the news of his disappearance from her, but it had been everywhere. Aubrey hadn't been allowed to go anywhere by herself, even to school or on her bicycle to her friend Meagan's house.

She'd been angry about the tighter restrictions, but then three months later, the news that they had discovered Jimmy's ruined body had changed her. For years afterward, she would glance over her shoulder to see whether anyone was following her, and if a stranger looked her way, her heart would speed up in fright.

Had Ethan ever learned to be wary of strangers?

The taxi continued in thick traffic down Le Jeune Road, past used-car dealerships, Latin American restaurants, and billboards in Spanish advertising health care and surgical procedures. The busy commercial streets felt alien until they crossed US 1 into the lush, dark forest of Coconut Grove. The driver turned onto a narrow street, palm fronds and overgrown banyan-tree branches brushing against the sides of the taxi. As her childhood home came into view, the vise around Aubrey's chest eased.

In the early-afternoon light, the house appeared just as it always had, like someplace where Sleeping Beauty might have comfortably slept for a hundred years, hidden away from the world. Vines grew over the faded, salmon-colored stucco walls, mildew darkened the once-red gabled roof, and magenta bougainvillea overhung the arched windows. Aubrey had left ten years earlier when she'd gone to college, and had come back only two or three times a year to visit her mother, yet she still thought of this place as home.

But her home was no longer a cloister.

Dozens of cars and news vans were parked helter-skelter on the torn-up lawn, blocking the driveway and much of the road, and a crowd of reporters stood at the edge of the property. The tightness in her chest returned.

Twenty-four hours after Ethan's disappearance and the vultures were already circling. They knew, just as she did, that with every passing hour, the odds of getting Ethan home safely diminished.

She paid the driver and stepped into the heat, anxious to get to her mother, concerned about what the stress of Ethan's disappearance might be doing to her. Aubrey had seen her mother debilitated from vertigo several times—most recently two years ago when she'd been sued by the parents of a little boy who had died while under her care. Aubrey could only imagine how Mama was coping with the disappearance of her own grandson.

She made her way through the reporters, trying to avoid eye contact with them. She hoped her mother had called Jonathan and asked him to stay at the house and protect her from this. In the last couple of years, Jonathan had become Mama's main support system, not only helping her through the malpractice lawsuit and problems with her medical-practice partners, but also keeping her from falling apart when things went wrong. Like now.

"Excuse me." A woman jumped in front of Aubrey and shoved a microphone in her face. "Are you a member of the family? Is there any news on Ethan? How is the family holding up?"

Aubrey pushed past the woman and hurried down the cracked coquina walkway toward the front door. These people didn't care about Ethan. They just wanted a good story. She fumbled through her handbag for her house keys.

"Will the police activate an AMBER alert?" one of the reporters called out. "Have they confirmed Ethan has been abducted?"

Aubrey got her key into the lock, opened the door, then slammed it behind her. She dropped her coat and suitcase and leaned against the door. She stood there, wanting to be strong when she saw her family, and took in the familiar musty smell, like old, damp towels—the result of roof leaks that had dripped through the walls. A smell Mama had been trying unsuccessfully to erase all the years they'd lived here, but which was as much a part of the house as the creaky Dade-pine floors and coral-stone fireplaces.

But there were sounds that didn't belong. Constant ringing, like phones in a telethon. And a droning noise, like from swarming bees.

"Are you Aubrey?"

She turned toward the stranger who had stepped into the foyer: a woman with too-thick eyebrows and jet-black hair, pulled back from a face that had been scarred by acne. She was probably in her early thirties, a few years older than Aubrey, and wore a gray, crumpled pantsuit. Her thumb was hooked on her waistband, over a gold badge.

"Yes. I'm Aubrey Lynd."

"Detective Gonzalez with the MDPD Missing Persons Unit." She had an accent Aubrey recognized from growing up in Miami—northeastern with a hint of Latino. "Your mother said you were coming."

"Tell me about my nephew. Is there any news?"

"Nothing yet, but we're doing everything we can."

"Where is my mother? I need to see her."

"In the other room, speaking with the FBI."

"The FBI?" Aubrey wasn't sure if she should be alarmed. "Are they involved?"

"Apparently your brother's in-laws have quite a bit of clout," the detective said. Aubrey picked up an edge of irritation in her voice. "The FBI deployed a CARD team to work with us."

"Card?"

"Child Abduction Rapid Deployment."

Aubrey's heart bounced. "Has Ethan been abducted? The reporters were asking about an AMBER alert."

The detective scratched a tattoo that stuck out from under her wristwatch. It could have been a nervous tic, not a good sign. "We don't issue an AMBER alert without a known suspect or a vehicle," she said. "We have neither. But we've put out a media alert. We're being aggressive in trying to find Ethan quickly."

They're trying to find him quickly. Aubrey wanted to believe the detective's confident words, not her faltering body language. *He's going to be fine.*

She took a deep breath to settle herself and glanced around the small foyer.

The walls were plastered in thick swirls, as had been the style in the 1920s, but the pattern made her dizzy.

Or maybe it was lack of sleep.

She caught her reflection in the mottled mirror over the foyer table. Her long, dark hair and stick-straight bangs looked the same as always, but her eyes were wrong—too large and shadowed, like a terrified character in a silent film.

Aubrey turned to the detective. "I have to let my mother know I'm here."

"You can't interrupt right now, but she should be finished soon."

"What about my brother? Is Kevin here?"

"He and his wife left a little while ago with Kimberly's parents."

"Left? For where?"

"They're all staying at the Coconut Grove Ritz."

So she wasn't going to see Kevin just yet. She felt a mix of disappointment and something resembling jealousy. Her brother was in the grip of the Simmers, not his own family.

"The Simmers have also arranged for several meeting rooms at the Ritz," Gonzalez said. "They're bringing in their own private investigators."

Aubrey was confused. "And the police and FBI—you're okay with that?"

"As long as their investigators don't interfere with our investigation," Gonzalez replied. "The FBI will continue to use your mother's home as its command post. I'll be back and forth between here, my office, and the Simmers' hotel. Someone will be with Kevin, Kimberly, and her parents in case whoever took Ethan tries to make contact with one of them. If this is a ransom situation, we still don't know who they're targeting."

"Well, the Simmers, of course," Aubrey said. The detective had to know that Prudence Simmer was a Baer heiress.

The detective frowned. "Do you know Ernest or Prudence Simmer well?"

"No. Not well." Aubrey had only seen them a few times, but she doubted anyone knew the Simmers well. They wore their money and power like gold-plated armor, keeping at a distance all but those in their inner circle. And even though Kevin had married into the family and worked at Baer Business Machines, Aubrey sensed they would never treat him as one of their own.

"Here you are, Detective," said a brusque voice behind Gonzalez.

A tall, stiff man stood in the archway of the foyer. He had a buzz cut and wore a white shirt, tie, and dark tailored suit. Something about the way he held his shoulders back and kept one hand in his pants pocket made him seem as if he thought he were better than everyone else. Aubrey wondered if he was one of the private investigators the Simmers had hired. His light-gray eyes roamed over Aubrey, then returned to the detective. "Do you have a minute?"

"Of course," Gonzalez said.

"What is it?" Aubrey asked, feeling the prickle of panic at the man's cold efficiency. "Have you found Ethan?"

The man stared at her, lips flattened, as though surprised by her question. "And you are?"

His tone irked her. "Aubrey Lynd. Ethan's aunt. And who are you?"

"Special Agent Smolleck. I'm heading up the FBI CARD team. And no, we haven't found your nephew." He hesitated, then added, "Yet."

Aubrey watched the two strangers walk across the dark wood floor of her childhood home and listened to the cacophony coming from the other end of the house.

Twenty-four hours ago, she had been sealed in her own private bubble, concerned about things that no longer mattered.

Twenty-four hours ago, Ethan had been laughing at a carnival in his grandmother's arms.

And just like that, everything changed.

Chapter 4

A stale smell hit Aubrey when she pushed open the door to her upstairs bedroom. She hadn't been home since Thanksgiving a couple of months before, but at least her room was as she had left it. The delft-blue wallpaper was still peeling away at the seams, still covered by the dozen or so oil paintings of fruit, vases, and favorite objects she had made when she was a teenager. She threw her coat on the white quilted bedspread and set her suitcase on the old footstool, then went to open one of the windows. Her room faced the front of the house, and as soon as she got the window open, reporters shouted up at her.

"Has Ethan been found? Is there a ransom demand?"

She slammed the window shut, then paced on the faded, blue-and-beige Oriental rug, reminding herself it wasn't the reporters' fault Ethan was missing.

Her breathing slowed as her eyes settled on familiar, much-loved mementos—her snow globes on the shelf above her desk, and the photo on the wicker nightstand she hadn't been able to part with, even after Mama had put away all the other photos of Aubrey's dad.

It was what Aubrey classified in her memory as a "before" photo of the four of them. *Before* Mama had begun working late most nights and Dad started traveling all the time. *Before* something had changed her parents' relationship, which Aubrey had never understood and was afraid to ask about. The photo had been taken twenty years ago, when Aubrey was eight and Kevin was eleven. They were standing on top of a mountain somewhere in Colorado. She and Kevin were smiling at the camera, but the reason Aubrey had kept the photo was because of the way her parents were looking at each other. Not in the polite-but-distant way she'd become accustomed to, but as though they were remembering the first time they'd fallen in love. Aubrey had always wanted to believe this was how they'd really felt about each other.

Even now—or maybe especially now, after her disappointing experience with Jackson—she still did.

How she wished her family could be together to support one another while they waited for news about Ethan! But Mama was unavailable, Dad probably hadn't arrived yet from Los Angeles, and Kevin was with Kim and her parents. But Aubrey was Kevin's family, too, and despite his angry words about their mother, she was certain he would want the comfort of the people who loved him unconditionally.

She got her phone out and speed-dialed his number, taken aback when a strange man's voice answered.

"I want to speak with Kevin," she said. "This is his sister."

"Mr. Lynd isn't taking calls right now."

"Would you please tell him it's Aubrey?"

"I'm sorry. He's not taking any calls."

"Who are you?" Aubrey asked.

"I've been hired by the family," the man said.

The family, she wanted to scream. *I'm his family.*

"I'll tell Mr. Lynd you called. I'm sure he'll return your call when he's able." He disconnected.

What the heck was that about? What if someone called with a ransom demand? Would they talk to a stranger? Or maybe the caller wouldn't know it wasn't Kevin answering his phone.

She sent her brother a text, not sure he would see it, but she had to try. I'm at the house. Can come see you anytime. Just say when.

She hesitated. Should she say she was here for him? That she loved him? But it would sound false after the distance between them for so many years. She pressed "Send," hoping he would write back or call.

Hoping his silence didn't mean the war with Mama was back on.

She stuck her phone in her pocket, then went across the hall to her mother's room. It was cool in the large corner bedroom, which was shaded by towering bamboos that blocked the sun from this part of the house. The bed was made, throw pillows piled up against the brass headboard, no indentation on the old patchwork quilt. She ran her hand over the satin squares in crimson, emerald green, and navy blue. It didn't look like her mother had slept, or even lain down for a rest.

Two faded-pink brocade armchairs were pulled close to the fireplace; a small table with a book on it stood between them. Now that she lived up north, she realized how odd it was to have fireplaces in Miami.

When she was little, she had longed for a fire, like in the Hans Christian Andersen stories she read, but her parents had never made one. So one winter when she was eight or nine, she'd talked Kevin into helping her gather wood. They'd filled the hearth with twigs and dead leaves, threw in some wadded-up toilet paper, then lit the mess with matches. It flamed and smoked, and Mama had coming running into the room, shouting hysterically. Aubrey had never seen her so upset. Mama had doused the fire with water, and had then climbed into bed beneath the patchwork quilt, suffering from one of her dizzy spells.

After that, with the smell of burned leaves lingering in the upstairs hallway, Aubrey and Kev had tried to follow the rules and be exemplary children. They only had themselves to rely on and became each other's best friends and confidants. Aubrey missed that so much . . . Kev's whispered dreams about reclaiming the Lonely Mountain, like Bilbo Baggins in *The Hobbit*. Promising her someday they'd be a real family again.

Well, maybe they could be, once they got Ethan back. One thing was for certain—she wasn't giving up on their family, even if Kevin had.

She went downstairs toward the dissonance of multiple voices talking at the same time. The family room had been transformed, crammed with folding tables and people talking on cell phones and tapping on computers. These strangers didn't belong here, surrounded by photos of her and her brother in front of their bunks at summer camp, hiking in the Rockies, throwing snowballs in Breckenridge. But Ethan wasn't supposed to be missing, either.

Neither Detective Gonzalez nor Special Agent Smolleck was in the room, so she went over to a youngish Asian man in a suit who was frowning at several computer screens.

He sat taller in his chair when he noticed her. "You're not allowed in here."

"I'm Aubrey Lynd. I'm looking for my mother, Diana Lynd. Do you know where she is?"

"Sorry. No."

She left the family room and pushed open a French door that led to the backyard. The mildewed-brick patio was shaded by so many trees—crepe myrtle, gumbo limbos, palms, and soaring bamboos—that the sun could hardly break through, and the little areas of grass around the rock garden were perennially thin. Unlike the inside of the house, transformed by all the people who didn't belong, out here nothing had changed. Still the same impossible-to-lift wrought iron chairs and filigreed table with a hole for an umbrella that Mama had never got around to buying.

Aubrey followed the brick path that meandered around the side of the house. This was the one area that was sunny, where the grass grew so fast it always looked like it needed mowing.

When they were kids, Aubrey and Kevin had begged their parents to put in a swimming pool. Dad had finally agreed, but Mama had dug in her heels. She'd said she had enough to worry about with her sick patients, without imagining her own children diving in and breaking their necks.

Mama was always waiting for a catastrophe to happen.

It finally had.

A couple of lawn chairs faced a small fountain near the tall hedge that separated their property from the neighbor's. Someone was stretched out on one of the chairs. Soft-brown leather loafers, pressed navy slacks, pale-blue shirt.

Dad.

For a moment she was a child again, remembering the joy she'd felt when her father would return home from an out-of-town trial and sweep her up in the air.

How's my beautiful princess?

She had adored him. Then he'd let her down.

He must have heard her coming, because he put his feet in the grass and turned toward her. "Aubrey."

His expression brightened, then his mouth fell, as though he'd remembered the circumstances. His full head of hair looked whiter than ever against his red face, but his blue eyes were the same—clear and concerned. Eyes that were known to sway the toughest juries.

And, once upon a time, even her.

He came toward her with outstretched arms, then hugged her tightly. Her mind told her to resist, but her body didn't listen, and she felt herself swaddled in his embrace. She clung to him, closing her eyes and taking in the familiar, fusty airplane smell of her childhood. He stroked her hair, and the sensation made her feel sleepy, just like when she was a little girl.

She wished they could go back to how they once were, but then he loosened his grip.

She took a step back.

She hadn't seen her father in more than a year, at a party for Ethan. He had a few extra wrinkles, but he was a handsome man, even at sixty-five. Kevin had inherited his lean, fit build, though both Aubrey and her brother more closely resembled their mother, with her dark hair and eyes and often-solemn disposition.

"I'm surprised to see you," she said.

"Did you think I wouldn't be here for my grandson and family?" His voice reflected hurt.

She backed off, ashamed to have implied that he didn't care about Ethan. "No, of course not. I didn't think you could get here so quickly from LA."

"I would have bought a plane to get here, if I'd had to."

She believed that. Even though he'd traveled a lot, her father had always put family first, which was one reason why it had been so bewildering to see him turn on her mother so heartlessly eight years ago.

"Have you spoken to Mama?" she asked.

"No. She's been busy with the police and FBI. I didn't want to get in the way." He clasped her hand. "It's been a long time. Too long."

"Yes," she said, feeling the firmness of his grip.

"I'm in shock over this," he said. "I could barely put one foot in front of the other. But Star's been my savior. Made all the arrangements to get here."

Aubrey pulled her hand away. She couldn't stomach the way her father seemed to worship the woman for whom he'd abandoned his wife.

He and Jackson were the same. Both of them oblivious to the pain they'd caused by succumbing to their self-centered needs.

"I wish you wouldn't resent her," her father said. "Star flew over with me. She's just as worried about Ethan as we are."

Aubrey felt a visceral loathing. It came on every time Star's name was mentioned, bringing up a memory of the first time they'd met.

Aubrey had been in her father's apartment, taking in the view of downtown LA, when she'd realized she wasn't alone. She had turned to see a ghostlike person in a darkened alcove of the room. Aubrey registered pale skin, flowing white scarves, and a perfectly shaped head with light hair so short it appeared naked. The apparition all but faded away—except for the bright, glassy-blue eyes studying her.

Then Star had stepped forward, arms extended, a smile pasted on her face. *Hello, dear,* she'd said, her words oozing like poisoned honey from an oleander flower. *I would so like us to be friends.*

"Please, Aubrey," her father was saying, "we need to stick together right now. For Ethan's sake."

"You're right," she said, erasing the vision of Star. She had to try to put old grievances aside and stand by both her parents. She knew how difficult Ethan's disappearance had to be for her father, too. He doted on his grandson, always sending Aubrey photos of Ethan's frequent visits to LA.

"I can't wrap my mind around it," he said. "Our little man." His voice quivered, and he ran his fingers through his hair. There was a dark perspiration stain under his arm on his light-blue button-down shirt.

"Do you want to go inside and get some water?" she asked.

"Thanks, but I'll be okay." The sun glinted off his white hair as he wiped his eyes with a handkerchief.

There was a spot he'd missed while shaving, near the cleft of his chin.

She remembered how immaculate he'd always been when he would leave to consult with one of the Innocence Projects he was involved with, looking like a movie star in his dark suit and white shirt, carrying the monogrammed cordovan briefcase Mama had gotten him.

She had been so proud of her father in his mission to save the innocent from death row. But at the same time, she was despondent about his leaving—sometimes for weeks at a time.

"Why don't we sit?" She led him back to the lounge chairs. He looked older, suddenly. Old and tired.

"Have you seen Kevin?" she asked.

He shook his head. "They'd already left for their hotel by the time I arrived." He put the handkerchief back in his pocket. "But I spoke to the FBI agent in charge. Special Agent Smolleck. I'm glad they've been brought in so early."

"Yes. Me, too." She didn't share her negative impression of the FBI agent with him. Maybe Smolleck's arrogance would be a good thing in getting Ethan back quickly.

"Smolleck told me they've set up a couple of phone lines for tips," her father said. "They've got some geek coordinating with the National Center for Missing and Exploited Children, to get the word out on Facebook and other social media."

"I'm glad you were able to get him to fill you in," she said.

"Well, it wasn't easy. He was more interested in asking me questions, but I've always had a knack for getting people to talk to me. At least most people." He searched her eyes. "I've missed you, Princess." It had been his nickname for her. His Sleeping Beauty princess, though she had never understood why he called her that. Now it occurred to her that he had always known she was closing her eyes to what was around her. "I've missed you and me."

She looked away. He was tugging on her heart, the way he always did, but she was wary of being taken in by his charm once again. "What else did he tell you?" she asked.

Her father let out a soft sigh. "Well, the good news is that the FBI moves very quickly in these situations. They're evaluating all contingencies, though I'm not sure I necessarily agree with the direction they're going. They've given the immediate family polygraphs."

Aubrey wondered if that's where her mother was—taking a lie detector test. "No one in the family would have taken Ethan," she said.

"Of course no one in the family is involved," he said. "The polygraph is a routine procedure. The FBI also has a mapping tool for sex offenders."

"Oh, God," she said. "They think Ethan was abducted by a *sex offender*?"

"No, no," he said quickly. "Not necessarily. That's just another angle they're pursuing."

"Did he tell you anything else?" she asked.

"He didn't, but one of the detectives informed me they brought in bloodhounds last night and searched the entire carnival area. They got his scent from his New York Mets baseball cap." He stopped, as though realizing this was his grandson he was talking about. He cleared his throat and continued. "Behind the fun house was a dumpster the dogs were interested in."

The sun pierced her eyes, sending sharp pains to the back of her head. "What did they find?"

"A paper napkin," he said. "They're analyzing it for prints."

"It could have been something he used while he was with Mama."

"Yes."

Or it could have the kidnapper's prints.

She stared at the fountain, the water barely dribbling into a basin that was green with algae.

"Then they took the dogs outside the carnival area to search for his scent," her father continued. "But other than in the parking lot, the dogs didn't pick up anything beyond the carnival grounds."

Aubrey considered this. "So it's unlikely Ethan wandered off by himself."

Her father nodded.

The significance of this hit her. The possibility that this was all a false alarm and that Ethan would miraculously appear, safe and sound, was now gone.

She didn't want to say it aloud, but she knew that denying the facts could hurt rather than help Ethan. "And since Ethan didn't simply vanish, someone must have picked him up and taken him away, probably in a car."

"That's what they're thinking," he said.

Her mother shouldn't be alone.

"I have to find Mama." She stood up and started back toward the house.

"She was negligent, you know."

The hardness in his voice stopped her. Aubrey turned to face him, anger warming her cheeks. "No, she wasn't. She lost him in the fun house. It could have happened to any parent or grandparent."

"That doesn't excuse her."

"Maybe not completely, but what happened wasn't her fault."

"You sound just like her defense attorneys."

She clenched her jaw and thought about the malpractice lawsuit and trial that had consumed her mother for much of the last two years. No doubt her father had read the transcript.

"And her lawyers were right," she said. "It wasn't Mama's fault. The little boy fell off the monkey bars. There was no indication of a brain hemorrhage when she examined him. The expert testimony confirmed she had been as thorough as any other physician would have been."

"Nonetheless, a little boy died. If your mother had taken a few more precautions, maybe that child would still be alive."

The unspoken words hung between them. *Maybe Ethan wouldn't have gone missing.*

"You're using hindsight," Aubrey said. "And why are you being such a bastard and bringing it up now? Why are you hitting Mama while she's down?"

"My grandson is missing."

"Yes. And Ethan's her grandson, too. She loves him, too. We all love him. But instead of being supportive, you attack her." She was breathing hard. "What's *wrong* with you? You used to be loving and caring, but I don't know you anymore. I haven't recognized you in eight years."

"When are you going to stop defending her?" he asked.

"When are you going to stop blaming her?"

And she stormed away, through the thick grass, out of the sharp sun, and back into the shadows, more determined than ever to get to her mother's side.

CHAPTER 5

She deserved to be blamed. A grandmother who'd lost her own grand-child. But would blaming herself bring Ethan home safely?

Diana was shaken as she stepped outside her small home office where the FBI was conducting interviews with the family members. The agent's questions had felt like personal attacks, opening old wounds and reminding her how tenuous her hold on happiness was. Questions about her relationship with Kevin and his family, with her ex-husband, and about her recent engagement to Jonathan Woodward and his possible Supreme Court nomination. Then more questions about the Coles and the malpractice lawsuit.

She had answered as honestly and completely as she could, understanding that someone in her life—or something she may have done to someone—could be behind Ethan's kidnapping. But she'd felt the implied blame behind the agent's questions and wondered, *How far back would the FBI dig to try to find a motive?*

She wandered through the downstairs rooms, a stranger in her own home. And so completely alone.

Had Aubrey arrived?

She wanted very much to see her daughter, but also felt guilty about putting her through this, too.

She glanced into the family room at the makeshift command post. There was no sign of the detectives who'd been keeping her informed about their progress. The FBI was monitoring her cell-phone and e-mail activity, as well as those of Kevin, Kim, and Kim's parents. She wondered whether anyone had received a ransom demand. That was looking like their best hope—that Ethan had been taken for money. And the Simmers were the likely target because of their wealth and public visibility.

Of course, that was no excuse for losing him, in their eyes or in hers.

In the kitchen, the coffeemaker was on, the coffee burned down to the dregs. She turned the machine off. Plastic cups and Styrofoam containers with sandwich crusts and uneaten salad had been abandoned on the scratched wood countertops. She gathered them up and dumped them in the garbage beneath the sink. She couldn't remember when she'd last eaten, but she had no appetite.

She glanced up at the photo of her mother as a young woman on a shelf beside the brass Sabbath candleholders she'd brought on her journey to America. Her mother had escaped the Holocaust, but her parents and older siblings had not.

Diana pressed her fingers to her lips, then touched her mother's face. *Please watch over our precious Ethan and keep him safe,* she prayed.

She turned from her mother's large, sad eyes. On the table was a pile of mail someone must have brought in. She picked it up and started to sort through the letters, just to have something to do. The envelopes had already been slit open. But why? Then she realized the FBI had probably gone through the mail, checking for a ransom note.

Seemingly out of nowhere, she was hit with such a powerful wave of exhaustion she could barely remain standing. During her residency, she had sometimes gone without sleep for forty-eight hours or more, but she'd never felt like this.

She hadn't slept since Saturday, the night before last, when the Simmers had dropped Ethan off. She'd lain awake much of that night, listening for sounds coming from Kevin's old room, where her grandson slept in his father's bed, surrounded by posters of hobbits and Middle-earth, Kevin's obsession all through his teens. But Ethan hadn't awakened.

She could only pray he'd slept soundly last night, too, wherever he'd been. That whoever had taken him—because by now it was clear that Ethan had been taken—would be gentle with her grandson.

She held the mail with one hand, and clinging to the banister with the other, went upstairs.

Aubrey's bedroom door was open. Diana's heart sped up. Aubrey was here. Her winter coat lay across the white bedspread, and her unopened suitcase sat near the foot of the bed.

But she wasn't in her room.

Diana felt a powerful letdown.

Maybe it was all a mistake. Maybe Ethan was asleep in his father's bed.

She took a few running steps and opened the door to Kevin's room. Ethan's little suitcase still on a chair, a pair of red sneakers on the floor, the sweatshirt he'd worn at breakfast then discarded before they'd left for the carnival, lying inside out on the bed.

But no Ethan.

She held her hand over her heart and sank onto the bed. On the wall across from her was Kevin in cap and gown. It was his high school graduation photo, which he never would have agreed to keep in his room with his favorite posters. But he had gone off to Dartmouth, so she'd hung the photo and occasionally sat here, not quite over her guilt for missing his graduation. Wondering whether Kevin had forgiven her for choosing a critically ill patient over him.

At the time, she'd been certain her son would understand, but something in his cool manner when she joined the family after he'd already received his diploma had told her she had failed him—that she'd been failing him for a long time.

Then, she had messed up yet again when she was unable to be at his wedding.

He stared back at her now with dark, solemn eyes.

It was how he'd looked at her last month, right after Christmas, when she'd flown up to New York, to see him for the first time in eight years and meet her grandson.

She had taken a taxi to her son's Manhattan apartment from La Guardia, surprised to find him waiting for her in the lobby of his building. They hadn't hugged, just greeted each other formally, which tore at her heart. He said he wanted to talk to her before they went up to see Kim and Ethan. After leaving her luggage with the doorman, they crossed over to Central Park and sat on a bench beneath a bare tree, surrounded by piles of dirty snow and wet, brown leaves.

"I've missed you so much," she said. "Thank you. Thank you for letting me back into your life."

Kevin looked away, his lower lip trembling. Her little prince. He would always be her little prince, no matter what.

"I'm sorry about what happened," she said. "My illness, your wedding. Please believe me that I never did anything to deliberately hurt you." She reached for his hand.

He continued to gaze across the park in the direction of Belvedere Castle, where she had fallen in love with his father. But Kevin didn't know about that, or about all the difficult things they had shared, so he couldn't possibly understand the extent of her devastation when Larry left her for another woman.

Kevin turned back to her, his eyes dark and serious. "I told Kim that Ethan should have all his grandparents in his life. She may be a little aloof toward you at first, but I'm sure she'll be fine. The most important thing is that you and Ethan get to know each other."

Diana didn't know why Kevin and Kim had agreed to forgive her, and it wasn't important. All she cared about was having her son back, getting to know his wife, and most of all, having her grandson in her life.

Over the next few days, the four of them went to museums and plays, and ice skating in Rockefeller Center beneath the magnificent Christmas tree. She and Kim, and sometimes Kevin, took Ethan to his karate and gymnastics classes. Ethan called her "Grandma," and even Kim laughed and seemed at ease around her. When Diana asked whether Ethan could spend a few days with her in Miami, they agreed. Kevin thought it would be cool for his son to sleep in his old room and to see the park where he'd learned to play ball.

"Kim is nervous about Ethan staying with you," Kevin told her privately. "But I reassured her. You're his grandmother, and I know Ethan will be safe with you."

And she had let him down.

"I'm sorry, Kevin," she said to the photo.

She left the bedroom and closed the door. Barely able to stand, she used the wall for support to get to her own room and collapsed on her bed, dropping the mail beside her. The room began spinning, and she was reminded of the dreadful teacup ride, the turning barrel in the fun house, and those even-worse times when vertigo had taken over her life. She shifted onto her side and shut her eyes.

She was jarred by soft ringing. Her cell phone. This could be the ransom demand they'd been waiting for. But why call her and not the Simmers? She fumbled in her pocket for the phone, hand trembling.

Caller ID showed it was Jonathan.

She sat up against the pillows and answered, disappointed this wasn't the break in Ethan's ordeal but comforted to hear her fiancé's gentle voice.

"Am I catching you at a bad time?" he asked. "Are you with the FBI agent?"

"No, I'm in my bedroom."

"Oh, gee. You're resting. I should have waited for you to call me, but I've been very anxious about you, darling."

"I'm glad you called."

"Any news?"

"No. Nothing yet." She blinked away the fuzziness in her brain. "How's the vetting going?"

"It's going, but I can hardly think about that right now."

"You have to, Jonathan. I know how much the nomination means to you."

"It doesn't mean as much to me as you do. Say the word and I'll fly home. I can't stand being here in DC while you're going through this alone."

"You're an angel, but Aubrey's here. I'll be okay. I don't want you turning your world upside down for me."

She could hear him breathing, as though he were weighing what he was about to say next. "You *are* my world, Diana. We don't need to wait until we're married to lean on each other."

Her eyes filled with tears. This was one of the reasons she hadn't wanted him to come back. She needed to be strong on her own. But she was also concerned about dragging him into the national spotlight when he was already being scrutinized. The FBI agent had been curious about Jonathan and even suggested there could be some connection between his possible nomination and Ethan's disappearance.

If the press picked up on that, it wouldn't do anyone any good.

"I love you, Jonathan. So very much. But if you come to Miami, I'm afraid it will turn Ethan's disappearance into a national media event. Everyone will wonder whether they want a Supreme Court justice with so much personal drama in his life. First, his fiancée is accused of being responsible for a child's death out of negligence, then she loses her own grandson."

"You know I would never put my career ahead of my family."

"That's the point. You won't put yourself first, which is why I need to protect you right now. You deserve to be on the Supreme Court. The country needs people like you. I won't allow you to jeopardize that."

He released a sigh.

"I'm holding up for now, but if that changes, I'll call you. I promise."

"I don't like it, but I'll do as you ask," he said.

"Thank you," she said. "Thank you, my darling."

She ended the call but held the phone against her chest. Jonathan had become her rock. They had met two years before, introduced at a Columbia University alumni event by the attorney who'd been handling her malpractice lawsuit. The eminent Judge Jonathan Woodward had recently moved back to Miami, his birthplace, after his appointment as circuit-court judge for the Eleventh District. They'd begun dating shortly thereafter, and then more seriously a few months ago, once the malpractice trial was over.

Jonathan had been supportive throughout, especially when her medical partners had hinted that she should consider retiring. A number of patients had lost confidence in their practice and had moved to other pediatricians. Jonathan had helped her through her initial anger and to the realization that the patients weren't the only ones who'd lost confidence. She had begun second-guessing many of her own diagnoses, to the point where she was barely functional. Leaving the practice three months ago had probably been the best thing for her as well.

The weight of her phone pressed against her heart. She'd fallen in love with him unexpectedly. She'd gotten the flu and could barely get out of bed. He had stayed with her against her protests, holding her hair back when she vomited into the toilet, cuddling against her when she shook with chills, feeding her spoonfuls of soup he'd made from a package.

Call him back. Tell him you need him. Don't let your pride keep you from seeking comfort.

She picked up the phone, her finger poised to call him.

"Mama," said the voice in the doorway. "Oh, Mama."

Diana dropped the phone, sprang out of bed, and rushed to her daughter. She squeezed Aubrey with all her might. She could smell her daughter's spicy scent, barely masking twenty-four hours of airports and travel.

Through all Diana's ups and downs, her battles with vertigo and taunting demons, Aubrey, unlike her father and brother, had never deserted her.

Reluctantly, Diana released her grip and took a step back to examine her. "Oh, my poor sweetheart. You're exhausted." She pushed a strand of hair away from Aubrey's pale face. There were dark shadows beneath her large brown eyes, like smudged charcoal. "You shouldn't have come. Not with everything you have going on. Classes starting this week. Jackson."

"Of course I had to come," Aubrey said. "You know I'll always be here for you." She paused. "And for Kevin. Have you seen him? Is he holding up?"

"Yes. They were all at the house earlier." She couldn't tell Aubrey how shattered he'd been this morning—a broken zombie. And Diana had broken him. "His in-laws have been taking charge of everything. Taking some of the burden off Kevin."

"That's our job, Mama."

"Kevin doesn't want us, Aubrey."

"Yes, he does. He needs both of us." Her daughter squeezed her hand. "But tell me how you're doing." Aubrey's eyes seemed to do a quick assessment of Diana's face and clothes, which she hadn't thought to change since yesterday. "Have you eaten anything?"

"I've grabbed a bite here and there."

Her daughter looked skeptical, then led her to sit on the edge of the bed. "They told me the FBI was interviewing you."

"They're talking to everyone in the family. Kevin, Kim, the Simmers."

"I heard the Simmers are bringing in their own investigators," Aubrey said. "The more people looking for Ethan, the better."

Diana reached for the mail strewn over the quilt and jogged the envelopes into alignment. "They blame me," she said. "Everyone does. And they're right. I should never have let go of his hand."

"Mama, stop it. It's impossible to watch a child one hundred percent of the time. You were not negligent."

"I'm hearing those words a little too often."

"Then let's just say beating yourself up is counterproductive. It doesn't help you, and it doesn't help Ethan."

She set the mail back down on the bed. "Okay, sweetheart. No more self-flagellation."

"Good." Aubrey ran her finger over a crimson satin square on the old patchwork quilt. A few stitches holding it in place had come out. "You've had this for as long as I can remember. Since Dad lived with us."

"It's a perfectly good quilt. I wasn't going to throw it away just because—" Diana stopped. She hadn't thrown *him* away. He threw *her* away.

"He's downstairs, you know," Aubrey said. "Sitting in the backyard."

"Who is? Your father? How did he get here so quickly?"

"I guess he took the red-eye."

Larry. There had been a time when they had faced terrible things together, but they were no longer the impregnable entity they had once been. "I'd rather not see him."

"I'm sure he understands that, but Ethan's his grandson, too. It was the right thing for him to come."

"Yes. Of course. I wish . . ." Diana shook her head. She was having a hard time holding on to her thoughts.

There was a soft knock on the doorjamb. "Excuse me, Dr. Lynd. I hate to intrude." Gonzalez, the woman detective, stood in the doorway. "I wanted to give you a quick update. Kevin and Kimberly will be making a statement to the press at five at their hotel. I understand the Simmers will be offering a sizable reward."

"We should go to support them, Mama," Aubrey said. "I want to see Kevin."

"Actually," the detective said, "the Simmers asked that you not be present. They don't want your mother distracting the press."

"What?" Aubrey said. "That's outrageous."

"She's right, Aubrey," Diana said, ashamed in front of the detective and her daughter. "The attention needs to be on finding Ethan, not on the one who lost him."

"I'm not so sure about that," Aubrey said. "I think the entire family should be together to show solidarity."

"I'm afraid it's the Simmers' show," Gonzalez said. "They've arranged the press conference and can handle it as they choose."

A sense of helplessness settled over Diana. The Simmers were controlling her family, and there was nothing she could do about it.

"And we can use your help here," Gonzalez said to Aubrey. "Special Agent Smolleck would like to have a word with you."

"With me?"

"FBI is speaking to all family members."

Aubrey gave Diana a hug. "I'll be back with something for you to eat." She got up and followed the detective out of the room.

Diana leaned back against the throw pillows. Her phone was on the bed next to the pile of mail she had brought up. She'd been ready to call Jonathan, but maybe she would wait. Aubrey was here now, taking charge of things. And did she want to bring him into this mess with Larry here and the Simmers asserting themselves? Maybe it would be best for things to settle a bit.

She hoisted herself up on one elbow and spread out the mail on the quilt, hoping a mindless task would calm her growing fears for Ethan. The open envelopes contained bills—credit cards, FPL, DishNET. There were also some advertisements, a medical journal, and a square sealed envelope that looked like a greeting card or an invitation to something. No return address, and the stamp hadn't been postmarked. That was odd. It was hand-addressed to "Di Lynd." But Diana had stopped using her nickname when she had married Larry in her sophomore year of college.

At that point, Di Hartfeld no longer existed.

Why hadn't the FBI opened this envelope?

She slipped a finger under the flap and pulled out a greeting card for a child. There was a cartoon depiction of a smiling little boy on a red tricycle, and above him the printed words, TODAY IS YOUR SPECIAL DAY.

A chill ran down her back. No one she knew would send her a card like this. Her hands began to shake uncontrollably as she struggled to open the card. A small piece of paper drifted onto the bed. Inside the card was the same grinning boy, waving from the tricycle, and the words, BECAUSE YOU ARE SPECIAL!

She picked up the paper that had fallen out, trying to hold it steady. The words blurred, then came into petrifying focus.

WE HAVE ETHAN. HE IS SAFE.

WE WILL RETURN HIM UNHARMED IF YOU DO ONE THING.

KILL JONATHAN WOODWARD.

CHAPTER 6

The door to her mother's office was open. Aubrey peered into the small, cluttered room with its large, low window that overlooked the jungle in the backyard.

Special Agent Smolleck's back was to her, something in his out-stretched arms. He took up too much space as he sat stiffly in Mama's rickety wood swivel chair at the scratched oak desk that faced the window. Except for this man, the office was like it had always been, with piles of paid and unpaid bills on the desk, and stacks of medical journals on top of the wooden file cabinets.

Beside the desk were shelves with dozens of old photos of Aubrey and Kevin, a few of Aubrey and Mama, and several of Ethan that she had sent her mother over the years. On the top shelf was a gaping space between a childhood photo of Aubrey and Kevin and a recent one of Kevin and Kim.

She stepped into the room.

Smolleck was holding a picture frame. Aubrey could make out Ethan's grinning face, and her first reaction was to grab it out of Smolleck's big hands. Then she reminded herself that the agent was just doing his job.

The picture was the "Tooth" photo she had taken two weeks before in Manhattan. Aubrey had taken Ethan to a matinee to see *The Lion King*. Afterward, they went to Ellen's Stardust Diner where Ethan had lost a front tooth and was proudly displaying it in the photo. It was the first baby tooth he'd lost.

"Detective Gonzalez said you wanted to see me."

Smolleck glanced over his shoulder, startled, but quickly regained his composure. His face settled into a mask, making it difficult for her to read him, and he put the picture frame on the desk. "Yes, thank you, Ms. Lynd. I'd like to talk to you for a few minutes. Would you mind getting the door?"

She closed it and sat down on a ladder-back chair at the side of the desk, catty-corner to Smolleck. The chair belonged in the kitchen and had probably been brought in here for the interviews. On the desk was an iPad, a yellow legal pad covered with writing, and a machine the size of a cell phone that was likely a recorder.

"You can call me Aubrey," she said, hoping to dispel some of the formality in the room.

"Aubrey, then." His voice retained its coolness. He scrolled through his iPad.

Although she'd seen him in the foyer when she'd first arrived, she now had an opportunity to study him, to decide whether he was as self-important as he had initially appeared. He was probably in his early thirties but seemed older because of his rigid manner, which she guessed came from a stint in the military. His reserve was very different from Jackson's charming and easygoing veneer. And unlike Jackson, who went in for the "grunge" look, the FBI agent was immaculate, from his perfectly knotted tie to his buffed fingernails.

"Okay, then." Smolleck picked up an expensive-looking pen and leaned back in her mother's chair, which creaked under his weight. "I would appreciate your help in sorting through a few things."

"Whatever I can do, if it will help find Ethan more quickly."

"Great." He scratched his eyebrow with the push button of the pen. That's when she noticed the tiny indentation and missing hairs, and realized that at some point in his life he had pierced his eyebrow. "Would you mind if I tape this?" His index finger hovered over the small recorder.

"That's fine," she said.

He pressed a button. "Special Agent Tom Smolleck interviewing Aubrey Lynd, aunt of Ethan Lynd. There are no others present in the room."

She felt surprisingly unsettled. Did the FBI believe the family was somehow involved with Ethan's disappearance? Of course they would. The family was always suspected first. Dad had said they'd given everyone lie detector tests. They would probably give her one, too. Well, she had nothing to hide.

"Tell me about your relationship with your nephew," Smolleck said.

"I live in Rhode Island, and Ethan lives with his parents in Manhattan, so I don't get to see him as often as I'd like."

"How often do you see him?"

"Several times a year."

"So you've never been estranged from your brother?"

It was a funny word—*estranged*. She and Kevin seemed like strangers these days, but that was more than she cared to share with Smolleck. She had worked hard to keep communication between them open, but Kevin deserved credit for allowing her in. Perhaps, on some level, he'd never stopped seeing her as his kid sister and childhood ally. Or maybe he hoped that someday she'd be the life raft that would bring him and Mama back together.

"No," she said. "We've never been estranged."

"Unlike your mother," Smolleck said.

"That's right," she said softly.

Smolleck twirled the pen between his fingers like a baton. "You see, I'm confused by the family dynamics. Maybe you can straighten me out." He didn't wait for her to respond. "I understand your mother and brother weren't speaking to each other until recently. Can you tell me what caused their estrangement?"

He had probably heard Mama's and Kevin and Kim's versions of what had happened, so why ask about it again? Unless Smolleck was looking for inconsistencies for some reason?

"My parents decided to get divorced eight years ago, right around the time of Kevin's wedding. My mother got sick and wasn't able to attend."

"Was she seriously ill?"

"Serious enough for her to be hospitalized." She tried to keep her anger at her father from rising up. His timing for telling Mama he was leaving her for another woman, just days before Kevin's wedding, had been inexcusable. Mama had been shattered and barely able to function.

"I'm not quite following," Smolleck said. "Why would your brother be angry about her being ill?"

"He believed she had faked it."

"Why would he have thought that?"

Her eyes roamed over the photos on the shelves. None of Kevin and Mama.

"Our father told Kevin she was putting on an act. That she wasn't really sick, but was trying to get sympathy or attention by not going to the wedding." Aubrey had been stunned when Dad transferred blame away from himself to Mama, and then behaved so damn righteous about it. His self-serving lies had turned Kevin completely against Mama and—whether or not that had been her father's intention—had been the cruelest part of his betrayal.

"And your brother chose to believe your father?" Smolleck asked. "I'm surprised he didn't cut your mom some slack."

Aubrey felt uneasy, as though she were being disloyal to her mother. "It wasn't just about the wedding," she said. "My brother had issues with my mom that went back a while."

"What kind of issues?"

She didn't like the direction his questions were taking. It was as though he were considering that Mama was behind Ethan's kidnapping. She needed to make sure he understood that was impossible.

"Typical child-parent things," Aubrey said, hoping to minimize the situation. "Kevin was a sensitive kid. He sometimes felt our mother wasn't always there for him."

"Did you feel that way?"

"Absolutely not. Our mother loves us. She always put us first." At least that was Aubrey's perception. But she knew from studies that children from the same family rarely viewed their parents in the same way.

"Okay," Smolleck said. "Back to the wedding. Your mother was hospitalized and didn't attend. Tell me about her illness."

"She suffered from severe vertigo, from an old injury. It flares up when she's under stress."

He looked at something on the yellow pad. "An injury she got when she was in college, is that right? At Barnard. And your father was at Columbia University. That's where they met, wasn't it?"

"Yes."

"Do you know how she got injured?"

"Not really. She was in an accident. That's all I know." He was making her defensive. "Does this have something to do with Ethan?"

"Ah, sorry." He scratched the indentation in his eyebrow with his pen. "You're studying psychiatry, right? You're probably busy analyzing me and my questions."

"I'm working on my PhD in psychology," she said. "I'm not in medical school."

It seemed he gave her a little wink, but she must have imagined it. "Glad we cleared that up," he said. "So, are you in a relationship with anyone?"

"Was." She glanced at her bare hand. Jackson had never gotten around to getting her a ring, though he'd been hinting at it for years.

She now knew he had never intended to take things to the next level. "I ended it with him a couple of days ago."

"A couple of days ago," he repeated, then pressed his lips together. "Had your boyfriend ever met Ethan? Did he know you were close to your nephew?"

"Well, yes, but . . ." Smolleck couldn't be thinking Jackson was involved.

"Is it possible your boyfriend was angry enough over the breakup to try to get even with you?"

"By kidnapping Ethan?" She shook her head. "No. Definitely not. It isn't in his nature."

"I suppose you're pretty good at knowing what people will and won't do from your studies in psychology."

"That's right." She sat up straighter. "In particular, I know Jackson." She stopped herself. She had thought she knew him, but she had closed her eyes to the real person. "I, I think it's very unlikely that he's involved."

"May I have Jackson's contact info so we can rule him out?"

She gave Smolleck his phone and e-mail address, feeling violated somehow. She had heard that Jackson had moved in with a graduate student in the English department, but didn't know the specifics.

The agent jotted down what she told him on the yellow pad, then looked back up at her. "So tell me about your brother and his wife," he said, changing direction so abruptly that Aubrey started. "Do they have a good marriage?"

"I guess."

"Kevin's a financial guy at BBM," Smolleck said. "Baer Business Machines is a nice family business to marry into."

"I suppose so. Is there some reason you're bringing it up?"

"Does Kevin get along well with his in-laws?" he asked without answering her question.

This FBI agent was all over the place. First, he hinted at Mama's involvement with the kidnapping, then Jackson's, and now it seemed he was considering the Simmers, or maybe BBM. But, of course, anyone might be a suspect. Was she?

"I couldn't say what his relationship is with the Simmers," she replied. Or more accurately, it wasn't her place to say.

A couple of years before, when she and her brother had been sharing a rare fraternal moment, Kevin had confided that he hated working at BBM. Ernest Simmer treated him like an errand boy, but Kevin felt trapped because his father-in-law was paying him so well. Kevin had told Kim he wanted to quit, but she was clearly not a fan of taking a hit to their comfortable lifestyle. Of course, it had been two years since that conversation. Maybe things had changed.

Smolleck leaned forward in her mother's chair. It creaked. "So what happened with your mother?"

Back to Mama. Why was he playing this head game? "What do you mean?" she asked.

"For eight years Kevin and Kim cut her out of their life; then when Ethan is six, they welcome her back." His voice had softened, no longer in attack mode. "Why'd they forgive her after all this time?"

It was a good question. One she'd given some thought to, but there had been no particular event or change that she knew of.

Smolleck's eyes were still on her.

"I don't know for sure," she said. "Maybe Kevin and Kim decided it was time for Ethan to get to know his other grandmother."

He picked up the photo of Ethan holding out his baby tooth. "It's kind of interesting that they would trust your mother with Ethan after she was sued for negligence that led to a child's death."

Aubrey winced. "My mother was cleared of those charges."

"Yes, I understand. But the timing seems odd to me."

"If you're trying to build a case against my mother, that's absurd. Why would she kidnap Ethan now, when she and my brother are finally reconciled and she's able to see her grandson freely?"

"An interesting paradox."

"Not a paradox at all, since my mother didn't kidnap him." Her voice had gotten higher, the way it did when she was upset. She took a breath, trying to bring it—and herself—back under control. "Agent Smolleck," she said, "I can appreciate that investigating the family is part of your due diligence, but shouldn't the FBI be considering other possible abduction suspects? Sex offenders, that kind of thing."

"There are several of us down here on the CARD team, Ms. Lynd. Excuse me, I mean Aubrey." His voice had resumed its clipped formality. "We're each investigating different areas. Does that answer your question?"

Her face got warm. She wasn't accustomed to being spoken to this way.

"So let's talk about this malpractice lawsuit," Smolleck said, not waiting for an answer. "Are you aware of any threats against your mother from Ryan Cole's family?"

"I'm not, but have you asked her?" She didn't like that he was getting to her, causing her to respond irritably to his questions. He was on *their* side, she reminded herself.

"The lawsuit unsettled your mother quite a bit, didn't it? I understand she resigned from her medical practice shortly after the trial was over."

Aubrey pulled the wool collar of her sweater away from her neck. It was too hot in here. She should have changed clothes when she arrived.

Smolleck was staring at her with his damn iridescent eyes.

"My mother and her fiancé decided it was a good time for her to retire."

"That's right," Smolleck said. "Her fiancé. Jonathan Woodward. He's being considered for the Supreme Court nomination. Tough to have two strong careers in one family. Is that why she resigned?"

Was he trying to bait her again? She didn't answer.

"You've met him, I assume," Smolleck said.

"Jonathan? Of course."

"And you like him?"

"Very much."

"Did your mother ever mention that he has any enemies? Anyone they were concerned might be upset if he was appointed to the Supreme Court?"

Aubrey glanced out the window at the thick jumble of trees, then turned back to him. She had assumed Ethan's kidnapping was a random child abduction or someone trying to get at Prudence Simmer's money. It hadn't occurred to her that it might be politically motivated. "You think someone kidnapped Ethan to get at Jonathan?"

"Do you think that's a possibility?"

"I suppose, but I don't have much to offer you on that. My mother never mentioned any concerns to me. Wouldn't it be better if you asked her or Jonathan directly?"

"Good idea," he said. "Moving on. Judge Woodward went to Columbia Law School right around when your mother and father were undergraduates there." He tapped the pen against his chin. "Is that where your mother met him?"

"No. They met in Miami a couple of years ago."

"Did your father know the judge at Columbia?"

"I have no idea," Aubrey said. "Did you ask him? And what does this have to do with Ethan?"

"What's your relationship with your father like?"

His questions whipsawed her. It was clear he was trying to catch her off guard. But about what?

"My father and I aren't close."

"Since the divorce?"

"That's right." Her mouth was dry. She needed some water.

"How often do you see each other?"

"Not very."

Smolleck glanced at the yellow pad again. "Your father does quite a bit of work for Innocence Projects around the country. Has he made any professional enemies that you know of?"

"I doubt it," she replied. "My father gets innocent men wrongfully convicted of murder off death row. He's a hero. Everyone loves and admires him."

"Except you."

He had once been her hero, too. "Can children ever stop loving their parents?" she asked, more of herself than of Smolleck.

"I suppose you don't like his girlfriend."

"No, I don't. May I ask where you're going with these questions?"

He leaned back in the chair. "Did your father know about Ethan?"

"I'm not following you. Know what about Ethan?"

"That your mother was back in your brother's good graces and Ethan was coming to spend a few days with her."

"I suppose," Aubrey said. "Kevin probably told him. But why is that an issue? What difference does it make if my father knew Ethan was here? It's not like he kidnapped his own grandson."

Smolleck sat forward and held the ends of the pen with his index fingers. "So who do you think took Ethan?"

His direct question took her aback. She picked up the photo from the desk.

One tooth missing and a big grin on his face.

One tooth closer to being an adult, but still a child. And here she was, unable to protect him. "I wish I could tell you that."

She got up from her chair and put the photo back on the shelf with the others. Back where he was surrounded by family and loved ones.

At least she could do that for her nephew.

Chapter 7

Diana made it to the bathroom just in time to retch into the toilet. Nothing came up but bitter bile. She heaved again and again, until finally the nausea subsided, but not the sharp pain in her gut. She put her head down on the cold tile floor.

For the past six years, what she had wanted most was to be part of her grandson's life. Now that she had finally gotten to hold him and kiss him and smell his sweet hair, someone was threatening to harm him.

Unless she murdered her fiancé.

She sat up and looked again at the note in her hand.

WE HAVE ETHAN. HE IS SAFE.

Focus on that. Her grandson was alive. He was safe.

She studied the small paper in her hand, probably from a notepad. She turned it over.

you have until midnight tues. if we don't have physical proof of jonathan woodward's death, ethan will die.

if you talk to the cops or fbi, ethan will die.

Ethan will die.

She gagged on another wave of nausea. Kill Jonathan, or Ethan would die.

And there was no one she could turn to for help.

She got up from the floor and caught her face in the mirror, pale and haggard. Her hands shook as she turned on the faucet and filled a cup with cold water. It spilled on her chin and chest as she drank.

The note had fallen to the floor. She picked it up and put it back inside the greeting card. The picture of a little boy on a red tricycle jumped out at her, this time its significance registering.

She grabbed the vanity top for support, as the room and memory whirled around her.

The little boy pedaled past her on a red tricycle. He was wearing a blue-and-white-striped sweater. He rode the tricycle around and around on the cracked sidewalk in front of the old brick brownstone, stopping to smile and wave at her. She hurried past him to the weathered oak door and banged hard with the brass knocker. She needed to talk to them.

"Let me in." She pounded on the door.

A little boy on a red tricycle. It couldn't be a coincidence.

The note. The card.

If anyone saw them . . .

If anyone put it together . . .

She hurried to the bedroom, the walls closing in around her. *Hide it. Hide it quickly.* But where? In a drawer, the closet, a book?

Her heart was pounding. Aubrey or the detective—they might walk in at any moment.

She reached for her hobo bag beneath the nightstand and shoved the card inside.

Her cell phone was on the bed, on top of the pile of mail. She stared at it.

What choice did she have?

She picked up the phone and lay down, crumpling into a fetal position. Then she hit the speed-dial button that connected her to the first man she had loved in a long, long time.

He answered on the first ring. "Are you okay, darling?"

She closed her eyes, but the spinning wouldn't stop.

"Please come, Jonathan," she said, praying she was doing the right thing. "I need you."

CHAPTER 8

Aubrey hated that he'd gotten to her. That he'd made her so defensive. She had fled her mother's office after Smolleck had finished questioning her, given her his business card, and assured her the FBI and police were doing everything possible to get Ethan back safely.

She was surprised he hadn't asked her to take a polygraph, but maybe he was saving that for their next conversation.

She didn't know what to make of Special Agent Tom Smolleck. His line of questioning and confrontational approach made no sense. Her parents' college years and Mama's illness couldn't possibly be connected to Ethan's disappearance. And Smolleck's harping on the family dynamics and relationships disturbed her. Even the Simmers—as disagreeable as she found them—loved their grandson.

She couldn't imagine them or anyone else in the family staging a kidnapping.

She checked the time. A little after four thirty. Kevin and Kim were making a statement to the press at five at their hotel. It infuriated her that the Simmers didn't want her mother to be there. Through the dining-room casement window, she could see a couple of black sedans, a police car, and her mother's old red BMW in the driveway. All the news vans were gone and had left behind deep, black ruts in the grass. She wondered where her father was—whether he had been invited to the press event or had returned to his girlfriend, wherever they were staying.

And how was Kevin doing with all this?

Did he know about the Simmers' directive, or was he expecting Mama to be at the press conference?

She checked her phone for messages. No response from Kevin to her earlier text. She speed-dialed his number. The call went to voice mail. "Call me, please," she said, then sent another text. **Mama and I want to be at press conference. Simmers say no. What do you want?**

Kevin probably wouldn't get her messages if the man who had answered his phone earlier still had it, but she had to keep trying.

She went to the kitchen to get her mother something to eat and was momentarily calmed by the familiar sight of the round, white kitchen table, sunset-colored chintz curtains, and glass-fronted wood cabinets that had been painted white long before Aubrey's family had moved here. On a small shelf was a photo of Aubrey's grandmother as a young woman. Nana had lived nearby and had always been here when Aubrey came home from school.

With Mama and Dad preoccupied by their careers, Nana was the one who provided most of the hugs, reassurances, and Mallomars cookies—always with a glass of milk.

Aubrey often missed her grandmother, but she especially could have used a hug and a Mallomars cookie now.

She opened the refrigerator, surprised to find it fully stocked. Whole milk, orange juice, containers of fruit salad, string-cheese sticks, hot dogs, and snack-size bags of baby carrots. Her mother rarely kept much food in the house.

This was all here for Ethan.

She picked up the bag of carrots. The last time she'd been with Ethan, he had taken two small carrots and stuck one in each nostril, pretending to be a dragon.

"Do dragons eat carrots?" she'd asked.

He'd taken them out of his nose, then said with a big grin, "Only carrots with boogers."

It was one of his favorite words. *Boogers.*

She transferred fruit salad to a plate with a few cheese sticks and a bag of carrots, then went upstairs.

A vague smell like vomit hit her when she opened the door to her mother's room.

Mama was in a fetal position on top of the patchwork quilt, eyes closed. She was surrounded by mail and magazines, her phone close to her open hand. Her shoulder-length dark hair was uncombed, and her white button-down blouse was badly wrinkled and damp, as though she had spilled water on herself. The blouse looked like the one her mother had been wearing the previous day in the photo at the carnival. It was Mama's typical uniform—white shirt and jeans—but Aubrey wondered whether her mother had bothered changing her clothes since yesterday.

The scene before her reminded her of those times when she was a child, and then again when Dad left eight years ago—her mother curled up in bed, eyes squeezed shut against some terrible pain.

Aubrey would darken the room and put cool washcloths on her head, whispering over and over, *Mama, please be okay.*

"Mama?" she said softly. "Are you sick?"

Her mother blinked. She seemed to be trying to focus on one point, as though the room were spinning.

"Is it the vertigo?"

"I was a little dizzy, but it stopped."

"I brought you some food."

"No, thank you."

"You have to eat."

Her mother sighed, then propped herself up against the brass head-board. She took the plate and fork and fed herself a few bites.

Aubrey sat down on the bed. "I just spoke to Special Agent Smolleck."

Her mother toyed with a cheese stick.

"He asked a lot of questions about our family. About Dad and Jonathan."

"Jonathan?" Mama's head swung up. "Why was he asking about Jonathan?"

She was surprised by her mother's defensiveness. "It makes sense that the FBI would consider the Supreme Court angle," Aubrey said. "Has Jonathan mentioned any enemies to you?"

Her mother shook her head, then put the plate of food on the nightstand.

"Smolleck also asked about the family of the little boy who died. Do you think it's possible the Coles kidnapped Ethan to get back at you?"

"I don't know, Aubrey." She lay back down.

Something was definitely wrong. A half hour before, her mother had been sharp and alert, very much herself, despite the trauma of Ethan's disappearance, but now she was exhibiting signs of deep depression.

"Did something just happen?" Aubrey asked. "Did Dad come in here when I was downstairs and say something that upset you?"

"Please let me be." Her voice was flat. "I want to sleep."

Aubrey glanced at the mail strewn over the bed. Bills, flyers, and magazines, but something was missing. She thought back to her mother aligning the envelopes earlier. A square white one had stuck out above the others. She had noted a stamp on the envelope, which suggested a personal letter or card, but hadn't thought more about it.

Until now.

She surveyed the mail on the patchwork quilt, but the square envelope wasn't on the bed with the others. Had there been a ransom demand? That would bring them a step closer to getting Ethan back.

"Mama?" she said. "Was there something in the mail?"

Her mother opened her eyes and searched Aubrey's, as though she wanted desperately to communicate something. Then she shook her head.

Whatever had happened while Aubrey was downstairs with the FBI agent, it was clear that Mama wasn't willing to talk about it—at least not here in the house.

Aubrey breathed in the smell of vomit. She needed to get her mother away from here to somewhere less toxic. To a place where her mother would feel safe and tell her what was terrifying her.

For Ethan's sake, she needed to do it quickly.

CHAPTER 9

They walked in silence toward the park, along the route Aubrey used to take on her bicycle, zigzagging through narrow streets of dense foliage, past old wood-frame and stucco houses, then down the gentle slope from the top of the bluff to South Bayshore Drive.

It was close to five and the shadows were deepening.

Her mother clutched her hobo bag against her chest like a shield, her face in a tense frown. As desperate as Aubrey was to find out whether Mama had received a ransom note, she had to approach her delicately. Rushing her mother might cause her to shut down, and that would be the worst thing for Ethan.

They reached the corner of South Bayshore and waited for the traffic light as cars streamed by. Mama stared straight ahead, lips moving, as though she were working out a complex problem. The light changed and they crossed to the bay-front park, passing young people who were working out on the fitness circuit and running along the jogging path. The sky was a rich blue, the air sweet and crisp. It seemed incongruous with the anxiety Aubrey felt inside.

She and her mother sat on a shaded bench near where the water lapped against a low wall of coral rocks and they could see the boats docked at Dinner Key. Behind them, a dog barked plaintively in the fenced-in dog park.

Where was Ethan now? Crying for his mom or dad, or even Aunt Aubrey to come and rescue him?

They had to find him.

"Talk to me, Mama," Aubrey said. "Please tell me what's wrong."

Her mother held her bag more tightly against her chest but didn't answer.

"You can't do this alone."

"Let it go, Aubrey."

"What are you so terrified of?"

"Don't you understand? I have to protect Ethan."

"Protect him from what?"

Mama stared at the water sloshing against the rocks. "They said . . ." She shook her head.

Aubrey took in a sharp breath. "They?"

"Nothing. I'm not thinking clearly."

"Mama, did you get a ransom demand?"

Several dogs began barking in the dog park.

"I saw a square envelope with the rest of the mail," Aubrey said. "Did it contain a ransom note?"

Her mother nodded ever so slightly.

"Oh, my God," Aubrey said. "We have to tell the FBI."

"No."

Her mother wasn't being rational. "Tell me. What did the note say? Is Ethan okay?"

"Please, Aubrey. It's not safe for you to get involved."

"I am involved, so let's talk about this." Her voice sounded stronger in her own ears than she felt. "Why are you afraid to tell the FBI?"

"They said . . ." Her mother took a breath. "They said not to tell the police or FBI."

"But Ethan—is he safe?"

"I think so."

"What does that mean?"

"The note said they have him. That he's safe."

Safe. Ethan was safe. And if this was a ransom situation, the kidnappers would hopefully try to keep him comfortable until they traded him for what they wanted.

"Do they want money?" Aubrey asked. "Let's give them whatever they're demanding so we can get him back."

"It's not so simple."

"I'm sure the Simmers will contribute whatever is needed."

"They don't want money."

"Then what? What do they want?"

Mama looked down at her right hand, at the engagement ring Jonathan had given her, a small sapphire surrounded by a halo of tiny diamonds. Her mother mumbled something so softly Aubrey wasn't sure she'd heard her correctly.

"Did you say Jonathan?"

Her mother's eyes met hers. They were filled with a darkness Aubrey had never seen before. "Yes."

Aubrey tried to make sense of what her mother was telling her. "They want Jonathan in exchange for Ethan?"

Her mother nodded.

That was crazy. Or maybe it wasn't. Smolleck had suggested the kidnapping was politically motivated. "You must tell the FBI about this, Mama. They'll figure out how to handle it so no one gets hurt. Maybe some kind of swap."

"They don't want a swap."

"But you said . . ."

"They want Jonathan dead."

"*What?*"

"And they want me to kill him."

She stared at her mother, certain she must have misheard. Someone wanted her mother to kill the man she loved in exchange for her grandson's life. *Impossible!* It was the kind of thing you saw in movies. But life had already taken a turn for the bizarre—Ethan had been kidnapped. That wasn't supposed to happen in real life, either.

"You must get the FBI involved," Aubrey said.

"I can't. The note said . . ." Her mother licked her lips. "They said if I told the authorities, they would harm Ethan."

Aubrey felt faint. She wasn't naive. She had known since Ethan disappeared that the outcome could be devastating, but now there was a note and a threat that made the awful possibility that much more real.

She thought about her nephew grinning as he pulled the carrots out of his nostrils. *Boogers,* he'd said, laughing. Dragons only ate carrots with boogers.

The entire situation boggled her mind, but it was now twenty-six hours since Ethan had been taken. "Did the kidnappers give you a deadline?"

"They want proof of Jonathan's death by midnight Tuesday," her mother said. "I called him. I told him to come to Miami. I didn't say why."

An icicle slid down Aubrey's spine. "And what are you planning to do when he gets here?"

"I don't know. I figured if they're watching me, they would expect me to get Jonathan down here. It's the first step."

The first step in planning his murder?

"And the second step?" Aubrey asked.

"I haven't gotten that far."

"Mama, you can't be considering . . ."

"I've been trying to come up with a plan. I might tell Jonathan about the note. Then, if he agrees, I could give him a drug that would slow his heart down sufficiently for him to be declared dead."

"Whoa," Aubrey said. "You're thinking of giving him a drug? Isn't that risky to him?"

"Yes, but I have to do something."

"Then what? You said they want proof of his death."

"I'm not sure. I haven't thought it through."

Her mother was clearly desperate, coming up with this Romeo-and-Juliet solution, but trying to fake Jonathan's death could turn into another disaster.

"There's no guarantee these people will return Ethan even if they believe Jonathan is dead," Aubrey said.

Her mother turned her engagement ring around on her finger.

"And this isn't something you could pull off alone. You would need the medical examiner and lots of other people to help you. You'd have to get the FBI involved."

"No," her mother said. "No FBI."

What if her mother was right? Notifying the FBI could put Ethan in greater jeopardy. But coming up with a plan to fake Jonathan's death would never work. They had to figure out something better.

Aubrey watched the boats bobbing in the water. A few clouds had formed and reflected a hint of pink as the sun began to set. It was almost six. The note had given her mother a deadline of midnight tomorrow. Thirty hours from now.

Thirty hours in which to get Ethan back safely.

And they had to do it without the FBI.

CHAPTER 10

Her mind settled into a familiar track. Step one, make observations. Step two, gather data. Step three, derive predictions as a logical consequence. Step four, test hypothesis by conducting experiments. Step five, interpret results.

But the scientific method only worked in a controlled environment, which this definitely was not. Aubrey was outside her comfort zone.

A sailboat glided across the bay, glowing in the fading sunlight.

Thirty hours.

She sat up straighter. Just because she couldn't test the hypothesis didn't mean she couldn't analyze the situation in a logical manner.

"Let's start with the note," she said to her mother. "You said it was in the square envelope. I noticed it on the bed. It was stamped but not postmarked. Isn't the FBI checking the mail for ransom notes? How could they have missed it?"

"I don't know."

"Someone must have slipped it in with the mail after the FBI went through it."

Her mother frowned, as though considering this.

"Which means someone who was in the house today most likely put it there." Aubrey took out her iPhone. "Let's make a list of everyone in the house." She started tapping in names as she said them aloud. "Detective Gonzalez, Special Agent Smolleck, and the people on their teams."

"You think someone with the police or FBI is involved?" her mother asked.

"We have to consider it." Aubrey thought for a minute. "Unfortunately, there's no way we'll be able to figure out if there's some rogue agent or cop embedded with the legitimate team without revealing we know about the note."

"And then the kidnappers might harm Ethan," her mother said.

Her mother was right. Telling the FBI, even if they were able to do it secretively, could end any chance for Ethan's safe return.

Several joggers pounded the path as they ran behind the bench. Aubrey turned to look at them as they continued around toward the bay. A man in sunglasses glanced back at her, slowing his pace, then he took off after the others. Had he been sent to watch them?

There was no one she and her mother could trust. They were on their own.

"What about the reporters?" she asked her mother. "Did any of them come inside? Maybe to use the bathroom?"

"I don't know."

"Anyone else come inside the house?"

"I don't think so."

Aubrey continued tapping on her phone. "We also have Ernest and Prudence Simmer, Kevin and Kim, and Dad."

"You're putting them on the list?" her mother said. "But no one in the family would put Ethan in danger."

"We can't rule out anyone."

"Kevin and Kim wouldn't kidnap their own child," Mama said.

Aubrey didn't want to believe it, either, but she considered the possibility.

Her brother and his wife could have set up the kidnapping and the threat to Jonathan as a way of punishing Mama for the wedding incident, but it seemed like an over-the-top reaction, and they had never shown signs of being viciously vindictive. Besides, they were loving, protective parents—not the kind of people who would use their child as a pawn.

"I don't think they would," Aubrey agreed. "Let's focus on the others who were in the house earlier and consider if anyone else could have something against Jonathan." She thought about the Simmers. "Could Jonathan's appointment to the Supreme Court impact Prudence's interests in Baer Business Machines? BBM has come under fire recently for acquiring competitors, and Jonathan has been outspoken about being against large corporate mergers. If he's appointed, Prudence could take a major financial hit."

"You're right." Her mother leaned toward her, nodding. "The Simmers are bringing in their own investigators. That would make it easier for them to come up with their own facts and interpretations and keep attention away from themselves."

"True, but—"

"But that means Ethan is safe." Her mother's cheeks were flushed. "Prudence and Ernest would never hurt him. Never."

A scenario in which the Simmers had orchestrated the kidnapping had appeal. Her mother was right—they would never hurt their grandson—but their best chance for getting Ethan back safely was to consider every angle. "The Simmers might be behind this, but what if they're not?"

Her mother's face fell.

"I asked you earlier if Jonathan has enemies," Aubrey said. "Can you think of any? Someone upset by a ruling he made as a circuit-court judge or threatened by his possible nomination?"

"Not that I can recall." Her mother looked out toward the darkening horizon. "But wait . . . I don't know why I didn't think of this before. If this is about his Supreme Court nomination, I can just talk to him. I'm sure he'll withdraw from consideration."

It seemed like a good solution. Too good. "Did the kidnappers offer that as an option?" Aubrey asked.

"Well, no."

"Wouldn't they have? If this were just about keeping Jonathan off the bench, they could have simply demanded he withdraw. They wouldn't have told you to kill him."

"Maybe they knew I'd tell him about the note and are using it to frighten him into stepping away from the nomination."

"You could be right," Aubrey said, "but let's go back to the people who had an opportunity to leave the note in the house today." Like her father.

She watched a pelican sail across the sky, then abruptly dive into the water and scoop up a fish. So innocuous, then, without warning, going in for the kill. Just like her father had done eight years ago. And none of them had been prepared.

Was her father capable of kidnapping his own grandson?

He had been acting oddly in the backyard—his exaggerated anger at Mama, his body language not matching his words. He'd been lying about something.

"Could Dad have a reason for wanting Jonathan dead?"

"Your father?" Mama got quiet. A mockingbird's raspy call cut through the silence. "I don't see it," she said finally.

"Does Dad know him?"

"I don't think so, but it's possible. They may have met at a law convention or on a case."

Aubrey thought about Smolleck's questions. Now it occurred to her that he may have had something specific in mind. "What about back at Columbia?"

Her mother flinched. "Columbia?"

Something Aubrey had said had hit a nerve in her mother, but she couldn't imagine what.

"Jonathan was at the law school when your dad was an undergraduate," her mother said. "I doubt they knew each other there. But even if they had met, I think you're taking this in the wrong direction. Why would your father want me to kill Jonathan?"

"Jealousy that you're finally happy?"

"No, sweetheart. Put that out of your mind. Your father and I may have issues, but he's not capable of killing anyone, and he certainly wouldn't set me up to do so. And he never would have kidnapped Ethan."

"You don't think Star could manipulate him?"

"Not that far. And why would she want Jonathan dead?"

"Who knows? But what do we really know about her? Only that she appeared in Dad's life eight years ago, and suddenly he's obsessed with her. How could she have such power over him?"

Her mother looked sad. "It's not that hard to charm a man after he's been in a marriage for over thirty-five years, especially when his wife spends too much time with her patients and not enough with him."

Did her mother believe this? Aubrey knew her parents' marriage had been shaky for years, but all four of them had pretended everything was fine. Keeping the family together had been everyone's mission. At least, that's what Aubrey had always thought. Until Dad walked. But maybe he had become tired of pretending.

Maybe he had a point.

"Where's the note, Mama?"

Her mother squeezed her bag.

"You have it with you, don't you?" Aubrey said. "Show it to me."

"I don't see what that would accomplish."

"Please. Maybe when I read exactly what it says, I'll get an idea."

Her mother glanced around. It was growing dark and most everyone, including the joggers, had left. Only a couple of people remained in the dog park with their dogs.

Mama reached into her handbag and pulled out a square envelope, then slid out a greeting card. There was a picture of a child on the front.

Aubrey sucked in a sharp breath. An innocent-appearing greeting card. Someone's idea of a cruel joke? Who would do such a thing?

Her mother took a small piece of paper out of the card and handed it to Aubrey.

She read it, her pulse accelerating like a Geiger counter approaching radiation.

WE HAVE ETHAN. HE IS SAFE.

WE WILL RETURN HIM UNHARMED IF YOU DO ONE THING.

KILL JONATHAN WOODWARD.

Seeing the threat in print, holding the piece of paper—it wasn't just her mother's words.

It was real. Terrifyingly real.

Her mother mumbled something.

"What?" Aubrey couldn't hear anything over the pounding in her ears. "What did you say?"

"Turn the note over."

"There's more?" Aubrey looked at the other side of the paper. In smaller, lower-case letters was written:

you have until midnight tues. if we don't have physical proof of jonathan woodward's death, ethan will die.

if you talk to the cops or fbi, ethan will die.

Her mother had said they might hurt Ethan, but kill him? Kill a six-year-old boy who had just lost his first baby tooth and liked to make jokes about boogers? Then Aubrey reminded herself—Ethan wasn't their ultimate target, Jonathan was.

Or was he?

"Oh, God," Aubrey said.

"What is it?" her mother said.

Aubrey tried to formulate her thoughts, to make sure she got it right. "Why would someone go to the trouble of kidnapping Ethan if what they really want is to kill Jonathan?"

"I'm not following you."

"Kidnapping a child, planting an extortion note—it's very complicated. And when a child's life is threatened, look at all the publicity and law-enforcement involvement. Wouldn't it have been simpler for them to have killed Jonathan themselves?"

Her mother frowned. "That's true. Whoever is doing this can't be sure I would kill him."

"Which means killing Jonathan may not be their ultimate objective."

The last rays of sunlight fell on her mother's face, reflecting the recognition in her eyes. "Someone wants to hurt me by making me choose between my grandson and the man I love."

"Not just hurt you." Aubrey glanced down at the greeting card on her mother's lap, then met her eyes. "I think someone's trying to destroy you, Mama."

CHAPTER 11

Diana was numb. She was the real target of the kidnappers' ultimatum.

"Let's get out of here, Mama." Her daughter rose from the bench and tugged on her hand. "It's not safe to stay here."

"It wouldn't serve their purpose to hurt me," Diana said. "Not after they've gone to the trouble of kidnapping Ethan and sending me the note."

"Maybe, but we have to go back home. We need to figure out who put that envelope in the mail."

"You go."

"I'm not leaving you here alone. We don't know who these people are or what they're capable of."

"Please let me stay awhile. I need to think. If someone's out to get me, I must know this person."

Aubrey's brow formed a deep frown. "You think you know who it is?"

"I'm just being logical."

Aubrey seemed to hesitate. "Dad could have left the card."

Diana was glad the sun had gone down so Aubrey couldn't read the doubt on her face. She kept her voice even. "We've been through this. A lot of people could have left it."

"Are you protecting him?"

"Don't be ridiculous. Why would I protect him?"

"I don't know," Aubrey said. "Why would you?"

"I wouldn't. I told you that already." She took a breath to calm herself. "Now, please, leave me be for a little while. I have my phone. You and the police are on speed-dial if there's any kind of problem."

Her daughter looked around, as though considering what to do. There were lights on along the paths, and some brightness in the sky that would probably last for another half hour or so. A woman sat alone on a bench inside the dog park with her small dog.

"Please, Aubrey. I need a little time."

"Okay," she said, her tone skeptical. "If that's what you need."

Diana watched her leave the park, then turned back toward the boats bobbing in the grayish light.

Why had Aubrey asked whether she was protecting Larry? Neither she nor Larry ever talked about the past, so Aubrey had no way of knowing about the unspoken agreement between them. Yet, her daughter had asked the question as though she had some sixth sense.

Diana stared at the gray-black ripples tinged with red from the setting sun.

The same setting sun, the same bay, but so much was different.

They had moved here from New York when she was thirty-two, right after Kevin had been born. She'd wanted to be near her mother, who had been eager to watch the baby while Diana continued practicing medicine. In those first few years, she and Larry would often sit at the edge of the bay at sunset with a bottle of wine. Larry had liked to talk about the exciting adventures ahead of them. But maybe, even then, he could see through her fixed smile and know she didn't buy in to his programs the way she once had. Not that she hadn't loved him—she had. That was one thing that had never changed. Even after their charade almost disintegrated twenty years ago.

She hated thinking about it, but whether she acknowledged it or not, the appearance of a man claiming to be Jeffrey Schwartz and the terrible reminder of their college years had redefined their marriage.

Even after the media had reported that the man had been a fraud and the story had disappeared, she and Larry had realized the past was something they could never escape. They had tried to go back to their normal life, but it was as phony as the man who had garnered the headlines.

Maybe keeping up the facade was why Larry had sought refuge in another woman. Of course, at the time, Diana had been so shaken by his demand for a divorce that she had fallen apart, seized by an irrational fear of being on her own. In her distorted view of things, she had believed she and Larry had an obligation to each other—their own private, mutual-protection pact. How dare he throw her aside? Then, on top of that, Larry had told Kevin she had faked her illness, further driving a wedge between her and her son.

She had stewed in fear and anger until finally, with Jonathan, she had rediscovered joy. Now someone wanted to rip that happiness away from her.

Was it possible that just as she had felt when Larry deserted her, her ex-husband now viewed her engagement to Jonathan as a breach of their shared bond—a violation of their ugly secret?

Impossible, she thought, as another memory seeped in. The Larry she had once known would never turn on her like this.

———

They were calling it Indian summer, and no one wanted to do any work, even though it was the end of September, a month into classes, and everyone should have been in study mode. The stagnant ninety-degree air, heavy with smoke, made them all lazy, including Di. She leaned back on a patch of dried grass on Columbia University's sprawling lawn, surrounded by dozens of other students. Beyond loomed what looked like the Pantheon with its Ionic columns and domed roof, but was actually Columbia's Low Library, the soul of the campus, as its statue of Alma Mater proclaimed. The building's broad steps were covered with students. Many, like the ones on the lawn, were smoking pot, and even though Di wasn't a fan of marijuana, she couldn't help but inhale the sweet fumes that seemed to be part of the atmosphere.

She stretched out her legs and examined her faded tan, a remnant of sunbathing at Crandon Park Beach, back home in Miami. She hadn't expected to need summer clothes up in New York, but her mother had packed this pair of pastel madras shorts and a pink sleeveless blouse, just in case. She knew she was different from most of the other Barnard College women in their blue jeans and tie-dyed shirts, and it bothered her that she looked like someone who didn't know that the *Donna Reed Show* had been off the air for three years. But mostly, she was genuinely mystified by how different people were in New York from those in Miami. And it wasn't as though she were a hick. But something had happened this summer while she was off in Europe with her parents. Maybe it was Woodstock. Or the first man to walk on the moon. Or maybe the escalation of the Vietnam War. But when she'd returned home from vacation, then left for college with a suitcase filled with tailored dresses from Burdines Sunshine Fashions, she had found herself in a very different world.

She glanced at the lethargic students parked on blankets or tossing Frisbees in their cut-off shorts and T-shirts, some of the guys with their long hair in ponytails, strumming guitars or passing joints, the girls holding sun reflectors to tan their faces. A number of professors had brought their classes outside, where the students sat in semicircles beneath spreading oak trees, pretending to listen to lectures on the wisdom of Sophocles and the declines of Rome and civilization.

She took in another lungful of sweet, sleepy air, surprised to see her roommate hurrying toward her, full of energy and purpose, a jarring contrast to everyone else. But then, Gertrude was unlike anyone Di had ever known before. So much her own person, she even bragged about her ugly name as though it were a badge of honor.

Gertrude was puffing on a cigarette, her black hair in a single braid that swung from side to side behind her as she glided between the students on the lawn. She wore what she always wore, regardless of the weather: a long-sleeved white-cotton blouse with embroidery around the scooped neckline, which was not quite sheer enough to show her braless breasts, but close, and tattered blue jeans that dragged in the dirt and hadn't been washed since the two girls had moved into their freshman-dorm room a month before.

She stopped beside Di and extended her free hand. "Come on," Gertrude said, blowing out a stream of smoke. "Time to split."

Di took her hand, slick with sweat, and allowed herself to be pulled up. "Where are we going?"

"A meeting," Gertrude said. Behind her rose-tinted glasses, her eyes looked violet. "We're already late." She had an awful Brooklyn accent that was incongruous with the graceful way she moved.

"What kind of meeting?" Di asked, trying to keep up with Gertrude's rushed pace.

"Some guys I know," Gertrude said. The sun glinted off the stainless-steel dog tag she wore around her neck that had belonged to her brother. She never took it off, even to shower. "We're gonna fix this damn world."

"Fine," Di said. "But don't get angry if I leave in the middle. I told you I don't care about political stuff."

"I don't care about political stuff," Gertrude mimicked, capturing Di's hyperenunciated speech pattern and hand gestures. She was a natural chameleon. "I can't believe I'm rooming with goddamn Pollyanna." Gertrude said it lightly, in her coarse voice. It was their roomie joke, how they referred to themselves. Pollyanna and Che Guevara.

They walked around the outside of the imposing library, through a courtyard, then into a building Di had never been inside. Since all her classes were at Barnard this semester, she usually only came over to Columbia to use the main library.

Gertrude threw down her cigarette, pulled open the door to a stairwell, and ran up the stairs, the pounding of her wooden clogs echoing against the concrete steps. Di stomped out the cigarette, then followed her friend to the second floor.

The hallway was deserted. There were classrooms on both sides but no classes in session. Gertrude stopped by a door and looked in through the glass upper half, as though she were deciding what to do. She scratched the beauty mark on her right cheek. It made her look sexy, but Di knew better than to ever tell Gertrude that. Gertrude was an intellectual, not a sex object. She had no interest in attracting men, she'd said often enough. Fucking them was a different matter.

She tugged on the classroom door, shooting a quick glance at Di. "Okay, let's go."

They stepped into a room where a half-dozen students, mostly young men with mutton-chop sideburns and longish hair, sat in a semicircle. There was one pretty blonde girl, whose darting blue eyes and long neck made her resemble a fledgling egret. Di recognized her from the dorms. Linda something.

Di followed their gazes to the front of the room. A lean, good-looking guy with a white bandanna over wavy blond hair that reached his shoulders was perched on the desk. He had on torn jeans and a flowing white shirt that a Renaissance poet might have worn, except his was open almost to his waist, revealing a tanned chest with golden hair.

"Peace," Gertrude said, holding up two fingers in the symbolic gesture. She went over to him and kissed him deeply on the mouth. Then she pulled away and said, "I brought my roommate. Di Hartfeld."

The guy smiled at Di. He had clear blue eyes and an adorable cleft in his chin. "I'm Lawrence Lyndberger," he said. "Welcome to the coolest group of revolutionaries on campus."

———

The light was almost completely gone from the sky, and dark waves lapped against the rocks. Diana had once believed she knew Larry as well as she knew herself. The truth was, she didn't know him at all. She wondered whether she ever had.

CHAPTER 12

The walk home from the park had done nothing to settle the disturbing questions in Aubrey's head. Who had left the greeting card with the devastating threat? Was her father somehow involved? And how could she get answers without revealing that she knew about the note and putting Ethan at even greater risk?

The smell of garlic and sausage overpowered the usual musty one as she stepped inside the house. She followed the scent to the family room, where she hoped to find Smolleck.

He was a good place to start, but she would have to be cautious about what she said and asked, so as not to raise his suspicions.

She stopped in the entryway of the family room, disoriented by the unexpected brightness. All the lights had been turned on—something she or her mother rarely did—and the room had been further altered from when she had come by earlier. Portable whiteboards with writing and blowups of photos stood in front of the bookshelves. The coffee and end tables, which had been shoved against the walls, were heaped with Coke bottles, plastic cups, and pizza boxes. Several FBI agents were eating pizza at their makeshift work stations, temporary folding tables in the center of the room.

Aubrey stepped closer to the whiteboards and examined the enlarged photos. Ethan at the carnival. Photos her mother had probably taken. She wondered why they were here, then noticed in the background of each photo were crowds of people. One of them was very possibly Ethan's kidnapper.

She shuddered as she imagined someone scooping up her little nephew, then carrying him kicking and crying to a nearby car or truck.

But that wasn't likely. Ethan would have made a scene, and people would have interceded, or at least mentioned it to the police.

Which meant Ethan probably knew whoever had enticed him to leave the carnival.

"You shouldn't be in here." The clipped voice startled her.

She turned to face Special Agent Smolleck. He stood as though at attention, still in his suit jacket, crisp white shirt, and perfectly knotted tie.

"This is my house," she said.

"I'm sorry, but this is an active investigation. It's a breach of protocol for any family members to see what we're working on."

He was as arrogant as when he had interviewed her a couple of hours before.

"I understand," she said. "But wouldn't it help if you showed the family these photos to see if we recognize anyone in the crowds?"

His face colored. "I'll get you and the others a set."

"Thank you." She softened her voice. If she hoped to get information from him, it wouldn't be by putting him on the defensive. "Could I talk to you for a few minutes?"

Smolleck studied her with a frown, as though he could read in her face that she was withholding something. She was surprised when he grabbed a closed pizza box, a bottle of Coke, and a couple of plastic cups, then said, "Let's sit outside."

She followed him out the French doors to the wrought iron table and chairs in the patio. The small area was lit by a rusting outdoor sconce that had at least two of its bulbs burned out. It cast shadows over the brick pavers and rock garden. Beyond were the lounge chairs where she had sat with her father earlier, but they were in total darkness.

Smolleck sat on one of the chairs and opened the box of pizza. "Have some," he said, taking a slice for himself. "I'm guessing you haven't eaten in a while."

She hesitated, but the smell of cheese and sausage was too much to resist. She picked up a slice and took a bite.

"So this is where you grew up." He took in the dimly lit bamboos, palms, and shade trees. "Nice."

She glanced behind her through the French doors at the strangers in the too-bright family room. "Yes. It was." She could hear the wistful note in her voice, but there was no time for thinking about what once had been. She needed information from Smolleck.

"I was wondering if you could give me an update," she said. "Did you get any leads from Kevin and Kim's press conference?"

He poured Coke into the plastic cups. "Did you see it?"

She shook her head. "My mother and I were down at the park. She wanted to get some air."

Smolleck's features softened, or maybe it was the lighting. "Sometimes it's good to get a change of scene, even perspective."

What was with this sensitivity? A new FBI strategy?

"Anyway," he said, taking another bite of pizza, "you asked about Kevin and Kim's statement to the press. It's already generating a number of phone calls. Not surprising considering the size of the reward."

She didn't ask how much the Simmers were offering. She knew it would be a lot. "Anything useful?" she asked.

"Hard to tell. We're following up on everything."

"Is anyone in the family a suspect?"

He stopped chewing. "Why do you ask?"

"Because you didn't want me in the investigation area. If none of us are suspects, you wouldn't care if I saw what you were doing."

"Do you have reason to believe someone in your family is involved?"

He was turning her questions back on her. Well, she could play this game, too. "What did the polygraphs show?" she asked. "You tested Kim and Kevin, the Simmers, and my parents. Were any of the results suspicious?"

He scratched the tiny indentation in his eyebrow. A tell. Something in the lie detector tests had been suspicious. "Like whose?" he asked.

"I don't know," she said. "That's why I'm asking."

"We didn't polygraph your father," he said.

This was news. She tried not to look surprised.

"Or you." He paused. "Should we?"

"Why didn't you test my father?"

"It's a voluntary procedure," he said. "A way to rule out members of the family so we can concentrate on other possible suspects."

She looked down at the tiny clusters of green weeds growing between the mildewed pavers. "You didn't ask me to take a polygraph," she said. "Did you ask my father?"

"Would you be willing to take a polygraph?"

Her face got hot. She hoped he couldn't see the flush in the dim light. A lie detector test would likely force her to reveal what she knew about the ransom note. "Of course I'll take one," she bluffed. "But you didn't answer my question about my father."

He gave a little smile, as though he believed he'd scored a point. "Your father said he'd be willing to take it if we had a basis for suspecting his involvement, but would pass until then."

"Very lawyerly," Aubrey said, but her mind was racing. Was her father hiding something, or had he refused on principle? Ethan very likely knew the person he left the carnival with. "I assume you've confirmed my father's flight from California got in after Ethan disappeared, and that he isn't a suspect?"

Smolleck gave her a hard look. "Yes, we confirmed the flight times and whereabouts of everyone in your family when Ethan disappeared. Is there a reason you believe your father should be a suspect?"

"Of course not," she said quickly, relieved her father couldn't have been the one who took Ethan. "I'm just making a logical assumption about why you didn't press for the polygraph."

Smolleck scowled, obviously annoyed with her questions. He took another bite of pizza. A bit of cheese and sauce fell on his tie, but he didn't notice. For some reason, this gave her satisfaction.

"Why were you asking me about my mother's and father's past?"

"What do you know about their political leanings back in college?" he asked.

"Political leanings?" She wondered whether this could have something to do with Jonathan. "My parents never felt strongly about politics."

"That you know about."

"Why would they hide that from me?"

"I don't know. Do they hide things from you?"

She didn't answer.

He was watching her, waiting.

"We don't talk about a lot of things," she said. "It isn't a question of hiding."

"Sorry," he said. "I didn't mean to upset you."

Of course you did. She was breathing too hard. He had gotten to her again, and she was failing miserably at getting information. She took a long drink of soda, conscious of the way he was watching her for tells, just like the way she was watching him. "We've gotten away from what I wanted to talk to you about," she said.

"Have we?"

"Yes. What progress have you made? You said you were checking into sex offenders. Have you found any leads?"

"We've identified all registered SOs in the area, and we're investigating them. We're also looking into all of the carnival employees." He tried to lean back in the wrought iron chair, as though he were getting comfortable, but the heavy chair didn't budge. He gave up and rested his arms on the table, steepling his fingers.

What the heck was he feeling so confident about? "What about Ryan Cole's parents?" she asked. "Did you know that after the civil trial was over, they tried to bring criminal charges against my mother?"

"We know that."

"And that in the courthouse, Mr. Cole made a scene and swore they would get even with my mother?"

He flattened his hands against the table. "What kind of scene?"

She was back in control. "Cole shouted across the room at my mother. Called her a murderer."

"I see." He reached into his pocket and tapped something into his phone. "I'll make sure Detective Gonzalez knows about that. The police are following up on the Coles." He met her eye. "Is there anything else you want to ask about to confirm we're doing our job?"

She ignored his sarcasm. It was time to ask the questions that really mattered. "Has anyone gotten a ransom demand?"

"You mean other than you or your mother?"

Her face heated up again. Was it possible he knew about the note her mother had received and was playing her?

"You would obviously know if you had been contacted, and I imagine your mother would have told you if she had." His tone was gentler. For some reason, he was retreating from their little sparring match. "And, no. No one's contacted your brother, his wife, or the Simmers, but we're monitoring their cell phones and e-mail accounts."

"Not mine or my dad's?"

"Not at this time," he said. "We only got a court order for family members who were likely to be contacted with a ransom demand."

Aubrey looked at the pizza crust in her hand so that Smolleck couldn't read her face. "What about regular mail? Are you checking that?"

"Obviously," he said.

She tried to keep her voice neutral. "Did one of your people bring the mail in today and check it?"

She followed his glance back at the FBI crew inside the brightly lit family room. "Yes," he said.

"There were a lot of people in the house today," Aubrey said. "FBI, police. Are you keeping track of everyone? Have they all been background-checked?"

He stiffened. "Do you have any reason to believe someone tampered with the mail?"

This wasn't going the way she wanted. She needed to back off before she inadvertently revealed anything about the ransom note. She met his gaze. "Special Agent Smolleck. We don't know who took Ethan or why. I want to be sure my mother and I aren't in any danger sleeping in our own home."

"Is that what you're really worried about?" He didn't look away.

Blood pounded in her ears. "What I'm really worried about is getting Ethan back." She stood up. "And I hope you are, too."

She hurried out of the patio before he could ask her any more questions, because it was becoming clear that all her expertise in analyzing human behavior was worthless in a sparring match with a master.

CHAPTER 13

Diana left the park and stood on South Bayshore Drive waiting for traffic to break. A number of cars sped past, heading toward downtown Coconut Grove. Probably people heading out to dinner or going home after working late.

She couldn't go home.

Not yet.

Not with the FBI creeping around.

She flagged down a passing taxi and got in. It was a little past seven, and Jonathan wouldn't arrive in Miami for a half hour or so, but she could wait for him at his apartment.

She gave the driver his Brickell Avenue address, a couple of miles away, then called Aubrey to tell her where she was going so she wouldn't worry. There was no point in calling Smolleck. Her phone had GPS if they were interested in locating her. Instead, she texted Jonathan to meet her at his apartment. He'd see the message when his plane landed.

She pressed "Send," and shuddered. Jonathan and the FBI now knew where she would be. Did whoever was threatening her know, too? The taxi turned onto Brickell Avenue and headed toward downtown, passing luxury high-rises that overlooked Biscayne Bay. She was uncertain about what she would do when she saw Jonathan. Whether she would tell him about the note. He had a brilliant mind; maybe he could help figure out who had sent it and what to do next.

She was jolted out of her thoughts as the taxi stopped in front of Jonathan's towering building, a recently built condo with all the amenities of a five-star hotel. She'd been surprised the first time Jonathan had brought her here. The building's modern marble facade didn't fit her image of the unassuming man who loved to talk about economic theory and ancient civilizations. But Jonathan had explained that he'd bought the condo shortly after his wife died. A place with twenty-four-hour room service had been a good choice for a widower who didn't know how to cook and had no interest in learning.

She paid the driver, then walked through the high-ceilinged lobby filled with abstract art to the elevator bank. She input the security code, and the private elevator zipped her up to Jonathan's apartment on the forty-second floor. In the outer foyer to the apartment, she input the code again and was hit by a blast of icy air as she opened the door. She shivered as she turned on the lights, which bounced off white-marble floors, white furnishings, and white walls. There were a few bursts of crimson from strategically placed paintings and heavy glass paperweights on the coffee table and on the shelves on either side of the gigantic flat-screen TV.

A decorator had designed the interior, clearly with no understanding of the sensibilities of the man who would be living here. A man who loved books, not television, and who wore ten-year-old suits, not the latest fashion. But maybe Jonathan had wanted something devoid of warmth and personality when his wife died after battling cancer for several years.

Diana glanced at the rectangular Lalique crystal tray on the entry-way table. It was an antique piece with three compartments, a piece the decorator had been very pleased with. But Jonathan had altered it to serve his own purposes. With a labeling gun, he had made blue stickers that he'd affixed to each compartment that held his keys: Car, House, Office. *What's wrong with labels?* he'd asked when the horrified decorator saw his handiwork.

Diana picked up the keys to the black Ford SUV, which he'd owned forever and had no intention of getting rid of. She put the keys down, turned the A/C up to seventy-five, then went into the bedroom and got Jonathan's burgundy sweater from his closet. He was a small man, and the sweater was only slightly large on her. She could smell his scent on it, the aftershave he often used. Eau Sauvage. He had once told her he'd been wearing it since college, which didn't surprise her at all.

She heaved open the balky balcony door and stepped outside. The wind was strong out there, so she closed the door behind her to keep it from blowing everything around inside.

The balcony was narrow, barely wide enough for furniture, but it wrapped around the entire apartment. She leaned against the balustrade, taking in the impressive view.

To the north were buildings that had once been the skyscrapers of Miami but now looked like mere toys relative to the new construction. To the south, the bay stretched off into darkness until it reached the bridge from the mainland to Key Biscayne. She could see the lights of the cars crossing, like two rows of tiny diamonds.

She looked down at the engagement ring Jonathan had given her, with its halo of diamonds.

Did someone really believe she would kill Jonathan in exchange for Ethan's life?

She held on to the railing. Directly below was a square of green, where she and Jonathan sometimes sat. She was overcome by a powerful wave of dizziness. She pulled herself back. The wind whipped her hair around. Forty-two stories up.

No one would survive a fall from this height.

Could she do it to save Ethan's life?

She looked out toward the black bay, at the tiny lights on the bridge. They began to blur.

Was saving her grandson worth the price of Jonathan's life?

A rolling noise behind her startled her.

"Here you are, darling." Jonathan was beside her in one stride. He hugged her against him. "I'm so, so sorry."

She buried her head against his neck and felt the light scratch of his evening whiskers, smelled the Eau Sauvage and his own scent that she had come to love. He was wearing an overcoat. He had come from Washington to be with her. Because he loved her.

She cupped his gentle face with her trembling hands and looked at him. A few wrinkles on his freckled skin, mostly laugh lines behind the horn-rimmed glasses, around his hazel eyes. The wind blew a few reddish-gray hairs across his bald spot.

"I'm here now, darling," he said. "I've come to take care of you."

The pressure and pain that had been building since Ethan disappeared rose to the surface, and the terror she had held back broke loose.

She clung to the man she loved and whom she had, for one brief instant, considered killing.

And for the first time since her grandson had gone missing, she began to cry.

CHAPTER 14

The shower hadn't cleared her head. Aubrey was annoyed that she had opened herself up to Smolleck's scrutiny, but at least she had taken a couple of things away from her talk with him. For some reason, the FBI continued to be interested in her parents' past. Smolleck had also brought up something disturbing about her father—his unwillingness to take a lie detector test.

She thought about her mother's odd behavior at the park when Aubrey had suggested Dad may have left the note. Mama's language was too emphatic, too defensive.

Don't be ridiculous. Why would I protect him?

It had reminded Aubrey of the stonewalling she'd gotten as a child when she'd asked her parents whether anything was wrong. She'd always retreated, afraid to upset them further.

But she was no longer a child.

Although she was satisfied her father hadn't been directly involved in Ethan's kidnapping, she sensed he knew something. Something that might help them get Ethan back.

She dressed in jeans and a long-sleeved jersey, then went into her mother's bedroom. She grabbed the extra set of car keys Mama always left for her in the top drawer of her dresser, then hurried down the stairs, hoping not to attract the attention of the FBI team.

Smolleck would expect some explanation of where she was going and why, and a visit to her father might arouse his suspicions further.

She left the house and walked around to the driveway where her mother's old red BMW 325i convertible was parked. She backed out of the driveway, maneuvered her way through the narrow streets to US 1, then headed toward South Beach.

When she'd called her father earlier, he had told her that he and Star were staying at a time-share, and invited Aubrey to come up for a drink. She wasn't happy about seeing Star again but didn't want to suggest someplace else and risk having her father change his mind. She had to confront him and try to unravel this mess before someone got seriously hurt.

The traffic was light, and she drove the old car just over the speed limit. She remembered when her mother had gotten it, shortly before Aubrey's eighth birthday. Mama had put the top down and taken Aubrey and Kevin for a ride across the bridge to Key Biscayne, singing along to an oldies station, then stopping at the marina for conch fritters and Cokes.

It had been a great day.

It was also the only time Aubrey could remember her mother taking the top down.

A short time after Mama had gotten the car, everything changed in the Lynd household. Her parents began fighting, then Mama had gotten sick and stayed in bed for what seemed like weeks or months to Aubrey, though it had probably only been a few days. Years later, she realized Mama had been suffering from a vertigo attack, and she'd wondered whether Jimmy Ryce's kidnapping and murder had changed Mama, too.

It took Aubrey twenty minutes to get to Meridian Avenue in Miami Beach: a pretty, tree-lined street of old pastel-colored apartment buildings and narrow houses. The address her father had given her was of a three-story, mustard-colored art-deco building that looked more like someone's residence than the luxury time-share she'd been expecting. It was across from a neighborhood park, which was enclosed by a chain-link fence.

She found a spot by the park and crossed over to the building, which was surrounded by tall hedges and heavy foliage. Decorative, wrought iron bars covered the windows and front glass door. Definitely not a place her dad, whose taste ran to modern, would choose. A narrow, warped garage door was on one side of the entrance, but weeds grew in the pebbled driveway, as though the garage were rarely used.

Aubrey examined the old-fashioned intercom system by the recessed front door that had a buzzer for each of the five apartments. She pressed the one for "100" to announce her arrival and noticed the outer door was slightly ajar. She was immediately buzzed into a small foyer with a dull terrazzo floor. She glanced around, noting a staircase that led up to the other apartments, a utilitarian doorway on the left that probably provided access to the garage, and a hallway that went straight through to a rear door. Beneath a row of mailboxes sat a cardboard box with several short metal pipes—probably a plumbing project in one of the apartments.

The door to the right opened, and her father came out, his white hair damp and neatly combed as though he'd recently showered. He'd changed out of the light-blue button-down he'd had on back at the house and was wearing a short-sleeved, untucked shirt with a pattern of palm trees.

"Come on in," he said. "We're glad you called."

She hated that he included Star in his welcome, but at least he didn't seem angry with her after their quarrel earlier.

She stepped directly into the living room, which smelled of over-cooled air and looked as if it had been furnished in the eighties with catty-corner rattan sofas in a tropical print, a matching rattan dining-room set, and a shelving unit covered with knickknacks made of sea-shells and pastel-colored glass. A ceiling fan hung in the middle of the living room, and another in the small, open kitchen which, judging from the mica countertop, hadn't been updated in many years. The one concession to the present was the flat-screen TV on the wall opposite one of the sofas.

"I know," her father said, as though reading her mind. "It's not the usual time-share property, but it's very convenient, and Star was able to secure it for us for as long as we need it." He touched her shoulder lightly. "And the bar is fully stocked, so what can I get you?"

"Is she here?" Aubrey asked, looking toward a closed door beyond the kitchen that was probably the bedroom.

"Star's off buying some snacks for us, but she should be back any minute." He went into the kitchen and opened a cabinet. "So what'll it be? A cocktail? Wine?"

"Wine's good," she said, speaking over the hum of a noisy, in-wall air-conditioning unit. "Doesn't matter what kind."

He took three wineglasses down from a cabinet, then opened a bottle of red and poured it.

She watched his competent movements, his frown of concentra-tion. She remembered him making her scrambled eggs one Saturday morning when Mama had gone to the hospital to check on a patient. How delicious those eggs had tasted.

He came back into the living room and handed her one of the glasses, which was filled almost to the brim, then sat on one of the sofas.

She took a seat on the other sofa and set her wineglass on the bub-blegum-colored mica coffee table, next to an ashtray made of seashells and a remote for the TV.

Her father took a long sip of wine. "Pretty tough watching that press conference tonight, wasn't it?"

"Tougher for Kev," she said softly. Although going to the park with her mother had been crucial, Aubrey regretted that she had missed seeing her brother. Missed being there to support him. He still hadn't responded to her texts, but the best help she could give him would be to find Ethan and get him home safely.

She leaned toward her father. "Dad. I need to ask you something."

"Sure. Ask."

"Smolleck told me you refused to take a polygraph test."

His white eyebrows rose. "What business does he have talking about me to you?"

"It just came up," she said. "Why didn't you take it?"

He studied her. The whites of his blue eyes were laced with red. They'd been clear when she'd seen him earlier, and she wondered whether he'd been crying, or perhaps drinking. "There's no legal requirement to take it," he said. "And no point for me. I was in California when he was taken."

"But they use it to eliminate suspects. Not taking it raises questions."

"For whom?" His face got red. "You think I kidnapped my own grandson?"

"I think the FBI is interested in you for some reason."

"Then they're a bunch of morons," he said. "Why are they wasting their time?"

"Smolleck asked me questions about your past political interests."

"What?" He put the wineglass down on the table a little too hard. "And this is supposed to be connected to Ethan's disappearance?"

"I don't know," she said. "Could there be a connection? Were you ever affiliated with any groups that might try to use Ethan as leverage?"

"Affiliated? What the hell are you talking about, Aubrey?"

"I'm trying to understand why Smolleck was asking about you. He brought up Columbia University. He asked if you knew Jonathan there."

Her father's eyes widened, then he looked away quickly. He picked up his wineglass and swirled it. He was hiding something.

"Did you know Jonathan before he started dating Mom?"

He shook his head, then took a sip of wine.

"Did something happen when you were at college? Something connected to the accident Mom was in?" She was grasping at straws, throwing at him the questions Smolleck had asked her, because why would the FBI care about those things? And why was her father acting as though he were holding something back?

Her father took in a deep breath. He looked like he was about to explode. Then he let it out. "Why are you here, Aubrey? What the hell are you doing?"

He had never used an accusatory, belligerent tone with her. Of course, she had never confronted him about anything while she was growing up. Maybe because she'd been afraid he would react like this and shatter the already-cracking glass bubble they'd been living under.

She tried to keep her voice even. "Someone has Ethan," she said. "I'm wondering if you have some idea who, and where Ethan is. And I think someone is playing some kind of sick psychological game. I don't know why, but maybe you do. I'm worried about Ethan, and I'm worried about you."

He continued staring at her as a vein pulsed in his neck.

"Please, Dad. If you know, tell me what's going on. Tell me before Ethan or someone gets hurt."

He slammed his hand on the coffee table, and the ashtray went flying, crashing onto the terrazzo floor. "Did she put you up to this?" he said, spit coming out with his words.

Aubrey was stunned. She had never known him to get so angry.

"Your mother, did she send you here? All I've tried to do these past eight years is make things right with her. To get Kev and Kim to drop their grudge and let her see her grandson. And they finally listened to me. But does your mother ever see the good I've done? No. She's a bitter woman and she wants her revenge."

"You're wrong," Aubrey said, bewildered. "Mama knows nothing about this."

"I'll *bet* she knows nothing," he snapped. "Columbia? Politics? Why is the FBI asking about that unless she put them up to it? And if she did, she's a fool, because it will all come back around to her."

"What do you mean?"

"That, little girl, is something you should ask your dear mother about."

CHAPTER 15

Heat rose to Aubrey's cheeks. Never in her childhood had her father yelled at her. Of course, she had practically backed him into a corner, so what did she expect—a pat on the back and a "good job"? Still, she didn't understand why he was suggesting that Mama had some secret past.

He picked up his glass of wine and froze. She followed his gaze to the front door, where Star stood holding a grocery bag with one arm. Aubrey hadn't heard her father's girlfriend come in, but she'd probably been there for a good bit of the argument. It was just like the first time Aubrey had met her years after Kevin's wedding, when Star had lurked in the shadows before announcing herself. Aubrey again felt a visceral tug of bitterness.

"Hello, Aubrey." Star crossed to the sofa, moving gracefully in a yellow tunic and flowing pants, like someone who'd practiced yoga for years. "I'm so sorry about Ethan and what your family is going through." Her soft accent made her sound like she came from southern aristocracy.

Aubrey was far too agitated to have a civil conversation, especially with the woman who had broken up her parents' marriage and hurt her mother so deeply. She stood. "Thank you, Star. I'm sorry, but I was just leaving."

"Oh, please don't go. I ran over to the store to pick up cheese and crackers for us."

Aubrey glanced at her father. After their quarrel, she was sure he would want her to leave quickly, but he looked sad rather than angry. Maybe once he had some time to absorb their conversation, he would reconsider confiding in her.

"Stay, Aubrey," he said. "I don't want you to leave on a bad note." He got up from the sofa, took the bag of groceries from Star, then went into the kitchen.

She sat back down, partially to appease her father, but she was also curious about this woman and the possibility she'd been involved with Ethan's disappearance in some way. As she and Mama had discussed, they didn't know very much about her.

Star took her father's place on the sofa and folded her hands on her lap. Her nails were short, with pale-pink polish, and there were rings on all her fingers. Aubrey hadn't seen her since they'd all been in New York for Ethan's fourth birthday.

She was as attractive and youthful as ever—though she was probably close to Mama's age, with a similar height and build. She wore her white, wispy hair very short, hugging her scalp. The pixie bangs, arched black eyebrows, and dangling hoop earrings accentuated her large blue eyes, which were doing a quick assessment of Aubrey.

"Please tell me what's going on," Star said. She glanced at the broken ashtray on the floor, making no move to pick up the pieces, then looked back at Aubrey. "Any news about Ethan?"

"No. No news."

Star tugged on one of her earrings. "I hoped the press conference would have shaken loose some leads."

Aubrey tried to be polite without saying too much. "I believe there have been a number of calls. The FBI is following up on them."

Her father returned with a tray of cheese and crackers and a glass of wine for Star, then sat down beside her. He didn't make eye contact with Aubrey. She wondered whether he regretted blowing up at her earlier.

"Thank you, dearest," Star said, accepting the wine and taking a sip. She held her glass delicately, her pinkie extended. On it was an unusual silver ring that wound up to the lower joint and ended with a garnet stone. Aubrey remembered her father once mentioning Star had a jewelry business and sold her designs to small boutiques.

"How is your mother holding up?" Star asked.

"She's managing," Aubrey said.

"She's lucky to have you. I know you two have always been close."

"Yes," Aubrey said. "And I'm happy you're here for my father."

Star raised an eyebrow, as though she had picked up on Aubrey's sarcasm. "That's very nice of you to say, dear. I'm glad to be able to help organize things so your father can be here for your family. And, of course, I'm very worried about little Ethan."

Aubrey glanced at her father, who was frowning at her. She'd already gotten his nose out of joint, so she might as well continue asking questions, even if he didn't like where she was going. "I know you've spent some time with Ethan in LA," she said to Star. "My dad sent me some photos of the three of you together."

"Oh, yes," Star said. "I've gotten to know Ethan quite well. He's an engaging little boy. I think of him almost as though he's my own grandson."

She wondered whether Star was taunting her, reminding her that all those years Mama had been kept from Ethan, this woman had been in his life. Aubrey tried to keep the anger out of her voice, and asked lightly, "Do you have grandchildren yourself?"

Star seemed taken aback, then said, "I'm afraid I don't have that blessing."

"But you have children?"

Star nibbled on a cracker with a piece of cheese. "I do. I have a daughter."

Aubrey picked up on Star's discomfort. This was something new. Some skeleton in her closet? "I don't mean to sound like I'm prying," Aubrey said. "It's just that you and my dad have been together for eight years, and we've never had a chance to get to know each other."

Star gave her a little smile that didn't reach her eyes. "It's never too late to start."

"Does your daughter live near you in LA?"

Star took another sip of wine. She could have been thirsty, or she could have been avoiding the question. The air conditioner kicked in with a cough, then made a humming noise.

Her father sat forward on the sofa. "Janice lives in Atlanta, Aubrey," he said loudly, possibly to be heard over the A/C, but Aubrey picked up an edge of impatience.

"Oh," Aubrey said. "So you've met her, Dad?"

Star put a hand on his arm. "It's okay, Larry." She turned to Aubrey. "Unfortunately, my daughter and I haven't spoken in years. It's been very difficult for me, which is why I understand how your mother must have felt being estranged from your brother and his family." She stood up. "I'm afraid you'll have to excuse me, but I'm feeling a migraine coming on. We haven't had much sleep, and I imagine you haven't, either."

Her father started to stand.

"No, no, don't get up, Larry. Talk to your daughter. You get to see each other so infrequently that I'm sure you'd like to catch up."

Aubrey watched her glide across the terrazzo floor and go into the room that was probably the bedroom.

"So now you think Star is involved?" her father said in a low voice. His arms were folded across his chest. "Because you couldn't be more wrong."

"I was just making conversation. You've been telling me to get to know her."

"Star is one of the kindest, most selfless people I've ever known," he said. "Did you know she's been your mother's biggest advocate all these years? She's the one who pushed me to get Kev and Kim to let your mother see Ethan. Star knows how painful it is when your children don't want you."

"I'm sorry, Dad. I didn't mean to come across as if I'm accusing anyone." Even if Star's intentions were selfless, it infuriated Aubrey that her father continued to defend her.

She got up to leave. "But I'm going to keep asking questions until we find Ethan. And if you care about him the way you say you do, then you'll start asking questions, too."

CHAPTER 16

Diana watched Jonathan pour her a brandy and one for himself. Then he took off his overcoat and sat down beside her on the white-leather sofa.

Her hands trembled as she held the snifter.

"My poor darling." Jonathan got up, went into the bedroom, and came back with a crocheted afghan Diana had never seen. As he wrapped it around her shoulders, she wondered whether his dead wife had made it. "I should have come sooner," he said. "There was no need for you to try to deal with this by yourself."

The lenses on his horn-rim glasses were scratched and pockmarked with age. He was still wearing his suit jacket, though he had loosened his tie. Blue-and-gray stripes.

It was one of the ties she had bought him for the judgeship interviews, because all his old ties were too wide and out of fashion.

He had laughed when she'd given him the box of ties. *Thank you, my darling,* he'd said. *But this is where we draw the line in you trying to change me.*

And she had replied, *I would never dream of changing you. I love you, even if you are hopelessly outdated.*

"Someone wants me to kill you," she said softly.

He blinked his hazel eyes rapidly and frowned.

"There was a note," she said. "Someone left it in a greeting card at my house this afternoon. It said that Ethan would be returned unharmed if I killed you."

"Good God. Have you shown it to the FBI?"

She shook her head. "It said not to tell the authorities or they would kill Ethan."

His eyes wandered around the room, though he didn't seem to be looking at anything. His face was paler than usual, the freckles more pronounced. "It doesn't make sense," he said finally. "I can understand there are people who would want me dead, but why involve you and Ethan? Why not assassinate me directly?"

She took a sip of brandy, hoping the burn would deaden her nerves. "The only explanation that makes sense is that I'm the primary target. Someone wants to hurt me as deeply as they can by forcing me to choose between two people I love."

He stared at his glass. Age spots covered his hands, and a few golden hairs grew between his knuckles, which were knobby from arthritis. "Do you think it's the Coles?"

"Possibly," she said.

"But how do they know about Ethan? Or about me?"

"They could have been stalking me. Maybe they've been watching my house and saw Ethan arrive. And they could have read about our engagement in the profiles that came out after you became a contender for the Supreme Court nomination." She took another drink. "But there are others who may have motives against both of us."

"But you just said you believe you're the extorters' target."

"*Primary* target. We shouldn't rule out that they may also want to eliminate you."

"True," he said. "So who might be out to get both of us?"

"The Simmers?"

He raised an eyebrow. "You think they have some grudge against me?"

"You may be a threat to them if you get the nomination."

Jonathan nodded. "Of course. Baer Business Machines would be hurt by my policy on large corporate mergers."

She stared at the three crimson paperweights on the coffee table. "But then, there's also Larry," she said.

"Your ex-husband? I never got the impression from you that he was vindictive or even jealous."

"Aubrey believes he could be manipulated by his girlfriend."

"So Aubrey knows about the note?"

"Yes."

"I'm glad you haven't been dealing with this alone," he said. "And now you have me as well." He reached over and squeezed her shoulder. "So why do you believe Larry and his girlfriend may be involved?"

"I don't know very much about Star, which means anything's possible."

"And Larry?" His face was full of concern, even though his own life was being threatened. She had to tell him.

"I'm worried this may relate to something that happened back when I was in college," she said.

"What do you mean?"

"April Fool." She barely managed to get the words out before her throat closed up.

Even after all these years, she couldn't talk about it, but she didn't have to.

Jonathan's eyes widened behind his glasses. He knew the reference to April 1, 1970, the day of the explosion. For anyone who had attended Barnard College and Columbia University back then, April Fools' Day would never again be thought of as a day for playing silly pranks.

She waited for him to confront her, to ask what she could possibly have done more than forty-five years ago that someone would try to threaten her over today. But Jonathan finished his drink, then went to the bar to refill his glass.

He stood there looking out the sliding glass door, his face thoughtful, as though he were weighing legal arguments. And a ghost passed through her.

What if he knew?

Jonathan had been at Columbia Law at the time. He could have known people, maybe even had some personal connection to April Fool. Some hurt he had hidden from her, waiting for the right moment to mete out revenge. This entire, terrible situation might be his doing.

Was Jonathan her enemy?

No. It wasn't possible. She would have known if he'd been deceiving her.

Besides, Jonathan would never turn on her. And setting up an ultimatum that involved his own death made no sense. She wasn't thinking clearly. Fear for Ethan and lack of sleep were making her paranoid.

Jonathan returned to the sofa, sat beside her, and reached for her hand. "You're still cold." He ran his fingers against her cheek. "You know I love you very much. If there's something in your past, I don't care about it."

She shivered.

He adjusted the afghan around her shoulders. "You believe me, darling, don't you?"

"Of course," she said, then quickly looked away.

CHAPTER 17

Aubrey left her mother's car in the dark driveway near the two black sedans, then went in the front door, half expecting Smolleck to be standing in the foyer, arms folded in front of his too-stylish suit, with a "gotcha" expression on his face.

But no one was there.

She listened for sounds coming from the back of the house. No phones were ringing, but the tip calls were probably being routed to the command post the Simmers had established over at the Ritz.

It was almost nine thirty, over thirty hours since Ethan had gone missing. Thirty hours! Because of the ransom note, she believed he was alive, but that didn't mean he was in a safe place. He was just a little boy. She hoped he wasn't frightened.

Only a few months ago, Ethan had spent the night at her Providence apartment while Kevin and Kim attended a gala in Newport. Jackson had gone off somewhere for the night, so she and Ethan wouldn't have to contend with a "third wheel," or so Jackson had said. Aubrey now realized what he'd really been up to.

She and Ethan had been propped up against pillows in her bed, watching a movie about a kid who was trying to outsmart a couple of bad guys. At one point, the little boy hid in the back of his parents' car. The bad guys looked for the boy in the car, but didn't notice him hidden beneath a dog carrier that was wedged behind the driver's seat.

Ethan had been delighted that the boy had outfoxed them, but later that night, he awoke from a nightmare about the movie and cried for his mother. Aubrey had comforted him, telling him the little boy was safe and that he had been very brave—just like Ethan.

Was someone comforting her nephew tonight when he cried for his mother?

She hurried upstairs. After checking and finding her mother hadn't gotten back from Jonathan's, she went to her own room and got out her laptop.

She had a lot to do.

There was a message and attachment from Smolleck. It had been sent to everyone in her family. Smolleck had written:

> Please review the attached photos, pay-
> ing particular attention to people in the
> background. Let me know if you recognize
> anyone.

So he had followed up on her suggestion. Her respect for him edged upward. She opened the attachment. There were six photos, taken at the carnival, probably with her mother's iPhone.

Ethan, in his sky-blue T-shirt with a jumping dolphin, was in all of them.

She enlarged each photo and studied the people in the background crowds, one by one. No one familiar, but she also checked to see whether anyone happened to be looking at Ethan or otherwise appeared suspicious.

She examined the last photo, the selfie of Ethan and Mama.

A woman was standing by a booth facing the camera. She appeared to be frowning at Ethan.

Aubrey enlarged her face until it began to get blurry, then she brought it back into focus. The woman had a pronounced chin, was wearing large sunglasses, and had her wild dark hair pulled back from her face. She looked to be around forty and had something above her bowed lip—a mole or a pimple—Aubrey couldn't tell.

She checked for the woman in the other photos, but couldn't find her. Then, she noticed something else—a man who didn't look like someone who went to carnivals. He was in another photo as well. He was large and muscled, with tattoo sleeves covering both arms. Aubrey enlarged the photo. The tattoos appeared to be of intertwining snakes. The man had a scraggly reddish beard, shaved head, and he wore dark glasses. He was probably in his thirties. And while he wasn't looking at Ethan, it was suspicious that he was in two photos taken at two different places in the carnival. He could have been one of the carnival workers the FBI was checking out, but she'd make sure Smolleck knew about him.

She replied to his message:

> Don't recognize anyone, but check out woman in Photo 6—dark hair, sunglasses and mole above lip—who's looking in Ethan's direction. Also bulky, bearded man with tattoo sleeves in Photos 1 and 5. Carny worker?

She hesitated. Smolleck was doing his job, even being responsive to her suggestions. She needed to stop reacting to him as if he were the enemy.

She added: *Thanks for forwarding photos*, pressed "Send," and leaned back in her desk chair.

Her eyes settled on her snow globes. Two children pulling a sled, a mother and daughter in a forest of snow-covered fir trees, a family having a snowball fight.

When Aubrey had pressed her father for answers at the time-share, he'd angrily pointed a finger at Mama. She recognized the bullying technique. Her father was hiding something. Why else would he have become so defensive when she'd asked him about politics and Columbia?

Yet, she couldn't imagine the man who had held her close as he guided her down a ski trail, when she'd been too scared to go by herself, being involved with the kidnapping of his own grandson.

Unless someone else was calling the shots.

And the woman, who had beguiled him from day one, was a likely candidate.

Star Matin.

When Aubrey had first met her, Star had introduced herself, pronouncing her surname like the French word for "morning," and Aubrey had thought it was spelled "Matanne." She'd since learned otherwise.

She entered "Star Matin" in Google search and had only a few hits, all having to do with Star's jewelry business. She followed each link and finally found a write-up in a small magazine called *Southern Comfort.* The article was an old one, from ten years ago, before Star had become involved with Aubrey's father.

Star Matin was born a southern belle in Charleston. To please her parents, she wore frilly dresses, learned how to curtsy, and didn't drink too much at her debutante ball, when what she really wanted to be was a tomboy. She studied art at Agnes Scott College in Decatur, Georgia, then worked in advertising and marketing before going off on her own and creating her own line of stunning jewelry, The

Star Collection, which can be found right here
in Buckhead, where for the last ten years, Star
has had her own boutique in the upscale shopping mall of Peachtree Shoppes. As Star says,
"I always thought I wanted to be a tomboy, but
the truth is I love being a girl!"

A puff piece without much content, but it was consistent with what
Aubrey knew. She looked for images and found a couple of photos of
Star at various events with Aubrey's father. She returned to her original
search and hunted for older links, but there was nothing.

It was time to check into her father's background. Maybe she'd find
some answers to her growing list of questions.

Why hadn't he taken the polygraph? Why was Smolleck asking
about his political views and his time at Columbia University? And had
her father known Jonathan in the past?

She would start with what she knew and build out from there.

Her dad had been an undergraduate at Columbia from 1967 to 1971.

Her mother had attended Barnard, its sister school, from 1969 to 1973.

Aubrey went online to see whether she could access either of their
college yearbooks, but they were password-protected, so she tried a
different tack. She recalled her parents had met in '69, so she googled
"Columbia University 1969" to get a sense of what was happening at
that time.

Articles with references to student protests and strikes popped up.
She already knew a little about this period—the unpopular Vietnam
War, opposition to the draft, racial tensions, the emergence of the hip-
pie culture, and flamboyant drug use.

She clicked on a link to a YouTube video—a documentary made in
1969 of a student strike and university takeover. She watched it, taken

aback by the anger of the fist-shaking students that had been captured on the choppy black-and-white film.

Rebellion and activism were completely alien to her experiences as an undergraduate at Brown, and now in graduate school. Her college years had been about getting good grades and studying under respected professors. But these Columbia students, led by a group called SDS, or Students for a Democratic Society, as the narrator explained, were at war against the university's administration. They claimed that Columbia University was hooked into serving big corporations that were financing the war machine. Companies whose CEOs were either on Columbia's board of trustees or providing substantial endowments to the university, like Lockheed, General Dynamics, CBS, and Baer Business Machines.

Aubrey paused the documentary. She hadn't realized there had been a link between Prudence's family business and Columbia, but it wasn't a surprise. BBM was one of the most powerful corporations in the country. They probably had their fingers in lots of pies, even back in 1969.

She did a search of Columbia's board of trustees and found that Emmet Baer, founder of BBM, had been on the board from 1965 through 1970.

Kevin once mentioned that Prudence had wanted him and Kim to name their son Emmet after her grandfather, but for once Kim had sided with Kevin, and they had agreed on Ethan. But Aubrey couldn't imagine what Emmet Baer being on Columbia's board might have to do with Ethan's kidnapping.

She returned to the documentary and continued watching the jerky footage of student protestors capturing five university buildings, then barricading themselves in against the police.

Her parents had both been at Columbia during this radical period, but Aubrey had told Smolleck her parents were not political people. Her father's reaction tonight suggested she may have been mistaken. She searched for her mother and father in the documentary, trying to match the long-haired students to what she imagined her parents might have looked like then, but if they had been there that day, Aubrey couldn't identify them.

She googled "Larry or Lawrence Lynd" and "Columbia University," which returned a number of references in recent bios of him being a graduate of Columbia. She narrowed the search, including "1969" and "1970." Nothing came up.

If her father had been involved with any student activism, he hadn't been very visible.

Then she googled "Diana Hartfeld" and "Diana Lynd," since her mother had married her sophomore year, and first "Columbia," then "Barnard."

Nothing on her mother, either.

She searched for "Larry Lynd and Jonathan Woodward," but came up with no hits on the two of them together.

Then something else crossed her mind. Smolleck had brought up the accident her mother had been injured in, as though that were somehow connected to Ethan's disappearance.

She googled "Accident, Columbia University, 1969."

No specific hits, but on WikiCU, the wiki site for Columbia University, there was a list of notable incidents in 1969. Protests, students seizing university buildings, the elimination of ROTC from campus, and more references to the SDS organization. She clicked on WikiCU's link to 1970 and skimmed the entries, stopping on one that caught her eye:

Revolutionary student group Stormdrain accidentally blows up its headquarters in brownstone.

Aubrey followed a link to the article. A black-and-white photo taken at night showed several police standing in front of a row of brick townhouses. Barricades and rubble lined the street, but most noteworthy was the black, gaping space between two stately brick brownstones. The building between them had been leveled.

The caption below the photo read: SITE OF MORNINGSIDE HEIGHTS BROWNSTONE THAT BLEW UP APRIL 1970, KILLING FOUR, INCLUDING THREE COLUMBIA UNIVERSITY STUDENTS.

Could this be the accident her mother was in?

Do they hide things from you? Smolleck had asked.

Aubrey hadn't responded, disturbed by the answer that came to mind.

Yes, they did hide things.

But she was as much at fault. She had never asked her parents about their past, sensing the topic was off-limits. She had grown up trying not to rock the boat because she knew her parents' marriage wasn't entirely stable. Then, eight years ago, after Dad left and the boat had capsized, she had felt an even greater need to protect her mother by not wading into treacherous waters.

But those days were over. Aubrey had questions only Mama could answer, and she would ask them. Even if they finally caused the boat to sink.

CHAPTER 18

The wooden floorboard outside her bedroom door groaned.

"Mama?" Aubrey called. "Is that you?"

Her mother opened the door and poked her head in. She was ghostly white.

"What's wrong?" Aubrey started to rise. "Is Ethan—?"

Her mother held up her hand. "No news." She came into the room, then sat on the bed.

"Something happened. You're upset." Aubrey's mind jumped to the ultimatum in the note. Her mother couldn't have . . . "Where's Jonathan?"

Mama looked at her, as though confused, then her expression cleared. "Jonathan wanted to come back here with me, but I told him not to." Her eyes were reassuring. "He's fine, sweetheart. We're both fine."

Aubrey released a breath. "Okay. Good."

"What about you?" Her mother pointed at the laptop. "What have you been doing?"

"Research."

"On what?"

Aubrey watched her mother for a reaction as she answered her. "The revolutionary movement when you and Dad were students at Columbia."

Her mother's eyes widened. "Why do you care about that?"

"Because Smolleck seems to care. And because Dad acts like you know about something important that happened back then."

"Your father?"

"I went to see him tonight. I wanted to ask him some questions about the past, but he turned everything back around at you."

Mama gripped the bedspread. "I don't understand what you're talking about, sweetheart," she said, in an unnaturally calm voice. "Turn what back on me?"

What was she hiding? "Mama. Were you involved with the brownstone explosion in 1970?"

Her mother looked away.

Oh no, Aubrey thought. *Please, no.*

"I was outside the brownstone when it exploded," her mother said, meeting her eye. "That's how I got injured. The blast ruptured my eardrum, and I was hit by flying debris."

"But were you involved?"

"What do you mean?"

"Did you have something to do with the explosion?"

"It was an accident," her mother said. "A bomb went off by accident."

"I know. I read that."

"I wasn't responsible for that explosion." Her mother's voice was loud, but maybe she was upset that Aubrey would consider such a thing.

"Do you think the explosion could be connected to Ethan's kidnapping?"

"I don't see how."

Aubrey looked up at the snow globes on the shelf above her desk. She had finally shaken up the flakes, but they had settled, and everything was just as before, with Aubrey no closer to finding the truth.

"Come here, sweetheart." Mama patted the bed.

It was the comforting voice her mother had used when Aubrey had been upset or frustrated as a child. And like a child, Aubrey went to sit beside her. She let her mother hug her, even though she felt as if she had compromised herself. She had acquiesced too easily by not pressing her mother further, but she had spent most of her life placating Mama—a pattern that was difficult to break.

"It's almost ten," Aubrey said, gently pulling away. "They're probably replaying Kevin and Kim's press conference from earlier. We should watch it." She turned on the TV in the armoire opposite her bed. A commercial was on. Two women jogging around a lake, laughing.

"Remember when we used to watch *The Gilmore Girls* together?" Mama asked. "We would lie here on your bed. I miss those days."

"Me, too." Aubrey had been thinking about the show herself. The special bond between the mother and daughter. She and Mama. They were both under tremendous stress. For now, it was important to trust and support her mother, not confront her.

The female newscaster's voice came on, explaining how six-year-old Ethan Lynd had disappeared from a neighborhood carnival on Sunday, at around three p.m.

Crawling across the bottom of the screen was a number to call with tips or sightings. One of the photos Mama had taken at the carnival appeared on the screen—Ethan with his big grin and dimples, golden curls flying around him.

Her mother's breath snagged. "Oh, God. Just like Jimmy Ryce."

"No. *Not* like Jimmy Ryce," Aubrey said. "We're going to get Ethan back safe and sound."

The newscaster's voice continued. "Ethan's parents held a news conference earlier today, begging for help in finding their son."

The camera cut to footage of Kevin and Kim.

Aubrey's chest felt as though it would cave in as she watched her brother and his wife. Kevin seemed to be holding Kim up as she stared ahead blankly. A large poster of Ethan was on one side of them, Prudence and Ernest Simmer on the other.

And then, anger overtook sadness.

She and her mother should have been there for Kevin. How dare the Simmers try to widen the chasm between them at a time like this?

Kevin spoke, struggling with each word as though he were cutting teeth. His brown hair was uncombed and his cheeks unshaven, but what got Aubrey were his eyes—dark, solemn eyes that held so much pain.

And she hadn't been there to support him.

Kevin and Kim stepped back from the microphones, and Prudence and Ernest came forward, first hugging their daughter and son-in-law, then turning toward the cameras. Everything about Prudence was colorless, even her lips. Her blonde bob touched the shoulders of her beige silk blouse. Prudence Baer Simmer looked nothing like a haughty heiress, but rather a desperate grandmother. Her pale eyes searched the cameras, a disoriented expression on her face. Ernest loomed over her, bald head shining in the glare of camera lights, shoulders hunched, one arm supporting his wife. These people weren't faking it.

Aubrey had considered the possibility of the Simmers being behind Ethan's kidnapping and the threatening note, but how could they be so grief stricken if they were responsible?

Prudence leaned into the microphone. "We are offering a reward of one million dollars for information leading to the safe return of our grandson, Ethan Lynd."

"A million dollars," her mother whispered.

"If you have seen Ethan or know any of the people who took our little boy, please call this number." Prudence held up a poster with the number and recited it. It was also the number that crawled across the bottom of the screen.

Prudence and Ernest spoke for another minute about Ethan, and then, to Aubrey and apparently the Simmers' surprise, Kim pushed in front of them. Her blonde hair was in disarray, her eyes red and puffy.

"He's my baby," she said, tears streaming down her cheeks. "Please, if you have my little boy . . ." She struggled to get the words out.

Kevin stepped up beside her and held her as he stared at the camera. "Ethan, are you watching? We love you, little guy. We're going to get you home." And then his face crumpled.

Mama shook her head. "He'll never forgive me."

Aubrey didn't know how to comfort her. Her mother was probably right. There'd be no forgiveness from Kevin now, no matter the outcome.

The newscaster was speaking, and "Exclusive interview" flashed on the screen. "We have an exclusive interview with a family that can shed some light on this horrible tragedy. Are you there, Roberto?"

"Yes," he said. "Thank you, Lourdes. I'm talking to Rhonda and Chris Cole, the parents of Ryan Cole, a little boy who died three years ago under the care of Dr. Diana Lynd, Ethan's paternal grandmother."

"For God's sake," Aubrey said. "I can't believe this."

"Mr. and Mrs. Cole," the reporter continued, "can you tell us about your experience with Ethan's grandmother, Dr. Diana Lynd?"

The Coles glanced at each other. They were dressed formally—the husband in a suit, the wife in a high-necked black dress.

Rhonda spoke. Her listless brown hair hung loose to her shoulders, and she looked at her hands, not at the camera. "When we heard what happened, we felt we had to come forth and tell the world what we knew."

"What is that, Mrs. Cole?" the reporter prompted.

"That woman—the little boy's grandmother—well, she's a doctor. She was supposed to take care of our child, but she said there wasn't nothing wrong with him. And then our Ryan, he died."

"Do you think that has something to do with Ethan's disappearance?" the reporter asked.

"What kind of doctor says a child is fine and sends him home to die?" Rhonda Cole wiped her eyes, but there was a telltale leak of contempt as one lip curled up.

The Coles could have left the note, Aubrey realized. Maybe the red tricycle on the greeting card was a reference to their child.

"Dr. Lynd was cleared of any liability in the malpractice lawsuit you brought against her, isn't that right?" the reporter asked.

"Yes, but she shouldn't have been," Chris Cole said.

"She's irresponsible," Rhonda Cole said. "She killed our son and showed no remorse, and now her grandson is missing. Why wasn't she at the press conference if she has nothing to hide? Why haven't the police taken her into custody?"

"The woman is a child killer," Chris Cole said, so loudly that he startled the reporter.

"I can't believe this," Aubrey said.

Mama grabbed Aubrey's hand and squeezed it hard.

The reporter looked upset. He touched his ear, as though listening to instructions. "Thank you, Mr. and Mrs. Cole," he said. "Back to you, Lourdes."

"Next up, a visit with some adorable puppies who need homes," Lourdes said, as a commercial came on.

"They're crackpots, Mama." Aubrey was fuming inside. She turned off the TV with the remote, then got up and slammed the doors of the armoire shut.

"The Coles are very angry." Mama pulled the sweater tighter around her. "They're parents who lost their child."

Aubrey leaned against the armoire, rubbing her arms. *Child killer.* The words chilled her, even though she knew they weren't true.

But Ethan was still missing, and Aubrey had no idea where to look or what to do, to keep her precious nephew from becoming someone else's victim.

CHAPTER 19

Child killer, they had called her.

Maybe they were right. Diana shivered in her too-cold bedroom. Maybe she was the real villain in all this. It wouldn't be the first time she believed she was on the side of good and turned out to be wrong.

She changed into a flannel nightgown, then slipped under the old, worn patchwork quilt, hoping the warmth would stop her chills. The attack by the Coles was upsetting, but she had become somewhat immune to their crazed outbursts during the trial. She was more concerned about what all this was doing to her family.

Kevin had looked close to a breaking point as he pled on TV for his son's return. But Aubrey was also caught in the maelstrom, experiencing the kind of outrage Diana had back when her eyes had first been opened to the injustices of the world.

The irony was that Diana's parents had tried so very hard to shelter their daughter, just as Diana had hoped she could do with her own children.

Her poor parents.

She never understood until recently how hard that year must have been for them.

———

Di could see the shock on her parents' faces as they took in her outfit—ratty jeans and a peasant blouse she had picked up at a flea market in the Village. They were in New York for a few days, and this was the first time they'd seen her in six weeks, since freshman year began. She hated the feeling that she had disappointed them, but knew she had to stay strong. This was her life now.

They took the subway to the Stage Deli for pastrami sandwiches, but Di didn't have much of an appetite. She was missing a meeting about an important antiwar demonstration. Or maybe it was Lawrence she hadn't wanted to miss.

"Why aren't you eating?" her mother asked.

Di played with the pickle on her plate. "Not hungry."

Her father put on his concerned physician face. "You're not taking drugs, are you?"

"Of course not, Daddy," she lied.

"Lysergide is a very dangerous drug," he said. "It can cause panic attacks, violence, even psychosis."

"I'm not taking LSD."

Her father continued, as though he hadn't heard her. "And there's data that years after use, there can be long-term perceptual changes."

"What I'm experiencing right now are short-term perceptual changes," Di said. "And not from drugs. It's as though I've been asleep my entire life. I'm finally waking up and seeing the terrible things that are taking place in the world. And more important, I'm trying to stop them."

"Vat's happened to you?" her mother asked, her Yiddish accent becoming more pronounced with her agitation. "You dress like a hippie, you talk like a revolutionary. We sent you to college to get an education."

"And I'm getting one," Di said. "A better education than I ever dreamed of."

Her father and mother exchanged a worried look. "This isn't good," her father said. "Come back to Miami with us. It's dangerous for you to stay here."

Di laughed. "What's dangerous? Standing up to our government? Not letting them herd us into ovens the way the Nazis did their citizens?"

Her mother's face went white.

"Oh, Mommy." Di reached for her hand. "Don't you understand it's important that we speak out? If the Jews had fought back, maybe more would have survived. Maybe your parents and brothers would still be alive."

Her mother pulled her hand away. "You know nothing about these things."

"And I'm not only talking about Jews," Di said. "The German people, too. They should have stood up to Hitler. Just like we have an obligation to tell our government they're doing the wrong thing."

Her mother pushed back her chair. "Let's go, Louie," she said. "I can't listen to any more of this. Our daughter has gone crazy."

———

Diana pulled the old quilt higher. Her mother had been right. She *had* gone crazy. But at the time, she saw only the heady excitement of doing something to make the world a better place. She'd been critical of her parents' fear of challenging authority and calling attention to themselves. She was ashamed to think of her brash naïveté and how she must have hurt them. But back then, she'd been intoxicated by a sense of righteousness.

And by *him*.

She closed her eyes and saw a flash of white against the darkness. And she remembered how it had felt, watching him.

———

He seemed to be flying as he led their group through the park, his blond hair loose on his shoulders beneath his white bandanna, his white shirt billowing around him.

Di was breathless as she hurried to keep up with the thirty-or-so other students who had followed Lawrence down from the university to Central Park. He had started referring to himself as Lawrence of Columbia, and it was hard not to make comparisons to *Lawrence of Arabia*, or at least to Peter O'Toole, who had played the man in the movie.

As they reached Central Park's Great Lawn, the crowd morphed into thousands, moving as one, like a giant, spreading amoeba. It seemed that everyone was here for what they were calling the Moratorium to End the War in Vietnam, and Di felt as though she was at its very center. Even the trees seemed to have dressed for the occasion in brilliant shades of red and orange. Above them, Belvedere Castle loomed from its perch on a hill.

The protestors held signs. "Make Love Not War," "Bring Our Boys Home," "War is not healthy for children and other living things." And chanted, "Hell no, we won't go!"

Di shouted with the others. She was finally doing something significant in her life. Helping to stop a terrible war that only benefited the government and corporate America.

She inhaled the sweet scent of pot and smoke from the small bonfires all around her and watched Lawrence climb up on the shoulders of Steve, by far the biggest guy in their group. Lawrence waved a small white card in the air. "Hell no, I won't go!" he shouted. He lit a match and held it to the edge of the card. "Burn it!"

The others in their group cheered and shouted, "Burn it! Burn it!"

His draft card went up in flames, but Lawrence didn't drop it, even as the fire touched his fingers. Di felt herself swoon. She didn't know whether it was from the pain she imagined he was experiencing or from his sexy bravado, and she didn't care. She only wished she had something to burn, to show him that he had reached her. That she would follow him wherever he led.

Gertrude had climbed up on Jeffrey's skinny shoulders. His wiry body was stronger than it looked, as it supported her weight. Gertrude waved her arms, eyes flashing violet behind her pink glasses, nipples visible beneath her sheer white blouse. "Come on, comrades," Di's roommate shouted. "Burn your fucking draft cards. Don't let them send you to kill innocent people, innocent children."

Jeffrey's scowling face, mostly hidden behind mutton-chop sideburns, came to life. "Burn them, comrades. Let it all burn!"

Several of the guys took out their cards and lit them on fire.

Linda was standing beside Di, flaxen hair pasted to her flushed cheeks, blue eyes bright as though she had a fever. She reached her arms behind her back, then triumphantly pulled her bra out of the sleeve of her T-shirt. "I don't have a draft card," Linda shouted, "but at least I can burn this."

Lawrence grinned and tossed her a book of matches.

Linda struck several matches at once and held them to her bra as the others cheered her on. The fire caught and flames shot out.

"Let's hear it, comrades," Gertrude cried. "Hell no, we won't go!"

"Hell no, we won't go!" they all chanted in response. Louder and louder. Faster and faster. "Hell no, we won't go!" Di felt the mounting frenzy around her, the blurry euphoria. "Hell no, we won't go!"

"To the castle!" Lawrence shouted, pointing up to Belvedere. "Let's storm the castle."

On Steve's broad shoulders, he charged up the hill. Gertrude was just behind, clinging to Jeffrey, her black braid bouncing against her back, as the rest of their group followed.

They made it up to the castle veranda that overlooked the Great Lawn and Belvedere Lake. Lawrence jumped down from Steve's back and climbed up on the retaining wall so they could all see him.

"Comrades," he shouted, "we need to make some decisions about who we are and what we want to accomplish."

"Hear, hear," someone called out.

"SDS has failed us," Lawrence said. "The organization is ridden with dissension and power struggles. How can we fight for peace when we're busy fighting each other?"

Everyone applauded.

Di looked around for Gertrude. She was standing off to the side, puffing on a cigarette as she leaned against Jeffrey. Leaning in a comfortable way, as if she would soon be taking her clothes off for him.

Undoubtedly in the name of peace.

"We need cooperation," Lawrence shouted, "Not condemnation."

The group cheered.

"Why don't we join the Weathermen?" Linda called out.

Lawrence turned toward her, a patient expression on his face. Linda looked almost like a child with her large eyes and narrow dancer's body. Then he shook his fist and shouted, "Because we can do it better."

Everyone cheered.

"The Weathermen want a revolution on American soil," Lawrence said. "Well, we want peace on American soil." He stretched out his arms as he stood on the wall, a crowd of thousands behind him on the Great Lawn, in front of him, his own small but passionate group. "And peace throughout the world!"

They exploded in another round of shouts and clapping.

Peace, Di thought. They were going to fight for peace. They were taking a stand, like the German people should have done. Like the Jews should have done.

"The fat cats are brewing up a storm of destruction," Lawrence said. "It's up to us to drain away their filthy poison and leave behind a cleaner, better world." He made a fist. "We are Stormdrain, and we want peace on American soil and peace throughout the world."

"Stormdrain!" Steve shouted, and everyone cheered.

"Lawrence of Columbia!" Another cheer went out. "Lawrence of Columbia is our leader!"

"We are all leaders," Lawrence called back. "We are in this together." He pulled off his white headscarf and waved it in the air. "And if we need to use revolutionary tactics to achieve our goals, so be it!" he bellowed.

Di shuddered. Revolutionary tactics?

Someone began to sing John Lennon's song about giving peace a chance, and everyone joined in.

She linked arms with Steve and Albert, who were on either side of her. Everyone had entwined arms with his or her neighbors' and swayed back and forth as they sang.

Lawrence surveyed his minions, searching the crowd with his blue eyes. *Look at me,* Di prayed silently. *Look at me.*

But his eyes fell on Gertrude. She had her arms around Jeffrey's neck and was rubbing up against him.

Poor Lawrence, Di thought, just as his eyes pulled away from Gertrude and connected with hers.

And when he smiled at her, all she could think of was smiling back.

———

Diana touched the pillow on his side of the bed, where she never slept, even after eight years. "Oh, Larry," she whispered. "Our intentions were so good. How did things go so terribly wrong?"

CHAPTER 20

The fishy air from the bay clogged her brain as Aubrey jogged the route she used to take when she was in high school—Tigertail Avenue to Vizcaya Museum, then back along South Bayshore Drive. The overhanging oaks and banyans blocked the sharpness of the morning sun and left the cracked, parched pavement dappled, much like on her morning jogs ten, twelve years ago.

After those runs, she had always felt better, as though she actually had some control over her life. But her special tonic had lost its magic.

This morning, the pounding of her feet did nothing to free her of her anger toward the Coles after their attack on her mother the night before, or of her frustration from the lack of results in digging into her parents' past.

She was winded and covered with sweat when she got back to the house and took in the driveway and bushes. Her mom's car and one black sedan. No newspaper, but maybe the FBI agents had taken it to check for a ransom note hidden among the pages.

She went into the kitchen for a glass of orange juice, then poked her head into the family room. Smolleck wasn't there. Agent Tan Lee, whom she'd been introduced to the night before, sat alone in front of his computers. The newspaper was open to an inner page on the table beside him. She could make out the headline: No Leads in Missing Boy.

It had already become old news, hidden inside the paper. The world had moved on, but Ethan was still missing.

"Anything happening?" she asked.

Agent Lee glanced at the newspaper, then back at her. "Not too much."

She leaned against the doorjamb. She had read everything she could online before she'd left for her run but was hoping the FBI knew more than the reporters. "Please, Agent Lee. My mother and I are going crazy with worry. Ethan's been missing for over forty hours."

Lee looked around the room, as though he were concerned about someone walking in. They'd taken down the blown-up photos from the walls. Had they found a suspect in the crowds at the carnival?

"We cleared all known SOs in the vicinity," Lee said. "And the carnival employees."

"That's good," Aubrey said, though because of the note, she already knew a sex offender wasn't involved. "What about the Coles?"

"I'm guessing you've seen the tweets," he said.

She had. #where'sgrandma? #grannychildkiller? #doctordidie. And many others crucifying her mother. "I hope you're not distracted by them," she said. "The Coles have a vendetta against my mother."

"We know that." His phone rang. "Excuse me." He answered the call, turning away from Aubrey.

She went upstairs to shower. The door to her mother's room was closed. It was well after eight. She hoped her mother had gotten some sleep.

The hot water pounded over her as she considered whether the Coles could be behind Ethan's kidnapping.

She had googled them at length after their appearance on the news, looking for some reason they might want to hurt or even kill Jonathan, in addition to wanting to get even with her mother.

She'd found nothing.

But even though she believed there was a reasonable possibility that the Coles had sent the threatening note, she wasn't willing to tell the FBI and risk that the kidnappers would act on their threat to kill Ethan.

She quickly dried herself and put her hair up in a ponytail. After she dressed, she went to her mother's bedroom. The bed was made, and her mother, wearing a flannel nightgown, sat on one of the wingback chairs near the fireplace, a small box and some color snapshots on her lap.

"Morning," Aubrey said, as she sat down on the other chair. "Did you sleep?"

"A little." Her mother scooped up the photos and put them back in the box, which was decorated with neon colors and old-fashioned peace symbols. Aubrey had never seen it before.

"Can I bring you some breakfast?" Aubrey asked.

"I'm fine, thanks. I'll go down in a bit and fix my own."

"What are you looking at?"

"Old photos."

"Of what?" The feeling that Mama was hiding something reemerged, even though Aubrey wanted so much to quell it.

"Just some old friends," her mother said. "Your father and me."

"Any reason you're looking at them now?"

"Your questions last night started me thinking about the past. Some terrible things happened, like that explosion, but there were a lot of good memories, too." She reached into the box and handed Aubrey a photo. "I don't believe I ever showed you this."

It took Aubrey a moment to realize the man wearing a white bandanna was her father. Young Larry had shoulder-length blond hair, a cleft in his strong chin, and intense blue eyes that seemed to be searching for something.

"He seemed larger than life to me," her mother said. "My white knight on a snowy stallion."

A knot formed in Aubrey's throat. It had been a favorite song of Aubrey and Mama's—"My Hero Knight." She remembered how her mother's face would change when she listened to the lyrics. It occurred to her only now that for her mother, the song had been about Dad.

"He looks like a movie star," Aubrey said. "Was he in costume for something?"

"That's how he dressed back then. Back in the late sixties, everyone was playing some part." Her mother rubbed her left hand with her right one, as though feeling for the wedding band she had once worn. "I never met a man as charismatic as he was."

Aubrey studied the photo. He had once been a hero—to Aubrey and her mother. And she realized she and her mother had been attracted to the same kind of charismatic men. "I'm sorry, Mama."

"Sorry? About what?"

"That he hurt you so much."

"It was my fault as much as his. I changed a lot more than he did." She took another photo out of the box. "Look at this one."

Aubrey examined the second photo. It was of both her parents. How beautiful her mother was! Long dark hair framing her heart-shaped face, large brown eyes filled with light. Her parents had their arms around each other's waists. Behind them in the distance was a large crowd, a lake, and trees with red-and-orange leaves. Mama was smiling. No—it was more like she was laughing. Aubrey couldn't recall ever seeing such pure joy on her face.

"It was taken the day we fell in love," Mama said.

The nagging feeling in her gut was back. It didn't make sense that her mother was sitting here reminiscing and looking at old photos when they both needed to figure out who'd taken Ethan.

Unless she was looking for something in the photos.

Aubrey picked one up from the top of the pile. "Who are they?"

"Friends. The one with the glasses was my roommate."

Three very pretty young women holding up two fingers in the 1960s symbol for peace. They were all roughly the same height, but otherwise very different. Her mother was in the middle, smiling broadly, her dark brown hair loose on her shoulders. The girl to her left was blonde and meek-looking. The girl to her mother's right had a muted smile and a strong chin. She wore wire-rim glasses with pink lenses, and her black hair fell in a single braid across her embroidered white blouse. With her other hand, she fingered the rectangular shape on her necklace.

"Your roommate looks awfully intense."

"She was."

"What's she holding? It seems very dear to her."

"Her brother's dog tag," her mother said. "She never took it off, even when she showered."

"Did you stay in touch with either of these women?"

Her mother stiffened, then took the photo out of Aubrey's hand. "No. We lost touch." She dropped the photo into the box and put the lid on.

End of subject.

But for Aubrey, something was opening up. These girls, or something else in the box, might have a connection to Ethan's disappearance. At least, that was what she was certain her mother believed.

Why else would she be looking at these photos?

Aubrey wasn't buying that it was because of nostalgia. Unfortunately, it was also clear to her that Mama wasn't ready to share.

"I'm going to the hotel to check on Kevin and Kim," Aubrey said. She knew her mother wouldn't be comfortable going into Simmer territory herself. "Will you be okay?"

"Yes, of course." Mama held the small box tightly against her, as though she were protecting it, or its secrets.

Aubrey left the room, wondering what secrets could possibly be worth protecting when Ethan's life was at stake?

CHAPTER 21

She held the small box tightly against her. It had been a reflex to grab the photo from Aubrey, but Diana knew it would serve no purpose to tell her daughter about that time of her life.

She took the lid off and went through the photos one more time, lingering on the one of her with Gertrude and Linda. She had forgotten how close the three of them had been at the beginning of freshman year. Before things changed.

She put the photos back in the box, trying to ignore the small white envelope, yellowed with age, but finally gave in to the nagging sensation and slid the card out of the envelope. It had accompanied a dozen roses sent to her dorm room the day after the Central Park antiwar demonstration.

Diana studied the cursive writing, similar to his careful script once he became a lawyer, but stronger and more determined, as he had once been.

D-Our love is stronger than the pain.
Love, L-

Maybe that had been true once, but not anymore.

She put the card back in the envelope, stuck it between the photos, then tucked the box back into the old blue suitcase where she had kept it all these years. It wasn't a hiding place, exactly—or was it? But if she'd been hiding the box, it had been to keep the memories from herself.

She leaned back in her chair and closed her eyes, shivering with the memory of her bare midriff on that chilly night.

———

The brownstone belonged to a freshman named Michael Shernovsky, who had recently joined Stormdrain. Although *belonged* wasn't quite the right word. The building was owned by Michael's parents, who were letting him live there with a couple of roommates. It was on the border of East Harlem and Morningside Heights. But if Michael had told people that, many of them might not come—the whiteys who attended Columbia weren't big favorites in the black community. At least, that was what Lawrence said when he explained about the Halloween party they were going to.

Di held Lawrence's arm more tightly as they stepped around broken bottles on a cracked sidewalk lined by three-story, reddish-brown townhouses that had probably once been elegant but were now mostly in a state of disrepair. Boarded-up windows covered with graffiti proclaimed: **Black Is Beautiful. Be Yourself. MLK Jr. Died For Us.**

She followed Lawrence up a stoop to a weathered oak door that was covered with gauzy webs, a hanging skeleton, and a peace sign. Now that they were here, Di was questioning the wisdom of her Halloween costume. She had rejected wearing her everyday clothes because she wanted to stand out from the rest of the girls, who she was pretty sure would be dressed in headbands and long, loose cotton shifts, or torn jeans and peasant blouses. Instead, beneath the green army jacket she'd gotten at an Army Navy Surplus store, she wore harem pants and a top that left her midriff bare, in the style of *I Dream of Jeannie*. Unfortunately, instead of sexy, she was feeling self-conscious. She and Lawrence had only been seeing each other a couple of weeks and hadn't crossed the line her roommate did with so little thought, but she was afraid her outfit screamed, "Make love, not war."

Lawrence used the tarnished brass knocker and gave her a smile, as though reading her mind. He was dressed as himself, wearing his white headscarf and flowing white shirt, though she knew he would be just as gratified if people mistook him for Lawrence of Arabia.

The door opened, though Di couldn't have said by whom, since the person disappeared by the time she stepped into the dark foyer and blinked the smoke out of her eyes. She smelled pot, tobacco, and incense, but there was another smell that she dragged deep into her lungs.

Chocolate.

Music hit her from different directions. Jimi Hendrix on the electric guitar, Ravi Shankar on the sitar, and the hoarse screaming voice of Janis Joplin.

People stood in the rooms to the left and right of her—smoking, drinking, and talking animatedly. Most everyone was from Stormdrain and not wearing costumes, but she noticed a Richard Nixon, and someone trying to be Paul or Ringo—she couldn't tell which.

Steve was talking to Albert in front of a boarded-up fireplace. He wore a football jersey with shoulder pads, and Albert was dressed as

Groucho Marx. They both held red plastic cups, probably rum-and-Cokes, which Stormdrainers liked to refer to as Cuba Libres, because they were, after all, revolutionaries.

Their host, Michael, dressed in an astronaut suit, approached and gave Lawrence a bear hug. "Hey, man. Got some good shit." He passed Lawrence a joint, who took a hit and handed it to Di.

She'd smoked pot a few times at their meetings, but this burned her lungs and made her cough.

Michael grinned. "Like I said. Good shit." He pointed to the stairs behind him. "Coats in the mudroom. There's a keg in the kitchen, and plenty of rum, and some dark-haired sorceress baked us Alice B. Toklas brownies."

"I'm getting one of those," Di said, heading toward the kitchen. Lawrence followed, stopping to greet various people in the hallway.

A waifish girl with very short blonde hair, wearing a quilted pink bathrobe, was arranging brownies on a tray in the kitchen. Di did a double take. "Linda?"

Her friend turned and touched her head. "Do you like it?" she asked, widening her blue eyes as if there was any doubt that she was utterly adorable. "I cut it like Allison cut hers in *Peyton Place*."

"It's great," Di said. "Now you really look like Mia Farrow."

Lawrence reached for two brownies and handed one to Di. "I'd better not find any hair in these, Linda."

Linda giggled. "Don't worry. I didn't make them, but I've had one. There's plenty of grass. Have fun getting stoned."

Di took a big bite of the brownie. The rich fudge didn't quite mask the bitter taste of the pot.

"What's wrong?" Lawrence asked.

"It has a chalky undertaste," she said with a straight face, hoping he'd get the movie reference.

He laughed and grabbed her arm. "Come on, Rosemary, before the devil gets you."

He got it. He "got" her. They had their own inside joke now.

He led her past people slumped against the hallway walls leading into the mudroom. A door with peeling paint led out to the back of the house. A few coats hung from pegs on the wall, but there was a bigger pile of coats on the floor.

"Take off your jacket," Lawrence said, removing his own and dropping it on top of the pile.

She thought about her skimpy costume and wrapped her arms around herself. She should have worn something else. "I think I'll leave it on. It's cold in here."

"I'll keep you warm, baby." He shoved the rest of his brownie in his mouth and slipped his hands under her coat, his fingers spreading over her bare midriff.

His hands were surprisingly warm, but she shivered at his touch.

"Mmm. Nice," he said, pulling her closer and pressing his lips against hers.

His tongue darted into her mouth, all warm and wet and chocolatey. She went slack in his arms, feeling light-headed and delicious from the brownie.

A raspy voice was crooning about love being stronger than pain.

"Oh, man," he said, gently pulling away. He grinned at her, a crumb of chocolate wedged between his front teeth. "Primo."

She laughed, though she wasn't sure whether he meant her or the brownie. She finished the rest of hers, the buzz growing.

"Good girl," he said. "Now, off with that jacket. I want to see what I've been touching."

She slipped it off, then threw it on top of his.

He stared at her, making her feel naked.

"Our love is stronger than the pain," the singer spat out, the words rubbing between them.

Don't stop. Never stop looking at me, Di thought.

A guy in fatigues staggered into the tiny room, pushing past them and throwing open the back door. A blast of cold air surrounded her, along with the sound of retching as the guy puked in the backyard.

"Let's split," Lawrence said, taking her hand. He opened a door that seemed to lead to the basement. "I want to see what's down here." He touched the inside wall, then she heard a click and a light came on. "Man, this is great." He dropped her hand and bounded down the stairs.

She held on to an unfinished wood railing and went halfway down the wooden steps leading into a large, cold room that smelled damp and musty. There were no basements in the houses in Miami, and this one definitely creeped her out. She quickly took in the wood shelves, hanging pipes, rusting water heater, and some other mechanisms she couldn't identify. A large workbench was shoved up against a brick wall that oozed mortar.

Lawrence was poking around in some cobwebs and seemed to be enjoying himself.

"Lovely," she said. "Can we go now?"

"You want to go? But this place is far out. I'll ask Michael if we can use it as Stormdrain headquarters. We can get some folding tables and chairs. Maybe a printing press to do our own flyers." He wandered from one side of the room to the other. "This area will be great for supplies."

What kind of supplies? she almost asked, but she didn't really care. She just wanted to get out of there. "I'm going up for another brownie," she said.

"Okay, baby. I'm coming, too." He raced up the steps behind her, stopping when he was inches away. "But wouldn't you rather check out the rest of the house?" he whispered in her ear.

"What did you have in mind?" she said, though she knew exactly what he had in mind. She did, too.

He led her up the stairs to the second floor, past people drunk or stoned, blocking the way.

Joe Cocker was screaming about needing help from his friends.

They reached the top of the stairs, and Lawrence opened a door, releasing the smell of incense, candle wax, pot, and something more human. She peeked inside the room. Candles threw shadows against the walls. Flesh-colored blobs were writhing on the white rectangle on the floor. Arms and legs and heads and tongues and breasts and penises.

Di took a step back.

Lawrence laughed. "I'm guessing this is a little too groovy for you."

One of the bodies separated from the others and slid off the mattress. The naked goddess came to the door, her black braid mostly undone, her brother's dog tag hanging between her perfect naked breasts.

"Come back here, Gert," a voice called from the room. Di recognized the growl as Jeffrey's and was surprised Gertrude let him call her by a nickname.

"Go fuck a law book, Jeff," Gertrude called back, then turned to smile at them.

"Have you had a brownie?" Gertrude asked Lawrence, though it sounded like she was offering him something else.

He stared at her just like he had ogled Di earlier, with the same hunger. "Yes," he said. "They were primo."

Di flinched. That word belonged to her.

"I made them," Gertrude said. "Old family recipe."

He smiled at her. "I'll always be Alice Toklas," he said, "if you'll be Gertrude Stein."

An inside joke between them, and Di was very much outside.

"So are you coming?" Gertrude grinned as she reached for his hand.

He glanced back at Di.

"Pollyanna, too." Gertrude grabbed Di's hand. "Come join the huddled masses."

Di felt herself being pulled into the room, into the frenzy.

But this was all wrong. Sex was supposed to be about love, not just groping bodies. Di jerked her hand out of Gertrude's and ran back into the hallway.

Hot tears ran down her cheeks. She was a fake. A poseur. Not the real thing like Gertrude. And she had lost him, probably forever.

Jefferson Airplane was crying about truth and lies.

Then his warm hands encircled her waist, his warm breath on her neck. He spun her toward him. She closed her eyes and licked the chocolate from his lips, melting into this man she wanted so desperately. She felt a burning sensation on her back, as though a pair of eyes were boring into her.

She turned, expecting to see Gertrude watching them.

But no one was there.

———

Diana's eyes flew open. Her heart was pounding. There was something in the memory she'd forgotten, but it wasn't about Gertrude. It was Jeff. Jeffrey Schwartz. She hadn't thought about him in twenty years, so why now? She tried to slow her breathing. Jeff had had a thing for Gertrude—Diana had always known that. But what she'd forgotten was that Jeff had been a law student at Columbia. At the same time as Jonathan.

It couldn't mean anything, could it? Then why couldn't she shake this feeling that Jeff was just beyond the door, watching her. Laughing at her.

Chapter 22

The Coconut Grove Ritz was on a slight bluff overlooking the bay, a ten-minute walk from Aubrey's house, but it had taken her six. She had hurried in order to see Kevin and check on what was happening at the Simmers' command post, but she was also eager to get back home to her computer to continue digging into her mother's past. She hoped to find something on those two women in the photo, or anything that might relate to the brownstone explosion.

She stepped into a hushed, sumptuous lobby filled with earth-tone marble and grand columns, where a number of reporters were milling about. She followed the desk clerk's directions to one of the meeting rooms off the lobby. A man in a dark suit stood at the door with an iPad. He checked for her name on his tablet, then asked for ID before allowing her into the room. She wondered whether the police had been so careful the day before when someone slipped the greeting card in with the mail.

The large room buzzed with voices. Aubrey took in the different stations of the Simmers' command post. Two women in T-shirts that said "National Center for Missing & Exploited Children" sat at a table near the front of the room. They were both wearing headphones and typing on their laptops, probably fielding calls from the hotline. At a nearby table, Detective Gonzalez was talking to another police officer.

A half-dozen men and women in suits had commandeered several tables in the back and were busy at their computers or on their phones.

They looked like FBI but were probably the private investigators the Simmers had hired.

Kevin, Kim, and the Simmers weren't in the room.

Aubrey approached Detective Gonzalez. She looked more haggard than the day before, her black hair greasy and pulled back from her pale face.

"Do you have a minute?" Aubrey asked.

"Sure." Gonzalez led Aubrey to a corner where they had some privacy.

"I was wondering about your reaction to the Coles' attack on my mother. Could they have Ethan, and are hoping to misdirect the police?"

"We considered that possibility. I went to see them last night after the interview."

"And?"

Gonzalez shook her head. "They admitted they had no basis for accusing your mother. They saw an opportunity to publicly hurt her, and they took it."

"Yes, of course. But it shows their motive to kidnap Ethan."

"We've already confirmed their alibis regarding their whereabouts when Ethan was taken. We've also had them under surveillance since the kidnapping. At this point, it's unlikely they're involved."

"So you're dropping them as suspects?"

"We're not dropping anyone." Her voice was a bit impatient, and Aubrey wondered whether she'd crossed a line by suggesting the police weren't doing their job. "And I'm sure the Simmers will let us know if we missed anything," Gonzalez added.

"What do you mean?" Aubrey asked

"Their investigators are all over the Coles, despite their alibis."

"They are?"

"Why does that surprise you?"

Aubrey glanced across the room at the Simmers' investigators. They looked purposeful as they conversed with each other and pointed at their computer screens. "I would have expected the Simmers to find a reason to blame my mother, not her enemies."

Gonzalez frowned, her thick eyebrows almost merging. Aubrey wondered whether the detective was able to read her thoughts. That the Simmers were leading the charge against the Coles, because they were hoping to deflect suspicion from themselves. But the possibility that the Simmers were behind Ethan's kidnapping continued to baffle her, especially after seeing their genuine grief during the press conference.

"Whatever agenda the Simmers have," Gonzalez said, "they'd better keep their people from interfering with the police investigation." The detective seemed to stiffen. Aubrey followed her gaze. Prudence and Ernest had come in and were heading toward the back of the room. No Kevin or Kim.

The Simmers looked as tired and wilted as they had on TV the day before. Nothing like people who had kidnapped their own grandchild, but rather like devastated grandparents. Aubrey had seen them a handful of times since Kevin and Kim's wedding, usually at one of Ethan's birthday celebrations. Prudence had always been cool toward Aubrey, though never quite rude.

Rudeness was unbecoming to a Baer.

Ernest stopped to talk to one of the dark-suited men while Prudence took a seat at a long table and pulled a laptop from her tote bag.

"Excuse me," Aubrey said to the detective. "I need to speak with them."

She approached the Simmers, standing back a few feet so as not to appear to be eavesdropping. The man Ernest was talking to had his hand on his hip, revealing an ID of some sort. The familiar logo of

BBM caught her by surprise. She'd thought these people were with a private security firm.

It occurred to her that the reward money and investigation wasn't being financed by the Simmers' personal funds, as she had assumed, but by Baer Business Machines. That was odd. Unless the Simmers believed the kidnappers were targeting BBM for some reason. She thought about the documentary she'd watched the night before and wondered whether there could be a connection between BBM and the brownstone explosion.

She stepped up to the Simmers' table, hoping she'd be more effective getting information from Prudence than she had been with Smolleck.

Prudence frowned, as though trying to place her.

"Hello, Mrs. Simmer." She had never been able to call her by her first name.

"Audrey," Prudence said, accepting her hand. "How awful that we have to see each other again under such circumstances."

"Yes, it is awful," Aubrey said, deciding not to correct her name.

Prudence clung to Aubrey. The woman's hand felt bony and cold. The red polish on her nails was partially chewed away.

"I wanted to tell you how much my mother and I appreciate your providing the reward money and private investigators."

Prudence got a faraway look. An amoeba-shaped splotch of coffee stained her beige-silk blouse. "We'd give far more if we believed it would help us get Ethan back, but thank you."

"It's great that you have the resources of Baer Business Machines at your disposal."

Prudence pulled her hand away from Aubrey's. "We're using all our resources to find Ethan." Her voice was clipped.

"Yes, of course." This was clearly not the best way to get information from Prudence. She needed to try something else. "Have your investigators found anything suspicious on the Coles?"

"Not yet," Prudence said.

"The police say they have an alibi."

"Alibis are easy to manufacture, dear." Something across the room caught Prudence's attention. "This is unacceptable," she mumbled.

Aubrey turned to see her brother staggering across the room. His white-cotton shirt was wrinkled and untucked from his slacks. Kevin stopped and rubbed an unshaven cheek, seemingly mystified by the people busy trying to find his son.

Her heart ached for him. Her big brother. A memory surfaced. Kevin holding on to her pink bicycle as he ran alongside her, then how he shouted with delight when he let go and she pedaled down the street by herself. She'd been six. The same age Ethan was now.

She started toward him, then hesitated. Given the stress he was under, he might make a public display and take all this out on her—his grief, his ineffectualness, his anger toward their mother. So let him, she decided, and continued walking. Let him use her as his whipping post if that was what he needed. His child was missing.

"Hey, Kev."

He blinked, as though trying to figure out what she was doing there. "Oh. Hey."

It was not even ten, but she could smell alcohol on his breath. She wasn't going to judge him if that was what he needed to cope with his son's disappearance.

He glanced toward his disapproving mother-in-law.

"Do you want to go outside?" Aubrey asked.

"Sure."

She led him to a terraced area near the pool, where they sat on a couple of square wicker chairs beneath a palm tree. A gardener was trimming the hedges and plants, but there were no hotel guests around.

"Is Kim back in your room?" she asked.

"Yeah. Prudence has her doped up on something. Doctor's orders, or so she says." He reached into his pants pocket and took out a miniature bottle of scotch he'd probably gotten out of the minibar. He opened it, then gave her a dare-you look. "Got a problem with this?"

She shook her head and he took a swig.

"I called and texted you a few times," she said.

He shrugged. "One of Prudence and Ernie's people has our phones. They're handling stuff. Works for me." He took another drink.

It didn't work for Aubrey. She wished her brother were stronger and could take charge of himself and Kim. "Where's Bilbo Baggins?" she asked softly.

"I'm no Bilbo Baggins. Never was."

She took his hand. If he couldn't be strong, at least she wanted him to know he wasn't alone.

The gardener clipped off several stray vines of fuchsia bougainvillea, and they dropped to the keystone tiles. One strand fell into the pool and floated on the blue-green water.

"Remember the time you almost drowned?" Kevin asked, pulling his hand away from hers.

"I almost drowned?"

He nodded. "We were at a birthday party for that kid who lived down the street. Matt. Dad took us because Mom was working. It was a pool party with a clown. I guess Dad figured it would be okay to leave us. Maybe he thought the clown was a lifeguard."

"I don't remember any of this."

"You were five, I guess. I remember I was in third grade. We both knew how to swim. There was a slide going into the pool. I went down headfirst. Got a mouthful of water." He took another slug from the bottle. "Maybe I was embarrassed. I don't know. You were watching me cough, so I dared you to do it."

She tried to bring up the memory, but it wasn't there.

"You went up the slide and lay down headfirst, like I'd done. Except you had one of those plastic swimming rings around your waist."

"What happened?"

"You slid down and landed upside down in the water, feet kicking up in the air. I realized you were stuck, that you couldn't right yourself. The swimming ring was too tight for you to slip out of, and it was keeping your head under."

Something was coming back to her. A sensation of being beneath the water, but she didn't remember being scared.

"What did you do?" she asked.

He took another drink and stared at the pool. "I watched your feet kicking. I remember thinking what little feet you had." He rubbed his cheek. His eyes were completely bloodshot.

"Did you jump in after me?"

"I should have, right? I was eight years old. I was a good swimmer. I could have saved you with no problem."

"But you didn't."

He studied the small scotch bottle. "Nope."

She felt sad for him, not angry. "Do you know why you didn't?"

"It was like I was paralyzed," he said. "I kept watching your little feet kick in the air, until somehow you righted yourself."

"Did Mom and Dad ever find out?"

"Someone told them. I remember Mom yelling at Dad for leaving us unsupervised at the party. I'd never seen her so angry." He thought for a moment. "That's when it started with Mom."

"What started?"

"I wasn't her little prince after that."

He rolled the bottle between his fingers. Above his gold watch, his wrist was knobby and red, just like when he was a teenager.

"Mama's always loved you," she said.

"Nope." Kevin took another swig. "She blamed me for everything that went wrong and has been punishing me ever since."

"But Kev—"

"No. Listen to me. Remember that big fight Mom and Dad had when we were kids? The one that seemed to last forever?"

"You mean when Jimmy Ryce went missing?"

He cocked his head, as though confused. "The kid who was kidnapped, then found dead?" His face sagged.

She never should have mentioned Jimmy Ryce. It would only make Kevin more fearful of what might happen to Ethan.

Kevin let out a heavy sigh. "Yeah. It was right around that time. I was eleven when the War of the Lynds got going."

War of the Lynds. Aubrey had always thought of those weeks as the nightmarish time between "before" and "after."

"The war was my fault," Kevin said. "They were fighting because of me."

"They were upset about Jimmy Ryce, Kev. Worried that something like that might happen to you and me." At least, that was how she had classified that memory in her mind.

"No." He gave his head an emphatic shake. "It was my fault. They hated my friend Jeff. They said he was a bad influence, but I disobeyed them and kept hanging out with him."

"That doesn't make sense."

"I heard them arguing," Kevin said. "I remember Mom saying, 'Jeff's going to be the end of us.' But Dad was on my side. He told her to stop concerning herself about Jeff."

He stared into the pool. The bougainvillea branch had sunk to the bottom. "But Mom was right. Jeff was the end of them," Kevin said. "After that fight, they started hating each other." He put the empty bottle to his lips, then shook it with frustration when nothing came out. "Mom never forgave me," he said, his body starting to shake. "I screwed up their marriage. I screwed up our family."

"That's not so, Kev."

"You don't know, Aubrey." His voice was like a shard of glass. "She blamed me for almost letting you drown and for that big fight with Dad. My whole life, she's been punishing me. First, she misses my graduation, then my wedding. And now . . ." His voice broke. "Now she loses my son."

She opened her mouth to defend their mother, then closed it. Kevin was hurting, and arguing with him wasn't going to help. She gently took the bottle out of his clenched hand, then put her arms around him and held his trembling body close. "We're going to find him, Kev. Ethan will be home soon, happy and safe."

He jerked his head back. His eyes were filled with pain. "Do you promise?"

Her heart clenched. Who was she to promise such a thing?

"Yes," she said. "I promise."

CHAPTER 23

Diana wondered whether Jonathan had already arrived at Frazier's. It had taken her over a half hour from the time she'd called and asked him to meet her to shower, dress in a white blouse and jeans, and then get to downtown Coconut Grove.

She had walked slowly, her mind in turmoil.

Jonathan couldn't possibly have known Jeffrey Schwartz. There had been hundreds of students in the law school. But if he had, then Jonathan likely knew more than he had let on about Stormdrain and April Fool. He might even be involved with Ethan's kidnapping.

But this was the man who made her tea when he sensed she was down. The man she was engaged to marry. It wasn't possible he had some secret past or agenda. The problem was in her mind. She was anxious and stressed, and lack of sleep was making her imagine villains where none existed.

She turned off onto a side street, almost an alley, where a red-and-white-striped awning protruded from the white brick front of a small building. The sight of it calmed her. Frazier's Ice Cream and News. The combination newsstand, ice-cream parlor, and luncheonette was one of the oldest establishments in the Grove and had been considered quaint even when Diana and Larry had moved here thirty years ago.

The window was covered with local postings of "Apartments for Rent," "Loving Dog Walkers Available," and "Today's Specials—Chili, Tuna salad, Pistachio ice cream." They were the same specials they'd had for the last thirty years.

She used to come here with Aubrey and Kevin and buy them ice-cream cones. Kevin always got vanilla, but Aubrey would order pistachio. Diana had been planning to bring Ethan here as a treat. She stood straighter.

She *would* bring Ethan here!

The bell on the front door chimed as she stepped inside, just as it used to. The place was empty except for Jonathan, who was sitting at a rickety table for two. He stood when he saw her—his pale, freckled face in a worried frown. He wore a faded, short-sleeved madras shirt tucked into a pair of khaki slacks.

A wave of guilt swept over her. He was still Jonathan. How could she doubt him?

He came toward her and gave her a light hug, not the usual bear-squeeze. She wondered whether he was responding to her remoteness or if he had some secret of his own.

"You got here quickly," she said.

"As quickly as I could. You sounded very distressed."

"Sorry if I worried you."

He glanced around at the newsstand and magazines, then at the counter. "Well, this is a charming place. Shall we get something to eat?"

"Their chili has always been great." She said it lightly, trying to hide the darkness that was threatening to reveal itself.

Jonathan signaled to the young man behind the counter. "Two chilis, please." He looked back at her. "Coffee?"

"Just water, thanks."

Jonathan ordered a couple of waters, then sat down across from her at the small table. He pushed his glasses up on his nose. "When you called, I was just finishing up with the man heading up the FBI investigation."

"Tom Smolleck?" She tensed. "He came to your apartment?"

"That's right. He wanted to ask me a few questions." Jonathan scratched his bald spot. "It was a bit awkward for me after what you told me last night about the note."

"You spoke with him?"

"Well, yes. Of course. How could I not?"

If Jonathan had mentioned the note to the FBI, then Ethan was likely lost to them. "What did you talk about?" she asked.

"Nothing about the note." He reached for her hand and gave it a squeeze.

She nodded, relieved.

"He asked about people who might use Ethan as a political pawn in my nomination, or anyone I may have angered in the past. Since I'd already given that quite a bit of thought, I gave him a few names."

"Anything else?" she asked.

He stared at the dulled marble tabletop. "Well, he asked about you and Larry, and about your relationship with your son and the Simmers. Whether I knew of any threats by the Coles."

"Anything else?" She could hear the strain in her voice and realized she probably sounded unhinged, repeating her question.

He met her eyes. "You seem anxious about my interview with him. I told you, Diana. I said nothing about the note."

She looked away. The newspapers and magazines were neatly stacked in the racks, everything in its proper place. So unlike the rest of the world.

"Diana," he said softly, "I don't want to make this about me, because I understand how frightened and upset you are, but . . ." He cleared his throat. "I feel you're withdrawing from me. Almost like you're afraid to confide in me."

The young man put the chili on the table, along with their water and silverware.

"Talk to me, Diana," Jonathan said when the man left. "Why did you want to meet me here?"

She took a bite of chili, then another, not sure how to ask him what she needed to ask him. Not sure what she would do if his answers showed him to be a villain in all this.

"Is it about April Fool?" he asked.

Her heart skipped a beat. So he did know something.

"What's wrong?" he asked. "Why are you looking at me like that? You told me last night you thought April Fool might have something to do with the kidnapping and the note."

She took a long sip of water. She *had* been the one to bring up April Fool last night. His question could have been perfectly innocent. She needed to get herself under control. "You're right," she said. "I am worried about that."

He pulled in a deep breath, then let it out slowly. "I understand you want to leave no stone unturned," he said, "but isn't looking for a connection to something that happened over forty-five years ago a bit far-fetched?"

Far-fetched. She bristled. Was he trying to divert her from discovering the truth about him?

"Nothing is too far-fetched," she said, holding his eyes.

He blinked and turned away. "I'm sorry," he said. "You're right. You should be pursuing every possibility. What can I do to help?"

It could have been a lawyerly tactic to cover his own involvement, but she would play along.

"One of the members of Stormdrain attended Columbia Law School," she said. "He would have been a student when you were."

"You mean Jeffrey Schwartz?"

Her chin shot up. "How did you know I meant him?"

"Everyone knew about Jeffrey. It was quite a big deal at the law school back then. One of our own being involved with April Fool and going underground. Then, of course, he became big news in '81 after the killings at the bank, and again about twenty years ago when that crazy man came forward claiming to be Jeffrey Schwartz."

She was relieved he was so matter-of-fact in the way he talked about him. "Sometimes I forget these were once front-page stories," she said.

Jonathan rubbed one of his inflamed knuckles. "But I had also known Jeffrey personally. He started with me in '68. We were in the same Constitutional Law study group."

"You knew him? How well?"

"Not very, I'm afraid. Jeffrey was brilliant—I remember that. He had the sharpest mind in our group when he spoke, which wasn't often."

"Did you have contact with him outside of your study group and class?"

He shook his head.

"Did you know he was involved with Stormdrain?"

"Not until after April Fool." He took a bite of chili. "In fact, now that I think of it, I can't say I recall Jeffrey in any of my classes during our second year. I probably would never have given him another thought except for his involvement with those terrible tragedies."

"Have you seen or spoken to Jeffrey since?"

He had a shocked expression on his face. "Of course not. Why are you asking me this?"

"As you said, I'm leaving no stone unturned."

He shook his head. "These things happened long ago, Diana. It was an awful time for many of us. Must you exhume it?"

"Yes, I must," she said. "Did you know anyone else involved with Stormdrain?"

He dropped his eyes abruptly, as though she had hit a nerve. He took a sip of water, then smoothed his few graying hairs over the bald spot on the top of his head. "I knew a woman in the group. We dated for a short while."

"Jesus," she said. "You dated someone in Stormdrain and never told me?"

"Why would I have told you? I dated several women in college and law school."

Under ordinary circumstances, this would have made sense. Jonathan hadn't known about her own involvement with Stormdrain, so there would have been no reason to bring up some woman he had once dated. Yet, with Ethan's disappearance, this took on a whole new significance.

"I don't know what she saw in me," he said. "I was a boring law student, and she was this wild firebrand."

Wild firebrand. There was only one woman in Stormdrain who fit that description. "What was her name?" Diana asked.

"What does it matter?" he said.

"Who was she, Jonathan?"

He shied back like a horse at the question. Or maybe it was her tone of voice.

"Gertrude," he said. "Gertrude Morgenstern."

He had dated Gertrude. How could she not have known?

"Why didn't you ever tell me?" Her voice was too loud in her own ears.

He stared at his freckled hands, folded in front of him on the table. "It wasn't something I was proud of."

The bell on the front door chimed. A young man and woman in their jogging clothes came inside. It registered that the man had one prosthetic leg.

Diana made an effort to slow down her breathing. If she wanted Jonathan to open up, she had to stop being accusatory.

"I never told anyone about my relationship with Gertrude," Jonathan said. "Can you imagine what it might have done to me politically if it had come out that I once dated one of the organizers of Stormdrain?"

Diana knew exactly what it would have done. It would have leveled his career. He never would have been considered for the Supreme Court. She took another sip of water. Her brain was getting foggy with overload. Jonathan had dated Gertrude. Jeffrey Schwartz had dated Gertrude.

"How long did you see each other?" she asked, making an effort to keep her voice even.

"Three months or so. Rarely in public. I'm not sure if she didn't want us to be seen together, or she enjoyed our private time as much as I did. I'm a little ashamed to say, I was happy enough with the arrangement. She would come to my room late at night, then leave a few hours later. I didn't get very much sleep those three months."

"Did you know she was also seeing Jeffrey Schwartz?"

He sighed. "It doesn't surprise me."

Her mind was racing. "Do you think it's possible Jeff is behind Ethan's kidnapping and the ultimatum?"

His brow creased. "That doesn't make sense. Why now, after forty-five years?"

To punish her, of course, but how could she explain that to Jonathan? "What happened between you and Gertrude?" she asked instead.

"Well, I can't say we went out with a whimper," he said. "It was quite a scene, actually. Not like anything I'd experienced before, or since."

He glanced over at the young man and woman who were tasting each other's ice-cream cones at the counter. "She was very angry with me," he said. "I would say disappointed, but it went much deeper than that."

"Why? What did she want from you?"

"To share her ideals. To join her."

"But you didn't want to commit to something political that might hurt your future?"

"Oh, dear, Diana. That sounds a bit harsh."

"Help me understand."

"I'm afraid it's true," he said. "I admired what SDS and the Weathermen and Stormdrain wanted to accomplish. At least, initially. Stop the war. Fight prejudice against blacks. Make government accountable for its actions. But once the organizations decided violence was a justified means to their end, I wanted nothing to do with them."

The doorbell chimed. The young couple left with their ice creams. The man walked naturally, completely at ease in his artificial limb.

"But Gertrude did," she said.

"Gertrude not only advocated violence, she demanded it." His eyes had become moist and shiny. "She insisted I join her in her ultimate grand gesture, or else. I told her I wanted no part of it, or of her. She left my room, angrier than I've ever seen anyone." He took off his glasses and rubbed his eyes. "Maybe I could have stopped it. Maybe I could have saved her."

"Nothing could have saved her," Diana said.

He put his glasses back on. "I imagine you tried."

The breath snagged in her chest. "What do you mean?"

"Nothing." He waved his hand ineffectually. His face was flushed.

Jonathan was holding something back.

"What else haven't you told me?" she said.

He ran his tongue over his lips. "I knew you back then."

"You *knew* me?"

"Well, not exactly. I knew who you were. I knew you were Gertrude's roommate."

His face went in and out of focus. This man she loved and was planning to marry had lied to her.

Deceived her.

Just like Larry had.

"Please don't be upset with me, Diana."

"Did you know who I was when we met?" she asked.

"I wasn't sure. When we were first introduced at the Columbia event, I thought it was you, even though your name was different. You haven't changed much, though I certainly have." He touched his bald spot, a feeble attempt to lighten the mood. "I once had a full head of long red hair, a moustache and a beard." He paused. "Did you remember me when we first met?"

"No. I would have said something if I had. Why didn't you?"

"And tell you what, exactly? That I knew you'd been the roommate of an extremist from Stormdrain? A woman I'd had a relationship with? It would have been uncomfortable for both of us."

"And later?" she asked. "When we got to know each other better? There were plenty of opportunities for you to have mentioned it."

"As more time passed, it became awkward to bring it up."

"Well, it's no longer awkward, Jonathan. Now it simply feels like you've deliberately lied to me."

"No, Diana. It isn't like that." He reached across the table for her hand. His fingers were cold. She pulled away.

She had trusted Jonathan. But if he had deceived her about knowing her in college and had never told her about his relationship with Gertrude, what else had he lied about?

"Tell me the truth, Jonathan. Why didn't you ever talk to me about Gertrude or Stormdrain or April Fool?"

"I've tried very hard to block out those days."

"Why?" she asked. "What was it to you?"

He stared at the white tiled floor, yellowed and cracked with age. "Losing Gertrude was devastating," he said. "I loved her very much."

The words smacked Diana across her cheek with an old, familiar sting. She felt violated and hurt, but she wasn't sure whether it was because Jonathan had lied to her, or because the old rivalry between her and Gertrude was still alive.

But how could that be? Gertrude was dead.

CHAPTER 24

Two blond children around Ethan's age were splashing each other at the shallow end of the hotel pool. Aubrey watched their parents put water wings on their arms and set out a pail with an assortment of plastic animals on the steps.

If only we could always be around to watch over our children. To forever be like the untouched family in her snow globe. She was glad Kevin had gone back up to his room and didn't have to see this happy family. He had left abruptly after their talk, clearly upset. She had hoped to comfort him, but had only succeeded in bringing his feelings of guilt to the surface.

Given what she knew of family relationships, she shouldn't have been surprised that she and Kevin had viewed that awful period in their childhood so differently, but she had been. For Kev, it had been the "War of the Lynds," something he blamed himself for, while she had always associated the change in her parents with the kidnapping of Jimmy Ryce. Regardless of what had caused it, their parents' subsequent coldness toward each other had left its mark on both her and Kev. They had spent much of their childhood careful not to do anything that might upset either parent.

They had been a dysfunctional family, but she and Kev had both believed that was better than a broken family. Considering the scars she could see in herself and her brother, maybe it would have been better if they had just let go.

But "what ifs" didn't matter right now, not with Ethan missing. She got up and went back inside the hotel. She would check on whether there were any new developments, then head home so she could get back to her own research.

The command center was as busy as when she had left nearly an hour earlier. Prudence and Ernest were still at a table in the midst of their investigators. Her father and Star had arrived while she was with Kevin and were standing by themselves in a corner of the room. They were agitated, as though in the midst of a disagreement. Her father's face was flushed, and Star stood stiffly, her short white hair standing on end like the crest of a cockatoo. Star turned and walked quickly toward the main door, silky-blue pants and top flowing behind her, a huge Louis Vuitton tote over her shoulder. She caught Aubrey watching her, changed direction as subtly as a navigator adjusting her course, and came toward her. The muscles in Star's face shifted from tense to concerned.

"Well, hello, Aubrey," she said, in her slow southern drawl. "I didn't see you before. Is your mother here, too?"

"No. Just me."

She brushed nonexistent hair back from her face with her jeweled fingers in what seemed to be a nervous or distracted gesture. There were dark circles under her blue eyes and a web of fine lines beneath her makeup that Aubrey hadn't noticed the night before in the time-share apartment. She didn't believe Star was genuinely concerned about Ethan and wondered what she was losing sleep over.

"I imagine her fiancé is a comfort to her," Star said.

"We're all trying to comfort each other."

"I only ask because I care about her," Star said, possibly picking up the coolness in Aubrey's voice. "And, yes, perhaps I'm also feeling a little guilty that your father is here with me when your mother's the one who could use his support." Star patted her arm. "I'm not a witch, dear. I hope you'll believe that."

Not a witch, but certainly witchlike.

Her father stepped between them. "Hello, Aubrey," he said with a formal nod, probably still angry about their argument the night before.

"Dad."

"I'm going to get a cup of tea," Star said. "Can I bring back something for either of you?" They both said no and thanked her, and Star left them.

Her father rubbed the back of his neck and surveyed the room, as though at a loss for something to say. "Quite an operation they put together," he said. "You've got to give the Simmers that much."

"What were you and Star arguing about?"

He pressed his lips together and stared at the door Star had left through. The flatness of his expression was very different from the passionate man in the photo that her mother had shown her this morning. A white knight upon a snowy stallion. But no more. At least not for Mama or Aubrey.

"Star's exhausted," he said. "We both are. It's put us on edge."

"I see."

"I'm sorry. I didn't mean to sound dismissive." He touched her arm. "Why don't we step outside?"

They left the room and found a couple of chairs at the end of the hallway.

"This is better," he said, sitting down. "There are a lot of ears in there."

"And you don't want them to hear something?"

He looked down at the gold-and-blue swirl-patterned carpet. "You never know who's on your team and who isn't."

A memory nagged at her. She had been eight and was playing in a neighborhood soccer league. Mama hadn't been able to get to the game, but Dad was home from a long out-of-town trial and came to cheer her on. She was so proud of her handsome father shouting to her from the bleachers.

"Run, Princess!" Somehow, she got turned around and kicked the ball into her own team's goal. She didn't understand why her teammates were yelling at her, why some of the grown-ups had angry faces.

"Stupid kid," one of the mothers said.

Her father glared at the woman, scooped Aubrey up, and carried her away from the field. He let her cry against his chest until she ran out of tears. Then he took her to Frazier's and bought her a pistachio ice-cream sundae.

He told her something she had forgotten until now.

I'm proud of you for trying your best, Princess. That's what matters. Sometimes things happen. You get confused. You want so much to help your team, but you end up hurting them. But you can't keep punishing yourself. You have to try to move on.

Now, she couldn't help but wonder what team he had hurt and whether he had ever moved on.

"Tell me about your mother," he said, turning his attention from the carpet. His voice was uncharacteristically gentle. "How's she holding up?"

Mama had been looking at photos of him this morning. Thinking of him, too. But was he genuinely concerned about her, or asking to be polite?

She met his eyes. Bloodshot like Kevin's. "She's doing okay."

He let out a small sigh. "You don't believe I have a right to worry about her, but I do. Especially after the attack against her by those people last night."

"You attacked her, too, yesterday. Blamed her for Ethan going missing."

"I was upset. I never had any doubt that your mother loves Ethan and only has the best intentions toward him. But the Coles are a couple of contemptible slanderers."

"The Simmers seem to believe they're behind the kidnapping."

"They have their own reasons for diverting the investigation toward the Coles," her father said. "It takes the heat off them."

"You think the Simmers are involved?"

He shook his head. "I almost wish that were the case."

"Then who do you think has Ethan?"

"Last night, you were very hard on me."

Why was he changing the subject? "I'm sorry," she said. "I was frustrated. Ethan's missing, and I don't understand why you—"

He held up his hand. "You made me think about things I would have preferred to keep buried."

She shuddered with apprehension. But this was what she wanted. To know whether her parents were keeping secrets from her. Secrets that might be connected to Ethan's disappearance. "What things?"

"In the past. My past, your mother's past. And I began to wonder whether someone from those days could have kidnapped Ethan to get back at us."

She sat up straighter. Her mother had denied this possibility last night. "Back at you for what? Tell me, Dad. You're talking in riddles."

A little girl in a long party dress with ribbons streaming from her hair came racing down the long hallway, giggling. She stopped a short distance from them and darted behind a heavy drape.

Her father stared at the shifting drape.

"What would someone want to get back at you for?" Aubrey asked again.

"Your mother and I were involved with a radical organization in college."

Why hadn't Mama told her this?

"Things went very wrong," her father said. "Three of our friends died."

"Jesus, Dad. Were you and Mom members of Stormdrain?"

His face paled. He covered it with his hands.

Aubrey became dizzy, as though she were standing on top of a ladder, about to fall over. "Were you?" she asked again. "Were you involved with Stormdrain?"

He didn't answer. Just sat with his hands over his eyes.

She felt a sensation like hundreds of ants crawling over her arms and back. Her mother had said she'd been walking past the brownstone when it exploded, but she had specifically said she hadn't been responsible.

Had Mama lied to her?

She couldn't imagine either of her parents knowingly killing anyone. If they had, they would have been arrested and convicted.

"Dad. I need to know. Did you or Mom have something to do with the brownstone explosion?"

He met her eyes. They were filled with a pain she'd never seen before. "No," he said. "Of course not."

"Casey, come out," a child's voice called. A little boy wearing a bow tie and dress shorts was trotting down the hallway, looking left and right. "I don't want to play anymore."

Aubrey took a deep breath. She wanted so much to believe her father. "But you said things went very wrong, and your friends died."

He hesitated. "Yes, but not because of us."

Her parents were not murderers. Her father had to be telling the truth. "Is it possible someone might blame you anyway?" she asked.

"Casey," the boy called. "Casey, come out now!"

"That's what's concerning me." He blinked at something in the distance and tensed. Star was at the other end of the hallway, coming toward them. "Let's not talk about this in front of her."

"But if you think you know why someone kidnapped Ethan, you must tell the FBI."

"Not now," he said quietly as Star came within earshot.

"Hope I'm not interrupting," Star said. "May I join you?"

He stood and offered Star his chair. He didn't look happy. Neither was Aubrey. The clock was ticking. If her father knew something, they needed to act on it quickly.

Star sat down with her back straight, like someone taught in cotillion. "So what have you two been talking about?"

Her father's eyes met Aubrey's. They said, *later*. "Just about how worried we both are," he said to Star.

"Of course." Star reached over and patted his hand.

Aubrey needed to get her father away from Star. She was about to suggest that he go with her to check on Kevin, when her phone rang. *Our love is stronger than the pain.*

"That's probably your mother," Star said. "Please answer. Don't mind us."

Aubrey glanced at her father. He had a troubled expression on his face. She pressed "Answer." "Are you okay, Mama?"

"I'm fine," her mother said. "I didn't want you to worry. I'm going to Jonathan's apartment."

"Jonathan's? Wouldn't it be better if you stayed home?"

"Home doesn't feel like home."

"I understand. I'll let you know if anything happens here."

Aubrey heard giggles erupt into laughter as she ended the call.

The little boy had pulled back the drape, exposing the little girl. "I found you!" he shouted.

"Is she all right?" her father asked.

"Yes," Aubrey said.

"I wish I could say the same about me," Star said, massaging her temples. "Here I'm supposed to be holding you up, Larry, and I keep fading."

"Can I get you something?" His voice sounded off, like a mechanical recording.

"No, thank you, dearest." She stood up. "The best thing for me is a little shut-eye. I'll take a taxi back to the apartment."

"I'll drive you," he said.

No! Aubrey wanted to shout at her father. *I need you to stay here and talk to me.*

"Absolutely not." Star pushed her wispy white bangs back from her forehead. "You need to be here in case something happens. I'll take a little nap; then I'll be back later."

She gave him a pat on the chest, nodded at Aubrey, then turned and walked down the hallway.

The two children ran past her, chasing each other.

"Okay," Aubrey said. "She's gone. Now tell me. Why do you think someone might blame you or Mama for the brownstone explosion?"

Her father was looking after Star, a frown on his face, though she was no longer in sight.

"What?" he said, clearly distracted.

Something was going on between her father and Star, but Aubrey had no idea what it was. She needed to bring him back to what mattered. "You said someone may have kidnapped Ethan to get back at you."

He blinked. "Did I say that?"

"Yes. Dad, what's going on? If you have a lead about Ethan, we have to let the FBI know."

"A lead?" He shook his head. "Forget that. I was rambling. This is all so stressful. I'm becoming paranoid about everything and everyone." He glanced back at the door to the command past. "I'd better go. I want to make sure Star's okay."

He hurried away, leaving Aubrey with the same confused feeling she had at that soccer game when she'd gone running in the wrong direction, mixed up about who was on her team . . . and who wasn't.

CHAPTER 25

Diana sat on the white sofa in Jonathan's living room. Beyond the sliding glass doors, the sky was the same shade of blue as the suitcase she'd brought to college when she was a freshman. The suitcase she kept in her closet filled with mementos.

The past was everywhere, but she didn't know if or how it might help her figure out who had taken Ethan so she could get him back.

She heard the clink of glassware and glanced over at Jonathan, who was hunched over the bar. They had come here straight from the luncheonette and hadn't spoken on the short drive. She'd been thinking about Gertrude and how much Jonathan had said he loved her. Was it possible he blamed Diana for her death? Could he have kidnapped Ethan as an act of revenge? Vengeance was a powerful motive that led people to do unthinkable things, but this theory made sense only if Jonathan knew what really happened on April Fool.

"It's just after noon," Jonathan said, his soft voice breaking into her thoughts. "I think it's acceptable to start drinking." He handed her a snifter, then sat down beside her with his own.

She took a swallow of brandy. "After you and Gertrude had the fight, did you ever see each other again?"

"You still want to talk about her?" He sounded exasperated.

"Yes."

He shook his head and released a puff of air. "Okay. We'll talk about Gertrude." He set his brandy down on the coffee table and picked up the crimson paperweight that encased a butterfly.

Gertrude had been a butterfly. Free and beautiful. But there had always been something hard surrounding her. Diana wondered if that was the person Jonathan had known, or whether he had seen a different side of her.

"We split up a week or so before the April Fool explosion," he said. "I never saw her again." He cradled the paperweight in his hands. "I keep thinking back to our last fight. It was just after the news came out that the army was bringing charges against several officers involved with the My Lai Massacre." He carefully set the paperweight back down on the coffee table. "Gertrude was enraged that there hadn't been a full-blown investigation. She said the government was covering up the truth, that the slaughter of innocent villagers in My Lai wasn't an isolated incident but rather the norm. She swore she would avenge them somehow."

Diana remembered Gertrude's fury, too. Then, a few days before April Fool, something changed. Her roommate seemed calmer—happy, even.

Gertrude's lighter mood would have been right around when Jonathan said he and Gertrude had had their big fight. So why would she have been happy?

A buried memory came to her. Gertrude dancing around the dorm room in a brightly colored scarf, singing, *La cucaracha, la cucaracha.* Then she laughed. *I think I'll brush up on my Spanish, Pollyanna. Might come in handy.*

As though she was planning to go away. Was she? With whom? Jonathan, Jeffrey Schwartz, or with someone else?

A couple of days later, Gertrude was dead.

Diana drank the rest of the brandy and put her glass down too hard on the table. The sudden sound made Jonathan jump.

"How did you feel when you learned Gertrude had died in the explosion?" Diana asked.

His reddish-gray eyebrows came together. "I was devastated, of course. Why are you asking?"

"Were you angry?"

"Angry?" He looked genuinely perplexed. "Well, after I got over my grief, I was angry with her, of course. Angry that she'd put herself in that situation."

"And you didn't blame Stormdrain?"

"No more than I blamed the government or the university for their pigheaded policies." He rubbed his cheek. "What is it, Diana? I don't understand where you're going with these questions."

She wasn't sure where she was going, either. Jonathan didn't seem to know anything about her own connection with Stormdrain, which meant it was unlikely he had anything to do with Ethan's kidnapping.

But there was still Jeffrey. If he knew the truth about April Fool and blamed her for Gertrude's death, might he have been further enraged by Diana's relationship with Jonathan, the man who had competed with Jeffrey for Gertrude's attention forty-five years ago?

Could Jeffrey have kidnapped Ethan and presented the ultimatum, which would both punish Diana and eliminate his former adversary? Or had Gertrude had other secret lovers and confidants? The truth was, Diana didn't know who was behind the death demand. She only knew she had to do something to get Ethan back.

"Diana?" Jonathan's tone was gentle.

She didn't like the way he was studying her, like she was a mental patient.

He opened his mouth to say something, then closed it.

"What?" she asked.

He shook his head, then released a heavy sigh. "Please don't get angry, but I have to say this. You must tell the FBI about the note. It's the only reasonable thing to do."

"No."

"Diana, the FBI is trained to handle this kind of situation."

"I said no." Her voice came out louder than she'd intended. Jonathan looked like she'd slapped him. "I'm sorry, but I won't put Ethan at risk."

She stared out at the railing, focusing on one point to keep the room from spinning. She felt trapped. *Calm down. Think.* There might be no connection between Jonathan, Jeffrey, or someone else from those days, and the ultimatum. It was her own guilt that had her believing April Fool was involved. What if she were wrong, and there was a much simpler solution? A solution where no one had to die.

She turned back to her fiancé. "There are things we can try before turning this over to the FBI."

"What things?"

When Diana had brought the idea up to Aubrey, they had considered it a long shot, but they were running out of options. If it worked, both Ethan and Jonathan would be saved. "Would you be willing to withdraw from consideration for the Supreme Court?"

He studied her over the rims of his glasses, his brow in a frown. "You want me to withdraw."

"Yes."

He rolled the brandy snifter between his hands.

"You said you would never put your career ahead of family," she said. "Were you just trying to placate me?"

"Of course not, but I'm not going to act rashly."

"Rashly?"

"We need to think this through, darling. The note said they wanted you to kill me. It said nothing about me withdrawing."

"But maybe your stepping down would satisfy them. Maybe they made the threat about harming Ethan to frighten us. To make sure you wouldn't accept the nomination."

"But there's no guarantee we'd get Ethan back if I did withdraw."

"If there's a chance it would work, we have to take it."

He tossed back the rest of the brandy. "These people, whoever they are, are trying to terrorize us with their threats of violence. Giving in to them goes against everything I believe in."

"If we don't try to appease them, they'll kill Ethan."

He got up and refilled his glass at the bar. He took a long drink.

Why was he procrastinating when in a few hours the kidnappers' deadline would run out? Or were his political aspirations too important, just as they'd been when he turned away from Gertrude?

"Will you do it, Jonathan?"

"I want to think it through."

"Then think it through." She got up from the sofa. She was trembling.

"Diana," he said, coming toward her.

She held up her hand for him to stop. "I'm leaving. You'll be able to think about it more clearly if I'm not here."

"Don't go," he said. "Not like this. Not when you're angry with me."

He followed her through the foyer to the front door. "Please, Diana. Let me at least drive you home."

"I'd rather walk." She looked back at the cold white room splotched with crimson, the blue sky just beyond. "I have my own thinking to do."

CHAPTER 26

The midday sun beat down on Diana, pounding on her head and burning through the back of her white cotton blouse as she walked south on Brickell Avenue, away from downtown and Jonathan's building.

The street was airless, the breezes blocked by tall, wide condos, so that even the palm trees that lined the sidewalk were motionless. Diana found it difficult to catch her breath.

Jonathan wasn't willing to save her grandson. And, yes, she understood his argument that withdrawing from the Supreme Court might not be what the kidnappers were after, but he should have been willing to give it a shot. Now their options were running out. The kidnappers wanted a response in less than twelve hours, and she had nothing for them.

If we don't have physical proof of Jonathan Woodward's death, Ethan will die.

She had no doubt they meant it.

The white sidewalk began to swirl in front of her. She reached for a palm tree, regretting the brandy she'd had at Jonathan's, and waited for the dizziness to pass.

It was foolish of her to walk home in this agitated state. She pulled in a few deep breaths and noticed a bus stop a few feet away. She staggered toward it and collapsed on the bench, grateful for the shade of a nearby palm.

She was scared. Not sure what she was capable of doing. She needed Aubrey.

She touched her phone, but the screen remained blank, the battery very likely dead.

She was alone.

A bus heading in the wrong direction pulled up to the stop. The driver looked at her, waiting. She shook her head and waved him on. The bus roared away, leaving the stench of diesel exhaust in its wake.

Jonathan didn't want to give in to threats of violence. His words had lit up a feeling of déjà vu. About how they had all believed in violence back then. They had accepted it as the only way to get what they wanted.

Someone still believed it was the answer. But to what end? What did these people who had taken her little grandson want from her? Was it Jonathan's death?

The thought sickened her. She was a physician, for God's sake. A healer, not a murderer.

Their battle cry echoed in her head. *Someone must die!* In order to go forward, you needed to destroy. In order to be noticed, you had to kill.

Maybe it was as simple as that.

———

Di sat with Linda in the front row of folding chairs, close to the boarded-up fireplace in the cold, damp brownstone. It was late November, but there was no heat, so everyone wore coats and jackets.

Michael had painted a giant peace symbol over the mantel, and magazine photos of war atrocities were taped to the walls. One of the other girls lit candles on the mantel and around the room, casting everyone in sputtering shadows. Sheets hung over the windows so people in the street couldn't see inside.

Most of the girls were crying, herself included. They had seen the photos on the news, and all the magazines had carried them—*Time*, *Life*, *Newsweek*.

The massacre at My Lai. It had happened months ago, back in March, but the news had been quashed, until one determined investigative reporter, Seymour Hersh, had finally brought it all to light. Since the story had broken a few days ago, it was all anyone could talk about. The murder of hundreds of Vietnamese women, children, old men—ordinary people. Murdered in cold blood. By American soldiers.

They went too far this time, Lawrence had said. Now the world will finally take notice of this immoral war.

Members of Stormdrain streamed into the living room and sat down. The sweet smell of marijuana wafted in with them. Everyone spoke in low voices, but Di sensed a nervous energy in the room.

She searched the young men for Lawrence, but he wasn't among them. She wished he would come and hug her before the meeting began. They had become a couple on Halloween—twenty-two days ago. It was Di's first serious relationship, and she treated each day as an anniversary. Except that since the news of My Lai, Lawrence had become distracted, almost as though something inside him was taking root and growing.

Di got that about him—loved it about him. That he cared so much about these people who lived on the other side of the world. Lawrence had cried when he read that the women had been gang-raped, then mutilated. Some of the mothers had lain over their babies, hoping to protect them, but the soldiers threw their dead bodies aside, then murdered their children, too.

"Just like the Holocaust," Di had said.

Lawrence had held her hands and replied, "We'll stop them this time. I promise you, Di. We'll stop them."

"What do you think Lawrence will tell us to do?" Linda asked. Her eyes were eerily large, shadowed by mascara smeared by her tears. A few weeks before, her close-cropped blonde hair had looked chic, but now it made her resemble photos of Auschwitz survivors. Or maybe it was Di's raw emotions in play.

We're all victims, Di thought. *Now, then, forever. Unless we stop them.*

She was about to answer Linda when she noticed her friend's lips open and eyes widen with an almost religious adoration. Di turned to see Lawrence striding toward the front of the room. His face was uncharacteristically flushed, his jaw clenched.

Everyone became quiet as he faced them from the fireplace.

"Thank you for coming, comrades," he said in such a soft voice that she sensed everyone around her lean toward him.

A shape came into the room and stood in the front corner, just beyond the glow of candles, but Di would know her roommate anywhere, even in shadows.

Lawrence glanced at Gertrude, then continued speaking. But Di only half paid attention. She wondered whether the two of them had just been *together*. If *that* was the reason for his flushed cheeks.

"The government has screwed itself this time," Lawrence was saying. "There's a movement building, and not just students like us. Ordinary citizens are becoming outraged as the facts come out. The US military is murdering hundreds, maybe thousands, of innocent civilians."

His words caught hold of Di, causing everything else to flee from her mind.

"Burning to death women, children, people like us, with napalm." Lawrence's voice became louder, angrier. "Destroying their villages with air strikes and bombardments." His nostrils flared. "Murdering for the sake of murder."

People shifted in their chairs. Di, too. It was impossible to sit still, listening to him.

Lawrence waved his hand at the photos on the walls. "We've become a country of baby killers."

Linda gasped. She was clenching the seat of her chair, as though afraid she might fall.

Lawrence made a fist. "We won't stand by and take it anymore!"

"We won't take it anymore!" shouted a new Stormdrain member named Gary. Others joined in, pounding the air with their fists.

"You've seen the outcry," Lawrence said. "A few days ago in Washington, DC, a half million of our comrades marched against these murderers. This isn't the last we'll see of protests. Next week, the government will hold a draft lottery to raise its military manpower. To try to send the rest of us into this immoral war. But we're not going to put up with that." His voice rose once again." We're not going to put up with killing babies in the name of democracy."

"No more killing!" they shouted.

Linda's voice was loud in her ear, almost hysterical. "No more killing!"

Lawrence held up his arms to quiet them, his loose white shirt reminding Di of a prophet's robes.

The shouting continued despite his efforts. "No more killing. No more killing." People were flailing their arms, standing on chairs, running between the aisles in a frenzy.

Di looked around for her roommate, but she was no longer standing in the corner, and Di couldn't spot her with all the movement in the room.

"Comrades," Lawrence said. The flickering candlelight played upon his cleft chin, his hollowed cheeks. "Comrades, we need to plan."

The noise died down. People returned to their seats or leaned against the walls. All eyes were on Lawrence.

"I feel your rage, comrades," he said. "I share it."

Another burst of voices.

He waited until they settled back down, then said, "When we formed Stormdrain, our mission was clear. Peace on American soil. And peace throughout the world." He held out his hand for quiet, as he continued. "But we've learned that to achieve peace, sometimes violence is necessary."

"Let's blow the motherfuckers to pieces!" Jeffrey shouted from the back of the room.

Lawrence shook his head. "Not that way."

"Then what the fuck are we supposed to do?" Steve called out. "Sit on our asses while they keep killing babies?"

"We need to show them we mean business," Lawrence said, "but we won't resort to the government's tactics. That will make us no better than they are."

Heads nodded in agreement.

"We're currently working on a plan to destroy certain significant targets," Lawrence said. "Statues of historical significance. Government property. And property belonging to corporations that support the war industry."

"Yeah, man," a voice called out.

Di shifted in her chair, uneasy about what Lawrence was suggesting. People could get hurt. But Lawrence would never take a risk like that. She was sure he knew what he was doing.

"Every act of violence must be related to a specific injustice, and it's crucial that we explain what we're doing and why in a Manifesto." Lawrence paused. "Our first Manifesto and first act of retribution will be dedicated to the victims of the My Lai Massacre."

People began to talk all at once, but Lawrence held up his hand. "We'll call it Project George," he said. "We're going to blow up the statue of George Washington in Union Square Park."

"Finally," Steve called out. "Count me in."

"Me, too," Albert said.

"How are we going to blow up anything?" Gary asked. "Do we know anything about bombs?"

The room went quiet and everyone turned to Lawrence. In the wavering candlelight, his features seemed to sag, but then he forced out a smile. "Come with me, comrades." He strode out of the room to the little mudroom, then down into the basement.

Di pushed her way through the crowd on the stairwell and leaned over the rough wood banister. The basement had been transformed since she'd been down here with Lawrence a few weeks before at the Halloween party. In the center of the room was a printing press and folding tables piled with cartons. But of greater interest was the workbench against the brick wall where Lawrence stood beside Gertrude.

"This, comrades," Lawrence shouted over the noise. He waited until everyone quieted down. "This, comrades, is our bomb factory."

On the workbench, Di could make out bottles, pipes, small boxes of nails, metal cans of lighter fluid. She watched Lawrence glance at the table, then meet Gertrude's eyes. Di felt a pang of jealousy. Lawrence and Gertrude shared something she wasn't a part of.

"We must treat these bombs with respect," Lawrence said to the group, as Gertrude reached into her pocket and pulled out a cigarette and a matchbook. "Our goal is attention and recognition through destruction of property," he said. "We are not going to kill anyone."

Gertrude got ready to strike the match, just as Lawrence's hand closed over hers. "What the fuck are you doing?" he said.

She flicked her braid over her shoulder and stared at him. "Blow up a statue?" She pulled her hand out of his. "That's the best you can do?"

Lawrence clenched his jaw.

Gertrude turned to the group. "If we want to be heard, we need to make a bigger bang."

The people around Di seemed to shrink, as though they wanted to disappear.

"Who's with me on this?" Gertrude shouted.

No one spoke. Lawrence was breathing hard, his fists in tight balls.

"You say you want to change the world," Gertrude said, "but you don't mean it. None of you are ready to do what it takes." She met Di's eyes.

Di winced, exposed for all to see by her roommate. All her pronouncements about wanting to stop injustice, her mission to prevent another Holocaust. It was just talk.

"To stop violence, we must be violent," Gertrude said. "To stop murder, we have to kill. If we want to go forward, we have to destroy," she shouted. "Someone must die!"

———

The blare of a honking horn brought Diana back to the present. Back from an old nightmare to the one she was living.

In less than twelve hours, someone was planning to kill Ethan unless she killed Jonathan first.

That was the deal.

She shook her head. The dizziness had passed.

In order to go forward, you needed to destroy. That had been their mantra. Someone must die.

She watched the traffic streaming by on Brickell Avenue, then stood and slowly walked back in the blinding brightness toward Jonathan's towering building.

Hoping she could think of another way.

CHAPTER 27

The sun was too bright, almost painful, the angle different from what Aubrey had grown accustomed to in Rhode Island. Here in Miami, the colors were brighter, like a movie shown in high definition.

And yet, the things Aubrey needed most to see remained veiled to her. Her visit to the Simmers' command post had provided no more clarity. If anything, she had left there even more perplexed, especially by her father's erratic behavior—his implication, then denial, that he had some idea who was behind the kidnapping.

She turned the corner to her childhood home. Tom Smolleck was leaning against one of the black cars talking on his phone. He signaled to her to wait a minute while he finished up his call. The sun hit him directly, and there was a gleam of perspiration on his forehead just beneath his buzz cut. He ended his call and came toward her, his badge prominent at his waist.

"Do you have a few minutes?" he asked.

She was anxious to get back to her computer research, but he was, after all, the FBI. "Of course."

"Let's go for a ride."

She almost asked what he wanted from her, but decided she'd find out soon enough. Besides, she had questions for him.

"How are you doing with the investigation?" she asked as he drove down the narrow, bumpy street. "Any possible suspects from the crowd scenes at the carnival?"

He turned onto Tigertail. "Your observations about the two suspicious-looking people in the photos were good ones," he said. "We had also noticed the woman with the sunglasses and the man with the tattoo sleeves. We're in the process of identifying them."

"My father told me the K-9 dogs found a napkin with Ethan's scent on it at the carnival. Were there any usable prints?"

"The only prints we were able to pull were your mother's." He stopped at a traffic light, lips pursed as though he were trying to decide something, then he turned to her. "Let's get something to eat." Apparently, he was planning to turn this into a long conversation. "Is there someplace near here?"

"I like Scotty's, but it's outdoors, so you might prefer—"

"How do I get there?"

She gave him directions, and they made it to the restaurant in a couple of minutes. He pulled into the near-empty parking lot, and they got out. It was hot in the sun, but a breeze was coming off the bay.

He hesitated as he stood beside the car, as though he would have liked to take off his jacket, but he kept it on. He was probably carrying a gun.

They walked along a path to the restaurant, the smell of gasoline from the marina triggering memories of her childhood. Smolleck stopped when they came around to the bay. The water rippled, reflecting the white cloud puffs in the blue sky. The view was the same as from the park where she and her mom had sat the evening before, but she forgot how beautiful it must be to someone not from around here.

They continued to the seating area beneath a white-and-green awning. The lunch crowd hadn't arrived yet, and only a handful of people, mostly in T-shirts and shorts, were seated. The tables and chairs were plastic, menus held up by large red ketchup containers and salt and pepper shakers.

They seated themselves at a table closest to the dock where the breeze was the strongest. It whipped around beneath her ponytail, cooling her neck. Smolleck unbuttoned the top button on his shirt and loosened his tie. His white shirt was damp beneath his suit jacket. A waitress wearing a baseball cap, green T-shirt, and khaki shorts came by. They ordered conch fritters and coconut shrimp.

"We used to eat here when I was a kid," Aubrey said after the waitress left. "My mother worked late and hated cooking, but I think we would have come here anyway."

She looked out toward the bay, remembering those evenings, especially before her parents became strangers to each other: the reflection from the sunset in the clouds to the east, the coolness in the air after the sun went down, how her father and mother would occasionally exchange a look only they understood.

"Sounds like you had a happy childhood," Smolleck said.

"Happy enough," she said, wishing she knew him better to say more.

"It's funny how when we're in the midst of something, it becomes our whole world, and we can't imagine anything different." He had a faraway expression on his face, like when they'd sat on the patio the night before. "Almost as though we're in a glass bubble and nothing exists outside of it."

So he knew about bubbles. "Have you ever felt that way?" she asked.

"A few times." He rubbed the indentation in his eyebrow. "I was in with a bad crowd when I was in high school. We cut classes, did a lot of drugs, and didn't give a shit about the rest of the world."

"Something happened?"

He picked up the bottle of ketchup and scraped the crud off its neck with his thumbnail. "My mother died from breast cancer in my senior year. It happened very quickly. So quickly, I hadn't accepted she was dying, and then it was too late."

"That must have been very hard on you."

"And of course I felt guilty, as though my lifestyle had caused her cancer. So I stopped doing drugs, cut my hair, and joined the marines. Spent some time in Afghanistan."

"What was that like?"

He shrugged. "I had thought in the military I'd be taking control of my life, but I ended up in a different kind of bubble. No thinking. No questioning. Just following orders."

Not so different from what she'd been doing up until recently.

"Is that why you joined the FBI? So you could question things?"

He gave her that half smile. "Something like that."

A small, noisy motorboat backed into the dock space, roiling the water.

"So is the FBI working out for you?"

He stared out at the rippling water. "I would say I've grown more self-aware. I know people are subject to getting caught up in their environments. The FBI is no exception." He turned back to her. "What about you? Do you ever feel like you're trapped inside some airless space?"

She thought about Jackson. How she almost couldn't breathe when he and Wolvie first left. It was nothing compared to what she was experiencing now. "Losing Ethan feels like being trapped in a nightmare."

He nodded. "Of course it does."

The waitress put two waters down on the table, then went to take an order from the people who'd gotten out of the boat.

She reached for her glass of water. In the midst of all the anxiety relating to Ethan and her mom, it was a relief to have someone to talk to.

She had misread Smolleck. His tough FBI-agent act was a cover.

"We checked into your boyfriend," he said.

His unexpected change in direction startled her, causing her to spill the water. Apparently Smolleck was uncomfortable with the soft talk and had needed to return to his professional persona.

"He's not a suspect," Smolleck said, his voice gentler, as though he were sorry he'd shaken her.

"I didn't think he was."

He scratched a knuckle. What was he procrastinating about?

"Why are we here?" she asked. "You obviously have something on your mind."

"I spoke with Judge Woodward this morning."

Her cheeks grew warm. She hadn't seen that coming. If her mother had talked to Jonathan about the note, he may have told Smolleck about it.

"Is something the matter?" he asked.

She needed to feel out how much Smolleck knew. "Jonathan's possible nomination could be connected to Ethan's disappearance."

"It could," Smolleck said. "But is there something else going on?"

She put her hands under the table so he wouldn't notice the give-away tremor. "What do you mean?"

"Judge Woodward was unusually concerned about your mother."

"She's his fiancée. Of course he's worried about her."

"But Judge Woodward seemed convinced the kidnapping was related to her. Why wouldn't he also consider that the kidnappers' target could be the Simmers, or your father, or even your brother and his wife? Or, for that matter, since there's no ransom demand, that some child predator has taken Ethan?"

Her mother must have told Jonathan about the note, and now the FBI suspected its existence because of Jonathan's awkward behavior.

The waitress put their food on the table. It gave Aubrey a minute to compose herself and think of a response, but as soon as the waitress left, Smolleck continued. "Obviously if there were a ransom demand, it would help us tremendously. We would know who the kidnappers have targeted and what they want. Without it, we're forced to go in a dozen different directions, and we're losing valuable time."

He was right. The more the FBI knew, the more likely they'd be to find Ethan. She realized his purpose in bringing her here was to persuade her to tell him of the note's existence. Perhaps to shake her from what she may have perceived as the bubble she and her mother were sharing. But she worried the kidnappers would act on their threat and kill Ethan if the FBI was told.

Smolleck reached for one of the coconut shrimp and took a bite. "These are good," he said. "You should eat something."

She had no appetite, but she picked up a conch fritter.

"You know, Aubrey, most ransom notes specifically say not to contact the authorities, or the victim of the kidnapping will be hurt."

He was as much as telling her he knew, but she had to be careful that what she said would help, not hurt, Ethan.

"You said Jonathan seems unusually concerned that my mother is the target of the kidnappers," she said. "If you think it's because of a ransom note to that effect, wouldn't it make sense to pursue that possibility even without confirming that the note exists?"

He threw the shrimp's tail down on his plate, a look of disgust on his face. She was surprised she felt bad about disappointing him with her hedged response.

"Assuming my mother is the target," she continued, "is it possible someone from her college years is behind the kidnapping?"

"What interests me is why you think that's the most likely possibility."

"I didn't say it was most likely."

"But it's the one you're directing me to."

"You're right," she admitted. "I think there is something there. But you're the one who brought up my parents' past to me, so I started doing my own research."

"Okay. Fair enough," he said. "Tell me why you think there's a connection to Ethan's kidnapping."

"I believe my parents had some kind of involvement with a revolutionary group in college. Is it possible someone believes they had something to do with the 1970 explosion, which killed several students, and kidnapped Ethan out of revenge?"

"We've been looking into members of Stormdrain who may have had ties to your parents."

So the FBI was considering this theory as well. Finally, she was getting some information. She steeled herself against what he might reveal about her parents.

"One is a man named Jeffrey Schwartz," Smolleck said. "He went underground after the explosion, then was involved in a fatal bank robbery a few years later. We haven't been able to locate him." He ate another shrimp, as though he were sharing bureaucratic details, not revelations that might turn her world upside down.

"The interesting thing is that around twenty years ago, a man claiming to be Jeffrey Schwartz marched into an FBI office insisting he had secret information about the 1970 explosion."

"What information?"

"He said the brownstone explosion hadn't been an accident, and he knew who had blown it up."

This man knew who blew up the brownstone? She shuddered at the possible significance. But if her parents had been involved, Smolleck wouldn't be talking to her so matter-of-factly.

"Did he tell you who did it?" she asked.

Smolleck shook his head. "No. He didn't know anything. We checked out his story. He wasn't Schwartz, and he hadn't been anywhere near New York at the time of the explosion. Turns out he was psychotic, suffering from a delusional disorder. He was apparently obsessed with the incident and wanted to get himself in the limelight."

An idea nagged at her.

Twenty years ago her parents had had a major fight. Earlier today, Kevin had said he believed it had been about a friend of his, because he'd overheard Mama say, "Jeff's going to be the end of us." What if her parents had actually been arguing about *this* Jeffrey? Or was that too much of a stretch?

"And the real Jeffrey Schwartz?" she asked. "What happened to him?"

"We're trying to find him, as well as a woman named Linda Wilsen. She was badly burned in the explosion. She's also off the radar."

"People just disappear?"

"All the time," he said. "They go to Canada or Mexico, or even hide in plain view with a new identity."

A breeze brought a strong fishy smell into her nostrils. "What about BBM? Is it possible someone from the company is taking revenge on my parents?"

"BBM? Why are you bringing them up?"

"Baer Business Machines was started by Prudence's grandfather."

"We know that."

"I saw several BBM employees at the Simmers' command post."

He frowned, his gray eyes becoming eerily light from the angle of the sun. "Why does that concern you?"

"Because Prudence's grandfather, Emmet Baer, was on Columbia's board of trustees from 1965 through 1970."

He had stopped eating. "I'm listening."

"Stormdrain was active on campus from 1969 to 1970 and would have been a major thorn in the administration's side."

"What does that have to do with BBM?"

"I watched a documentary that was filmed in 1969 of a student take-over of several university buildings. In the documentary, the voiceover claimed that Columbia University was hooked into big corporations who were financing the war machine. One of the corporations they mentioned was Baer Business Machines."

"So you think there may be some residual anger toward members of Stormdrain from that period?"

"I have no idea what to think. I don't know what my parents had to do with Stormdrain. I've looked them both up on the Internet but found nothing on either of them." She swallowed. "Tell me. The FBI knows things the public doesn't. What did my mother or father have to do with the brownstone explosion in April 1970?"

He studied her for a long minute. "I'm sorry, Aubrey, but I'm not at liberty to say."

And her parents refused to say.

She looked out toward the bay. A couple of boats were sailing into the wind, doing a graceful pas de deux.

So many secrets.

So much she didn't know.

What she did know was that the FBI was trying to find Ethan and bring him home safely, but they were doing it with their hands tied. The note could help them. And the dark question she kept pushing away—what if her little nephew died because she hadn't told them?

"There is a note," she said softly, knowing she was going against her mother's wishes, hoping she'd made the best decision for Ethan.

He sat up straighter. "You have it?"

She shook her head and took a sip of water. "No, but I saw it."

"Tell me about it."

"Someone slipped it into Monday's mail after the FBI had checked everything. It was in a greeting card."

"Did you see the envelope? The card?" He took out his phone and started tapping into it.

"I only saw the top of the envelope. It had a postage stamp that hadn't been postmarked."

"I see," Smolleck said. "That's why you were so interested in who'd been inside the house. Where is it now?"

"My mother has the envelope and card. I saw the front of the card when she showed me the note."

"What can you tell me about it?"

"It was for a child. There was a drawing of a little boy on the front. And the card said, 'Today is your special day.'"

"Printed as part of the card?"

"Yes."

"Anything distinctive about the card? What did it say on the inside?"

"I didn't see the inside. Just the front. The little boy was riding a red tricycle."

Smolleck frowned. "If you didn't see the inside, how do you know about the threat?"

"The note was separate."

"And you saw that?"

"Yes. It was on a piece of paper, like from a small pad. The note was typed." She had committed it to memory. Had recited it to herself over and over, as though chanting the message might change it, or reveal some inner secret. "On one side it said in caps: We have Ethan. He is safe. We will return him unharmed if you do one thing."

She took another sip of water. Smolleck was waiting.

"On the back of the paper, it gave my mother until midnight tonight to do what they asked. They said if she told the authorities, Ethan would die." Her abdomen convulsed. It was out and she couldn't take it back. "Please say I did the right thing in telling you. That this will help get Ethan back safely."

"And the one thing they want your mother to do?" he asked, his voice formal.

She looked down at the discarded shrimp tails on his plate.

"They want my mother to kill Jonathan Woodward."

"Jesus." Smolleck's face got red. "And you kept this from us?"

Rage rose in her gorge. "Don't you dare judge me or my mother. They threatened to kill Ethan if we told you about the note. What would you have done if your child's life was at stake?"

He let out a breath. "You're right. I'm sorry. Thank you for telling me now. It's just, we've lost so much time."

He reached into his wallet and took out a couple of bills, which he threw down on the table.

"This changes everything," he said, standing up. "We need to get back."

"You'll be careful with what I told you, won't you?" she said, following him out to the car. "Promise me you won't do something that will endanger Ethan."

"Of course we'll be careful. But we'll need the note. It could contain forensic evidence."

"I told you, my mother has it."

His phone rang as they reached his car. He took the call. Aubrey watched his face change to something like disbelief.

"Okay," he said. "I'll head over in a minute."

He put his phone in his pocket and looked at Aubrey, a cold, unreadable expression on his face. "Where's your mother now?"

She didn't like the hard edge to his voice. "She went to Jonathan's apartment. Why?"

"Because Jonathan Woodward is dead."

CHAPTER 28

"Dead?" Aubrey was stunned. It wasn't possible. Then a more terrifying thought hit her. "Is my mother okay?"

"We don't know where your mother is," Smolleck said. "Her cell phone is off, so we can't track her with GPS."

Mama was okay, but Jonathan was dead. "What happened to him?"

"He apparently fell, or was pushed, from his balcony."

Pushed from his balcony.

"I have to go." Smolleck opened the car door.

"She didn't do it." Aubrey could hear the pleading in her own voice. "Agent Smolleck, my mother would never do such a thing."

"Even to save her grandson?" he barked.

What was he saying? Had the kidnappers' ultimatum been satisfied? She took a step toward him, hope pushing against fear. "Has someone been in touch about Ethan? Is he okay?"

The anger in Smolleck's face evaporated. He shook his head. "No news on Ethan."

"Nothing?"

"I'm sorry," Smolleck said.

She began trembling all over. Jonathan was dead. Because of what Aubrey had just told Smolleck, her mother was likely a suspect in his murder. And Ethan was still missing.

Smolleck was saying something to her.

She blinked, trying to focus. "What?"

"Do you need a ride back to your house?" His voice was gentle.

She shook her head, conscious of the tears running down her cheeks. "He's my nephew," she whispered. "We have to find him."

He put his hand on her shoulder. It was a light touch, like Wolvie's when he would rest his paws on her, knowing she was upset. "We're trying," Smolleck said. Then he turned, climbed into his car, and drove away.

The trembling became more intense. Aubrey wrapped her arms around herself and rubbed them. Her teeth chattered, and she went over to the curb and sat on a bollard. If she'd told Smolleck about the note sooner, maybe this tragedy could have been prevented. Jonathan might still be alive, and her mother might not be a suspect. Maybe the FBI could have found Ethan by now.

She wiped the tears away with a rough hand. Just like the compliant child she had always been, Aubrey had listened to her mother about the note, rather than doing what she believed was best.

She took out her phone and touched the speed dial. It went straight to her mother's voice mail. She left a message. "Call me. Please."

Shakily, she stood up. She had to find her. She hurried out of the parking lot and headed up the bluff toward her house, trying to convince herself of her mother's innocence. Mama had been considering giving Jonathan a drug to slow his heart and fake his death, but she would never have murdered him, even to save Ethan.

Then where was she, and why wasn't she answering her phone?

She slowed a short distance from her house, panting, but not only from exertion. The out-of-control feeling came from a place deep inside.

She had lost her center.

Her mother wasn't the person she had believed she knew so well. She may have been a college revolutionary. Someone who had been involved with something so terrible that now, many years later, it was likely that her grandson had been kidnapped and her fiancé killed because of her actions. But Aubrey still didn't know what her mother had done then, or what she was capable of doing now.

Her childhood home loomed in front of her. Faded salmon-colored walls covered with vines, dark-red gabled roof, bougainvillea that hung over the arched windows.

Sleeping Beauty. That's what her father had always called her. His Sleeping Beauty princess.

Sleeping Beauty had lived hidden away in this house, content to work on her still-life oil paintings, collecting snow globes of scenes that would never change.

Aubrey had been sleepwalking through her life. Unwilling to look beyond what she was told, sensing her questions would somehow alter things. It was time to wake up and confront the truth. Time to learn who her mother really was.

Because too much time had already elapsed, and Ethan was still missing.

CHAPTER 29

Diana put on her dark glasses and staggered toward the red-and-blue lights in front of Jonathan's building as sirens screamed around her.

Dozens of men and women pulled her along with them—horrified and excited by this intrusion in their routine lunch breaks.

"A jumper," someone next to her said. "My friend saw him falling."

"I heard he was pushed," someone else said.

Her abdomen convulsed. She knew she should run away, but she couldn't stop herself. She had to see.

Crowds had formed at the edge of the police barricades. Reporters stood near their vans as their cameramen filmed. She caught bits and pieces. *Don't yet know. Suicide or murder. Swarming with FBI agents. High-profile individual.*

She pressed through the gawking crowd and got up against a barricade. Everyone was filming with their phones, arms extended in Nazi salutes.

She took in the people in uniforms and suits who filled the small grassy square beneath Jonathan's balcony. She strained to see what was behind them. Several people were kneeling beside a tarp. The tarp that covered the body.

She looked up. Forty-two stories. People on Jonathan's balcony. So many people. But she knew none of them was Jonathan.

A scent wafted toward her. Eau Sauvage.

She heard a choking sound.

"Are you okay?" someone beside her asked.

No. Not okay. I'm dying inside. No words came out.

On the other side of the barricade, one of the men in suits was checking out the crowd. He looked familiar. Smolleck.

Quickly, she lowered her head and turned back into the crowd. Can't stay here. Run away.

I can't leave him, her heart screamed. *I love him. I love him.*

Her feet kept moving, weaving through the horde, carrying her away.

The voice in her head quieted the one in her heart.

Not now. Not here. You can grieve for him later.

You'll have all the time in the world later.

CHAPTER 30

Aubrey didn't know where she might find her. She only knew her mother had been at Jonathan's apartment earlier, so that was where she was driving.

Cars streamed past her. People everywhere, but Aubrey had never felt more alone. Her phone rang, startling her. She pulled it out of her handbag and glanced at it. "Unknown caller."

She answered. "Hello?"

"It's me," her mother said in a trembling, barely audible voice. "Meet me at the Circle." Before Aubrey could ask anything else, her mother had hung up.

Her heart pounded. This was what she'd wanted. To talk to her mother and find out what she'd done before the FBI caught up with her, but she hesitated. The right thing to do was to call Smolleck. But if someone from her mother's past had been behind Ethan's kidnapping, her mother was more likely to tell her than the FBI. It was their best chance to get Ethan back.

Aubrey glanced at the phone in her hand. She turned it off. With no GPS in her mother's old car and the phone off, no one would be able to track her.

No one would find them at the Circle.

She continued driving, feeling like a fugitive herself. If her mother was charged with murder, Aubrey might very well be arrested as an accessory by not turning her in. It was a disturbing and unfamiliar sensation. She had always been the good girl, the one who never bucked authority.

Except for the time she had insisted on marching at the Miami Circle. She had just turned twelve and was self-conscious about the new braces on her teeth. At school, she had learned about a real estate developer who had uncovered an archaeological site that was close to two thousand years old. A perfect thirty-eight-foot circle made by the Tequesta Indians. The developer wanted to relocate it so he could build a high-end condo. Aubrey had been furious about destroying the past and had begged her mother to take her to the protest march to "Save the Circle."

Mama had said absolutely not. Demonstrations were dangerous—people got hurt, and good rarely came of them. Aubrey had dug in her heels until Mama reluctantly agreed. They had marched together with dozens of others at the torn-up construction site, chanting, "Save the Circle!"

Aubrey had felt exhilarated and couldn't understand why her mother seemed so angry and upset, especially since they had been victorious. A couple of days after the march, Mama gave Aubrey an easel with canvases and oil paints, and books filled with still-life paintings. Mama never said so, but Aubrey understood that painting would make her mother happy; marching would not.

Now, she wondered if there was some special reason Mama wanted her to meet back there after all these years.

Traffic slowed as Aubrey continued up Brickell Avenue. In the distance, she could see flashing red-and-blue lights. The Circle was on the Miami River, a few blocks north of Jonathan's building, so she would have to pass the crime scene. As she got nearer, she could see the crowd that had amassed near the news vans and emergency vehicles, probably gawking at Jonathan's broken body.

She glanced up at the looming building. She wondered what Jonathan's last thoughts had been as he flew through the air. Whether he had seen the person who pushed him. If he had been pushed.

Part of her wanted to pull over and say good-bye to this man who had loved her mother. Whom she was certain her mother had loved. But Smolleck was probably there. If he saw Aubrey, he would very likely send someone to follow her when she left, and she didn't want to risk that.

She continued on toward the Circle, praying that when she saw her mother face-to-face, the doubts that were continuing to multiply in her head would miraculously evaporate.

CHAPTER 31

Her mother stood facing the narrow river at the edge of the Miami Circle. She wore a white blouse and jeans, and her dark hair flapped in the breeze. The torn-up construction site of Aubrey's childhood was now a small park at the base of a brand-new condominium tower.

She turned when Aubrey was a few feet away, as though sensing her presence. Despite the dark glasses, Aubrey could read the agony in her down-turned mouth and collapsed cheeks.

This was her mother, yet she no longer knew this woman.

Without speaking, they went over to one of the benches carved from rock that surrounded the ancient circle, which had been buried beneath plants and mulch.

"Jonathan's dead." Mama's voice was flat.

Aubrey took in a sharp breath. Did she know this, or was she seeking confirmation from her? Innocent, she told herself. Her mother was innocent. "Yes, he's dead."

Her mother nodded. Tears ran down her cheeks from behind her sunglasses. "I loved him very much." She reached into her bag and took out a tissue. "What do the police think happened?"

Why was she framing the question this way, as though she knew what had happened? Innocent. Her mother was innocent. "Smolleck said he may have jumped or been pushed. I don't know anything more."

"He didn't jump," her mother said. "Jonathan had everything to live for."

"Yes, he did." This was the man her mother had loved. Aubrey still believed that. "I'm sorry, Mama."

Her mother reached over and ran her hand over Aubrey's cheek, touching her as lightly as a silk scarf. "I'm sorry, too."

Aubrey tensed. "About what?"

"Who knows how much of this was my fault? Ethan. Jonathan."

Aubrey felt sick. "Why do you think any of this is your fault?"

Her mother stared down at the shrubs that covered the circle.

"Where were you, Mama? You told me you were going to his apartment."

Her mother took her sunglasses off and wiped her eyes with the tissue. "I did go, but then I left. I needed some time alone, so I decided to walk home."

"Did you and Jonathan have an argument?"

"Why are you asking me that?"

"Because that's the most logical explanation for you to have left and walked home."

"I told you I wanted to be alone."

"What did you argue about?"

"Are you listening to me? I told you I wanted to be alone."

Her mother sounded unhinged. Aubrey softened her voice. "Why did you turn your phone off?"

Mama looked confused. "It's not off. The battery's dead. I borrowed someone's phone to call you."

Should she ask to see her phone? But if it had been turned off, Aubrey would know she was lying.

Then she would have to accept that her mother was a murderer.

"Aubrey." Her mother's voice jolted her. "Look at me."

She met her mother's intense gaze. There was a resolve that hadn't been there a moment before.

"I didn't push Jonathan off that balcony."

Aubrey felt light-headed, but it was because she had stopped breathing. She wanted so much to believe her. She filled her lungs with river air, which carried the faint scent of gasoline. "Smolleck thinks you did."

"Why would he think that?"

"I told him about the note. He knows about the ultimatum to kill Jonathan and save Ethan."

"Dear God. You told him? But what will happen to Ethan? What if they hurt him?" Her mother looked panicked. She glanced at the people strolling along the river walk, at the boats, and the condominium that towered over them. "Why hasn't anyone gotten in touch about Ethan?"

Her mother's fear seemed genuine. She pulled her phone out of her bag and touched it, but the screen stayed dark.

"The battery's dead. I'd forgotten the battery's dead." She held the phone out to Aubrey. "How can they tell me where he is if they can't reach me?"

She hadn't lied about the phone.

"They don't have to call anyone to give Ethan back," Aubrey said. "They can just do it, if that's what they intended to do."

"But it wasn't," her mother said. "They want to watch me suffer. First, Jonathan. And now . . . oh, God." She stood up.

"Tell me who these people are. Why do they want you to suffer?"

"I need to go," her mother said. "I have an idea why all this is happening."

"Is this connected to your past?"

"It could be."

"Do you know who has Ethan? Where he is?"

"Not yet, but I may be able to figure it out."

"There's a better way," Aubrey said. "Come with me to Smolleck. Show them the note. Let them analyze it. Tell them your theory. Maybe they can help."

"They won't listen. They're focused on who's behind Jonathan's murder, not who has Ethan. They'll lock me up, then it'll be too late. We'll never get our little boy back."

Was Aubrey once again falling into the same trap, wanting so much to appease her mother that she was willing to go along with her, or was this Ethan's best chance?

"You have to trust me, sweetheart. Please, just a little longer. If I can't find what I'm looking for, I'll go to the FBI."

If she turned her mother in to Smolleck now, she was eliminating an important avenue for finding Ethan. Mama knew things about the people from her past and would be in a far better position to investigate if she weren't locked up in an interrogation room.

"Tell me where you're going," Aubrey said.

Her mother hesitated. "If I do, that will put you in a difficult spot with the FBI."

She was right. It was better if she didn't know. "Promise you'll call me if you find anything," Aubrey said.

"Of course." Her mother squeezed her hand. "I won't let you down, sweetheart."

Aubrey's throat tightened. This woman was her mother, not some stranger.

Mama put her sunglasses back on, hands shaking. Her fiancé had just been murdered, and her grandson was missing. Was she up to this? Would the people who had taken Ethan and killed Jonathan try to hurt her, too? Was Aubrey doing the right thing letting her go?

It was Ethan's best chance.

Her mother started walking away, then stopped and glanced down at the plants that covered the buried circle. "I was very proud of you that day, sweetheart."

"What day?"

"The day we 'Saved the Circle.'"

Why was she bringing this up now?

"If you feel I kept you from being the person you wanted to be, I'm sorry."

"I don't—"

Her mother held up her hand. "Wait, please. I need to say this." Her lower lip trembled ever so slightly. "I only wanted to protect you, to keep you safe, but maybe I smothered you somehow."

"We don't need to talk about this now."

"But we do. In case there is no other time."

"Mama, don't—"

"I want you to know." Her mother's voice broke. "I want you to know that even if . . . even if you end up hating me, I love you and Kevin more than life itself."

She walked away quickly, before Aubrey could say anything.

Aubrey stared at the pretty plants covering the old Indian circle, which was buried deep beneath. Most people didn't even know it was there.

She had once marched with Mama to save the Circle. All that trouble, all that passion to save the past, just so that it could be hidden again.

She wanted to cry out after her mother to come back. Because she was terrified she would never see her again.

And it wasn't fair to have come all this way and have it end like this.

CHAPTER 32

The vein in Smolleck's right temple throbbed as he stood in the foyer of her mother's house.

Aubrey had been hoping to avoid him—not only because she wasn't sure how she would talk her way out of where she'd been the last hour, but also because she was anxious to get to her computer.

I did the right thing, she repeated to herself. *Letting her go was Ethan's best chance.*

"Can you come with me, please?" Smolleck didn't wait for her to answer, just led the way to her mother's office in the back of the house.

He sat down at the desk and gestured for her to sit on the other chair.

"Where have you been?" he asked.

She glanced out the window at the trees in the backyard. A blue jay was perched on one of the branches. Stay as near to the truth as possible. "Looking for my mother."

"May I have your phone?"

She handed it to him, hoping he didn't notice her hands were shaking. She had turned the phone back on when she had pulled into the driveway.

He examined it. "Why did you have it turned off earlier?"

"Were you trying to reach me? Is there news about Ethan?"

"There's no news about Ethan, and yes, I've been trying to reach you. You received a call from your mother, didn't you?"

"Yes," she said.

"What did she say?"

Even though Smolleck had said they weren't monitoring her calls, she wouldn't be surprised if their entire conversation had been recorded. "My mother asked me to meet her at the Circle."

"Which is?"

"Well, I thought she meant the park where we used to go when I was a kid."

"What park?"

She hesitated. "Ponce Circle. It's in Coral Gables."

The vein in Smolleck's temple wasn't pulsing as furiously. "Was she there?"

"No," Aubrey said. "I drove over and waited, but she didn't show up. I guess I misunderstood where we were supposed to meet. She may have meant Alhambra Circle or Cocoplum Circle or even Miami Circle Park." She was explaining too much. Giving more than he had asked for, something liars often did thinking it made them look innocent.

He touched the face of her phone, probably checking her Received and Sent call lists.

She looked back out the window. The blue jay was gone.

He put her phone down on the desk, apparently not finding anything of interest to him. "We've put out an ATL on your mother."

"ATL?"

"'Attempt to Locate' bulletin. She's a suspect in the death of Jonathan Woodward."

"I assumed you would think so after I told you about the ransom note. But that's not enough to arrest her."

"So you're a lawyer now?"

Her face grew warm.

"Then you probably know that harboring a fugitive is a serious crime."

"Is my mother a fugitive? Has a warrant been issued for her arrest?"

"Not yet, but we have more than just your report about the note's existence."

"You do? What?"

They stared at each other until the vein in Smolleck's temple began pulsing hard again. "I'm not about to give you information until you start leveling with me."

"I don't know how I can help you," she said. "Are you certain Jonathan was pushed? Could he have fallen accidentally?"

"It's highly unlikely that it was an accident."

There was a discoloration in the oak desk where she had once spilled nail-polish remover when she was doing her nails. Her mother had been matter-of-fact about the ruined wood, but Aubrey had been very upset with herself. Would Mama forgive her if she told Smolleck the truth?

"I know you don't trust me right now," she said. "I understand why you wouldn't, but I told you about the ransom note. If you think about it, whoever wrote it was probably more interested in hurting my mother than in killing Jonathan."

"So why is he dead?"

"Maybe whoever sent the note intended to make it look like my mother killed him. They would know you or the police would automatically suspect her if you were aware of the note."

"It's a theory."

It was. A good one. "My mother is not an impulsive woman," she said. "I don't believe she killed Jonathan." Was she repeating the mantra to convince herself, or did she truly believe it?

Her eyes flitted over the photos of Ethan.

Some she had taken herself, but others she had gotten from her father and brother. She had sent them all to her mother, knowing how much joy she received from the photos of her grandson. There was one of Ethan on a horse, another at Disneyland, and a recent silly one Ethan had taken of himself making an ugly face.

He loved taking selfies and had learned how to send them to her.

Something about the "ugly face" photo stopped her. She got up and took the framed picture from the shelf. Ethan was in the foreground, but behind him was a woman she didn't recognize. An older woman with gray hair, who was staring at him, her chin pushed forward, her brow in a frown.

"What is it?" Smolleck asked.

"This woman. There's something familiar about her."

"You don't know her?"

Aubrey shook her head.

"Do you know where the photo was taken?"

She recognized the black-leather furniture and a black-and-white painting of a maze that was a favorite of her father's. "This is my father's apartment in LA. The photo was taken a couple of weeks ago. I can tell because Ethan was missing his front tooth."

"The woman could be a neighbor or a friend," Smolleck said.

"Yes. Probably." She put the photo back on the shelf. She had the original on her computer where she could study it more carefully. There was so much to do, and here she was using up precious time.

"Anything else you'd like to distract me with?" Smolleck asked.

"Agent Smolleck. My nephew is missing. I'm concerned that Jonathan's death and looking for my mother has shifted everyone's priorities away from finding him."

His shoulders stiffened. "Finding Ethan is our number one priority."

"Good," she said, as she headed out of the room. "I'm glad we're at least agreed on that."

CHAPTER 33

Aubrey closed her bedroom door behind her. She had just lied to the FBI, but that was the least of her problems. Her mother was definitely a suspect, and Ethan was still missing.

She opened her laptop.

Earlier today, her father had told her he believed someone involved with Stormdrain or the explosion at the brownstone could be connected to Ethan's kidnapping. He had hinted that he or her mother had played some role in that catastrophe, then denied it.

But Smolleck was also interested in Stormdrain, and Mama had gone off to do something related to her past.

Aubrey googled "Stormdrain, brownstone explosion, April 1970," and viewed the search results. A few were travel websites, identifying the brownstone as an interesting, off-the-beaten-path place to visit. There were before-and-after photos—the blackened shell of the brownstone in 1970 after the explosion, and a modern, angular building with large windows and a plaque out front. Then there were blogs and articles going back several years about Stormdrain, and a Wikipedia article she decided to read first.

According to the article, Stormdrain had been an American, radical left-wing organization that began in late 1969 on the campus of Columbia University and was briefly a faction of SDS, Students for a Democratic Society, before it broke away. Its goal was to create a revolutionary party for the overthrow of the US government.

Aubrey still had a difficult time seeing her parents as revolutionaries who wanted to overthrow the government.

She read on. Stormdrain had conducted a campaign of bombings from December 1969 through April 1970, targeting patriotic statues, like one of George Washington in Union Square Park, as well as banks and government and corporate buildings. Stormdrain had taken credit for explosions in the lobbies of the Manhattan headquarters of Mobil Oil, IBM, General Telephone and Electronics, and Baer Business Machines.

Another connection to BBM and Prudence.

She continued reading about the bombings. Although there was destruction of property, no one was ever injured or killed. Stormdrain always took precautions that people would not be around when they detonated their bombs.

The article went on to talk about the founding members of the group, all Columbia University and Barnard College students, though neither of her parents was mentioned.

She read the names of the founding members: Steve Robinson, Jeffrey Schwartz, Albert Jacobs, Linda Wilsen, and Gertrude Morgenstern, noting that Schwartz and Wilsen were two people Smolleck had said the FBI was looking for. Twenty years ago, a psychotic man had claimed to be Jeffrey Schwartz, a publicized event that coincided with her parents' big fight.

She clicked on the link to an article about Schwartz. The photo was a blurry black-and-white of a skinny, scowling man with longish dark hair and mutton-chop sideburns. She skimmed the article. Attended Columbia Law School. One of the leaders of Stormdrain Underground, a militant faction of Stormdrain that was associated with a number of bombings that occurred after April Fool, between late 1970 and 1981. Was involved in a foiled bank robbery in 1981, which resulted in the death of a teller, a security guard, and a police officer. Still at-large and on the FBI's Most Wanted List.

She read the paragraph entitled "Jeffrey Schwartz Sham," which essentially said what Smolleck had told her. A man claiming to be Jeffrey Schwartz had insisted he knew who was responsible for the 1970 brownstone bombing but had turned out to be lying.

Although this seemed to be an inconsequential footnote, she wondered whether someone had set up the fake "Jeffrey Schwartz" for the purpose of frightening her parents. There was no way of knowing without speaking to the man who had posed as Schwartz, something Aubrey couldn't do but planned to ask Smolleck to follow up on.

She pulled up the article on Linda Wilsen, the other person the FBI was looking for, hoping for a photo she could match to the one in her mother's box. There were none, just a brief write-up on how Linda had survived the April Fool explosion but had suffered severe and disfiguring burns over most of her body. She had never been charged with any crimes but had dropped out of Barnard and returned home to Arkansas. There was nothing about her life since. She googled "Linda Wilsen Arkansas" but came up with no matches that could be a sixty-something-year-old woman. Of course, if it had been so easy, the FBI would know where she was.

She returned to the main article on Stormdrain and clicked on the link to the explosion at the brownstone. Her mother had said she'd been injured when she was walking by, but hadn't provided any details.

Aubrey read on. Also known as April Fool, the explosion had taken place on April 1, 1970 in Morningside Heights, a neighborhood not far from Columbia University.

The explosion resulted from the premature detonation of a bomb being assembled by members of Stormdrain, which set off other explosives and reduced the brownstone to burning rubble. The bombs, according to Stormdrain member Steve Robinson, had been intended to be used to blow up the Lexington Avenue Armory.

Three Columbia University students had been killed on impact—Michael Shernovsky, Gary Cohen, and Gertrude Morgenstern. A fourth, Linda Wilsen, had escaped from the wreckage with third-degree burns and was hospitalized. A five-year-old child, Martin Smith, playing in front of the brownstone at the time of the explosion, was rescued from the scene, but died before he reached the hospital.

Damn. A child had died. This was something she hadn't known before. The little boy's parents might have held her parents accountable for his death if they believed Mama or Dad had had some connection to the explosion.

She returned to the article.

Over several days, a search of the rubble uncovered a "bomb factory" with several unexploded eight-stick packages of dynamite with fuses attached, six pipe bombs, remnants of Molotov cocktails, and timing devices.

All that, in addition to the makeshift bombs that had detonated in the explosion. The crime scene was gory, and it took a week to identify the three students. Gertrude Morgenstern was believed to have been holding the bomb when it exploded and suffered the greatest impact.

She was identified by her remains found at the site, including the tip of a finger, a scorched braid of hair, crushed wire-rim glasses, and shreds of clothing including a wooden clog shoe.

Aubrey sat back in her desk chair. Her father had said the people who died in the explosion had been their friends. She thought of her mother sitting in front of the fireplace this morning going through a box with photos in it. *Just some old friends.*

Aubrey went across the hall to her mother's room and closed the door after her. She opened the drawers in the dresser and bureau and sifted through the clothes. No box. She checked in shoe boxes and containers on the shelves of the closet. Nothing. She pulled out her

mother's luggage and unzipped each piece. There was an old blue suitcase that didn't have wheels. Aubrey set it on the floor and opened the
snap-down locks. The suitcase was filled with old clothes—worn jeans
and tie-dyed shirts and peasant blouses, harem-style pants and a halter
top—and a small box covered with neon peace symbols.

She pushed the suitcase back into the closet and returned to her
own room with the box. If Smolleck came upstairs, she didn't want
to have to explain to him why she was snooping around her mother's
bedroom.

She put the box on her desk and opened it. Inside were folded
papers and a handful of photos. On top were the photos Mama had
shown her earlier of her father alone, and the one of both her parents.
The papers were an assortment of class schedules, grade reports, and
commendations from Barnard College for Diana Hartfeld.

Nothing culpable.

She opened a tiny envelope, the kind that usually accompanied
a delivered floral arrangement. The envelope was yellowed with age.
In it was a small note card. Although it was a little different from his
handwriting these days, she recognized her father's strong script, each
letter pressed hard into the paper, revealing a high level of confidence,
even back in college.

D-Our love is stronger than the pain.
Love, L-

Her mother's ringtone.

The song was clearly special to both of them. She put the card back
in its envelope and examined the rest of the photos. Young men at a
party. Her father was in a couple of them, the white scarf covering his
hair. The men had longish hair and sideburns. Several wore beards. One
of the skinny men with mutton-chop sideburns resembled the photo
of Jeffrey Schwartz, but his face was turned away from the camera, so

she couldn't be certain it was he. She turned the photos over. No dates. No one identified.

She came to the photo of three women she had looked at with her mother. On the back, written in her mother's neat script, was: *With Linda and Gertrude at antiwar demonstration, Oct. 15, 1969.*

Linda Wilsen and Gertrude Morgenstern? Probably. Gertrude wasn't exactly a common name.

Both women had been in the brownstone explosion. Linda had suffered severe burns, and Gertrude had died.

Aubrey looked again at the three young, happy women in the photo.

And Mama?

What exactly had she been doing by the brownstone that day?

Chapter 34

There was something about grand buildings with their soaring ceilings and hushed echoes that made Diana's chest contract. Even the Miami-Dade Library with its Spanish-style architecture, terra-cotta tiled floors, and arched hallways reminded her of that other library, that other time. She darted into the cool, dark building from the too-hot, too-bright courtyard, bought a five-dollar guest card so she could use a computer, and then found a remote cubby.

"To stop murder, we have to kill." Gertrude's war chant. Her prophecy.

Now there was more death, and once again, Diana was to blame. But she wasn't going to think about Jonathan now. She just couldn't.

She logged on to the library computer and searched for articles about April Fool that had appeared shortly after the brownstone explosion.

Although she was unable to log in to the *New York Times* without a subscription and didn't want to create a trail to her whereabouts, she found references to a few articles on recent blogs. She read through them, but they all contained the same information. The explosion at the brownstone had been an accident.

Three Stormdrain members had died—Michael Shernovsky, Gary Cohen, and Gertrude Morgenstern. They had been assembling a bomb intended to be used to blow up the Lexington Avenue Armory. A fourth Stormdrain member, Linda Wilsen, escaped the explosion with third-degree burns.

Nothing more. No speculation. No uncertainty. The explosion had been an accident.

She entered "April Fool, Columbia Low Library" in the search engine. Dozens of hits, but only one that included both references. A human-interest story published in 2000. The journalist had interviewed several former Columbia students who had been attending the university in April 1970. She didn't recognize their names, and none of the interviewees claimed to have been involved with Stormdrain. She read the article, stopping at the line she'd been hoping to find.

Radicals from Stormdrain were making bombs to destroy property. There'd been rumors that Columbia's Low Library was a target, but it was never confirmed.

Never confirmed.

The brightness from the computer screen made her head hurt. She closed her eyes and listened to the hushed noises around her—footfalls and whispers.

———

Di walked through the Rotunda at Columbia's Low Library, hearing her own footfalls echo in the massive domed room, along with whispers from prospective freshmen and their parents admiring the neoclassical architecture and busts of Greek gods and goddesses.

She'd been taking notes for her art-history class, pretty sure there would be questions about Columbia's own art legacy on the exam, but now she had only a few hours to prepare for her calculus exam before she needed to leave to meet Lawrence.

She hurried down the broad steps of the library, past the bronze statue of Alma Mater with her raised arms and scepter, and wondered fleetingly whether that was going to be on the art exam, too. Mostly she was thinking about later. Lawrence was taking her to dinner at a restaurant he'd discovered down in the Village, then over to the Fillmore East to hear the Grateful Dead.

She unlocked the door to her dorm room, relieved Gertrude wasn't there. She didn't want to have to tell her roommate about her plans with Lawrence and listen to her sarcasm.

They each had a desk, but Gertrude was as bad with personal boundaries in their dorm room as she was in her sex life. Papers and open books that hadn't been there that morning were piled on Di's desk. Disgusted, Di gathered up the books. Chemistry, she noted. Gertrude wasn't taking chemistry.

A large piece of paper with blue diagrams was open on the desk. An architectural drawing. But Gertrude wasn't taking architecture.

Di examined the blueprint. Printed at the top of the page was "LOW LIBRARY," where she had just been. There was a diagram of each floor, including the basement. Notes had been written on the paper in black ink in a confident hand.

Administrative center. President's office.

Career Day, 4/3, Rotunda. Fortune 100 Corps. Several hundred students expected.

On the diagram of the basement, several points had been marked with a red *X*. Di matched the location of the *X*s to the floor above. The Rotunda, where major events were often held.

Including the upcoming Career Fair in a few days.

Dear God.

The door opened behind her. Gertrude came in, carrying several books. She frowned. "You said you'd be gone all afternoon."

"What is this?" Di held up the blueprint.

"What does it look like?" Gertrude dumped the books on her bed.

"Like a plan to blow up Low Library."

"We're planning to blow the armory," Gertrude said. "You know that."

"Then what's this all about?"

Gertrude shrugged. "An intellectual exercise."

"You're planning to kill innocent people, aren't you?"

"Innocent?" Gertrude said. The pupils in her eyes seemed to throb, like they always did when she was angry. "You don't mean the big corporations that are financing the war machine, do you?" She stepped closer. "Or the bourgeois students who want to go work for them? Are those the innocents you mean?"

Di could smell her breath—cigarettes and something minty. Gertrude took the blueprint from Di and folded it on the creases.

"Who knows about this?" Di asked.

"Just a couple of the anointed. They're helping me build the bombs. Real whoppers."

"I think you've gone crazy, Gertrude."

"Bring the war home, baby."

Di shook her head. "No, Gertrude. The point was to end the war. Not start a new one."

Gertrude laughed. "You really are a Pollyanna."

"Well, you're no Che Guevara." Di brushed past her to the door.

"Hey, Pollyanna."

Di turned to face her from the doorway.

"I was right about you," Gertrude said. "You don't have what it takes to change the world."

Di felt a flash of rage. "Is that so, Gertrude?" she said. "That just goes to show how little you really know about me."

———

Diana opened her eyes and faced the glaring computer screen. She checked the throwaway phone she had picked up before coming to the library so she could call Aubrey when she was ready. It was after three o'clock.

She knew what she had to do. It was the only way to finally make peace with herself.

She left the cool, dark library and stepped back outside into the sharp, harsh sunlight.

She would make her peace, and then she would tell Aubrey.

She prayed her daughter would understand.

CHAPTER 35

Aubrey put her mother's box in a drawer of her desk. If there was a connection between Ethan's kidnapping and either her mother or father, she was at a loss as to how to find it. She hoped her mother was having more success, whatever it was she was doing.

She checked the time. Just after three.

With Jonathan dead, the Tuesday midnight deadline no longer applied, but Ethan had been missing for forty-eight hours. Forty-eight hours away from his mom and dad. She didn't want to think about how terrified he must be. She needed to try something else.

Her laptop was synced with her iPhone and contained all her photos. She went to the album she had set up for Ethan, hoping there was some clue in the photo that had caught her attention in her mother's office. Ethan at his grandfather's apartment making an ugly face while an old woman watched him. As she had told Smolleck, something about the woman was familiar.

She scrolled through Ethan's baby pictures, photos of him learning how to walk, then the recent ones of him, until she came to the selfie he had taken with the old woman in the background. She checked to see whether the woman was in any other photos. She wasn't. She "snipped" out the woman's face and enlarged it. The woman's hair was short, gray, and curly. She had blue eyes that were a little out of focus, and a long chin. Her lips reminded Aubrey of a 1920s film star, the upper one thin and bowed, the lower full and pouty. Aubrey enlarged the photo further. Above her bowed lip was a small beauty mark. That's when she noticed what wasn't in the photo. Wrinkles. The woman wasn't old. She had the skin of someone around forty. She could have been prematurely gray, or had had a facelift, or maybe something else was going on here.

Aubrey studied the frown on the woman's face as she looked at Ethan. It was the expression that was familiar, but what did it remind her of?

Something recent.

She went to her e-mails, opened the one from Smolleck with the photos from the carnival, and found the photo of the woman in sunglasses staring in Ethan's direction. There it was. The same frown.

She "snipped" out the face of the woman at the carnival and put it next to the face of the gray-haired woman. Same bowed lips and prominent chin. Just above the upper lip, in the exact same place, was a tiny mole.

This must be the same woman.

She was about to call Smolleck when a disturbing thought stopped her.

The gray-haired woman had been at her father's apartment. What had she been doing there, and what was her father's involvement? Instead of Smolleck, she called her father's cell phone, impatient as it rang and he didn't pick up.

"Aubrey?" he said, answering on the fifth ring. He sounded breathless.

"Yes, it's me. Where are you?"

"At the time-share."

"I have to ask you something," she said.

"What is it?"

"There was a woman with gray hair at your house when Ethan visited you a couple of weeks ago. Who was she?"

Through the phone, she could hear the sound of things being moved around. Drawers opening and closing. What was he looking for? "Dad? Do you know who the woman was?"

"Woman? Oh, you must mean the babysitter." He paused. "Why are you asking about her?"

"Do you remember her name?"

"Let me think. She told Ethan to call her Miss Alice. She seemed very nice, and Ethan liked her. What's going on?"

"Where did she come from?"

"Some babysitting service. Star made the arrangements."

"Is Star there? Can you ask her?"

"She isn't here." His voice sounded strange.

"Tell me what you know about the babysitter."

She listened to him breathe and wondered whether he was trying to come up with a story.

"I remember it was last minute," he said finally. "I don't like going off without Ethan when he visits, but Star hadn't known he was coming. She surprised me with tickets to a concert. She said we didn't have to go, but I didn't want to disappoint her. She said she'd find a trustworthy babysitter. A grown-up, not some kid."

Through the phone, she heard a zipper open. Then another. As though he were going through their suitcases.

"Was that the only time Alice watched him?" she asked.

"She came the next night, too. Like I said, Ethan seemed to like her. I didn't think there was a problem. Is there a problem?"

"She looks like a woman who was in one of the photos at the carnival watching Ethan."

"What are you saying? You think the woman we hired to babysit Ethan kidnapped him? That's ridicu—" He stopped abruptly.

She heard a rustling, like her father was shaking out a large piece of paper, maybe a sheet of newspaper. "What the hell," he said.

"What's the matter? Did you find something?"

His breathing was all wrong, like he couldn't quite catch it. "What is it, Dad?"

"Nothing," he said. There was a muted shuffling noise, as though he were folding the paper.

Then she heard a woman's voice in the background. "Larry, are you here?"

"I've gotta go," he said, and before she could say another word, he had disconnected from the call.

She stared at the phone in her hand, wondering what the hell that was all about.

CHAPTER 36

Her father was behaving strangely, but at least Aubrey had gotten some information from him. Now she had something to work with.

Starting with Star. She had hired the babysitter, which meant that she might have something to do with the kidnapping.

But what about Dad? Was he involved? He had seemed genuinely surprised when Aubrey asked about the babysitter, so for now, she'd stay with the assumption he wasn't.

But that created a troublesome possibility. What if her father mentioned to Star that Aubrey was interested in the babysitter? Would he be putting himself in danger? But her father had seemed so preoccupied by whatever it was he had found, it seemed unlikely he would bring it up. Besides, it was possible Star had nothing to do with the kidnapping and that the babysitter had been working independently or for someone else.

Of course, all this hinged on the assumption that the babysitter and woman at the carnival were the same person, and that she was the kidnapper, which was yet to be proven.

"Alice," her father had called her, but who was she?

She sent Smolleck an e-mail with a brief explanation and attached the two photos:

> Woman at my father's apartment two weeks ago appears to be same as woman at carnival watching Ethan. Note similarities in lips, chin, and mole over lip. My father said she was a babysitter from an agency that Star contacted. She watched Ethan two evenings in a row and Ethan seemed to like her.

If they got lucky, the FBI would be able to identify her. Maybe even confirm that the babysitter and the woman at the carnival were the same. But would that lead them to Ethan?

A moment later, she got a reply from Smolleck.

> Thanks. Will check into it.

She was surprised he hadn't called or come upstairs. She went to the window. One of the black sedans was gone. Smolleck had probably left the house after their confrontation in her mother's office. She wondered whether he had returned to Jonathan's condo or was out looking for her mother.

She returned to her computer and stared at the screen.

If the babysitter had come from LA and was waiting for Ethan at the carnival, where would she have taken him?

Aubrey discounted a hotel, because with all the publicity about Ethan, someone might notice a woman and little boy checking in on Sunday. So where would a kidnapper bring a child and not expect to be noticed? Probably not a condo, because of nosy neighbors. Maybe they had rented a private house for the purpose, but Aubrey had a different idea.

It was a long shot, but she googled "How to find who owns property in Florida." There were several links to Miami Beach property records. She chose one that charged a small fee, figuring she would get access to more complete information. Because of Star's possible connection to the babysitter, she decided to start there. She entered Star Matin's name. There were no matches. She entered her father's name, and was relieved when only the house in Coconut Grove came up. Full ownership had been transferred to her mother eight years ago. Next, she tried the address of the time-share her father and Star were staying at. She was hoping to see Star's name, but the property had been acquired two years before by Time-Share Dreams for $1.2 million.

That sounded like a legitimate business, but she googled "Time-Share Dreams" to see what other properties the company owned. She found nothing, nor any online marketing presence, which she would have expected for a company selling time-share properties. She returned to the county-records website and went deeper into the ownership behind Time-Share Dreams, finally finding a document identifying J. W. Hendrix as the president, and an address in Atlanta.

J. W. as in Jonathan Woodward, or was that a coincidence?

She left the county website and googled "J. W. Hendrix, Atlanta." There were a couple of near hits, including Janis Hendrix. She pulled up images of "Janis Hendrix." The photos were all of Janis Joplin and Jimi Hendrix, two famous performers from Woodstock, who had died young. She went through the other images. If one of them was Janis Hendrix, she had no way of knowing. She searched every link for Janis Hendrix, but found nothing helpful, so she couldn't confirm that J. W. Hendrix was Janis Hendrix.

Her research into the time-share was another dead end, but it was very likely a flawed assumption anyway. If Ethan had been in the apartment with her father and Star, Aubrey would never have been invited to come over.

She had wasted almost an hour and was no closer to finding Ethan. Her eyes settled on her still-life paintings. A solitary apple. A vase. A bronze horse in the center of an empty table.

Maybe the problem was that she was looking at each aspect of Ethan's kidnapping in isolation. She needed to put all the pieces together. So far, she had photos of a woman who had babysat Ethan in LA and who also had appeared at the carnival. Then there was Smolleck and her parents' interest in Stormdrain, so she assembled the names of people involved with the organization: Steve Robinson, Jeffrey Schwartz, Albert Jacobs, Linda Wilsen, and Gertrude Morgenstern.

Linda Wilsen and Gertrude Morgenstern had been friends of her mother's. Someone claiming to be Jeffrey Schwartz had gone to the FBI twenty years ago, insisting that the brownstone explosion hadn't been an accident and that he knew who had blown it up. That had been right around the time her parents' marriage began to fall apart. Was there a connection?

There was still the big hole in her information. She didn't know what her parents' involvement had been in Stormdrain or with the explosion.

She opened her desk drawer and took out her mother's small box. She studied each photo again, but kept going back to the one with Linda and Gertrude, the two women who had been in the explosion.

Linda had been injured. No one knew what had become of her.

She set the photo down on the desk and pulled up the photos of the babysitter on her computer, but except for eye color, there wasn't even a remote resemblance to Linda. And of course, her age was all wrong. Linda would now be in her early sixties, and the babysitter was probably twenty years younger than that.

Aubrey looked at the pretty blonde, blue-eyed woman. Even in the photo, she could tell that Linda had been delicate and graceful.

A lot like Star.

Jesus. Could Star be Linda Wilsen?

Linda could have had extensive reconstructive surgery and no longer be recognizable as the Barnard College student in the photo. She
could have changed her identity and returned to seek revenge for her
friend's death and her own disfigurement. But why wait so long? Unless
she had been planning and waiting for every detail to be perfect.

Aubrey felt a flurry in the pit of her stomach as pieces started fitting together. Star had been responsible for Kevin and her mother's
reconciliation, which would have set up the opportunity for Ethan to
visit Mama. Star had hired the babysitter, perhaps to establish a rap-
port between the babysitter and Ethan so he would leave the carnival
with her willingly. And for the last eight years, Star had turned Aubrey's
father against her mother and had been manipulating him.

She needed to call her father now.

She touched his number on her phone and listened to it ring. Three,
four, five rings, then it went to voice mail. She grabbed her handbag and
car keys and ran down the stairs. Her phone rang as she stepped outside.

Smolleck. She answered. "Hello?"

"Aubrey." Smolleck's voice was raw.

Something must have happened with Mama. "What is it? What's
wrong?"

"You were just calling your father."

"What? How do you know that?"

"I have his phone."

"Oh," she said, confused. "Where is he? Is he there?"

"He's been in a car accident. Actually, he was hit by a car."

Her legs went weak. "He couldn't be. I spoke to him a little while
ago. He was in the apartment. It's a mistake."

"Aubrey?"

She sat down on the grass in the front yard and stared at the deep
ruts that had been made by the reporters' vans. She knew it wasn't a
mistake. "Is he . . ."

"Your father's in a coma. The ambulance brought him to Mount Sinai Medical Center in Miami Beach."

A coma. Her father was in a coma. He'd been hit by a car. Had Star tried to kill him when he asked her about the babysitter? Was this Aubrey's fault?

"Who," she said. "Who was driving the car?"

"It was hit-and-run," Smolleck said. He coughed to clear his throat. "But there was an eyewitness who saw the driver."

Hit-and-run.

Not Star.

"Have you apprehended him?"

"It was a woman," he said. "She was wearing sunglasses, but she had shoulder-length dark hair and a white blouse."

Her heart was pounding too hard. It hammered in her ears.

"Aubrey. You need to tell me where your mother is."

CHAPTER 37

The nurse on the ICU floor told her that her father was in surgery and would be for several more hours. They didn't know the extent of his injuries, or the prognosis. His wife was very upset and had to leave, the nurse said, and it took Aubrey a minute to realize the nurse meant Star, not Aubrey's mother.

Her mother may have been the one who tried to kill him.

Aubrey went to a small, empty, windowless waiting room, where a hanging TV was tuned to a man in a suit with a droning voice. She sat down on one of the chairs and stared at the man, trying to process what he was saying. Something about the economy and financial markets. She listened harder, making no sense of his words, but it was better than thinking about whether her father might die, whether her mother had been driving the car that had run him down, and where little Ethan was.

She blanked out her thoughts and watched a commercial that came on. An ad for a vacation getaway. Two people riding horses on a deserted beach. It reminded her of the time her own family had stayed on Sea Island in Georgia and went horseback riding one very hot day. Her dad rode a large white horse and had tied a scarf around his head to keep the sweat from dripping into his eyes. She remembered how her mother had looked at him. Her hero. Why would she try to kill her white knight on a snowy stallion?

The witness had to be wrong about the driver of the car.

Aubrey sensed someone standing the hallway. She took in the young man's wrinkled white shirt, unshaved face, and mussed brown hair before registering it was her brother. "Kev," she said. "You're here."

He staggered into the room and dropped into the chair next to hers. "Maybe Dad needs me." He was slurring his words. "Can't do anything for Ethan." He reached into his pockets and took out two miniature bottles, one scotch, one vodka. "This cleaned out the minibar. Want one?"

She was about to refuse, then changed her mind. "Thanks." She took the vodka from his outstretched hand.

He unscrewed the top of the scotch and took a swig. "They were happy to see me go," he said. "Prudence and Ernest." He said their names in a hyperarticulated, proper voice. "Don't think drinking is appropriate behavior." He took another swig. "Maybe they'll fire me."

She reached over and rubbed his shoulder. She wanted to say everything was going to be okay, but she didn't believe that. She doubted anything would ever be okay again.

"Who told you about Dad?" she asked.

"Detective Gonzalez. She's nice. She called a taxi to bring me here. Said she'd call if there was any news." His shoulder began to quiver beneath her hand. He was crying.

"Shhh, Kev," she said softly. "They'll find him."

He wiped his eyes with his shirtsleeve, drank back the rest of the scotch, and then put the empty bottle down on an end table covered with magazines. "It's her, isn't it?"

"What do you mean?"

"She's the devil, isn't she?"

Aubrey shivered.

"Why did I let her back in my life?"

Kevin was talking about Mama. Smolleck or someone must have told him that the driver of the car looked like her.

"I wanted her to love me," he said. "To be her little prince again. What an idiot!"

Their mother probably had no idea how much her aloofness had hurt both her kids.

"She does love you, Kev. She was dealing with her own issues and didn't know how to show it."

He gave his head an angry shake. "I should have known better. Dad did."

"But Dad was the one who said you should forgive her," Aubrey said.

"I mean years ago, when he left her. You don't believe it was just because he met someone new, do you?"

Aubrey had always assumed Star was the reason, but maybe their father had suspicions Mama might be capable of something terrible.

My mother did not try to kill my father. She did not kill Jonathan.

Kevin eyed the unopened bottle of vodka in her hand. "You drinking that?"

She hesitated, then handed it to him. He was probably better off numb.

He took a sip of vodka. "You're a good sister," he said. "I'm sorry I almost let you drown."

"It's okay, Kev."

"Do you think she'll try to kill us, too?" he asked.

A chill flew down her spine. "What do you mean?"

"I heard the investigators say she probably killed Jonathan. And the woman who was driving the car that hit Dad looked like her. Maybe she's trying to get rid of all of us."

"No, Kev. Don't think like that."

My mother did not try to kill my father. She did not kill her fiancé.

"I'm sorry, Aubrey," he said. "I'm sorry I didn't drown you."

Her brother was very drunk. His thoughts were getting mixed up. "You mean you're sorry you almost let me drown."

He shook his head like a stubborn child. "No. I'm sorry I didn't drown you, and me with you." He took another swig of vodka. "It would have been better than living through this."

She opened her mouth to tell him he was wrong. That this was all a terrible mistake. Their family would be together again, laughing and celebrating Ethan's next birthday. Happy and safe. Like she'd promised him earlier today.

But this time, the words got stuck in her heart.

CHAPTER 38

The droning voice on the TV or the alcohol had caught up to her brother. He was curled up on the chair, asleep, but gripping the empty vodka bottle like it was a lifesaving tonic. Aubrey left him in the waiting room and went for a walk down the linoleum-covered corridor, past the nurses' station and patient rooms and beeping machines.

She didn't like what was happening to her mind—the dark, negative feelings. She understood Kevin's need to succumb to them. It was almost too much to accept—Ethan, Jonathan, their father. There had to be some other explanation.

Her mother wasn't a murderer.

She turned back at the end of the corridor and saw Special Agent Smolleck coming in her direction. She hurried toward him, hope that he had something positive to tell her overpowering her fear of more bad news.

Then she saw the tense expression on his face.

"I understand your dad's in surgery," he said.

"Yes."

"Let's go somewhere to talk."

They were silent as they took the elevator down. She followed him outside to a small inner courtyard with several spindly trees. A few people she took to be visitors and some hospital staff were sitting on benches or talking in small groups.

Smolleck gestured toward a food cart. "Want something?"

"I'm good. Thanks."

They sat on one of the benches. His tie was crooked, and his shirt less crisp than earlier.

"We haven't located your mother. I'd really appreciate your help."

She didn't answer.

"I thought we had the same goal," he said. "To get Ethan back safely."

"I don't know where she is."

An orderly pushed an old woman in a wheelchair to the sunny corner of the courtyard. The old woman lifted her wrinkled face toward the sun and closed her eyes.

"Have you come up with anything on the babysitter at the carnival?" Aubrey asked.

He shook his head. "We spoke with Star. She told us she'd called a few agencies, but didn't remember which one had sent the babysitter. We're checking with each of them."

"But most agencies have photos of their babysitters, don't they? Wouldn't you be able to get a match with facial-recognition software?"

"We're working on that."

"What about an invoice from the agency? Didn't Star or my father get billed for her services?"

"We haven't found anything on their credit-card statements."

"So what does that mean? Is Star lying?"

"It's possible."

Of course Star was lying. Aubrey just needed to persuade Smolleck.

"You say we have the same goal," she said. "But you're holding back from me."

"There are a number of aspects of this investigation that—"

She had no patience for his posturing. "Why don't my parents come up when I do a search on Stormdrain or the explosion in 1970? We both know they had some involvement with the organization."

He frowned.

"What did they have to do with the explosion?"

"I already told you I'm not at liberty to say."

"Did they make a deal with the FBI? Is that why you can't tell me?"

"I'm not at liberty to say."

His stubbornness was infuriating. "Without saying it, you're telling me my parents were involved in some way. Which means a survivor of the explosion might be seeking revenge against them."

"I appreciate you trying to solve this, but help us do our job," he said. "Help us find your mother."

"Twenty years ago, a man claiming to be Jeffrey Schwartz approached the FBI and said he knew who set off the brownstone explosion. It made the headlines, and I think it spooked my parents. I believe they thought the real Jeffrey Schwartz was out to get them. Tell me why."

"I can't."

"Did my parents blow up the brownstone?"

He looked miserable. He gave his head a little shake. "It wasn't that."

"Then what was it? Why were they afraid of Schwartz?"

He pressed his lips together tightly. He was done sharing.

But she wasn't done asking questions. "Where is Schwartz now?"

"We don't know, Aubrey. Look, enough of this. Tell me where your mother is."

"What about the man who claimed to be Schwartz? Have you found him? Have you asked him why he went to the FBI? Who gave him the idea to say he was Schwartz?"

"He's a psychotic."

"Have you found him?"

He let out an exasperated sigh. "Yes, we found him and spoke to him."

"And?"

"He was useless. Said he didn't know what we were talking about."

"Found him where?"

Smolleck shook his head, annoyed. "He's still working as a janitor at some upscale shopping mall in Buckhead. He's been there forever."

Upscale shopping mall in Buckhead. Where had she heard that reference? "Peachtree Shoppes?"

He frowned. "How do you know that?"

Her heart was pounding. "Because Star owned a business there years ago." She made a quick calculation. The article was from ten years ago. It said Star had owned the business for ten years. That would have been twenty years. "If this man worked as a janitor when Star was there, she could have known him. She could have convinced him he was Jeffrey Schwartz and told him to go the FBI."

"Enough, Aubrey. You're pushing for impossible connections. How would Star even know about Schwartz?"

"Because she isn't Star. She's Linda Wilsen."

"She isn't, Aubrey. Stop this and tell me where your mother is."

"Think about it," she said. "There's a physical similarity between Star and Wilsen. They're the same age."

He shook his head. "You're completely off track here."

"Star could have been working on an elaborate plan to punish my parents all these years. First she convinces some guy with delusions to go to the FBI knowing that news about April Fool will rattle my parents, then she gets my father to leave my mother, and finally, when the timing is right for her, she gets my dad to convince Kevin to let my mother be part of Ethan's life and kidnaps him."

"Aubrey."

"I know. You need a motive," she said. "Linda Wilsen was completely disfigured in the explosion. If she blamed my parents, there's your motive."

"Aubrey." His voice was sharp. A couple of people at the next bench turned to stare at him. He shifted closer to Aubrey. "Star isn't Linda Wilsen," he said quietly.

"But—"

"Linda Wilsen is dead."

"No, she isn't. You said you couldn't find her."

"We found her. She moved to Canada in 1971 and changed her name. We've confirmed that she died in 1980."

"But—"

"Star isn't Linda Wilsen. We need to talk about your mother."

Aubrey looked at the old woman. Her face was now in shadows, but she kept her eyes closed and head back as though hoping the warmth would find her again.

Was Aubrey so desperate to prove her mother's innocence that she was finding patterns in unrelated events and creating a flawed, alternative narrative?

"I know you think you're doing the right thing by trying to protect her," Smolleck said, "but you aren't."

Aubrey wished the sun would come around to the bench where they were sitting. "Star could still be involved," she said.

"You're grasping at straws."

"Where was she when my father was hit by the car?"

Smolleck shook his head.

"Before you convict my mother, I want to know why you're so sure Star can't be a suspect."

"Star was in her apartment," Smolleck said. "She told us she had a migraine and asked your father to pick up her medicine from the drugstore."

"But doesn't that sound like a perfect opportunity for her to have followed him and tried to kill him?"

"Except that the driver of the car looked like your mother."

"Star could have been wearing a wig."

"The SUV was the same make and model as Jonathan's."

"*What?*"

"A valet saw a woman with shoulder-length dark hair and a white blouse drive out of the garage in Jonathan's SUV minutes after he fell to his death. Unfortunately, it doesn't have GPS, so we can't track it."

"It still could have been Star," Aubrey said. "Have you checked out her alibi? Have you looked into her background?"

"Where is your mother, Aubrey?"

"I don't know."

"Your mother was seen at Jonathan's condo shortly before he died. Someone who looked like her was seen driving Jonathan's SUV away from the building immediately after his death. An eyewitness described someone who fits the description of your mother as the driver of the SUV that ran down your father, almost killing him."

"But she didn't arrange for the babysitter," Aubrey said.

"I can't explain that yet."

"So you believe my mother was also behind Ethan's kidnapping?"

He didn't answer. Just kept his face in a rigid, unreadable mask.

Aubrey couldn't find her breath.

"Where is she?" Smolleck said.

The corner of the courtyard was completely in shadows, and the old woman in the wheelchair was gone. "I don't know," she said.

"If you did know, would you tell me?"

"I don't know," she repeated.

He stood up. "Well, I appreciate your honesty."

She watched him walk through the courtyard and back into the hospital. She wanted to call after him, tell him that he was chasing after the wrong person, that her mother wasn't a murderer. But she knew he wouldn't believe her.

Because neither did she.

CHAPTER 39

Aubrey left the courtyard and went around to the back of the hospital, past the emergency room and parking lots, to the broad bay.

Mount Sinai was on one of the most beautiful pieces of land in Miami Beach, once the site of a grand hotel. Now, a number of buildings made up the medical complex, most with fabulous views of the bay and downtown Miami.

She walked to the edge of the water. The sun was beginning its descent and hurt her eyes as she stared into it. She blinked. The bay spread out before her, clear and sparkling, but beneath the water, she could see shifting shadows.

She never should have let her mother leave the Circle. She should have called Smolleck and had the FBI pick her up, so another near-tragedy could have been avoided. Once again, Aubrey had allowed herself to be duped. She had wanted so much to believe her mother was innocent and that letting her go was best for Ethan that she'd ignored the signs of her mother unraveling—the angry denials, plaintive entreaties, ardent assurances. It should have been clear to Aubrey, given all her psychological training, that her mother was distraught and capable of doing things that would have been unthinkable in a sane state.

Mama could have killed Jonathan, believing that to be the only way she could get Ethan back. But why would she have tried to kill Dad, when just yesterday she had been defending him? Unless she feared he would reveal some incriminating secret from their past. One thing Aubrey knew for certain: both her parents had been hiding something from their college years.

Was Mama so unhinged that this killing spree was only just the beginning? Kevin had referred to their mother as the devil and believed she was lashing out at everyone close to her, that even her own children weren't safe. Aubrey didn't accept that. If her mother had killed Jonathan and attempted to kill Dad, it was because she believed their deaths would somehow save Ethan. Her mother may have murdered, but she wasn't a psychopath.

Smolleck had also implied that Mama was behind Ethan's kidnapping. Was that possible? Mama's grief over her grandson's disappearance appeared to be real, and unlike for Jonathan and Dad, she had no compelling motive to harm him. But that didn't mean her mother didn't know things that might help them get Ethan back.

She breathed in the muggy air. Shadows shifted beneath the water.

A few musical notes broke through Aubrey's musings. It was her cell's generic ringtone, but although she didn't recognize the number, it was very likely her mother.

She let it ring as a cloud drifted in front of the sun. She needed a moment to prepare herself for what might happen if she answered. The phone went silent after the sixth ring. Aubrey stared at the missed call icon.

She could call back and arrange to meet, but Smolleck would most certainly follow her. He would probably bring in the police with a SWAT team. Helicopters, people in Kevlar carrying M16s and shotguns. They'd surround Mama. Would she run? Would they shoot?

Her phone began ringing again. Same number.

Mama had said something disturbing as she was leaving Circle Park. *Even if you end up hating me, know that I love you more than life itself.*

Her mother may have killed her fiancé and tried to kill Aubrey's father.

But she might also know who had Ethan.

Aubrey pressed "Answer" and held the phone to her ear. "Hello?"

"Sweetheart," her mother said. Sweetheart, like Mama always called her.

She was still her mother.

"Meet me at Grandma's place," her mother said, then disconnected from the call.

Aubrey stared at her phone. *Grandma's place.* Once again, her mother was being cryptic, probably assuming the call was being monitored, but she knew Aubrey would recognize the reference. Her mind raced over her options.

She pressed Smolleck's number. "I need to talk to you."

"Okay," he said. "Talk."

The setting sun was behind a cloud, blocking the painful rays. *Mama, I hope you'll forgive me for this.*

"If I meet my mother, I'm concerned you'll follow me and arrest her."

"You can't protect her anymore."

"You said we have the same goal—to get Ethan back safely. I believe my mother may know who has him."

"Why would she keep that information from us?"

"I'm not sure. She may be protecting someone or something from her past. But if you arrest her, things might go wrong with Ethan."

"What do you have in mind?"

"My mother trusts me. Let me meet her alone."

"I'm not letting you out of my sight."

"I understand, but can you do it surreptitiously? Let me talk to her and try to find out who has Ethan, if she even knows."

He was quiet for a long time. "You're putting yourself in danger," he said.

The cloud in front of the sun had turned a bruised purple pink. "She's my mother. She would never hurt me."

"She's likely killed her fiancé and tried to kill your father."

"My mother would never hurt me."

"Let's hope not," he said.

Chapter 40

Aubrey hadn't been to the Miami Beach Holocaust Memorial since her grandmother died ten years before. The park and sculpture garden were located on Nineteenth Street and Meridian Avenue. She, Mama, and Kevin used to come here with Nana three or four times a year, for certain Jewish holidays and other occasions that were special to her grandmother.

As she pulled her mother's BMW into a parking spot just outside the memorial, she had the uncomfortable realization that this was only a few blocks away from the time-share and where her father had been hit by a car. Her mother had been in the vicinity, but Aubrey was relieved not to see Jonathan's black SUV parked nearby. She wondered where Smolleck's agents would station themselves.

She hurried toward the entrance, surprised there were no people around, but the memorial closed at sunset, and the sky was already beginning to darken. Her mother wasn't in the Garden of Meditation. Aubrey gazed at the giant bronze upstretched hand, which rose out of a lily pond toward the sky, and remembered the awe she had felt the first time she'd seen it. The sculpture was beautiful, until you noticed the tormented souls trying to climb up the hand and out of hell.

She continued past a statue of two terrified children clinging to their mother, then through the wooden arbor overhung with white-bougainvillea vines and past the black-granite slabs etched with photos of the Holocaust.

Her mother wasn't there, either.

As she stepped into the stone tunnel, the piped-in haunting voices of children singing surrounded her. She slowed as she got closer to the statue at the end of the tunnel. A small child reaching for help. Standing beside it was a woman in a white blouse with dark shoulder-length hair.

Her mother turned as Aubrey got nearer. Mama held out her arms toward her. "Sweetheart."

Aubrey couldn't hug her, she just couldn't.

Her mother dropped her arms.

This place was too quiet, too personal. Besides, Smolleck would have a difficult time watching them here.

"I'd rather not stay here," Aubrey said.

Her mother cocked her head but didn't question her. "All right." She followed Aubrey through the rest of the arbor, back to the giant hand sculpture in the lily pond.

Traffic went by in the street beyond the memorial. A couple of men stood on the other side of the pond. Probably Smolleck's.

Her mother sat on one of the benches near the last statue of the same woman who stood at the entrance of the memorial. Here at the end of her journey, the woman and her two children lay dead, in the shadow of Anne Frank's words about shattered dreams and ideals.

"Come sit, Aubrey."

Aubrey stayed where she was.

"You remember coming here?" her mother asked.

"Of course."

"This place was very special to my mother," Mama said. "You know she lost her parents and older brothers and many other relatives in the Holocaust."

"I know."

"My mother was lucky." Mama rubbed her hands together as though she were cold. "Her paperwork came through in 1939, so she was able to go to America. She was only sixteen. Then the door slammed shut. Very few Jews got out of Poland after that."

"Why are you telling me this?"

"I want you to understand why I did what I did."

Aubrey's legs went weak. She sat down on the bench, avoiding her mother's eyes, terrified that she was about to hear her mother's confession of guilt. Several white bougainvillea petals were scattered over the stone tiles with one crushed red petal.

"Your grandmother didn't talk about the Holocaust when I was growing up, but before I left for college, she told me what had become of everyone in her family. Of her guilt at not being able to save them." Her mother stared at her hands. "At first it made me sad, especially for my mother to have lost so much. But shortly after I got to college, I started thinking about things differently. I became angry that the people of Germany, as well as the Jews, hadn't protested more vehemently about what their government was doing. Maybe if they had, they could have stopped the Nazis, stopped the war, prevented the Holocaust."

Her mother turned to Aubrey. Her eyes were red. "I started college in 1969. The US government had pushed itself into a war with Vietnam. Many of us were angry, but I suppose I saw myself as being on a mission. I believed the aggression in Vietnam was a first step in curtailing the freedoms of Americans, and convinced myself that ordinary citizens had to stand up against the government or we would be opening ourselves up to another Holocaust. I wanted to do what my mother had been unable to. To save her family. To save her country." Her eyes drifted to the statue of the woman with her dead children. "I failed."

"You were a member of Stormdrain, weren't you?"

"Yes."

"And Dad?"

"Your father was the one who started Stormdrain."

Aubrey heard herself gasp. She had suspected he was involved, but not at that level. "But I did an online search. Neither of you came up in connection with Stormdrain. Was that because you made a deal with the FBI?"

Her mother nodded. "We also had different names, then. I was Di Hartfeld, and your father was Lawrence Lyndberger. We legally changed to Lynd when we married in 1971."

How could Aubrey have not known that? But her parents had many secrets they'd kept from her. "Why did you make a deal with the FBI?"

"Things changed," her mother said. "Your father and I had been naive to think we could remain pacifists."

"Pacifists? You were setting off bombs."

"Yes, we were, but we always took precautions that no one would get hurt. Then when some people in the organization decided to take things in a different direction, your father and I tried to stop them."

"How?" Aubrey asked.

Her mother looked back down at her hands. The sky had darkened. Cars went past on Meridian Avenue. The lights came on around them, casting the giant hand sculpture in an eerie green.

"Mama, what really happened at the brownstone explosion?"

CHAPTER 41

Diana turned toward the sculpture of souls trying to claw their way up out of hell. Would she ever make it out of her own hell?

"I found plans to blow up Columbia's Low Library," she said. "Someone had marked up the blueprint indicating where to plant bombs to kill hundreds of people, mostly students."

Her daughter made a little noise, like a kitten that's been kicked aside.

"I went to your father and told him things had gone too far and we needed to end Stormdrain. I wanted him to go with me to the FBI. We had to do whatever was necessary to stop it."

"Did he go with you?"

Diana could still see Larry's expression of fear when she'd told him what needed to be done. "He was worried," she said to her daughter. "Concerned our friends would all be arrested and probably go to prison, even those who knew nothing about the library." She took in a breath. "You see, he knew the FBI would never be able to ignore the intent to kill innocent people. He was adamant that we shouldn't mention the plan to blow up the library."

"You went along with that?"

"He persuaded me we could avoid the library disaster and protect our friends."

"How?"

"We made an agreement with the FBI that we would arrange for each Stormdrain member to come forward, sign an affidavit, and be granted immunity. Your father also insisted that my file and his be kept out of all public records."

"So you and Dad made a deal with the FBI and got off scot-free."

Diana winced. "Scot-free? Hardly."

"The FBI never knew there was a plan to blow up the library?"

The arbor of trees that led behind the Memorial was in shadows. "That's right," she said. "We told them about the bomb factory in the brownstone and Stormdrain's plans to blow up the armory on Lexington Avenue. We also took responsibility for a number of bombings Stormdrain had been involved with. But we assured the FBI that we always took precautions to avoid injuring or killing anyone."

"How could you be sure the people who'd planned to blow up the library wouldn't do it?"

"Once the FBI knew about the bomb factory, the plan couldn't go forward."

"How did the Stormdrain members feel about Dad and you going turncoat?"

"You have to understand something. Your father was like a god to everyone in Stormdrain. They listened to him. If he said it was time to retreat, they retreated."

"So what happened?"

"A group of our friends were supposed to be at a neighborhood bar that afternoon. Your father went there to tell them about the deal and persuade them to talk to the FBI in exchange for immunity."

"And you?" Aubrey asked. "Where did you go?"

"I went to the brownstone, where we held our meetings."

"Where the bomb factory was."

Diana nodded. "A few Stormdrain members were there. I wanted to warn them that the FBI would be coming to dismantle everything and let them know we had gotten everyone immunity."

"So what went wrong?"

"There was a ringleader," Diana said. "My roommate, Gertrude. I think she went a little crazy. She believed killing was the only answer to righting the wrongs of our society."

"Gertrude Morgenstern," Aubrey said.

"I don't know what I was thinking." Diana remembered the fury and arrogance on Gertrude's face when she had confronted her in their dorm room with the blueprint of the library. "Why I thought I'd be able to reason with her."

The memory pushed against her brain, as painful as ever. "A little boy on a red tricycle was riding around in front of the brownstone." She squeezed her eyes closed, but the memory remained.

The little boy pedaled past her on a red tricycle. He was wearing a blue-and-white-striped sweater. He rode the tricycle around and around on the cracked sidewalk in front of the old brick brownstone, stopping to smile and wave at her. She hurried past him to the weathered oak door and banged hard with the brass knocker. She needed to talk to them.

"Let me in." She pounded on the door. "Let me in!"

She opened her eyes. Aubrey was watching her, her daughter's face apprehensive, as though she were expecting a pail of water to be thrown at her.

"The door opened," Diana said. She ran her tongue over her dry lips. "It was Gertrude."

Her daughter didn't move, not even her eyes.

"I told her Larry and I had gone to the FBI. That we had told them about Stormdrain, and they had agreed to grant everyone immunity."

The memory ran through her mind, like sandpaper over raw skin.

"What about the library?" Gertrude asked.

"We didn't tell the FBI about that," Di said. "If they knew that any of us intended to kill, they'd have never agreed to immunity."

"Then it's over," Gertrude said. "It's all been for nothing."

"We've done what we could."

Gertrude stared at her, eyes throbbing like ancient stars before they explode. "Done what we could? They'll never remember. They'll never learn."

"It's our chance to start over."

"Whose chance?" Gertrude's voice was flat. She glanced down the street toward the boy on the red tricycle, then slammed the door.

Di's heart was beating too fast, as though her body sensed some danger that hadn't yet reached her brain. She turned from the door and watched the little boy pedal around and around, wondering whether she had done the right thing. She should have known Gertrude wouldn't take the news well. Maybe she should have told the FBI about Gertrude and the plan to blow up the library, no matter what Larry had said. Her roommate was unpredictable. In Gertrude's mind, there was no victory unless someone died.

Di glanced back at the weathered front door. It was too late now. She couldn't change what was done.

She went down the stoop past the little boy on his tricycle. He squeezed the little bulb horn, honked twice, then waved.

Di waved back and kept walking.

Diana shook her head, trying to clear it, but she couldn't erase the guilt.

Aubrey was as stiff as one of the statues, as she waited for her to continue.

"Gertrude was furious about the FBI deal," Diana said. "I never should have left her in that state, but I walked away."

"You did what you could, Mama."

Did I? I walked away.

"I was only a short distance from the brownstone when I was shaken by a blast. It was like a sudden thunderclap. Then a tidal wave of air flattened me against the sidewalk, and everything went black."

She blinked hard, clearing her vision. "I don't know how long I was out. Seconds, maybe longer. When I came to, something in my brain clicked. I needed to save my friends. I pulled myself up and ran back to the building."

She was breathing hard, running. Running with her feet mired in mud.

Aubrey touched her hand.

"That's when I saw the little boy who'd been riding the tricycle. He was lying on the sidewalk. Bleeding. I went to him. There was another blast. Something hit my head. I couldn't hear anything but ringing."

She could hear it now—that high-pitched squeal that erased all other sounds.

"I don't know how, but I picked up the little boy and carried him away."

The hellish, copper-green hand seemed to be emerging from the pond, the light playing on each of the tormented souls.

My fault. It was my fault.

"I couldn't save him," Diana whispered. "Or the others."

CHAPTER 42

Shadows from the sculptures and trees surrounded them. There was an unnatural lightness in the sky as the moon tried to push through the clouds.

"Do you believe Gertrude blew up the brownstone?" Aubrey asked.

Her mother didn't answer, just continued to stare at the tortured bronze hand in the pond.

"It wasn't your fault, Mama. You did the right thing. If you hadn't gone to the FBI, Gertrude or the others in the brownstone might have done much more damage. They might have blown up the library. Think how many more people may have died."

"Your father used to say that, but I could never forgive myself for my friends' deaths or that innocent child's."

The story explained a great deal, but not everything. Not enough to persuade Aubrey that her mother wasn't responsible for Jonathan's death and the attempt on her father's life.

"Mama," she said as gently as she could, "you've been through a lot of very terrible things. I'm sorry you've had to keep this inside all these years. But it's time to let the past go. Please, tell me, do you know who took Ethan?"

In the dim light, she could see disappointment in her mother's face. "Oh, Aubrey, do you really believe I wouldn't have gone straight to the police if I had some idea of who had him?"

Her mother sounded genuine, and her slumped body reflected grief, but Aubrey recognized she wanted so much to believe her mother that she could no longer read her accurately.

Aubrey sat up straighter. She had to distance herself and get to the truth. She had to find Ethan. "I think you know things you aren't telling me. That you're protecting someone or something."

"And put Ethan's life at risk?" her mother said. "Don't you know me, Aubrey?"

No, Mama. I don't. "Tell me everything that could have led to someone kidnapping Ethan."

Her mother stared at her tight, interlocked fingers. "I don't know who took him. I only know it's someone from Stormdrain."

"Why?" It had been the question Aubrey had been unable to answer.

"Someone may have seen your father and me as traitors or blamed us for the brownstone explosion and the deaths of Gertrude, Michael, and Gary."

"Why would they blame you? Didn't Dad tell your friends at the bar about the deal you made with the FBI to get immunity for everyone?"

Her mother shook her head. "They weren't at the bar when he got there. Then, once the brownstone blew up, the FBI withdrew the deal. There was too much public outrage to let any of the other Stormdrain members go free."

"So that's why they all went into hiding." Aubrey thought for a moment. "I can see someone from Stormdrain resenting you and Dad for getting off, but it's just a theory. There's no proof."

"The greeting card is proof."

"How?"

"Because whoever left it wrote my college nickname on the envelope and knew the little boy outside the brownstone rode a red tricycle."

"Who knew about the tricycle?"

"The police and FBI. I told them what happened."

"Anyone else?"

"Gertrude saw the boy riding his tricycle." Her mother frowned. "Maybe someone else was in the brownstone and saw the child from a window."

Mama was doing something liars frequently did—making up things as they went along—but Aubrey couldn't tell whether her mother was trying to come up with a cover story or if she was genuinely searching for an explanation. She decided to see where this was going.

"Everyone in the brownstone died in the explosion," Aubrey said, "except Linda Wilsen, and the FBI confirmed she died in 1980."

"Linda's dead?"

"According to Smolleck," Aubrey said. "Who else knew about the tricycle?"

Mama rubbed the finger where she once wore her wedding ring. "I told your father about the little boy."

"Dad knew?" That meant her father was the only one alive from Stormdrain who knew everything. Aubrey felt sick. Mama had been leading her on. In a distorted way, her mother may have started seeing her onetime co-conspirator as an enemy. "Is that why you tried to kill him?"

Her mother's eyes grew large. "What are you talking about? Did something happen to your father?"

Was this an act, too?

Her mother grabbed Aubrey's wrist. "What happened to your father?"

Aubrey was torn, uncertain whether she was dealing with a pathological liar or a victim of a terrible scam. "He was hit by a car," she said, watching her mother's reaction. "He may not survive."

Her mother brought her hands to her face. "How did it happen?"

"Hit-and-run."

"Did they see the driver?"

"Yes. She looked like you, Mama."

"Like me?" She blinked, and Aubrey could see the confusion turn to recognition. "I see." Her mother ran her tongue over her lips. "That's why you've been so distant. You think I've done all these horrible things."

Aubrey glanced at the statue of the mother with her two dead children. The inscription talked about shattered dreams and ideals. "I don't want to believe it."

"Tell me all the evidence they have against me."

If only Mama could persuade her she was telling the truth. "Someone who looked like you was seen at Jonathan's building shortly before he died," Aubrey said. "She drove away in his car after he fell from the balcony. The car that hit Dad was the same make and model. The driver also looked like you."

Her mother frowned. "Someone is posing as me, making it look like I've gone crazy."

Aubrey studied her mother as a thin ray of moonlight broke through the clouds. Crow's-feet around her dark eyes. A few silver hairs at her temples. Lips that she sometimes pressed against Aubrey's forehead for no special reason.

"Who hates you that much?" Aubrey asked.

Her mother got a faraway look. "Gertrude did."

"But she died in the explosion. They found a piece of her finger, hair, clothes, her glasses." Aubrey stopped. No vital organs. Nothing that meant she was unquestionably dead. "What if Gertrude escaped from the brownstone? What if she's still alive?"

"Gertrude. Alive." The words came out softly, as though her mother were testing them out.

"Did Gertrude know Jonathan at Columbia?" Aubrey asked. "Did she have a reason to kill him and try to kill Dad?"

"She had once been in love with both of them."

The pieces were starting to fall into place. "But they loved you more?"

"I believe they did," her mother said.

Was that enough to connect the ghost of Gertrude to Jonathan's murder, the attempt on Dad's life, and Ethan's disappearance?

Aubrey considered the theory she had shared with Smolleck. She had been certain Star was involved, but she had thought Linda Wilsen was posing as Star, seeking to take revenge against Aubrey's parents for her ruined body. But Gertrude may have had an even stronger motive to destroy Aubrey's mother and father.

Was Star Matin really Gertrude Morgenstern?

Had Gertrude reinvented herself as a southern belle through surgery and a new veneer, or was Aubrey trying too hard to make the pieces fit?

She looked up at the black space between several shifting clouds. In the darkness, she could see a tiny glimmer. Star had arranged for the babysitter, disappeared around the time of Jonathan's murder, and had an unsubstantiated alibi when Aubrey's dad was hit by a car. All that was missing was motive, unless Star was Gertrude, then everything made sense. But other than a theory, there was no way to tie them together.

The star grew brighter.

And then it hit her. Of course Star was Gertrude.

Impostors often left a telltale sign of their true identities. On some level they either wanted to be caught or at least have someone acknowledge the cleverness of their deception. Star Matin was no exception. Her name was the giveaway.

Aubrey felt a powerful wave of relief. Mama was not a murderer. She had been telling the truth.

Then her heart dropped.

Because she knew where Ethan was and what Star was capable of doing to him.

CHAPTER 43

As they hurried to the car, Aubrey explained to her mother what she had only just put together. She asked her to drive so she could call Smolleck. They weren't going to be stupid and try to confront a murderer by themselves.

"Where the hell are you going?" Smolleck asked.

"To the time-share where my father and Star are staying," she said. "Ethan's probably there."

"Your mother confessed to taking him?"

"My mother is innocent," Aubrey said. "Star is behind everything. Like I told you earlier. Someone from my parents' past is trying to get even. I was wrong about Linda Wilsen, but I was right about Star. Star very likely persuaded the janitor who worked at the mall in Buckhead to tell the FBI he was Jeffrey Schwartz. She knew all about Schwartz and the explosion because Star is Gertrude Morgenstern. Star Matin, Morgenstern. She even used the same name. *Matin* is French for 'morning.' *Morgenstern* is 'morning star' in German."

"Go on," Smolleck said.

"The time-share is owned by J. W. Hendrix of Atlanta." She kept talking as her mother tried to drive through the crowd of people crossing

Lincoln Road against the light. "That's probably Janis Hendrix. Star has a daughter named Janis who lives in Atlanta." She took a breath. "Janis is probably also the babysitter."

Smolleck was quiet. Aubrey could hear a police radio in the background. "It's a pretty big leap," he said.

"Please," Aubrey said. "Can you try to get a match between the photo of the babysitter and Janis or J. W. Hendrix with facial-recognition software? Then you'll know I'm right."

"We'll check it out," he said. "Until we have a confirmation, your mother remains a suspect."

Their car made it past the crowd, crossed to the other side of Lincoln Road, and picked up speed.

"Park away from the apartment," Smolleck said. "I'm right behind you. I'll alert the police and the other teams in case Ethan is in there." He disconnected from the call.

The neighborhood changed abruptly from crowded tourist destination to a quiet residential quarter. Large, overhanging trees and widely spaced streetlights made the street eerily dark. They rode along with the neighborhood park on their right until they came to a couple of "resident only" parking spots a half block from the time-share. Aubrey told her mother to park. A black sedan pulled in behind them. Smolleck and three agents got out of the car.

Mama was staring out the windshield, her hands clutching the wheel.

"We have to get out and talk to the FBI," Aubrey said. "I don't think they'll arrest you."

"I don't care about that," her mother said. "We need to get Ethan out safely."

"We will, Mama."

She and her mother left their car and approached Smolleck, who was on the phone, standing outside the glare of one of the few streetlights.

Several police cars stopped at the corner behind them, blocking off the street. No sirens or flashing lights. Nothing to alert Star.

Smolleck finished his call and nodded at Aubrey and her mother. "We're trying to develop a possible timeline for Star's involvement with Judge Woodward and your father," he said. "Can you help me out with a couple of things?"

He believed her?

"We've been considering her all along," he continued, as though he could read the question on Aubrey's face. "Star left the Ritz around eleven thirty, just after your mother called you and said she was going to Jonathan's apartment. Did Star know about your conversation with your mother?"

"Yes," Aubrey said. "Star was with me at the hotel when my mother called. She could have picked up from my side of the conversation that my mother was going to Jonathan's."

Smolleck nodded. "After Star left the Ritz, she took a taxi to a shopping mall where we lost track of her."

"Maybe she changed into a wig and dark glasses," Aubrey said. "Then she could have gone to Jonathan's building from the mall and waited outside until she saw my mother leave."

"I left a little after noon," Mama said. "She could have called up to ask Jonathan to buzz her into the private elevator. He would have thought I'd come back."

"Wouldn't he have recognized it wasn't your voice?" Smolleck asked.

Mama shook her head. "Back in college, she could walk like me, talk like me. She had a real gift of mimicry."

"If she was disguised as my mother, Jonathan may not have realized who she was when she got up to the apartment. Star and my mom are about the same size. Once inside, if he recognized his mistake, she could have turned a gun or knife on him, forced him out to the balcony, and then pushed him over."

"Possibly," Smolleck said. "How would Star have known about his car?"

"Jonathan always left his car keys on the front foyer table," Mama said. "She could have grabbed them and driven away."

"Then returned to the time-share in Jonathan's car and run over my father," Aubrey said, thinking it through.

"It's still circumstantial," Smolleck said.

"Just like your case against my mother."

He rubbed his eyebrow. "Well, the tactical teams have been alerted in the event Star is involved and has Ethan in the building with her. It may take a little while for the Hostage Rescue Team to get here, but we're coordinating with the local police and have our own negotiator."

He believed her. But relief was quickly replaced by fear of what was to come.

Aubrey looked down the half block at the time-share. Although it was dark outside, the lights in every window of the small residence were off. Was Star even in there? Was Ethan?

"You've met Special Agent McDonough." Smolleck gestured toward one of the three agents that had gotten out of the car with him. He'd been at her mother's house. A balding, middle-aged man with tortoise-framed glasses and a gentle face. "Special Agent McDonough is trained in hostage negotiation. He'll try to start a dialogue with Ms. Matin to ascertain if she has Ethan and what she wants."

"So you're not convinced she kidnapped Ethan?"

"Convinced enough to request tactical-team backup." Smolleck turned from her to take a call.

Aubrey watched as heavily armed officers emerged from vehicles, spreading out around several small buildings.

"Which one is the time-share?" her mother asked.

"The mustard-colored one with the hedges around it."

Her mother shook her head. "I don't like this. Star may be at a window watching all of this."

Mama was on her same wavelength. What if Star reacted to all the law enforcement like a cornered animal? Would she take it out on Ethan?

Aubrey stepped closer to Smolleck. He was turned away from her, but she could hear his side of a phone conversation. "We got the floor plan of the building," Smolleck was saying. "It's wood-frame construction with stucco over lath. Two one-bedroom apartments on the second and third floors, one one-bedroom apartment, and a garage on the first floor. The building is owned by Time-Share Dreams but doesn't appear to have been rented out or occupied in the last couple of years. We're pretty sure there are no civilians in the building, aside from the suspect and little boy, and possibly the woman who took him from the carnival." The person on the line said something else. "Good," Smolleck said. "Did you speak with her boss?" He listened for a while. "Okay, thanks," he said, then disconnected from the call.

"What's going on?" Aubrey asked.

"We got a confirmation on the facial-recognition software. Janis Hendrix is a match with the babysitter."

It wasn't a surprise, but Aubrey felt a twinge of edginess. They were homing in.

A large dark van pulled up in the street near them. Agent McDonough opened the side door and climbed inside. There were two men sitting at the front. Aubrey could make out electronic equipment, a narrow table against one side of the van, and a couple of chairs. McDonough sat down on one of the chairs and put on headphones.

"I'll need the two of you to move outside the perimeter," Smolleck said to Aubrey and her mother. He gestured to where the police cars had blocked off the street.

"What do you mean?" Aubrey said. "Won't we be able to listen to your conversation with her?"

"No," he said.

"But my mother and I may be able to help. We know this woman. We have some idea of how her mind works."

He glanced at McDonough, who was watching them from inside the van, perhaps waiting for a signal from Smolleck.

"Please," Aubrey said. "Let us help."

Smolleck filled his cheeks with air, then blew it out. "Okay. Go on in. You can listen, but you mustn't speak under any circumstances."

Aubrey and her mother stepped into the van. Smolleck followed, then closed the door after them. He leaned against the narrow table where McDonough sat, while Aubrey and her mother stood in the small space. The two men in the front were involved with what seemed to be communications equipment.

Mama looked pale and wobbly, as though she might pass out. Smolleck must have noticed. He gestured to the other chair, and Mama sat down with a grateful nod.

McDonough pressed a button on one of the machines, and a phone somewhere began to ring.

Aubrey was startled by the sudden clarity of Star's voice coming through speakers, as though she were in the van with them. "Yes?" Star said.

"Ms. Matin, I'm Special Agent McDonough of the Federal Bureau of Investigation."

"Hello, Special Agent McDonough," she said in her soft southern voice.

"I would like to speak with you," McDonough said. "Are you comfortable having a conversation over the phone?"

"Yes, of course."

"Good," he said. "Is Ethan Lynd in there with you?"

Star hesitated. "He is."

Mama let out a tiny sound. Smolleck glared at her.

"Ethan's in there with you," McDonough repeated. "Very good. Is he in good health?"

"For the moment."

Aubrey glanced at her mother. Her eyes were wide with distress.

"May I speak with him?" McDonough asked.

"No, I'm sorry. That's not possible."

"I understand," he said. He pushed his glasses up on his nose. "Who else is there?"

Star didn't answer, as though she were considering what to say. "My daughter," she said finally.

Smolleck nodded.

"I see," McDonough said. "Your daughter is in there with you and Ethan. Anyone else?"

"No."

"Well, you have certainly gone to a great deal of trouble, Ms. Matin. Tell me what it is you want, and let's see if we can work something out."

"Thank you, Agent McDonough. I appreciate your solicitude. For starters I will ask you to please have your agents and the police move away from my building," she said. "And let me warn you, if anyone tries to storm it, I will kill Ethan without hesitation."

Aubrey clasped her hand over her mouth.

McDonough exchanged a look with Smolleck. The overhead lights showed beads of perspiration on McDonough's forehead.

"I will have the agents and police move away, Ms. Matin," McDonough said.

"Thank you."

Smolleck spoke in a low voice into his phone, then nodded at McDonough.

"They're moving away from the building, Ms. Matin," McDonough said. "Now before we continue our conversation, please let Ethan come outside."

"No," she said.

McDonough pressed a button that probably disabled the mike on their end and took a deep breath. Then, he pressed it again. "Okay, I understand, Ms. Matin. So tell me what it is you want."

"Justice," she said.

"You want justice," he repeated. "Justice for what?"

She was quiet for a long time. "Justice for what, Ms. Matin?" McDonough asked again.

"Something you'll never be able to remedy," she said finally.

"We can try, Ms. Matin," McDonough said.

"Can you change the past?" she asked.

"What about the past would you like to change?"

"Maybe Di can help you with that."

McDonough's head swung around so he could look at Smolleck, who was scowling.

"Who is Di?" McDonough asked.

"Diana Hartfeld Lynd."

Smolleck fixed his eyes on Aubrey's mother.

"I see," McDonough said. "But it would be helpful if you told us, Ms. Matin."

Star was silent. Aubrey listened for background noises and could make out a humming sound, like one from the air conditioner. She wondered whether Star was in the downstairs apartment. Where were Ethan and Janis?

Smolleck had written something on the pad that was on the table and pushed it over to McDonough to read.

"Ms. Matin," McDonough said. "Are you Gertrude Morgenstern?"

Star let out a little laugh. "Gertrude Morgenstern is dead."

"Do you blame Diana Lynd for her death?"

"I do."

Her mother made a small noise.

Smolleck brought a finger to his lips and frowned.

"Is Di there with ya? Far out." Star's voice had changed from its southern accent to something coarser. "Hi there, Polly."

Smolleck tilted his head at Mama.

She scribbled on the pad, and Aubrey leaned over to read it. *Gertrude's nickname for me.*

Smolleck nodded at McDonough to continue.

"Ms. Matin," McDonough said, "what is your relationship to Gertrude Morgenstern?"

Star gave a little cough. "Star was born when Gertrude died," she said, back to her southern drawl.

"I don't understand," McDonough said. "Please tell me what that means."

The van was silent, except for the magnified sound of Star's breathing.

"Are you doing okay, Ms. Matin?" McDonough said.

She didn't answer.

"Please tell me what you want," he said.

"Di."

Aubrey tensed. She looked at her mother, but Mama's face hadn't changed expression. She had probably been expecting this.

"Please explain that, Ms. Matin," McDonough said.

"I want to talk to Di," she said. "Here, in the apartment."

Mama started to stand up. Aubrey shook her head "no" vehemently.

Her mother wrote something on the pad.

Smolleck read it, made a note on the pad, and pushed it to McDonough.

McDonough nodded. "Ms. Matin," he said, "we'll consider letting Di inside to speak with you. But first, you will have to let Ethan leave."

"Oh, but I'm afraid I can't do that," she said. "If I let Ethan go, I'll lose my leverage. No, that won't work. But I have a proposition for you."

"What's that?" McDonough asked.

"Let Di inside to talk to me. Then, after we've settled old business, everyone can leave."

Smolleck shook his head hard.

"We won't be able to do that, Ms. Matin," McDonough said.

"Oh, that's too bad," she said. "Because if you don't, I'll blow up the entire building, with Ethan in it."

CHAPTER 44

Aubrey opened her mouth, but no words came out. *How dare you. How dare you hurt my loved ones and threaten my family!*

McDonough seemed to be struggling to keep his voice even, but sweat was running down his cheeks. "Is there a bomb in the building, Ms. Matin?"

"Yes, there is, Agent McDonough."

The two men at the front of the van were working frantically on their equipment, possibly communicating the bomb threat to other agencies.

"What kind of bomb is it?"

"There wouldn't be much fun in me telling you," Star said.

"Is it possible that cell phones would trigger it?"

She hesitated. "Probably not, but I want to reiterate what you can do to prevent its detonation."

"What is that, Ms. Matin?"

"Send Di in to speak with me."

Smolleck leaned over and said something to McDonough, then ushered Aubrey and her mother out of the van.

The street was unnaturally quiet, as if all the hidden officers, and not just Aubrey, were frozen in suspended animation. She released a shaky breath. Her mother's eyes were moving back and forth, as though looking for a possible escape.

Smolleck's jaw was tight, the vein in his temple throbbing. "If she does have a bomb, we have to be careful using cell phones or two-way radios, regardless of what she said."

"She has a bomb," Aubrey's mother said. "I'm sure of it, but I don't think she's used modern technology."

"What do you mean?" Smolleck asked.

"Gertrude's more likely to try to reenact the 1970 brownstone explosion than try something new."

"You don't know that."

"I think my mother's right," Aubrey said. "When I visited my dad yesterday, I noticed a box with short plumbing pipes in the hallway of the building. I hadn't thought anything of it, but pipe bombs were found in the brownstone."

Smolleck frowned. "Damn. You could be right. Janis Hendrix worked for a demolition company in Atlanta. She took a leave of absence a few weeks ago. Around that time, a case of dynamite went missing."

"So if she's planning to re-create the brownstone explosion, what do we do?" Aubrey said.

"We're considering our options, but it's a very difficult situation."

"Of course it's difficult," Aubrey said, feeling the rise of frustration and anger. "But you're the FBI. You have sharpshooters, don't you? And what about the SWAT team?"

She could see his face redden, even in the darkness. "Yes, we have sharpshooters. But it may be difficult for them to distinguish between Star, her daughter, and Ethan. And if we hit the wrong target, Star will still most likely blow up the building."

"I'm sorry," Aubrey said. "I shouldn't have—"

"I'm not finished," Smolleck said. "The SWAT team could storm the building, using stun grenades to disorient Star, but she's controlling a bomb. It's too risky."

"Let me go in," her mother said.

"That won't stop her, Mama."

"It will delay her."

Smolleck shook his head.

"Ethan is in there," her mother said. "We have to get him out. Tell her I will go in, but only if she releases him."

"We already tried that," Smolleck said. "She refused."

"She was bluffing," Mama said. "She won't give up the opportunity to speak to me. To look me in the eye and gloat. She will let Ethan out."

Aubrey looked over at the small building with its dark windows. "I have an idea," she said to Smolleck. "Star's daughter. Can you use her as a bargaining chip?"

He thought for a moment, then nodded. "We'll give it a try."

He went back inside the van.

Her mother's hand touched her cheek. Aubrey met her eyes. They glistened in the streetlight.

"I started all this," Mama said. "And now I have to finish it."

"You don't, Mama. You don't have to go in there."

"But I do. You know I do."

The pain in Aubrey's gut took her breath away. Her mother. This might be the last time they would ever be together.

"I've always been so proud of you, sweetheart. You know that, don't you?"

Aubrey nodded. Tears ran down her cheeks. She looked at her mother. The woman who had been her center. Who had only wanted to protect her. She couldn't lose her.

The van door slammed shut, causing Aubrey to jump.

Smolleck came toward them. There was something in his eyes she hadn't seen before—doubt? Or was it fear?

"Star's agreed to swap."

CHAPTER 45

Aubrey's heart plummeted. It was what they wanted, but she wasn't ready to say good-bye to Mama if something went wrong.

"What are her terms?" her mother asked.

Smolleck glanced at the dark building, then back at her. "She'll allow Janis to bring Ethan out in exchange for a guarantee of leniency for her daughter. Star claims she pressured Janis into kidnapping Ethan and doesn't want her daughter to pay for her scheme." He rubbed his eyebrow. "She said this is between you and her and is willing to leave it that way."

Her mother nodded. There was a look of determination on her face.

"Then what?" Aubrey said. "Once my mother is inside a building with this murderer and a bomb, how are you going to protect her?"

"This is my choice," Mama said. "I would rather put myself in danger than leave Ethan in that building."

"We don't have a lot of options here, Aubrey," Smolleck said. "Do you have a better idea?"

If only she did. She would gladly go inside herself in exchange for Ethan, but it was clear Star wanted her mother. She shook her head.

"Tell me what I'm supposed to do," her mother said.

"You'll go to the front door of the residence at the same time Janis carries Ethan out the rear door."

"Can I bring a weapon in with me?"

"No. She wants you to approach the building with your hands in the air. No Kevlar. No phone. She said she'll frisk you when you get inside, and if she finds a weapon, she'll blow up the building. She also warned that if we try to storm the building once Ethan is out, she'll detonate the bomb."

Aubrey heard a noise escape her throat. It reminded her of the sound her childhood doll made when it was dropped. And that was exactly how she felt—as though she'd been dropped, hard.

"Will you get Ethan away from the building quickly when he comes out?" her mother asked.

"Yes. We'll have agents in position to grab him and get him to safety."

"Then I'm ready."

"Wait, Mama. There must be some other way."

Her mother's face sagged. "Oh, my sweetheart. You know there isn't." She pulled Aubrey close and squeezed so hard it took her breath away. Then she released her abruptly and gave Smolleck a nod.

"Okay," he said. "Let's go."

"Be safe, Mama," Aubrey called after her.

Aubrey watched her mother follow Smolleck to the mustard-colored building.

"This isn't good-bye, Mama," she whispered. "Promise me. It's not good-bye."

CHAPTER 46

Diana stopped on the sidewalk, about twenty feet from the three-story yellow building. There was a warped garage door on one side of the entranceway and windows to a ground-floor apartment on the other. Tall hedges surrounded the property, blocking most of the windows on the bottom floor. The glass entrance door was covered with decorative bars, as were all the windows. It would be impossible for someone to jump out. Although the lights inside were off, she could see shadows in the hallway beyond the door.

She felt the creeping terror in her gut she had experienced so many years before in front of the brownstone, but then she realized something she wasn't feeling. No dizziness, no disorientation.

There was only clarity.

She needed to save her grandson. She needed to end this with Gertrude.

Smolleck seemed to be listening into his earpiece, then spoke to her. "Someone—probably Janis—is approaching the back door."

Diana could see a shadow moving down the hallway. "Does she have Ethan?" she asked.

"She's carrying what appears to be a child wrapped in a blanket." Smolleck's body was tense, like an animal ready to spring into an attack. "She's at the back door."

Diana's heart was pounding so hard she could hardly hear anything else.

"Walk slowly toward the front door with your hands in the air," Smolleck said. "When you get to the door, press the button on the intercom for apartment one hundred. Star's instructed me to stay here, but I'll call to you with instructions. Okay?"

"Yes."

"Do not go inside the building until I say so. We must be certain Ethan has gotten out safely."

"I understand." She started walking slowly, her hands in the air. Her body was shaking. It wasn't fear of Gertrude but terror for her grandson's life. She reached the front door and studied the old, corroded intercom.

That last time, at the brownstone, she had banged on the door, screaming, *Let me in! Let me in!* And Gertrude had opened the door.

She didn't want to think about the aftermath of that conversation. She pressed the button for "100" and waited. And waited. Perspiration ran down her back.

Diana pressed the button again. No answer. That's when she noticed that the door, with its wrought iron frame, wasn't completely closed. She heaved open the door, but stopped and glanced over her shoulder at Smolleck. He signaled to stay where she was.

She looked inside. Lights were on in the alley behind the building, and she could see down the hallway through to the rear door. A woman was by the door, holding a large bundle over her shoulder and chest like a shield.

Please, God, let Ethan be all right.

The rear door opened a few inches. She willed the woman, *Go, go, go! Get my grandson out of this place.*

The woman turned back to look at her. There was an instant of déjà vu. A flash of Gertrude's blue eyes and her defiant chin.

But it wasn't Gertrude.

It was Gertrude's daughter using Diana's innocent grandson for protection.

They were locked in a stalemate. Janis wouldn't leave the building until she was sure Diana was inside, and Diana wouldn't go all the way in until Ethan was safely out.

Diana opened the door a few more inches and put one foot inside the small foyer.

"Not yet, Diana," Smolleck's voice boomed behind her.

Janis turned to look at her again. Why wasn't the bundle moving? Was that even Ethan?

Janis pushed the rear door open another few inches.

Diana eased herself inside a little more as Janis watched.

Janis opened the rear door a little wider.

Good girl. "Janis," Diana called, "let's do this on the count of three."

Janis nodded.

"One," she said, coming inside as she watched Janis with Ethan continue cautiously out the door.

"Two." They each inched forward.

"Three." Diana started to step farther into the foyer just as something rushed toward her, smashing painfully into her legs and upsetting her balance.

She heard Smolleck yell, "Wait, Diana!" as she toppled over the low, rolling object and fell hard on the floor.

The hallway was dark. Was Ethan out? Was he safe?

She struggled to stand up, but someone was restraining her. She felt a stinging sensation in her leg.

And saw a tangle of metal, spokes on wheels going round and round.

A red tricycle just beyond her reach.

CHAPTER 47

Something was wrong.

Aubrey paced by the van, where one of the agents had instructed her to stay. She had lost sight of her mother when Mama had gone up to the front door.

Had she made it inside the building?

Was Ethan out?

The area closest to the small apartment building had been cordoned off, and there were no pedestrians, no moving vehicles. She strained to see Smolleck in the dim light. He was talking to several people in uniforms and suits, including Detective Gonzalez. Smolleck was shaking his head in a way that couldn't be good.

She ignored a loud voice behind her to stay where she was, and ran down the street toward Smolleck. He gestured for her to stop. She slowed her pace as she watched him say something to the others and then come toward her.

His face was grim as he approached. "You need to stay back, Aubrey."

"Where's my mother? Where's Ethan?"

"Your mother's inside. She seems to have tripped or fallen over something."

"So you don't know if she's okay?"

He shook his head.

"And Ethan?"

"Star set us up," he said.

"Set you up?" Her heart bounced. "What do you mean?"

"Star's daughter was carrying a pillow wrapped in a blanket."

"A pillow? Oh, my God. Ethan's still inside?"

"Our medics are trying to calm down the daughter so we can debrief her, but she's hysterical."

Failed. Their plan failed. "But Ethan's in that building. And now my mother's in there, too."

"She understood the risks."

"But you let her do it." She heard the panic in her own voice.

"We all agreed it was the best chance to get Ethan out of there." His face was red. "We had no way of knowing Star was bluffing."

She took a deep breath. It wasn't his fault, even though she sensed he blamed himself, but that didn't change the situation. Star was capable of doing anything. "How are you planning to get my mother and Ethan out?"

"We're working on it. Everyone seems to have an opinion." He glanced back toward the group he'd been talking to.

"You're not thinking of doing something that would endanger my mother and Ethan, are you?" If they stormed the building, Mama and Ethan wouldn't have much of a chance.

"We haven't decided on a plan."

"But—"

He held up his hand and listened to his earpiece, then replied, "Okay. I'm coming." He motioned with his head at Aubrey. "Come to the van. We'll talk."

She hurried alongside as he loped away from the time-share.

"Star's back in communication with us," he said.

"Back? You mean she was out of communication with McDonough?"

"Yes," he said. "For a few minutes."

"Did she say anything about my mother and Ethan?"

"She said your mom's okay. But McDonough said she seemed surprised Ethan hadn't come out with her daughter. He couldn't tell if she was playing dumb or if something really went wrong with the swap."

None of this made sense. "So where's Ethan?"

"Hopefully Janis will have some answers when we debrief her."

Aubrey took in a shaky breath. "What happens now?"

They reached the van. Smolleck rubbed the back of his neck. "We continue trying to negotiate with Star."

A crowd had gathered behind the police line at the end of the street. Aubrey could make out news vans and reporters pushing up against the barricades. She felt completely helpless. The FBI would continue to negotiate. But what was there to negotiate? Star had both Ethan and Mama. Her own daughter was out of danger, and Star didn't seem to care about her own life.

Aubrey thought about the behavioral-psych classes she'd taken. She turned to Smolleck. "The problem is that Star has nothing to lose."

"It's a big problem," Smolleck said.

"But what if she had something to gain?"

He frowned. "What are you thinking?"

"What does Star really want in all this?"

"She said she wanted your mother."

Aubrey shook her head. "She told McDonough she wanted justice. But justice for what?"

"You don't believe your mother is her end game?"

Aubrey thought about the photo of the three friends that her mother had kept hidden in her room. The way Gertrude fingered her brother's dog tag. Mama said Gertrude never took it off, even to shower.

"Maybe Star is looking for justice for some larger grievance," she said.

"What do you mean?"

"Why did Star—why did *Gertrude*—join a revolutionary group in college to begin with?"

"A lot of young people did back then."

"Yes, but very few of them took it to the level Gertrude did. Most of them, like my mother and father, disassociated from the organization when it advocated killing people to make a point."

"What are you saying?"

"My mother told me Gertrude wanted to blow up Columbia's library. She had believed people had to die in order for Stormdrain to be taken seriously." Aubrey stopped to catch her breath. "What made Gertrude willing to take lives?"

Smolleck seemed to be considering this.

"Whatever it was," she said, "I believe that's the injustice Gertrude has been trying to right since she was a freshman at Barnard."

"How the hell are we supposed to figure out what an eighteen-year-old was angry about over forty-five years ago?"

"She had a brother," Aubrey said. "She wore his dog tag. Can you find out what happened to him? Maybe we'll have something to offer her that she actually cares about."

Smolleck didn't look convinced. "It's worth a try."

Aubrey looked back at the mustard-colored building. In it were her mother and her nephew. With an unpredictable psychopath and a bomb.

"Try hard, Agent Smolleck," she said.

CHAPTER 48

Diana heard ringing. A phone? An alarm? She just wanted to sleep. She tried to roll over and hug her pillow, but her hands wouldn't move. She tugged on them again, but they were stuck behind her back. She kicked her feet, but they didn't move, either.

Something sharp and acrid crept up her sinuses. Gasoline fumes. She opened her eyes to darkness and felt a paralyzing terror. Where was she?

Her brain cleared abruptly. She remembered stepping into the foyer of the building, something crashing into her legs. The red tricycle. Gertrude was clearly determined to get all the details right in this reenactment of the past.

Then she remembered the sting in her thigh.

She had been drugged.

So where was Gertrude? And where was the smell of gasoline coming from?

She blinked to clear her vision. As her eyes adjusted to the dimness, she could make out a pale light coming in from behind closed drapes. She was in a small living room, on a sofa, facing an open kitchen.

Gertrude must have given her a shot of Versed, or something similar, then tied her up. How long had she been unconscious? Had Ethan gotten out safely?

Smolleck's shouting voice came back to her. *Wait, Diana.* Why had he told her to wait, unless Ethan was still inside?

A wall air conditioner coughed and began to hum.

Diana looked down at her ankles. They were bound with duct tape, and she assumed her wrists were as well. There was nothing covering her mouth, but who was she going to scream for? The FBI already knew she was in here.

Now that her eyes had adjusted, she took a more detailed inventory of the room. She could see ugly rattan furniture and a glass étagère, a light-colored mica coffee table, and another floral-patterned sofa, catty-corner to the one she was on. On the counter between the dining room and kitchen were several piles. A few short pipes with long fuses. Bottles with rags sticking out of them—Molotov cocktails. Rolls of what looked like thick candles, but knowing what she did of Gertrude's intentions, she assumed they were sticks of dynamite.

Gertrude had created a bomb factory just like the one that had brought down the brownstone on April Fool.

There was no sign of Gertrude, but she might return at any moment. Diana had to get out of here and find Ethan. She looked for something to cut the tape around her wrists and ankles. There were knickknacks on the upper shelves of the étagère, beyond her reach. Maybe there were knives in the kitchen. She struggled to stand up, then hopped around the coffee table until she reached the kitchen counters. She turned around and pulled open a drawer with her bound hands, then checked its contents. A pair of dark sunglasses and a wig of long hair, the same color as Diana's.

There was a note written on top of the wig in thick black marker:

DID YOU THINK I'D LEAVE YOU A KNIFE, POLLYANNA?

She tried the next drawer. A white blouse and jeans, just like Diana always wore.

The monster had taken her husband, her fiancé, her grandson, and her identity. Well, she wasn't going to let Gertrude win.

She grasped the knob of one of the upper cabinet doors with her teeth, pulling it open. Drinking glasses glinted in the thin light, but she had no way to reach them. She scoured the kitchen for something long to hold in her mouth to swipe at them, but saw nothing that would work. She didn't know what Gertrude's plan was or how much time she had until Gertrude returned.

Her eyes fell upon the Molotov cocktails on the counter. Glass bottles with pieces of rags. Filled with gasoline. If she broke one of them, the gasoline would spread over the floor. Harmless if not ignited.

Was the risk worth it?

She might be able to get herself out of the apartment and building without cutting her bindings, but she'd never be able to rescue Ethan without the use of her hands.

She hopped around to the other side of the counter. Using her forehead, she pushed one of the bottles toward the edge. It toppled off and fell against the terrazzo floor. Without breaking.

Damn. She pushed the next bottle toward the edge. This time, she gave it a hard shove with her head. It hit the floor with a crash. Glass and gasoline burst over the floor. She leaned against the wall and slid down until she was able to reach the broken glass. As her fingers closed over a long, sharp sliver, familiar laughter rang out from the far side of the kitchen. She frantically sawed at the tape on her wrists, feeling the edge of the glass slice into her hand. A searing pain from the gasoline radiated up the nerves in her arm.

She heard a click, and light flooded the kitchen.

"There. That's better," said a soft southern female voice. "Now we can see each other."

The stranger had short, wispy white hair, arched black eyebrows, and wide blue eyes. She wore a flowing blue tunic and slacks. Star—the woman she'd only seen in photos. If only Diana had recognized Gertrude in this impostor, all of this could have been prevented. But Star's disguise had been so masterful that no one had suspected, not even Larry.

"I know ya wanna split, Di," said the pretty woman, switching to Gertrude's Brooklyn-accented voice. "But that's not gonna happen."

In the next blink, Star dissolved. Gertrude stood before her. Haughty. Sexy. Confrontational. The surgeon's scalpel couldn't change who she really was.

Gertrude walked around and pushed Diana forward with one of her feet. "You're bleeding," she said. "Drop the broken glass. I'd hate for you to hurt yourself."

Diana released the shard and heard it clink against the terrazzo. Gertrude kicked it away.

"Good job," Gertrude said. "Now get your ass back up and over to the sofa."

Diana did as she was told. Her hand throbbed from the stinging gasoline.

Gertrude sat down on the other sofa.

Could sharpshooters see into the room through the heavy drapes, now that a light was on?

"They can't see in," Gertrude said. "And if they could, they're just as likely to shoot you."

Diana searched her old roommate's face for something familiar, but the prominent jaw had been reshaped in a delicate heart, the nose was smaller and narrower, and her upper lip, once bowed, was now puffy with cosmetic filler. Even the beauty mark on her cheek was gone. Only her probing eyes were the same.

"You look like shit, Di," Gertrude said. "Of course, you have been under a lot of strain the last couple of days."

"Where's Ethan?"

"That's the question of the hour."

"You were supposed to let him go," Diana said. "That was the deal."

"That was my plan, but the FBI tells me he never came out."

"Please let him go. This is between us."

"I would if I could find him."

Was she lying, or had Ethan hidden somewhere? Was Gertrude capable of blowing up the building with a little boy inside? Unfortunately, Diana knew the answer.

"They said you died in the brownstone explosion," Diana said.

"Obviously, they were mistaken."

Diana took in Gertrude's creamy pale hands, the rings that covered all her fingers.

Gertrude lifted her left hand and wagged her pinkie. "I'm sure you're curious about this."

She was. The finger appeared to be intact, but Gertrude had been identified by the print from her pinkie found in the aftermath of the explosion.

Gertrude gripped her left pinkie with her right hand, gave a tug, then held up the top joint of the finger with a spiraling ring still wound around it.

"Jesus," Diana said.

"I never take it off," she said. "Larry once asked why I always wear my pinkie ring. I told him it's sentimental." She pursed her lips. "I wonder if he's dead yet. I spoke with his physician before they took him in to surgery. He said Larry would probably have extensive brain damage if he lived."

Diana didn't believe the surgeon would have said that. More likely Gertrude was trying to get a rise out of her. All of this had been to get Diana's attention—Ethan's kidnapping, Jonathan's death, Larry's accident. And now, here they were for their final confrontation.

Gertrude's phone rang. She glanced at the display, touched a button, and the ringing stopped.

Diana needed to defuse her, to bring her down. At least until she could get Ethan to safety.

"How did you escape from the explosion?" Diana asked softly. "Everyone was sure you were dead."

Gertrude rubbed the knob of her finger. "I stumbled away from the blast. Some friends let me hide until I was able to get away to Mexico."

"I can't begin to imagine the agony you've been through," Diana said.

"That's right. You can't." Gertrude fixed her blue eyes on Diana. Back in college, her eyes often looked violet, altered by the pink-lensed glasses she always wore. Now, the black pupils throbbed in the way Diana remembered them doing when Gertrude became enraged.

"I'm sorry, Gertrude. I know you think I turned on you, but I didn't. I was trying to protect you and everyone in the group."

Gertrude shook her head. "You wanted to be sure we wouldn't blow up Low Library. Was that your idea of a good outcome?"

Diana didn't answer. Arguing would only inflame her further.

"Another revolutionary group fails, and the government gets to keep on murdering. That was your solution?" Gertrude practically spat the words. "Stormdrain would have been for nothing."

"We had an impact," Diana said. "Stormdrain and all the others who went out to protest the war. The government had started paying attention to us."

"They were killing our brothers," Gertrude said, her eyes roaming over the floral-patterned sofa as though she hadn't heard Diana. "Killing them to feed their own greed. We had to bring the war home. It was the only way to stop them." Her eyes paused on Diana. "I told you that was the only way to get their attention. Someone had to die."

"Yes, I know you believed that was the way."

Gertrude smacked the coffee table with her open hand. "It *was* the way! If you hadn't interfered, we would have succeeded. We could have killed hundreds. We would have been heard. Instead, we became hunted animals. I was forced to go into hiding."

"I'm so sorry," Diana said, but Gertrude didn't seem to be listening.

"He promised he would come for me," Gertrude said. Her eyes were no longer throbbing with anger. There was something else there. Sadness or hurt.

"He said we'd live in Mexico. Puerto Vallarta, or maybe Cabo. I believed him."

Who was she talking about?

"I found ways to get him messages, but he never replied." She turned to Diana abruptly. "He lied to me."

"Who? Jonathan?" Was that why Gertrude killed him?

Gertrude gave her an odd look. "You never got it, did you?"

"Got what?" Diana said. How was she going to save Ethan from this madwoman?

Gertrude gave her a little smile. "I was pregnant. I'll bet you didn't know that, either. It was Jonathan's."

Diana felt a spasm of pain. Pregnant? By Jonathan?

"Janis was born in October 1970. Janis Joplin and Jimi Hendrix had just died. I thought my daughter should begin her life with an important name."

Jonathan had told Diana none of this. But he was dead now. There would be no explanations from him.

"Did he know about Janis?" Diana asked.

Gertrude shook her head. "At least you can take some small comfort in that."

Poor Jonathan. Killed by this woman, and he'd never known about the deep grudge she'd carried against him all these years. Diana struggled to push her thoughts away from him. If she kept Gertrude talking, maybe that would satisfy her need for revenge. Maybe she'd realize she had already taken enough.

"How did you survive with a baby and no money?"

"I turned tricks for a while," Gertrude said. "Then when I realized my knight wasn't coming to rescue me, I reinvented myself into a sweet southern belle with a little surgery and cotillion lessons. I married an old crook who was happy to live out his final years in bliss. Of course, they ended sooner than he was expecting, and I came away with a few million and lots of free time to plan things."

"You mean getting even with me and Jonathan."

Gertrude smiled. "And Larry."

Of course. Gertrude hated both her and Larry for going to the FBI.

Gertrude's phone rang again. She glanced at the display, then over at the closed drapes. She ignored the call. "I kept up with you and Larry," Gertrude continued. "First with PIs, then things became easier with the Internet. I wanted to be sure you were thinking of me, too, so I had a little fun with a delusional janitor who believed I was an actual Greek goddess. I convinced him he was Jeffrey Schwartz, and with the facts and figures I fed him about April Fool, I understand he really had the FBI and media going. In fact, my PI told me that Schwartz's reemergence shook up your marriage quite a bit."

So Gertrude had been behind the mysterious Jeffrey Schwartz.

"I decided I didn't want to keep watching you two from the sidelines, but I was in no hurry to take Larry away from you. I knew the right moment would come along. And it did—just in time for a big wedding."

Kevin's wedding.

"I persuaded Larry to ask for a divorce when I knew you were most vulnerable." Gertrude touched her cheek where the beauty mark had once been. "I had Larry so bewitched, it was easy to convince him you didn't go to Kevin's wedding because you faked your illness."

Gertrude had even contrived the rift between Diana and her son.

"For six years, I enjoyed being on the inside and seeing you alienated from your family." She twirled the ring around her index finger. It was shaped like a serpent. "I probably would have been satisfied maintaining the status quo, but you ruined that yourself."

"I started dating Jonathan," Diana said.

"There didn't seem to be any justice in it, ya know what I mean? You get everything, and I get screwed."

"I never intentionally hurt you."

"No one ever does," Gertrude said. "People fuck you and don't know they're fucking you. They kill your dreams. They kill the ones you love." She was starting to speak more quickly, becoming agitated. "Where's the justice in that? Would you tell me? Where's the fucking justice?"

She was crazy, crazier than Diana had ever seen her in college. Talking her down only seemed to agitate her, which wasn't helping Ethan. Would begging help?

"You've won, Gertrude. You took Larry from me. You've killed Jonathan. You've broken me."

"You think so?" Gertrude said, staring at her ring. "And here I think I'm just getting started."

CHAPTER 49

Gertrude wasn't answering her phone. It was clear to Aubrey that everyone was becoming increasingly worried, especially McDonough, who paced back and forth in the small space in the van.

Aubrey watched McDonough hit Gertrude's number again—his third attempt.

It had been fifteen minutes since they'd last spoken.

Aubrey understood the agent's feeling of uselessness. She sat in the back of the van, picking up bits and pieces of information, mostly from Smolleck's phone conversations. He had contacted someone to check into Gertrude Morgenstern's brother but hadn't heard back. Then Detective Gonzalez came by to report that Janis Hendrix had calmed down enough to talk about what had happened.

Aubrey wasn't able to keep silent. "Where's Ethan?" she asked the detective. "Is he okay?"

Gonzalez looked exhausted. "Janis doesn't know where he is."

"What does that mean?" Aubrey said. "She was with him, wasn't she?"

"She said she left Ethan sleeping in a bedroom on the third floor and went downstairs to get instructions from her mother. When she got back to the bedroom, Ethan was gone."

"Gone?"

"She searched the apartments on the third floor but couldn't find him. She panicked and wrapped a pillow in a blanket, pretending it was Ethan."

"Why would she do that?" Aubrey said.

Gonzalez's thick eyebrows came together in a scowl. "She knew that without Ethan, the swap would never take place. And she had to get out of there. Apparently her mother told her that if she walked out on her own, the police would shoot her dead."

"And she believed that?" Smolleck asked.

"Janis is terrified of the woman. She told us Gertrude wouldn't give a second thought to blowing up the building, even with her own daughter in it."

An invisible hand squeezed Aubrey's gut. What if this madwoman decided she'd gotten what she wanted and blew up the building with Mama and Ethan in it?

Smolleck met Aubrey's eyes. He gave her a little nod, letting her know he understood what was at stake. He was doing what he could. *Hold it together,* he told her without words.

He turned to the detective. "I need to speak with Hendrix myself."

"I'm not sure you'll get much more from her right now," Gonzalez said. "She talked up a storm, then went silent, almost catatonic."

"Did she tell you how she got Ethan to leave the carnival with her?" Smolleck asked.

Gonzalez nodded. "She told us she put on the gray wig she'd worn when she babysat for him in LA and waited for him to be alone. When she saw Ethan come out of the fun house, she told him both his grandparents were in the parking lot. He trusted her because she'd babysat for him. Once behind the carnival and out of sight, she injected him with Versed."

"My God," Aubrey said. "He's being drugged?"

Smolleck frowned. "Then how could Ethan have hidden from her at the time-share?"

"Janis told us since bringing him to the apartment, she used only small doses of Valium," Gonzalez said. "Then she didn't give him anything after the first day because Ethan was very cooperative. He's been eating well and seemed happy enough watching movies in the bedroom."

Eating well. Watching movies. But that didn't free Aubrey of guilt. Ethan had been two floors above her yesterday. How could she have not known? She went over in her mind if there had been any indication, any hint, of his presence. But she was certain not even her father had realized how near Ethan had been to them.

"Why did Janis do it?" Aubrey asked. "What kind of person agrees to kidnap a little boy and keep him captive?"

"I wish I had an answer for you," Gonzalez said.

The detective had no other useful information about Janis or Ethan. Smolleck asked her to call him when Janis was communicative again. He wanted to interview Star's daughter himself.

After Gonzalez left, Smolleck took another call. Aubrey absorbed what the detective had told them and tried to focus on the positives. Ethan was alive. He had been alert enough to sneak out of the bedroom and hide. But where was he?

Then the negatives crept into her head. Janis was terrified of her own mother and believed Star would have been willing to sacrifice her. That meant if they didn't find some way to persuade Star to walk away from this, Aubrey's mother and nephew were doomed.

She glanced over at Smolleck, who was scribbling down notes, his cell phone held to his ear by his shoulder. He got off the phone, and she tried to read the tense expression on his face.

"Okay," he said. "Here's what we have on Gertrude's brother."

Wings fluttered in Aubrey's abdomen. They had found something.

"Willis Morgenstern was reported killed in action in June 1968 at the age of nineteen."

Aubrey thought about the timing. Gertrude would have been seventeen when her brother died, an impressionable age. Which explained the dog tag Gertrude never took off.

"Shortly after his death, a soldier who had served with Willis contacted the Morgensterns and told them Willis had been killed by friendly fire. The Morgensterns filed a complaint and demanded an investigation." Smolleck paused. "The government refused to investigate and denied the soldier's story."

Aubrey was beginning to understand the woman's psyche. "Gertrude would have been incensed about the government sending her brother off to fight, getting him killed in friendly fire, then denying its role."

Smolleck tensed. She remembered he had been a marine.

She continued. "It might explain why she became a revolutionary and believed violence was the answer."

"Possibly," Smolleck said. "But how can we use this information now?"

"By telling her the government made a mistake. By apologizing and reassuring her the case will be reopened so she can finally get justice for her brother."

"We can't make those promises," Smolleck said.

"Jesus," Aubrey said. "So lie. Stretch the truth. My mother's and nephew's lives are at stake."

Smolleck looked at McDonough. "What do you think?"

"I'll try anything," McDonough said. "The problem is, Star's not picking up when I call, and she hasn't been checking her messages." He glanced at his watch. "I can call her again."

"Well, let's see if she answers this time," Smolleck said.

McDonough hit the "Call" button. Aubrey could hear it ring, just like the last few times, then go to voice mail. "This is Star Matin. Please leave a message."

"Please call back, Ms. Matin," McDonough said. "We want to talk to you about your brother, Willis." He hung up and looked at Smolleck, his expression defeated. "She has Diana. I think she's finished with us."

Aubrey's gut cramped. She couldn't accept this was the end. That Gertrude would have her confrontation with Mama, then go out with a final blast, taking Ethan with them.

"There's something else we can try," Aubrey said.

Smolleck and McDonough both turned to her.

"Let me call her from my cell phone."

"Why would she take a call from you?" Smolleck asked.

"Because I'm Di Hartfeld's daughter. Because Gertrude is obsessed with everyone in my mother's life, and she'll be curious to hear why I'm calling."

"And if she takes your call?" Smolleck asked.

"I'll talk to her about her brother."

Smolleck shook his head. "You're not a qualified hostage negotiator."

"But I won't be negotiating," Aubrey said. "And I've taken dozens of behavioral-psychology and related courses. I can do this."

McDonough rubbed his bald scalp.

"Let me try," she said. "We have nothing else."

Smolleck nodded.

"Give me your phone," McDonough said. He took it from her, connected it to a machine, then put a pair of headphones over Aubrey's ears.

She could hear ringing. Three rings. Four. Five.

"Hullo?" said a coarse voice. Gertrude, not Star.

"This is Aubrey."

"Yeah. Your mother said she recognized your number."

"Is my mother okay?"

"Sure. She's fine."

"Good," Aubrey said. "I want to talk to you about something I believe is important to you."

"Oh, yeah? What's that?"

"Your brother, Willis."

It seemed to Aubrey that Gertrude's breathing had gotten heavier. *Don't hang up. Please, don't hang up.*

"The government did your family a huge disservice," Aubrey said. "They killed my brother."

"Yes, I know," Aubrey said. "I understand your anger."

"Do you?"

Wrong approach. "You're right," Aubrey said. "I can't understand how you feel, but I understand why you would be angry."

She heard what sounded like a sigh. "We were so normal," Gertrude said. "So wonderfully ordinary. My brother played football. I was a cheerleader. My parents went to all our games."

Not so different from how Aubrey's family had once been. A family in a snow globe. And then without warning, everything had changed.

"And then they took him," Gertrude said. "He had just turned eighteen. We were a trusting family. My parents didn't play games like a lot of people who got their kids doctor's excuse letters or had them join the National Guard. When Willis was called up, he went proudly. And we let him go."

Aubrey waited for her to continue.

"When they came to our door to tell us he'd been killed in action, my parents were heartbroken." Gertrude swallowed. "I thought I'd never recover. I had loved my brother more than anything." Her voice became a whisper. "I worshipped him."

Aubrey thought about the young, pretty girl in the photo, fingering her dead brother's dog tag.

"The letter came a few weeks later from a buddy of his saying Willis's death had been an awful accident. Their squad leader had mistakenly led them into a free-fire zone, and Willis was shot by one of our own soldiers. We contacted our congressman and asked him to look into it, but the government stuck to its story. They refused to apologize."

"They were wrong," Aubrey said.

"My parents never got over it," Gertrude said. "Dad died from a heart attack, and Mom ended up in a mental hospital." She didn't speak for a few seconds. "The government destroyed my family."

"And you want to get even," Aubrey said. "But hurting more people won't bring your brother back, or your family." She took a breath. "The government owes you justice for Willis. They have agreed to reopen his case."

Star didn't react.

"Get justice for you brother," Aubrey said. "For your mother, and for your father. Get justice for yourself. But please, don't hurt anyone else."

Star was silent.

"Please, Star. Let Ethan go. Let my mother go."

"Okay," Star said, so softly Aubrey wasn't sure she heard her correctly.

Smolleck nodded.

"Thank you," Aubrey said. "Thank you, Star."

The line went dead.

Aubrey's hands were shaking. Her whole body was shaking. Would Star do it? Would she let them go?

She didn't want to think about the alternative.

Chapter 50

It was strange, yet also familiar, for Diana to be sitting so close to her college roommate.

Gertrude's cell phone had been ringing every five minutes or so, but this last time, Gertrude had frowned at the number on the display and shown it to Diana. Aubrey's number.

Gertrude had sat down on the sofa beside her, so close that Diana could smell her scent—a not-unpleasant smell like spicy sausages. She was reminded of the early days of their freshman year when they'd go to the dorm lounge to watch a movie and share popcorn out of a chipped mixing bowl.

The memory was a distant whisper, as Diana strained to hear what Aubrey was saying on the other end of the phone.

Something about Gertrude's brother.

Then, Gertrude had become agitated as she told Aubrey things about her brother and parents Diana had never known. Diana was starting to understand what had made Gertrude the irreverent, passionate woman she had once admired, but also feared.

The government destroyed my family, she'd said to Aubrey on the phone.

No wonder Gertrude wanted to set off bombs.

Diana caught a word on Aubrey's end. *"Justice."* And it seemed Gertrude's face changed, but to what? Sadness? Defeat?

"Okay," Gertrude said softly, then put her phone down and sat without moving, as the air conditioner hummed.

"Justice for your brother," Diana said. "That's what you always wanted, wasn't it?"

Gertrude shifted, as though awakening. "It was in the beginning."

"That's why it was so important to you to make a statement," Diana said. "The library would have been that statement."

Gertrude got up from the sofa and went over to the kitchen counter. It was cluttered with pipe bombs, dynamite, and Molotov cocktails, just like the workbench in the brownstone basement had been.

Suddenly, Diana understood. "I took it away from you. Your only way to be heard, your voice. I left you with no choice."

Gertrude met her eyes. Blue and wide. She'd always had the prettiest eyes.

"That's why you blew up the brownstone," Diana said. "But how did you survive?"

Gertrude gave her a small smile.

The memory of that day pushed against Diana like a rough wave, but as it receded, she was left with clarity. "After I told you about the deal with the FBI, you went back inside," Diana said. "You thought it was all over."

"I knew it was over."

"So you ran back down to the basement where Gary and Michael were working on the bombs for the library."

Gertrude stood motionless at the counter, as though she were remembering it, too.

"From the top of the basement stairs, you could have thrown a Molotov cocktail against the brick wall. The explosion would have set off the other bombs on the workbench."

Gertrude remained still.

"You would have had a couple of seconds to get out before the explosions reached the stairs," Diana said. "You could have run out through the mudroom, then out the back door."

Gertrude seemed to awaken. She looked back at Diana. "But they found my remains."

"Because you planted them, didn't you?" Diana said. "The fires burned for six days, so no one was able to search the wreckage. What did you do? Cut off your finger and braid? Scorch them along with your clothes and go back to leave them in the ruins?"

"I see you've become an ace detective, too." Gertrude's voice sounded tired.

"Then you disappeared, hating Larry, hating Jonathan, and hating me. Waiting for the right moment to destroy each of us, because we took away your voice."

Gertrude picked up one of the Molotov cocktails and took a lighter from her pocket.

Diana knew nothing she could do or say would stop Gertrude from fulfilling what she saw as her destiny.

Gertrude lit the rag in the bottle. "You got it right, Di, except for one little thing." She drew her arm back, the bottle clasped in her hand. "I wasn't the one who blew up the brownstone."

What was she saying?

Gertrude let out a laugh that could have been a cry. She flung the flaming bottle toward the wall above the counter, as she sang out, "April Fool!"

CHAPTER 51

The fireball burst over the kitchen counter, hypnotizing Diana for barely an instant.

Ethan! she thought, dropping to the floor.

The second, louder explosion came a fraction of a second later, the force of it crushing her chest. Something flew across the room, as plaster and glass fell all around her. Then Diana could no longer hear anything, just shrill, high-pitched ringing.

But she was alive. She was still alive.

Something over her head was trapping her. She rolled away. The coffee table had protected her from the worst.

Ethan . . . she had to get to him.

Smoke burned her eyes as she felt around for a piece of broken glass and cut through the binding on her wrists, then ankles, trying not to breathe.

She covered her mouth and nose with her blouse and crawled behind the sofa toward the door, barely able to see through the thick smoke. Flames shot up around her, the floor shifted beneath her.

Ethan. Where was Ethan?

Something was lying in a heap. Red and blue and white.

The little boy on the tricycle. She had to save him.

She crept toward him on hands and knees.

The head was wrong, eyes wide open, neck broken, blood pouring from his face. Diana stared into his blue eyes.

Not the little boy. Gertrude.

The hot air was crushing her. Flames bursting. Ringing in her head like a relentless siren.

The little boy. She needed to save the little boy.

Di's head was filled with cotton, so no sound could break through. Only a shrill, high-pitched ringing. She ran from the brownstone as the ground fell from beneath her. She turned to see bricks flying through the air, the building collapsing.

On the sidewalk, a red tricycle. Near it, something blue, white, and red. The little boy.

Di crawled toward him. She needed to save the little boy. Something warm was running down her check, in her eye. The ringing sound screamed in her head.

She picked up the child and tried to run, but her feet were trapped in quicksand. The boy—he was so very heavy. She heaved her legs away from the smoke and fires and flying debris.

"You're going to be all right," she said to the bundle in her arms. She pulled herself down the street, past two people huddled by the stoop of another brownstone. A flash of white. A flash of black. Something familiar about them.

She kept dragging herself forward, the warm wetness in her mouth, in her eyes so she could no longer see. The ringing so loud that all she wanted to do was scream. Then she became weightless as she fell into darkness.

Diana coughed. She stretched out her arms and thrashed the air. She had to get to Ethan, but the darkness was too thick.

And there was nothing to break her fall.

CHAPTER 52

Aubrey felt it before she heard it. A tremor beneath her feet. Then came a blast so loud, so sudden, that even from a hundred feet away where she stood with Smolleck, the sound reverberated through her body.

She couldn't move, couldn't take her eyes off the small building that seemed to swell as though it had just taken a shallow breath. Hundreds of cracks appeared in the walls as windows burst out of their frames and mustard-colored stucco fell to the ground.

Blinding lights flashed in the downstairs apartment.

Aubrey found her voice. "Mama!" she screamed.

Something was restraining her arm, keeping her from running toward the exploding building, where black smoke flowed out like lava.

"Mama!" she cried, trying to run. "Let me go. Let me go!"

Someone pulled her back. He was stronger than she. She looked up. Smolleck.

"Aubrey. We have to get away from here. Now!"

She took deep breaths. *Calm down,* she willed herself. She stopped fighting him and went slack.

He eased his grip.

And then she took off and ran toward the building.

"Aubrey, stop!"

She didn't know whether he was following her, but she sprinted toward the building, charged with adrenaline.

She yanked on the outer door and ran into the building. Smoke poured into the hallway, coming out of the apartment on the right. She covered her mouth and nose, ducked down low, and tried not to inhale. Part of the wall to the apartment was missing. She stepped through the torn gap. Flames shot up where the kitchen had been. The outer wall of the building was gone, and part of the upper floor dangled above her.

She searched through the haze for her mother.

Two bodies were lying on the floor, head to head.

Aubrey crawled over.

Star's eyes were wide open, her head twisted like a broken doll's. Beside her, Mama was huddled in a fetal position, her shirt pulled up over her mouth and nose.

"Mama?" Aubrey shook her.

Her mother jerked and opened her eyes. She began to cough.

Aubrey grabbed her arm. "Come. Quick."

Her mother was confused as she glanced at Star's wrecked body. Then panic filled her eyes, and she crawled after Aubrey through the gaping wall into the hallway. Behind them, the spitting flames set off another blast.

"Ethan!" her mother shouted over the noise.

Aubrey rushed ahead and opened the door to the garage. She prayed she was right about Ethan, that the movie they'd watched together had left an impression.

Her mother pointed upstairs. "Ethan."

The upper floor was caving in around them. They had to get out.

"In here, Mama." Aubrey pulled her mother into the garage, then threw the door closed behind them. She could hear plaster and wood crashing down where they had just been. Only a thin haze of smoke had leaked into the small garage. A white sedan took up most of the space.

Please be here. She opened the rear car door. A blanket covered the space behind the driver's seat. Had he remembered the movie with the clever little boy?

"Ethan?"

The blanket moved.

She pulled it away.

There he was—wide-eyed, his damp blond curls matted around his head. A small indentation in his cheek from a crease in the blanket. A jumping dolphin on his wrinkled blue T-shirt.

Safe. He was safe.

"Was I brave enough, Aunt Aubrey?" he asked, in his pure, sweet voice.

Her eyes stung. "You were the bravest."

"Ethan," her mother said, taking him into her arms. "Oh, my precious boy. Oh, my Ethan."

Another blast shook the garage. A piece of ceiling crashed down on the top of the car.

"Mama, get in. Quick." Aubrey gave her a little shove, then slammed the door after her. No time for reunions. The garage was reverberating from the explosions. They needed to get out before the building collapsed.

She felt for a button to open the garage door, but found nothing.

She climbed into the driver's seat, praying that Janis had left the key in the ignition, in case she and Star had needed to make a quick getaway.

Yes! It was there. She started up the car.

"Hang on," she shouted.

"Grandma, get down," Ethan said.

Aubrey stepped on the accelerator. The car began to move. She floored it, squeezing her eyes shut and lowering her head. The wheels squealed.

The car crashed through the wood door. She heard the crack of glass.

Out. They were out!

She opened her eyes. The windshield was a giant cobweb of thin white lines. She couldn't see beyond. She eased the car into the street.

Behind them came an explosion that rocked the car, scattering pebbled glass.

Her arms shook so badly she was afraid to let go of the steering wheel. The sound of sirens surrounded her. People in uniforms rushed toward them. Smolleck, his tie askew and arms outstretched.

"Aunt Aubrey?" asked a little voice. "Is it safe to come out?"

Glass from the windshield glistened on the passenger seat, on her lap.

Glass like from a smashed snow globe.

"Yes, sweet boy." Her throat ached. "It's safe to come out now."

CHAPTER 53

Hours had gone by. Or maybe it had only been seconds. Someone had wrapped a blanket around her, but Aubrey couldn't stop shaking. The lights were disorienting, spilling out red, white, and blue, like a Fourth of July gone crazy. Then things came into focus. Sirens blared as people ran from firetrucks, ambulances, police cars.

Aubrey watched black smoke billow out of what once had been the time-share. It reminded her of the gaping hole between two intact buildings in the photo of the brownstone explosion.

Explosion. Where was Mama?

She looked around in a panic, but quickly spotted her mother sitting on an ambulance stretcher, her arms enveloping Ethan. His head rested against his grandmother's shoulder, eyes closed.

Safe now, and finally able to sleep.

Ethan was fine.

They were both fine, but Mama had refused to let go of her grandson when they were helped from the car. Everyone seemed to understand why and gave her some space with Ethan.

The burning smell lingered in Aubrey's nose and chest. She couldn't tell whether her nostrils and lungs were scorched from earlier, or if the acrid odor was hanging in the open air.

She noticed a woman standing beside Detective Gonzalez a short distance away. Feral black hair, a prominent chin. The woman was absolutely motionless as she stared at the burning building.

Aubrey drew nearer. Up close, she could see the woman's resemblance to the college photo of Gertrude Morgenstern. Gertrude, who had been her mother's roommate. *We were once very close,* her mother had said.

And now, here were their daughters. Two women whose lives had been shaped by their mothers.

What had Gertrude done to her daughter to make her willing to go along with her plan to kidnap a child and put his life at risk? Why hadn't Janis had sufficient will to resist her?

Gertrude's daughter seemed to sense Aubrey's presence. Their eyes met. Janis's were very blue. Pretty, even. Like Star's.

Like Gertrude's would have been, behind her pink-lensed glasses.

"Why did you do it?" Aubrey asked.

Janis sucked the thick air deep into her lungs. "My mother," she said. "She was so sad. I just wanted her to be happy." She turned back to stare at the smoke rising out of the building.

And Aubrey realized that was exactly what she had been doing her own entire life. Trying to make her parents happy, because she had wanted so desperately to preserve their family. A family she had sensed had been built on a weak foundation, which could collapse from pressure on the tiniest fault line.

The breeze shifted and it began to snow. Aubrey looked at the snowflakes on her arms.

Not flakes.

Ashes.

"She's dead, isn't she?" Janis asked. "My mother's dead."

"Yes," Aubrey said.

Janis nodded. She held up her arms, bound together by handcuffs. "Finally, I'm free." A smile grew on her face. "And so is Mom."

Free, Aubrey thought.

So why was it so difficult to breathe?

Chapter 54

Her ears hadn't stopped ringing, and her head felt as though it were filled with sawdust, but she was alive. More important, Ethan was safe, in good health, and reunited with his mother and father.

Diana rolled her wheelchair out of the hospital room where she had spent the last twenty-four hours. Her hands were in bandages, and it was painful to use them to operate the wheelchair, but she was too unstable on her own feet.

She had been to Larry's room earlier today, shortly after he'd regained consciousness, but she had wanted to wait until they were alone and he was stronger before she spoke to him.

If not for the misunderstanding, she might never have put it all together. The nurse had assumed she was Larry's wife, not ex-wife, and had brought her a large folded paper that had been tucked into Larry's waistband when the medics had brought him to the hospital. The old, yellowed paper was spotted with recent blood. She had unfolded the document and realized it was the blueprint of Low Library that she had seen forty-five years before. But it was only when she examined the notations in the margins that she recognized the handwriting.

Handwriting that had been so new to her when she first saw the blueprint, she hadn't made the connection.

That's when everything came together for her—Gertrude's last words before she blew up the time-share, Larry's reluctance to go to the FBI so many years ago, and Diana's confused memory of the two people huddled together a few doors down from the exploding brownstone.

The hallway was quiet, just the sounds of beeping coming from patients' rooms. It was after ten and the visitors were mostly gone. Aubrey had left a few minutes earlier. Diana had reprimanded her daughter for risking her life, but there was no heart in her motherly scolding, and Aubrey had known it. Without her daughter's intervention, Diana and Ethan would never have survived.

She stopped at the doorway to Larry's room. A basket of wildflowers from she didn't know whom. A balloon held by a coffee mug filled with candy—"Get Well Soon!" She eased the wheelchair closer to the bed, grimacing as her hands touched the wheels.

His bed was raised, and he was propped up against a couple of pillows. A white bandage covered his head. It reminded her of the white bandanna he'd worn when he'd been Lawrence of Columbia.

A million years ago. Mere seconds ago.

He opened his eyes—sky blue set in bloodred. "Diana," he said, his voice hoarse, "so glad to see you."

His words were muffled, almost drowned out by the ringing in her head.

"How do you feel?" she asked.

"Been better." He tried to smile. The cleft in his chin quivered. "How about you?"

"About like that."

"What about our girl Aubrey, eh? She really saved the day."

"She could have died." Her voice came out too harsh, but she didn't care. She wanted him to understand the magnitude of what could have been.

"How long have you known Star was Gertrude?" she asked.

He jerked, and the heart-monitoring machine he was attached to beeped his agitation. "Not until the day she tried to kill me," he said. "When she recognized the ringtone on Aubrey's phone as yours."

Our love is stronger than the pain. Sentimental nonsense. She should have moved on years ago.

"So for eight years you didn't realize who she was?"

"Everything about her was different," he said quietly. "Her face, her body, the way she talked and moved."

"How could you not have noticed her finger?"

"I don't know, Diana. The prosthetic was perfect, and she never took the ring off."

Or maybe he had seen what he'd wanted to see. "What about the ransom note?" she asked.

"What ransom note?"

"The one in the greeting card you left for me at the house."

"Greeting card?" he said. "My God. Star gave me an envelope when I went to the house to see you. She said it was a 'We're-thinking-of-you' card and asked me put it with the mail. She didn't want me to make a fuss about it. Was there a ransom demand?"

"There was." Diana was fairly certain he was telling the truth. At least about that. "I finally remembered," she said. "About April Fool."

He kept his bloodshot eyes on her.

"When I was carrying the little boy away from the explosion, I saw two people standing near a stoop a couple of doors down."

The heart monitor beeped again.

"Something about the two people seemed familiar," she said. "I don't know—maybe I was concentrating so hard on getting the boy to safety that I didn't pay attention. Or maybe I blocked the memory."

"You had a serious head injury."

"I did," she said. "Were you hoping either the injury or the trauma of the explosion would wipe away my memory?"

He seemed to go whiter. The monitor beeped more quickly.

"You were right," she said. "At least, for the last forty-five years or so. But today, I remembered."

He squeezed his eyes shut.

"The two people by the stoop," she said. "He was wearing a white bandanna, and she had a long black braid."

She waited for him to deny it, but he said nothing. Just lay there taking shallow breaths.

"I thought I had figured everything out, but I hadn't. Gertrude even told me I was mistaken just before she died."

His eyes flew open.

"You were the one who planned to blow up Low Library."

"No, Diana. I didn't."

"Stop *lying*." Her voice carried over the ringing in her ears. "I have the blueprint. It's your handwriting on it, Larry."

He closed his eyes. A tear ran over the purplish pouch beneath his eye, then down his sunken cheek.

"I'm trying to understand, Larry. We were lovers then. How could you have planned such a thing and me not know?"

He kept his eyes closed. "You saw what you wanted to," he said. "You believed I was a hero."

"I thought I knew you. You proclaimed to the world that murder wasn't the answer. Was that a cover story?"

He wet his lips with his tongue. "I didn't want to tell you. I knew you'd never accept killing. I didn't want to fall off the white horse you put me on."

But he had fallen. Far and hard.

"What changed you?" she asked, her voice hushed inside her sawdust brain.

"She did."

Diana felt a stab. So many years later, and she was still jealous of her.

"Gertrude had such intensity," he said. "She persuaded me that the only way to get the world's attention was to do something devastating."

"So you came up with the plan to blow up the library and kill hundreds of students."

He pulled in several labored breaths. He was talking too much. Wearing himself out. "I was caught up in her vison," he said finally. "She was always the one with the true convictions. Not me."

Lawrence of Columbia. He had been nothing more than an actor playing a part.

"When I asked you to come with me to the FBI to stop the plan, you were reluctant at first, then you agreed."

"I was relieved you'd discovered the plan," he said. "I hadn't wanted to go through with the bombing, but I didn't know how to stop it once it was in motion."

"Except you didn't want anyone to learn the truth about you. That it had been your plan."

He lay there, dead still.

She needed to get it out. All of it.

"Instead of going to the bar to tell the others that we had negotiated for their immunity, you snuck down to the brownstone basement. You decided to silence the people who knew the plan to blow up Low Library was your brainchild." She stopped to take a breath. "And that's what you did, didn't you? You silenced them. Michael Shernovsky, Gary Cohen, and Gertrude Morgenstern. And a five-year-old boy named Martin Smith, who happened to be riding his red tricycle that day."

He moved his head back and forth against the pillow, but she sensed it wasn't in denial, but rather some inner hell he was trying to block out.

"You were the one who blew up the brownstone on April Fool."

He let out a noise like he'd been kicked in the gut.

"Except you had expected Gertrude to be in the basement, but she wasn't. She was upstairs, where she'd been talking to me at the front door." The beeping of his monitor seemed to merge with the ringing in her head. "So what happened, Larry? Did you see her running from the building and stop her at the stoop where I saw the two of you? What promises did you make after convincing her you'd known she hadn't been in the basement when you threw the bomb? Did you tell her to plant her body parts and clothes to make it look like she had died in the explosion?"

"I panicked." His voice came out in a whisper. "I wasn't thinking clearly."

"Did you reassure her that the two of you would run away and hide in Mexico? Maybe Puerto Vallarta or Cabo?"

"I didn't know what else to do," he said.

Larry had been Gertrude's shining knight, too. That's what she'd called him. Her knight. It had been Larry who had made Gertrude promises, not Jonathan. It was all so clear now. So obvious.

"You had a relationship with Gertrude when I believed it was just you and me." The idea no longer hurt her. She was finally past that girlish pain.

"That's why Gertrude believed you. You two had already been planning to go off to Mexico." *La cucaracha. La cucaracha.*

The ringing in her head was too loud. She willed it to stop. "But you never replied to her messages after she went into hiding, did you? You discarded her."

"I was in love with you, Di. Never with Gertrude."

"Not until she came back as Star. Although you didn't know it was Gertrude, or that she had come back to get even with you and with me." She paused, a lump rising in her throat. "And with Jonathan."

Because of Larry, the man she loved was dead.

"I'm sorry," he said. "I'm a fraud."

Diana leaned back against the wheelchair, the sickly smell of flowers surrounding her, the ringing in her head finally quieting down. Jonathan's remains would be cremated, as he had wanted. There would be a memorial, but it wouldn't be enough. Not nearly enough.

"The sins of the fathers," Larry was saying. "I've brought terrible pain upon my children. Upon you." He met her eyes. "I'm sorry, Diana. I wish I knew what more I could say or do."

She turned away from the eyes that had once captured her heart.

"Will you tell the FBI?" he asked. "There's no statute of limitations on murder."

"No," she said.

"And the children? Are you going to tell Aubrey and Kevin what I did?" He wet his cracked lips with his tongue. "It would kill me if they knew, Di."

He had once been her hero, her white knight on a snowy stallion. The man she had sipped wine with on the shore of the bay. He was the father of her children.

"No. I won't tell anyone."

She rolled her wheelchair away from him, toward the door. "Enough have already suffered and died because of you."

CHAPTER 55

There was dried blood on his neck. Aubrey dampened a washcloth in the bathroom and cleaned it off as her father slept on the raised hospital bed. The blood turned the washcloth a brownish red and left a metallic smell that overpowered the sweet scent of wildflowers in the basket the Simmers had brought when they'd come by the day before.

Prudence had hugged Aubrey so tightly it took her breath away. Aubrey had saved her grandson. She had become the family hero, a designation she had never sought.

But at least everyone was safe now.

She watched her father's eyelids twitch, as though he were dreaming. Had he loved Star? She was certain he had no idea what his girlfriend had been planning all these years.

He opened his eyes, as though startled by something.

"I'm here, Daddy."

"Yes, Princess," he said, his voice hoarse.

He looked so helpless connected to machines, a turban bandage on his head. His blue eyes, completely rimmed in red, were defeated-looking.

"You know, Daddy, we've all been so relieved to get Ethan back that no one's thought about how Star's death affects you."

He winced as though in pain.

"I'm sorry," she said. "Would you rather not talk about it?"

"No, it's okay."

"Did you love her?"

He seemed to be battling with something.

"It's hard to turn love on and off," she said.

"Even when you realize the one you love is a murderer?" His eyes seemed to be pleading with her. But why? Because he wanted to be forgiven for still loving a monster?

She took his hand, avoiding the tubes in his arm and heart-monitoring contraption on his finger. "It's all right if you love her," she said.

He squeezed his eyes closed. "Not her," he whispered. "Me. Would you still love me, Princess?"

"I love you no matter what, Daddy."

He kept his eyes closed, but tears leaked out and ran down his face.

She dried them with her fingertips, then kissed his bruised forehead. "I'll let you rest."

She took the bloodied washcloth with her and rinsed it out in the bathroom sink. But the metallic smell stayed with her.

CHAPTER 56

The memorial service for Jonathan Woodward was held on Sunday, five days after his death, at a small bay-front park not far from where Aubrey had grown up. Her mother had made the arrangements quietly, without informing the news media, and kept it to a small group of family and friends.

Aubrey held her mother's elbow, careful not to touch her bandaged hands, as they walked from the wooded area across the grass to three rows of white folding chairs that faced the bay. Many of the seats were already occupied by people Aubrey didn't recognize, probably colleagues of Jonathan's.

"I'm fine, sweetheart," her mother said. "Really."

But Aubrey didn't release her grip on her mother's arm. Mama might insist she was no longer having dizzy spells, and that the ringing in her ears was mostly gone, but Aubrey worried the emotional impact of today's service might set her back.

She helped her mother into a chair in the front row next to a judge, a colleague and friend of Jonathan's who had agreed to officiate. She thanked the judge for coming, then nodded at Kevin and the Simmers, who had taken seats in the third row. Kevin had driven down from Palm

Beach with Prudence and Ernest. Kim had stayed behind with Ethan at the Simmers' house, not willing to entrust him to a babysitter's care. Aubrey certainly understood Kim's feelings.

The judge got up to speak about Jonathan. He had a low, soft voice that blended with the breeze coming off the bay. It was late afternoon, and the air was beginning to cool, like the night Aubrey had come here with her mother.

That was Monday. Six days ago. A lifetime ago.

Aubrey watched a sailboat tacking across the gray-blue water, coming toward shore.

A week ago, Ethan had been kidnapped. Since then, she had experienced more pain and fear than she'd had over her entire life. She'd been in an emotional vortex, anxious about Ethan, at times doubting her parents, and finally, terrified for all of their lives. Jonathan had been killed, Dad had almost died, and the trauma of almost losing her mother and Ethan in the time-share explosion haunted her daily. During the last couple of days, she would find herself suddenly shaking uncontrollably in the middle of some mundane task, her brain's way of reminding her it was far from healed.

The judge had sat down, and others got up to speak. A law clerk, who talked about how Jonathan had helped him through a tough personal time and gave him a fresh start. Other judges and lawyers, who spoke about Jonathan's inherent goodness and devotion to the law. Jonathan was not afraid of making tough decisions if they were the right decisions, someone said, even the ones that pained him personally.

Aubrey sensed her mother shift in her seat. "Are you okay?" Aubrey asked softly.

Her mother nodded. "I need to speak."

Aubrey helped her up, but her mother pulled out of her grasp and went to the podium alone. In her loose black dress, white bandaged hands in front of her, dark hair blowing in the breeze, Mama reminded Aubrey of a frail nun.

Mama looked over the heads of the assembled mourners, back at the trees, or perhaps at something only she was able to see. "Jonathan was one of the kindest, most loving people I've ever known. His death is a loss to humanity and utter heartbreak for me." She put one bandaged hand to her neck. "But there comes a time when we must say good-bye to our loves and to our dreams. A time when we must say good-bye to the past."

Her mother was finally leaving her demons behind, but she had lost a great deal in the process, including the man she had loved.

Life, Aubrey was learning, was filled with painful choices, and love didn't always prevail. She hoped her mother would at least find peace now.

No one spoke after Mama sat down. The judge thanked everyone on Mama's behalf for coming, then the mourners gathered around her.

Aubrey took a few steps back and waited under the shade of a big old banyan tree, ready to jump in and catch her mother if she appeared faint. She watched as people offered their condolences, awkward in their embraces because of her bandaged hands. Through it all, Mama nodded, her eyes unfocused, as though she were somewhere else.

Kevin said something in Mama's ear. She nodded and gave him a sad smile. He kissed her cheek and then came toward Aubrey.

"Hey," he said. He was still pale, but his eyes were no longer bloodshot. "This sucks for mom."

"Yeah," she said. "It does."

"I never understood her before this happened." He glanced back at their mother, who was talking to the Simmers.

"What do you mean?"

"I thought her coldness had to do with me. With something I had done to displease her. I didn't get that she was so angry at herself that she had a tough time showing love."

A ray of sunlight pushed between the leaves of the banyan tree. Aubrey had finally gotten it, too. All the years of trying to understand who she was, but it had taken the trauma of almost losing Ethan for Aubrey to finally appreciate her family's dynamics. Kevin had reacted to Mama's aloofness by pulling away, while Aubrey had become Mama's protector, sensing a wounded person who needed her support.

"Have you forgiven her?" she asked.

He nodded. "Now I'm trying to forgive myself."

"What do you mean?"

"I've been living a lie," he said. "I was angry with everyone around me, when it was me I was pissed off at." He met her eyes. They were the same dark-chocolate color as her own. "I'm sorry if I turned my own feelings of inadequacy against you."

"Don't beat yourself up. You'll always be my big brother."

"I know that, but I'm still working on fixing myself." He gave her a crooked grin. "I told Kim I'm quitting my job at BBM."

"What? You are?" This was a surprise. "What did Kim say?"

"To do what'll make me happy."

"Well, good. I'm glad she's being supportive."

Prudence and Ernest were each giving Mama a hug. It seemed Kim's parents no longer blamed her for Ethan's kidnapping. Well, they were bigger people than Aubrey had always assumed.

"Do you know what you want to do?" she asked.

"Not really." Kevin frowned. "I need to be happy with myself so I can be there for my family." He gave her a little smile. "And you're my family, too, kid. I'll never forget that again."

Her throat closed, making her unable to speak, unable to tell him how much his words meant to her.

Kevin glanced over at the Simmers, who were walking across the grass toward their limo. "Time to go." He hugged her but didn't release his grip. When he finally pulled away, his eyes were wet. "Thanks again for saving my little guy," he said, then hurried after his in-laws.

A breeze unsettled the tree, and a few leaves floated down. Kevin was back. She had her brother back.

She sensed someone standing near her and turned. Tom Smolleck. She hadn't expected to see him, but here he was, looking unflappable, once again, in his dark suit and white shirt.

"Nice service," he said.

"I didn't realize you were here. Thank you for coming."

"I wanted to say good-bye." He rubbed his eyebrow. "When are you heading up to Rhode Island?"

"In a couple of days. I have to get back to my classes, but I want to be sure everyone is okay before I leave."

"I heard your dad will be in rehab for a while."

"That's right," she said. "He's going to have to work very hard if he wants to walk again."

"Sounds like it's in his hands."

"Yes. I suppose it is." The sails on the sailboat were coming down. She wondered whether the boat was going to moor at Scotty's where she and Smolleck had had lunch. It wasn't far from here.

She wondered whether she would ever see him again.

"A few days ago you talked about living in a glass bubble," she said.

He nodded.

"The thing about bubbles is they inevitably burst," she said.

There was a sadness in his gray eyes. "I'm sorry about all you've been through," he said. "But sometimes leaving your sheltered world behind can free you to do other things."

She couldn't help but smile. There was an optimist hiding inside that dark suit.

He took her hand and held it. "If there's anything I can ever do for you, you'll call me, right?"

The heat of his hand warmed hers. "Yes," she said. "I will."

He met her eyes and hesitated. Either one of them could have leaned in a tiny bit, but the moment passed.

He released her hand. "Take care of yourself."

"You, too."

She watched him leave the park, shoulders stiff, head up. The perfect clothes, the rigid, formal way he moved and talked—it was his way of coping with impossible, heart-breaking situations. It was his armor.

And she realized, with her glass bubble gone, so was her own armor. No protective glass.

Just herself.

The thought was terrifying.

CHAPTER 57

She was choking, smoke stinging her nose and eyes. She had to find Ethan. She had to save Mama.

Aubrey woke with a start, her heart pounding. She blinked as the blurs around her came into focus. Grayish-blue wallpaper. White bedspread. Pillow crushed in her arms.

It had been a dream. Just another dream.

She sniffed the air. Smoke.

That was no dream.

She jumped out of bed and hurried into the hallway. The smell of something burning was stronger here. Like the time she and Kevin had made a fire in their parents' fireplace. The smoky smell had lingered in the upstairs bedrooms and hallway for weeks.

The door to her mother's bedroom was ajar. Aubrey went inside. The bed was made—all the throw pillows in place—but Mama wasn't there.

A thin haze floated around her, glowing in the morning light that spilled in from behind the curtains. Had her mother built a fire?

Aubrey knelt down on the cold stone slab in front of the fireplace. A couple of embers smoldered, and thin pieces of charred paper drifted like bats in the draft. She pushed through the ashes with the poker.

Several fragments of yellowed paper.

As recently as ten days ago, just before her epiphany about Jackson, she would have put the poker down and returned to her room. But she no longer ran from asking questions.

She picked out a few small pieces of paper caught beneath a leg of the andiron and examined one. On it was a line drawing of some kind. An architect's blueprint? She examined another fragment. Part of a printed word—LIBR. The Spanish word *libre*, meaning free?

Then she realized what she held in her hand—remnants of the blueprint for Columbia's library. The blueprint her mother had told her about. On another small piece were scorched words.

Several hundred students . . .

Written with a black pen in a strong, confident hand.

It was just like the handwriting on the notecard she had found in Mama's memento box.

Her father's handwriting.

Aubrey was falling. She leaned back against one of the armchairs.

Would you still love me, Princess? Even when you realize the one you love is a murderer?

Now she understood why he had asked that.

And Mama knew, too.

Chapter 58

Her mother sat in a chair at the patio table, shaded by the gumbo limbos, palms, and bamboo trees. Maybe it was the harsh morning light, or perhaps the recent lack of rain, but the plants seemed to droop around her.

She was staring off absently, unaware of Aubrey's presence, her bandaged hands upturned as though in supplication.

Aubrey pulled out the chair beside her. The loud scraping sound jarred Mama back. Her eyes flitted over the oversize T-shirt Aubrey had slept in, then paused on her fingertips, which were blackened by soot.

"Why did you burn the blueprint?" Aubrey was surprised by the strength in her voice, because it was nothing like the terrible weakness inside her.

Mama bit her lower lip and looked down at her bandaged hands.

That's when it hit her.

Her mother had *wanted* her to smell the smoke and find the few charred scraps of blueprint.

"Have you had it hidden away?" Aubrey asked. "Tell me. Why did you burn it now, after all these years?"

She continued to stare at her hands. "A nurse gave it to me at the hospital. It was with your father's things when the ambulance brought him in."

Had that been the paper her father had found when she'd called him about the babysitter? If so, had he taken it from the time-share, planning to destroy it, knowing it was the one remaining physical link to what he had planned to do?

"It was Dad's idea to blow up Columbia's library and kill innocent people, wasn't it?"

Her mother's face seemed to harden into stone. She was protecting him, the way she had always done.

"Can't you for once tell me the truth? For God's sake, Mama. My whole life you and Dad have tried to keep me in the dark. And I've let you. I've been afraid if I pressed you for answers, I would somehow rip whatever it was that held you and Dad together." She took a breath. Her heart was racing. "Why did I bother? You two were already broken."

Her mother's face was filled with agony. She extended her bandaged hands toward Aubrey.

"I'm sorry," Aubrey said, "but I can't do this anymore. I need to know the truth, and if you won't tell me, maybe Dad will." She pushed back the heavy wrought iron chair. The sound scraped painfully against her heart as she went toward the house.

Behind her, she could hear her mother's voice, barely a whisper. "I love you, sweetheart," she said. "Remember that, no matter what."

CHAPTER 59

Her father sat in a chair by the window in his hospital room, the basket of wildflowers from the Simmers, now wilted, on a side table. His head was wrapped in bandages, and his hands lay palms-up on his lap, like they'd already surrendered.

Her father. Would he finally tell her the truth?

Aubrey stepped into the room. It was larger than the one he had been in originally, and there was a patient in the second bed. An orderly was adjusting the bed, moving wires and tubes.

Her father stared at his writhing roommate, who was moaning over and over, "Kill me. Put me out of my misery. Kill me."

"I'm going to take you for your procedure now, Mr. Detweiler," the orderly said, pushing the rolling bed.

"Leave me alone," said the man. "I want to die."

"Dad," Aubrey said, "I have to talk to you."

He ignored her and continued watching the other man as the orderly rolled the gurney out of the room. "Why are they prolonging his agony?" her father said, frowning at the empty space where his roommate's bed had been. "He just wants to die."

"Dad. We have to talk." She stood directly in front of him, forcing him to look at her.

He sighed. "What is it, Aubrey?" His eyes were bloodshot, surrounded by purple bruises.

She held out her hand with the fragment of charred paper covered with his handwriting.

He seemed to shrink against the chair. "Where . . . where did you get that?"

"From the fireplace. Mama tried to burn it—not very successfully."

"It's not what you think, Aubrey. I swear."

He had the audacity to deny it? "Tell me the truth," she said. "What you did. All of it. I need to hear it from you."

"So she told you." His face drooped. "She promised she wouldn't."

There was something in his voice that stopped her. A plaintive tone like from the previous day. Was there another secret he believed Mama had revealed?

Would you still love me, Princess? Even when you realize the one you love is a murderer?

He couldn't have been referring to the library. Even though he may have planned it, the library bombing had never happened, and no one had died. Yet he had called himself a murderer.

A murderer.

The pieces came crashing together.

"Oh, my God. You blew up the brownstone, didn't you?" Her voice sounded discombobulated to herself.

Her father looked away abruptly.

In that single gesture, he confirmed what she didn't want to believe, but she had to hear him say it. Once and for all, she needed to hear the truth.

"Say it," she said.

He kept his head down.

"Say it!"

"Yes." His chin jerked up. "Yes. I did it. I blew up the brownstone. I killed my friends and an innocent child."

She sat on the edge of his bed, no longer able to support her own weight. His confession brought no relief, only a deeper pain. Her father was a weak, selfish person who was willing to kill others so he wouldn't go to jail. Her father was a murderer.

She slowed her breathing, trying to calm herself. "That's why you took on all those Innocence Projects. Freeing innocent men because you're the one who should have been behind bars."

He stared at the empty space where his roommate's bed had been.

"We almost lost Ethan because of you."

"I'm so sorry, Princess. So sorry about everything."

She took in a deep breath. "You must tell the FBI what you've done. You must pay for this."

He shook his bandaged head, his hands open, pleading.

"You're a coward," she said.

He met her eyes. "But you're not."

Maybe not a coward, but certainly no hero. She got up from the bed on unsteady feet, wondering how she would be able to walk out of this room, walk to her car, walk away from everything.

His voice followed her. It sounded as though he were begging her. "I love you, Princess. Remember that, no matter what."

"I'm not your princess," she said, and kept walking.

CHAPTER 60

The snow was falling lightly. Aubrey watched through the kitchen window in her apartment. She had been back in Rhode Island for more than two weeks, burying herself in her classes and dissertation, trying not to think about what she had left behind, unfinished. What she couldn't bring herself to do.

She dumped the empty bottle of wine she and Trish had drunk the night before in the garbage, along with the mostly empty Chinese-takeout containers. She and her friend had talked until almost two in the morning, and Aubrey had been too exhausted to clean up when Trish had finally left.

Trish was a good listener, and like the professional psychologist she was, she offered no solutions. They both understood the process. That getting it all out—the hurt, the fear, the letdown—might somehow free Aubrey to move on.

But Aubrey hadn't told Trish everything. She doubted that she'd ever admit to anyone what her father had done.

She put the teabags back into the blue-and-white porcelain canister and an open box of Triscuits into the fridge. The postcard Kevin had sent her a couple of days ago was stuck on the refrigerator door with a little doggy magnet.

Aubrey slipped the postcard off and examined it once again. A jumping dolphin against a blue-green lagoon and the printed words, "Dolphin Research Center, Marathon, Florida." On the back, Kevin had written:

Yeah—I know. I can't believe they still make post-cards. Ethan's loving the dolphins. He gave one a big hug. He's doing great. Mom's good. We're all good. I know it sounds corny, but wish you were here. Kev (aka Bilbo Baggins)

Her eyes stung, like the first time she'd read the postcard. Ethan was doing great, her brother was back to his old self, and Mama was good. Aubrey spoke to her every day. The conversations were slightly awkward, as they both struggled to acquaint themselves with the people they had become, but each day was a little easier. A little more natural.

They never talked about Dad.

He had been moved to a rehab center in Miami. He was still in a wheelchair, uninterested in trying to walk on his own, unwilling to take another step. At least, that was the most recent report Aubrey had gotten from his doctor yesterday.

She put the postcard back under the magnet and headed toward the front door. She turned at the sound of toenails skittering across the wood floor. She stooped over and hugged Wolvie, taking in his delicious musty-dog smell. Wolvie ran his cold, wet nose against her neck.

At least getting her dog back had been an easy decision for her. When she'd gotten home from Miami, the first thing she'd done was march over to the apartment where Jackson lived with his latest conquest. Wolvie had raced into Aubrey's arms, and she had refused to let him go.

"I'm taking him," she'd told Jackson. "For the last six years, I've been the one to feed him, walk him, and take care of him when he's sick. He's at least as much mine as yours."

"So take him," Jackson had said with a shrug. "I don't give a shit." And Aubrey had wondered what she'd ever seen in the man.

Wolvie rolled over on his back, and she scratched his belly. "I have to go to class, puppy," she said. "But I'll be back soon."

Her dog's tail thumped against the floor.

———

It was snowing hard when she got to the campus. She trudged across the slushy path toward her classroom. Benches and skeletal tree branches were coated with snow. In front of her, barely visible through a curtain of white, was the grayish-white facade of the library. She watched students climbing the steps and thought about another college library. Another era.

Snowflakes stung her cheeks like pinpricks.

She no longer had the protection of her snow-globe bubble. She was on her own, faced with a decision only she could make.

What was holding her back? It wasn't as though she hadn't already been making difficult choices during Ethan's ordeal. She had toughened her heart, first deciding whether to tell the FBI about the ransom note, then whether to turn her mother in to them. But those choices at least had the potential of a good outcome. They had been about getting Ethan back. This decision would make her a traitor to her family, and worse. Her father would likely go to prison, maybe even be subject to the death penalty.

How could she do that to her father? Just because it was the right thing?

But what was the right thing?

The snow fell around her. Flakes clung to her coat, reminding her of the ashes that fell when she had stood beside Janis, watching the time-share burn. *I'm free,* Gertrude's daughter had said, her wrists in handcuffs. *And so is Mom.*

Aubrey thought about her father in his wheelchair, already mummified and so paralyzed by guilt and shame he was unable to do what he needed to. She thought about her mother, reaching for her with bandaged hands. Mama didn't have the strength to take action, either. She had already been burned once too often trying to help her husband.

The answer came to Aubrey with a gust of glistening flakes. Her parents wanted her to free them. They needed her to free them.

She reached into her pocket for her phone.

"Smolleck," he said. His voice was strong and emboldening, but she didn't need his reassurance. She had made her decision.

"Tom. It's Aubrey."

A memory brushed her consciousness. A smiling blue-eyed man lifting her high in the air. *How's my beautiful princess?*

She blinked back tears and took a deep breath. "There's something I must tell you about my father."

ACKNOWLEDGMENTS

Whew. Finished the book. I never could have done it without an amazing support system.

My tough-but-always perspicacious critique group: Christine Jackson, Miriam Auerbach, Neil Plakcy, and Kristy Montee. An especially hearty thanks to Neil and Kristy for their in-depth, critical reading of the manuscript and their often-brilliant suggestions.

My technical support crew: Julie Hecht DeMay and David Hecht, for their patience and useful input on psychology in academia. Jack and Marilyn Turken, for their medical expertise. Detective John Perez, Miami-Dade County Special Victims Bureau, Missing Persons Unit, who graciously took time out of his busy day to help me understand police procedures.

My first-readers and cheerleaders: Arnold Weiss, Koula Papadopoulos, and, as always, Delia Foley, who did double duty as my tour guide around her native Coconut Grove, with a memorable lunch stop at Scotty's Landing.

My enthusiastic champion, Christine Kling, who guided me to the perfect home for *Someone Must Die*.

My very own visionaries, whose diligence and creativity helped me realize the potential of my manuscript: Mallory Braus, my discerning developmental editor, and my fantastic T&M team, led by the ever-supportive JoVon Sotak.

And finally, my much-cherished family:

Sarah, for her always sharp insights, this time into a twenty-eight-year-old woman's thinking and perceptions.

Ben, for taking me on a tour of South Beach, with a visit to the Holocaust Memorial and a stroll down Meridian Avenue (including sneaking into a building that looked like a perfect venue for my story).

Joe, for always being there to read, reread, and read yet again. And . . . for always being there.

ABOUT THE AUTHOR

Sharon Potts is the award-winning, critically acclaimed author of four psychological thrillers, including *In Their Blood*—winner of the Benjamin Franklin Award and recipient of a starred review in *Publishers Weekly*. A former CPA, corporate executive, and entrepreneur, Sharon has served as treasurer of the national board of Mystery Writers of America, as well as president of that organization's Florida chapter. She has also co-chaired SleuthFest, a national writers' conference. Sharon lives in Miami Beach with her husband and a spirited Australian shepherd named Gidget.